# VISIBLE SIGNS

*A Novel*

## GRACE MARCUS

*Relax. Read. Repeat.*

VISIBLE SIGNS
Grace Marcus
Published by TouchPoint Press
Brookland, AR 72417
www.touchpointpress.com

Copyright © 2022 Grace Marcus
All rights reserved.

ISBN-13: 978-1-956851-14-4

Editor: Kimberly Coghlan
Cover Design: ColbieMyles.com
Cover Images: Depositphotos
Author Photo: Al Sirois

Visit the author's website at www.gracemarcus.com

First Edition

Printed in the United States of America.

*In memory of my parents, authors of eight*

# CHAPTER 1

If God is calling her, she wishes He'd speak louder. Or send her a sign. Once again, she can't sleep, no matter how hard she tries to ignore her nagging heart.

Sister Jude rubs the bony ridge above her eyes, behind which pinpricks of light herald the throbbing pain. Sister Immaculata had said, "This too shall pass." But it hasn't. Not the sleepless nights or restless days eroding her peace of mind, capsizing the equilibrium of the life she chose, the life she'd loved.

She kneels next to her narrow bed and bows her head. *O God, come to my assistance. O Lord, make haste to help me.*

He had shown her the way once, so clearly, so completely. On her Confirmation day, returning from the communion rail at Our Lady of Sorrows and seeing her mother's face as luminous and nacreous as pearl, despite her useless body in the wheelchair. Jude was thirteen, and by then, all too knowledgeable about the disease, how it attacked the nerve cells in the spinal cord and the brain; how some people could live for decades and others just a few years; that whatever the manifestation, all had the same pitiful, inevitable end.

But on that day—for long, slow-motion seconds outside of time—she'd felt her mother's arms around her as real and warm and solid as muscle, flesh, and bone. She'd stood riveted in the aisle, transfixed by 'the peace which passeth understanding.' And her heart had stirred with the sudden, sure, ineffable desire to serve the radiant God who could lift her dying mother halfway to Heaven with His grace.

A desire burnished by the solace she found in her mother's daily devotions, her clear-eyed sacred journey to her death; a desire that withstood her father's furious opposition, her friends' shocked reactions, as if entering the convent were a deprivation greater than the one she'd already suffered by losing her mother in increments from the time she was a child of eight until she turned eighteen.

But her mother had remained incandescent throughout, despite the wasting. And dispassionate about her prognosis in a way that Jude had envied and her father had hated.

He had insisted on carting his wife to Mt. Sinai, Johns Hopkins, the Mayo Clinic, or anyplace else that offered a wisp of hope with experimental drugs or therapies.

She had begged her mother to stop allowing herself to be poked and prodded and tested. "It's what he can do; not doing it would murder him," her mother said. "Besides, I've no pain, love, and all my senses to drink in my last of this glorious world."

An ache blooms in Jude's chest. That's how her mother spoke, in words effusive and grand.

She brushes away the tears that ambush her frequently these days, outbursts that the others have learned to ignore, much the same way they abide Sister Theresa's menopausal mood swings. But Jude has come to realize that her own condition is neither biological nor transient, but what feels like the shifting of tectonic plates, the familiar terrain altered, and she cannot find her bearings. Although she's tried, roaming the acres of monastery grounds in silent meditation so frequently, she's had to tighten the cincture around her waist.

Jude slips on a robe and tiptoes downstairs to the chilly refectory kitchen. She turns on the burner under the kettle and stands there, mesmerized by the necklace of blue flames, their bright warmth, the odor redolent of those mornings when—her father long gone to work at the docks—she'd take tea to her mother, frail and shrinking under the chenille bedspread. With no one to check her homework, or braid her hair, still, she felt safe in the sanctuary of her mother's room, remembering the soft light from the silk-shaded lamp on the nightstand, the vase of flowers on the dresser, the emerald green rosary beads that matched her mother's eyes. She'd walk the six blocks to Connie's house, an alternate universe where Connie's sisters teased their hair and each other, their brothers roughhoused, Rose scolding her sons as if they were six years old instead of six feet tall. Where, as the years went on, Louis, Jr. and Carlo coached her through JV basketball, high-fiving her when she made varsity, griping when she regularly beat them at free throws. Her killer foul shot was more likely the result of the sheer physical release of hurling her body into the air and slamming the ball into the basket, rather than reaching her full height of five foot ten. Connie's house was as raucous and crowded as hers was quiet and spare, her home away from home until the convent.

The word primes her well of sadness, blurring her vision. Jude runs her hand over the worn countertop where she's spent hours in happy communion chopping vegetables, stirring batter, or slicing roasts; the sighing of the radiators as familiar to her as the pale blue coffee cups lined up for the morning, next to a stack of matching plates.

With trembling hands, Jude lifts the kettle before it whistles, fills a mug, stirs in Sanka, and carries it into the parlor, already set up as the reception area for this weekend's retreat. Their annual Advent retreat, three weeks before Christmas, is always well-attended by busy wives and mothers. Women—she knows by now—from elegant Westchester houses, East Side high-rises, duplexes in Queens seeking respite and reflection. There doesn't seem to be an equivalent for nuns, no way for her to slip into secular life for an occasional weekend.

She walks through the foyer past the statues of the Blessed Mother and the Sacred Heart of Jesus. A beautiful, tranquil Jesus holds his own red heart surrounded by flames. Her heart feels as combustible and unstable, made up of warring elements.

She climbs the stairs and hesitates outside Immaculata's door but resists the temptation to knock. At seventy-three, she needs her rest. Besides, what else can they say that hasn't been already said? She's been Jude's spiritual director for years, from before she entered the convent, when she was still Rita Mooney and came here on a retreat for young women considering religious life.

"That's God's plan for me, is it?" her father had said when she told him where she was going for the weekend. "That my wife and daughter leave me to be with Him?"

His words had stung and she carried them with her on the subway to the city, on the bus back upstate, in the taxi to Holy Name. She remembers the Shirelles crooning "Soldier Boy" on the radio. It aired endlessly that summer, an anthem for girls whose boyfriends were in Vietnam.

But they dissipated as soon as she entered the monastery grounds, the gradual rise to the weathered stone building surrounded by woodlands and crowned by high altitude clouds. All she could think of was that e.e. cummings poem her mother loved, "I thank You God for this most amazing."

That weekend Rita had prayed in the simple white chapel and attended the talks. Spent hours scrupulously examining her conscience. She had doubts. Of course, she had doubts, which she confided in Immaculata. *Was she compensating for the loss of her mother or indulging a prideful need to be extraordinary? Abandoning her father?*

"Perhaps it is grief, or guilt," Immaculata had told her then. "Perhaps not. But you're barely eighteen. See how you feel when you're twenty-one. If it's a true vocation, it will not only endure, but strengthen. And God is patient."

Even though Rita lived at home all through college, and dated and partied and flirted with temptation, those experiences never eclipsed the profound joy she'd felt at the monastery. She entered the cloister at twenty-one, gaining a precious peace in handing her heavy heart over to a loving God. Her father never once stepped foot on the grounds. And he never forgave her.

"Then you must forgive him," Immaculata said.

Jude had tried. Hadn't she? She trudges along the silent corridor to her own cell, past the rest—ten in all, each nun's room sacrosanct and off-limits to one another—to her own private purgatory.

She sets her coffee next to the letter from her father and draws her feet up onto the ladder-back chair, hugging her knees to her chest.

Except for her canonical year, when her contact with the outside world was completely restricted, she had dutifully visited her father each spring. Seven times over eight years. At first, their only common ground was the cemetery, where she would pray (silently) and he would tend her mother's grave. She spent more time at Connie's house or in her mother's sickroom—left untouched save for the absence of medical equipment—than in her father's company. Once, thinking it would be too painful for him, she'd offered to go through her mother's things and give what they could to charity. His horrified look angered her, as if she were adding to his burden instead of lifting it. She'd cook his favorite meals and they'd eat in an excruciating silence, which she interpreted as her punishment instead of his despair. Their infrequent exchanges bore no resemblance to affection let alone the love she'd enjoyed when she was a little girl and her mother had been well. The three of them at Rockefeller Center each Christmas, Jones Beach every summer, at the Macy's Thanksgiving Day parade.

Whatever the cause—the passing of time, the power of prayer—her last visit home offered her hope. One evening, they were watching Ed Sullivan when an Irish tenor began to sing "Danny Boy." Her father flinched and she reached for the remote. "Leave it," he told her. "If I shut out everything that reminds me of her, I'd never see or hear again."

It was the first time he spoke of his pain and her heart hurt for him, but it was also a crack in the veneer of their entrenched formality. So, with not a little trepidation, she offered to put the boxes of photos, which had been moldering in the attic, into albums. "For when you want to look at them," she told him. "They could get ruined. I know you wouldn't want that."

He nodded. "Okay, Reetie. The next time you're home."

The endearment disarmed her. She was his child again, his daughter.

He made her breakfast her last morning, the toad-in-a-hole that delighted her as a little girl. She was so choked up she could hardly eat. If he noticed her tears, he didn't say, but he'd given her a fierce hug when she left.

She'd taken the subway in a trance, hardly cognizant of the usual stares at her attire. Jude hadn't realized how much she'd missed him, *them*. Who else remembers her first day of school, carrying her weeping to the schoolyard, staying with her all day, despite the scowling nuns, standing sentry in the hallway, where she could see his reassuring grin; or her mother, rousting them out of bed at dawn to go sledding in the pristine snow in Prospect Park; or the summer nights, shooting hoops until one of them caved, staggering back inside sweaty and exhausted, her mother serving the biggest sundae to the loser?

*Next time*, the bus terminal thick with shamrocks and leprechauns and St. Patrick's Day revelers, they'll have their own celebration. They'll sit on the sofa, surrounded by piles of photos, and reminisce about her mother's rowdy laugh, her goofy jokes. Next time, she'll tell him she loves him, that she's sorry she'd hurt him; next time she'll call him her Da.

But the next time was a drear September day in a hospital room, after a stroke left him unable to comprehend speech or even recognize her. His room had been dark, except for the frenetic flickering of the TV. His eyes were closed and when she touched his arm, he turned his head and looked at her unseeing.

Her headache ratchets up a notch. Jude stands to open the tiny window, drinking in the cold air.

She tried to care for him at home, her big, strapping Da, as bewildered and frightened as a lost child. Jude was lost as well, unable to comfort him or to give him some small joy.

Even at her last, her mother insisted on being taken outdoors no matter the weather, dining with everyone else when all she could manage was a morsel, lavishing them with her fierce attention and affirmations. "You're strong," she'd tell them, or wise, or funny. And to her, always, "It's a beauty you are, daughter, through and through." She was extravagant with her praise, profligate with her love.

When it became clear that her father was too easily confused, too difficult for her to manage, his older brother, Raymond, helped her choose a nursing home, then ten days later, after a second, fatal stroke, his casket.

The desolation blindsided her. That was how she expected to feel when her mother died, their final words accompanied by the eerie sound of the ventilator's artificial breaths. She felt relief, however, at the end of her mother's temporal body, unable to swallow, or even breathe on its own. They had taken leave of each other with fullness and tenderness and tears.

No regrets, not one. But for her father, she had so many.

"You did the best you could," Immaculata told her.

She knew she hadn't. For years, she'd been as withholding as he, as unforgiving. The knowledge haunted her; she became pale and withdrawn.

Maybe she's had her signs. Maybe helping Tomás is simply a lesson in charity. And her father's bequest, a test of her faith. Maybe she's not meant to *do* anything, other than pray. She retrieves his letter from the nightstand. She believes her father loved her in his own cramped way, but his gift feels like a reproach. How did he put it?

*Daughter,*

*I've left my estate (such a grand word!) and such as it is to Raymond. I couldn't take the chance that naming you in my will would automatically give those crows a right to it. Your uncle (another foolish papist) knows it's meant for you and would cut off his thumbs sooner than touch a penny of it.*

*It's you I'm after protecting, don't be mad at your Da. The money is yours, throw it off Canarsie Pier, if that's what you want, but you're not to give it to them.*

When the carillon peals for Vigils, she puts the letter away and then slips the black tunic over her head. Covering her head with the coif, she tucks the front flaps (like a bib only hidden, Sister Immaculata had instructed that first time) inside her tunic. Jude places the white vinyl band like a crown over the coif. The trick to attaching the black veil, she's discovered, is a combination of safety and straight pins. Now for the stiff discipline of the starched wimple, which encases the sides of her face and her chin, circles her neck, and lies over her heart like a white shield. She reaches back to fasten it, forced then to hold her head high and keep it there. After looping her rosary under her belt, she kisses the worn silver crucifix and pins it over her heart.

She joins her Sisters crossing the courtyard, their serge habits sibilant, their clacking beads a counterpoint, her spirit rising with their first words—a prayer. The day breaks in a chalky mist so still the echoes of the monastery bells linger in the foothills and the cross at the crest of the drive seems suspended in mid-air.

Mother Superior stands at the lectern as they file into the modest chapel, the air silky with incense and candlelight. They take their places by seniority, Sister Immaculata first. Kneeling beside Sister Catherine John in the last pew, Jude begs God to have mercy on her father's soul, and to show her the way back to contentment. When she finally looks up, she meets Mother Superior's level gaze.

After chapel, Jude takes her place next to Immaculata in the dining room. When Mother Superior finishes saying grace, Jude leaves her breakfast untouched, savoring instead the skitter and hum of female voices, the crowded table, the food, plain but delicious because of their company, the youngest part of her thinking: Good. Solid. Mine.

"You won't find any answers by fasting," Immaculata tells her.

"I'm not hungry."

"You're losing too much weight. It does not go unnoticed." She inclines her head towards Mother Superior seated at the head of the table. "Eat something, Jude. Now." For such a tiny person, she wields a commanding tone.

Jude tears a roll in half and takes a bite; she forces herself to chew, to swallow. She doesn't taste a thing.

After breakfast, they scatter to their assigned chores. Hers begins with clearing up and washing the dishes, which she dispatches with alacrity. They expect twenty-six guests this weekend. It's going to be a hectic day.

She towels out a porthole on the refectory window. Across the courtyard, the midday sun bisects the chapel. The monastery wing is still in shadow, its mortared stone sugarcoated with frost. A lone figure trudges toward the convent, as happens occasionally. A car breaks down on the back road. Or perhaps it's an early arrival for the retreat. She hangs up her apron, rolls down her sleeves, adjusts her habit, and opens the back door.

"Tomás, what are you doing here? It's not allowed." She signals the boy to be quiet and motions him inside. "How on earth did you get here?" she whispers.

He sticks out a bony thumb. She warms it between her hands. "Has something happened to your mother?"

He shakes his head. "She sent me. The food place, it closed."

"The grocery store?"

"The free place."

"Oh, no! When? Never mind. Let me think." She throws open the cupboards. Nearly everything is allotted for the resident nuns or the retreatants. She grabs a box of graham crackers and glances at the clock. If she hurries, she can make it back in time—barely. She snatches the car keys from their hook and tugs a coat from the bulky assortment by the back door. "Let's go Tomás, I don't have much time."

Tucking her veil securely behind her head, she double-checks the rearview mirror then eases the station wagon down the steep hill, pausing at the entrance marked by the weathered sign, and then pulls onto the county road. She turns up the heater and drives faster than she should, past clumps of empty summer cabins, a scattering of year-round houses in various states of disrepair, a trailer park or two. The bleak homesteads are usually obscured by the Catskills' glorious seasonal palettes, but in winter, their splintered bones are a plain and sorry sight.

"Are you warm yet?" She hands him the crackers. "Where's your scarf, your gloves?"

"I'm okay."

He's rubbing his hands together, but he refuses to wear anything more than the coat she gave him. She shakes her head. Maybe it's boys. At least he has all the clothes he needs now, whether he wears them or not. The first time she saw Tomás—his long hair wild with cowlicks, his ankles bare—he was combing through trashcans along the street in the little town not twenty miles from here, not in the Bronx or Appalachia but close enough to hear, however faintly, the monastery bells. It still gives her the chills.

"Any word from your father?"

He nods. "He found work in St. Augustine."

At the A&P she parks between a car missing its front bumper, and a pea-soup green VW bus with paisley-curtained windows. "Wait here. I won't be long." She leaves the heater running full blast and sprints to hold the door open for an elderly man clinging to a shopping cart for balance, his shoelaces untied, trousers tight around his waist, baggy everyplace else.

"Thank you, Sister, God bless you," he says, as if she's performed an act beyond a common courtesy. Is kindness such a rare commodity? Or is it the veil? She's never sure.

In record time, she picks up the boy's favorites, franks and beans, raisin bread, Ovaltine. Gets butter and eggs, some ground beef. That should tide them over until she can figure something out. Jude hesitates before getting back in the car, grinning at the sight of him drumming a backbeat and singing along to the music cranked up on the radio. It's not until the rousing chorus of 'na-na-na-nas' that she recognizes her name and her laughter becomes a frozen lump in her throat.

Ten minutes later, she pulls up in front of the Liberty Launderette. Its plate glass window reflects the faded brick façade of an abandoned building where some hippies set up a makeshift way station, selling preserves and beaded jewelry and weavings from their commune, distributing mysteriously acquired foodstuffs from USDA handouts to vagrants, migrants, and burnouts. The front door is boarded up. "When did they leave?" she asks.

He shrugs. "A few days ago, after they gave everything away. Here, my mother says to take this." He hands her a neatly folded five-dollar bill.

"Tell her no. *Gracias*, but no." She smiles at him and tucks the money into one of the grocery bags. "I'll see you soon, okay? We'll figure something out."

She waits until he disappears into the narrow doorway between the launderette and the drug store window clotted with dusty advertisements before she pulls away. God only knows how many more there are like him, living God knows where, invisible as seraphim.

At least it's nice and warm in the apartment above the dryers. But now what? Without Social Security numbers, they depend on seasonal work, money from relatives, the erstwhile hippies, and her. And if the convent washer hadn't gone kaput, their paths would never have crossed. How do people manage?

In the city, soup kitchens serve daily meals but here the little villages are too scattered for people to travel to a central location every day. It's prohibitive anyway, subject to all kinds of regulations, to say nothing of the cost of equipment and labor. The hippies had the right idea, even if they may have stolen from Peter to pay—*that's it.*

Her father never said she couldn't give to the poor.

# CHAPTER 2

She turns the heater off and the radio on. When the oldies station hammers out the staccato beat of *Walk On By*, she sings along, belting it out the way she and Connie used to, clutching their hairbrushes as mikes. She tips her head back to shout, "Foolish pride!" and nearly hits the deer bounding into the road. Braking hard, she fishtails on an icy patch, sending her pulse rocketing. *Don't brake on ice. Steer slowly. Use the gas to pull out of a skid.* Danny Farrell taught her, making her practice on the icy lip along the Brooklyn Navy Yard. The deer pricks up her ears and bolts into the woods. Jude relaxes her grip on the steering wheel and moves her foot to the gas pedal. *Danny Farrell.* She wonders if he's still in Canada, as fierce and funny as he was at nineteen, and if he still thinks about her. By the time her heartbeat slows to normal, she's at the monastery entrance, safely home. Beneath the weathered 'Monastery of the Holy Name' sign is a new one:

### RETREAT THIS WEEKEND
*The Changing Role of Women in the Church*

Making her way through the parlor crowded with women Jude avoids Sister Immaculata's steady gaze and heads for the registration table where Sister Catherine John is taking payments and handing out room assignments. "Sorry I'm late."

"Where on earth have you been?" Catherine John's chubby cheeks are flushed, but she looks more relieved than annoyed.

"Where do you want me, cash or carry?"

"Carry." She nods toward a woman shivering in a stylish but flimsy wrap. "You can start with that one."

The woman reminds her of Connie. A bit younger, early twenties maybe, and her features are coarser, but her hair is a similar shade of blond, and she's slight like Connie used to be before the children. She sometimes wonders how she would fare in Connie's shoes. Jude had done her share of caretaking but it had been—except for those few weeks with her father, which totally exhausted her—for a grown woman who could speak for herself.

Jude remembers how terrified she felt holding Anna, eight weeks old on her baptism day, the wobble and weight of the child, her heavy head and fragile body, the translucent skin. This trusting creature wanting nothing of her but needing everything she had to give. Jude cradled her with trembling arms, her chest flooding with such a fierce joy she could hardly breathe.

"Oh no, thank you, Sister," the woman says when Jude picks up her suitcase, even though Jude's practically twice her size.

"I'm Sister Jude, and you are . . . "

"Kathleen."

She escorts Kathleen to the guest wing and leads her down a dim corridor, their footsteps echoing against the vaulted ceiling. "This one's yours," she says, opening the tall, narrow door. "They're called cells but we don't lock the doors. Honest."

Kathleen doesn't crack a smile. She drags her suitcase over the threshold and stands there, waiting for Jude to leave.

"Dinner's at six in the main building. Vespers are at five-fifteen in the chapel across the courtyard. Come if you like."

"Okay. Thanks. Sister."

The door closes as soon as Jude turns her back. She shakes her head. After nearly a decade, she can't get used to being regarded as some kind of wholesome freak. Just wait, though. She'll bet anything that Kathleen will be the one to ask how they get along without sex.

To be fair, there was a time Jude used to pity these women, who had so little time for prayer and reflection. Over the years, she has come to envy them: Peace Corps volunteers back from El Salvador and Nicaragua, wives and mothers who marched in Selma and Washington, women starting their own businesses or daycare co-ops in the Bronx. "Weary pilgrims," Sister Immaculata calls them. They call the nuns "The Lord's Handmaidens." Servants of God; troubled souls. From the inside looking out, Jude fails to see the difference.

Taking her place next to Immaculata at dinner Jude whispers, "It couldn't wait."

"You'll do them no favors if you neglect your obligations here."

"But I didn't, I—"

"You left without permission."

"No one was around."

"If it wasn't for your father," Immaculata sighs.

Jude feels the heat flooding her capillaries, reddening her skin. She shouldn't have disclosed her father's final wishes. He wouldn't have approved. "If it wasn't for my father, I couldn't help Tomás."

Immaculata rests a tiny hand on Jude's arm. "I'm not judging him, just saying that the Lord works in mysterious ways."

"He does. And if I'm not mistaken, I just found out what the money's for."

In the parlor that evening, as Immaculata works a jigsaw puzzle, Jude writes out all the details in a proposal to Mother Superior. "I can do this, Immaculata. And keep it afloat until I can get enough grants and donations to make it self-sustaining. It must be God's will."

Immaculata considers a puzzle piece then finds its place. "It has been my experience that we seldom recognize God's will if it differs from our own."

"But it's perfect. It will only be open one day a week to start. Of course, we'll have to order the groceries and stock the shelves. And write the grants, of course. And notify the—"

"We? You, you mean," Immaculata says.

Jude flushes. "Everyone can help, there's plenty to do—"

"That's hardly the point. We've more than enough to do here. You'll need Catherine John's help at the very least—"

"I can handle it alone if I have to. I feel it's what God's calling me to do."

Immaculata fixes her with a pointed stare. "Then you won't be doing it alone, will you?"

Jude slides the proposal under Mother Superior's door before retiring to her room. Preparing for bed Jude considers Immaculata's words. She's right, of course. As brusque and exacting as she can sometimes be, Immaculata has always steered her in the right direction. It was Immaculata who, a few weeks after Jude's father's funeral insisted on being chauffeured to the Old Rhinebeck Aerodrome where she surprised Jude by treating her to a ride in a biplane. How she loved the thrill of flying in the open cockpit, her veil flapping beneath the old-fashioned leather helmet, the Hudson Valley a green furze scrolling beneath her, pulling her focus back to the earth. She had surfaced for a while.

Until she had to pack up the house. Long days spent sorting out what her father saved, what her mother had left behind, navigating the landscape of her childhood. Her skin prickled at the ghostly remnants: her father's steel-toed boots on the back porch, as worn down as he was from work on the docks; the antique ivory lace mantilla her uncle brought back from Ireland that her mother wore every Sunday at Mass; her own basketball trophies for All-Star, state champion, MVP, artifacts of her former life, the figures frozen mid-leap, victorious.

The even longer nights when, too exhausted to cook, she'd have a bowl of cereal and lie on the sofa staring at the pale geometry on the walls where pictures used to hang. She had traveled back to the cloister in a fog, leaving some piece of herself behind.

For the first time in months, Jude sleeps through the night, waking the next morning with her heart plump with hope, and her favorite prayer, the first one her mother taught her, on her lips.

*I arise today*
*Through the strength of heaven*

*Light of sun,*
*Radiance of moon,*
*Splendour of Fire . . .*

"I'm giving you St. Patrick's Breastplate," her mother said, "to keep you safe. To keep you strong."

*I arise today*
*Through God's strength to pilot me:*
*God's might to uphold me,*
*God's wisdom to guide me,*

When she was little, she imagined the Breastplate as an invisible coat of armor and couldn't understand why her mother gave it away, didn't keep it to protect herself. And with a child's faith took it as a sign of her mother's great love, the ultimate sacrifice. Even now that she knows better, it still conjures up her mother's voice, and comforts her.

Jude matches her stride to Mother Superior's on their way through the courtyard after Vigils. "Have you read it?"

"I have."

"And?"

"It bears discussion. Come to my study after Vespers, Jude. We'll talk then."

It satisfies her, this pacing of prayer: Vigils, Lauds, Noon, Vespers, Compline, unfailing, reassuring, like God's love. Today Jude uses each time to ask God's blessing on Loaves and Fishes, as she's already christened the food bank.

The women do retreat, hour-by-hour, from the lives they left, she can see it in their faces, in their gait. There doesn't seem to be an equivalent for her. No way to slip into secular life for an occasional weekend. Sometimes she wonders how she would fare in Connie's shoes. In her last letter, she mentioned that Vince has been working long hours at Fields, he has a second call back at Circle in the Square; Anna's grades are excellent, and she's a big help with Ceci (thank God, this pregnancy's the worst).

Jude wrote back, including a note for Anna, and a brochure with the upcoming schedule for retreats. Circled the next one. January 6th: *Reflection and Renewal for the New Year.*

At Vespers, the chapel is full, the monastery no longer forbidding and the nuns less exotic to the retreatants, who are welcome to join them in the chapel. Tonight, some do, Kathleen among them. She waves to Jude from across the aisle.

As soon as they're done, Jude hurries back to the convent and enters the study on Mother Superior's sturdy heels.

Mother sits behind her desk and motions her to the opposite chair. "Please."

Since Mother's longish nose and narrow mouth give her a perpetually dour appearance, Jude can't read her mood. The older woman has a well-earned reputation for slow but fair deliberations. In light of the latitude granted by the Second Vatican Council, she's agreed to authorize whatever changes in habit the convent decides upon. But it's been eight long years since Vatican II and the Sisters of the Holy Name are still arguing about what to wear.

"What you propose is a noble enterprise, Jude, and a clever way to use your inheritance without violating either your vows or your father's wishes."

"Immaculata told you?"

"Only because she's been worried about you."

"Then you approve?"

"Of the project, not your involvement."

"It will not affect my work, Mother, I promise—"

"It already has," she says, not unkindly. "That is where you were yesterday, with that child?

"But it was an emergency—"

"No doubt. And if you do this, there will be other emergencies."

"So, what are you saying? I may fund a food bank but not administer it?"

"Why must it be you?"

"It doesn't, not in the long run, but they need help now; Tomás and his family, and the old man with the baggy pants and that little girl who reminds me of . . . " Her voice catches and she can't control her tears.

Mother reaches in her pocket and hands her a handkerchief. "I know you're passionate about this, Jude, but it is not our mission."

"I can do both, I know I can."

"That is not your decision." Mother's voice sounds oh so soft and gentle. "What if each of us wanted to do something else? And believe me, we have all felt that way at some point."

"But something must be done."

"There are social services—"

"They don't qualify. And even if they did, it's still not enough."

"I'm sorry, Jude. There will always be people in need; you can't take care of everyone. We can pray for them, entrust them to God's care. And hope for the best."

"There's always hope, Mother. It's justice that's scarce."

Mother stands. "Come, let's go to dinner."

"I'm not hungry."

"Get some rest then."

Jude presses the hankie to the fresh fall of tears. She pauses in the doorway. "What if I can't let this go?"

"Then you must choose whether or not you wish to remain here."

"But you're my family," she whispers. "This is my home."

"I do not say this lightly, Sister, but I see no other way."

After staring at the wedge of moonlight on the ceiling for hours, Jude gives up. Air. She needs air. And sky. She follows the flagstones to the front entrance, nearly slipping on the icy path.

Circling behind the dormitory wing, she sees a light in Kathleen's room. Just as she predicted, Kathleen finally did ask how they get along without sex. "Easier than you think," Jude answered, as she always does. But she had wondered too, at eighteen, still close to the season of Danny Farrell, when promising never to lie skin to naked skin with a man—holding fast, being held—seemed an exquisite sacrifice.

"What about money?" Kathleen wanted to know. The vow of poverty never fazed Jude. She'd watched her father divide his pay among tattered envelopes marked for "Hudson City Savings," "ConEd," "Bell Tel." He'd rattle his loose change into the cloudy crystal vase that used to be filled with flowers when her mother was well. Perhaps his scrimping was his way of denying them the comforts her mother had forfeited long ago, or maybe it was the only way he knew how to care for a child.

No one ever asks about obedience or what it's like to relinquish your judgment; surrender your will. If they did, she'd tell them it's the hardest vow of all.

She'd entered the convent happy to forfeit the trappings of a secular life for an abundant spiritual one. A road sometimes arduous, sometimes perplexing but always *there*. Until now. It no longer feels as if she is giving things up but that they are being taken from her, erasing her past, preempting her future. Things she hadn't realized she wanted.

Jude leaves with what she brought with her. Her simple wardrobe: two skirts, two blouses, two sweaters: one black, one white. Underwear, pajamas. Her winter coat and boots. Except for her prayer books, her Daily Office, she has no personal effects.

It takes her an hour to pack and all day to say goodbye.

She walks the cloister, the monastery grounds, leaving the chapel for last, where she knelt a long time in her usual place, grateful for His guidance, humbled by His grace.

Jude nearly changes her mind at the last minute, enduring Immaculata's mournful gaze, Catherine John's false cheer, Mother Superior's formal farewell, the weight of her decision like a mantle of stone.

# CHAPTER 3

"Whoa, Ceci." Connie corrals her five-year-old. "Let Anna in the door first."

"You *promised*." Ceci hurls herself at her sister. "The snow's almost gone."

Connie squints at Anna's frayed suede jacket. "Sweetie. Stop wearing that to school. You look like a tatterdemalion."

"Spell it, Mama," Anna says, tossing her jacket on the banister.

"See if you can first."

Anna opens the dictionary on the shelf near the Scrabble board. "Tatter, tatter, then d-e?"

"Right. Then—"

"Wait. Don't tell me." Anna runs her finger down the page. "A person wearing ragged or tattered clothing. Ragamuffin."

"Can I have a muffin?" Ceci says. "I'm hungry."

"You can have a snack with Anna before you go out," Connie tells her. "Unless she has a lot of homework?"

"Not really." Anna sets her backpack on the stairs.

"Again? Maybe you should have skipped third grade like Daddy wanted."

The anxious look on Anna's face tells Connie she was right to intercede when Vince was badgering her. "Standout and standup, Anna." Anna dislikes the spotlight as much as Ceci adores it. Anna may resemble Vince, but she's her mother's daughter.

When Anna goes upstairs to change, Connie bundles Ceci into leggings and boots, zips up her parka. "One hour, okay? And mind Anna."

Ceci nods and bolts out the back door, leaving Anna to catch up with her.

Connie shakes her head. Maybe she would want more children if they were all like Anna, but one more like Ceci and she'll be worn to a nubbin. She can barely cope with two. How did her mother manage with six? No, not manage . . . *excel.* Rose not only cleaned and ironed, baked and sewed but also took them to the botanical gardens, the Bronx Zoo, Radio City Music Hall. She's saved every drawing and lock of hair, their baby teeth, report cards. Now nearly seventy, her mother still drops by to lend a hand and seizes any opportunity to babysit her thirteen grandchildren.

When Vince isn't home by nine-thirty, Connie indulges her hope that this is the turning point, that he'll come home triumphant. He was wild about the script. She loved watching him rehearse, his gaze fixed in the middle distance, his features suddenly stilled by grief or clenched in fear, or loose and languid with lust. Last night, he hardly slept. He pampered her with a breakfast tray this morning, and then joined her under the covers.

"This guy's going to be the next O'Neill," he had said, rubbing the small of her back. Vince slid his hand over her belly. "Maybe we should name this one Eugene. What do you think, Con?"

"Better than Tennessee," she laughed.

"No, seriously. If it's a boy, we'll name him after the next great American playwright." He tapped the curled-up script on the nightstand.

"Whose name is ?"

"Oh, right. It's Joseph," he said, releasing her. "Forget it."

"Would it be so awful to name the baby after your father?"

"I wouldn't give him the satisfaction."

Connie sighs. Vince is his father's son, hotheaded the two of them, unbending. To be fair, that same stubbornness is what keeps Vince going. His audition was scheduled at six. This wasn't a cattle call—he was asked to read. Along with others, she knows, but still. Maybe they're running late, or they've called him back, or maybe he's with Arthur, negotiating his contract, or maybe—*shit*. Something smells scorched.

She shuffles to the kitchen. Her ankles are swollen, and the baby's been kicking field goal after field goal. *Must be a boy, this pregnancy is nothing like the others.* She turns off the burner under the minestrone, as thick with fresh vegetables as stew, pours all but the bottom inch into another pan, leaves the burnt part to soak in the sink. She's hungry but takes a handful of Saltines to tide her over until Vince gets home. She fed the girls in-between loads of laundry and finally—Ceci wheedling for an extra kiss, Anna for one more story—tucked them in an hour ago.

If she had the energy, she'd climb the stairs, change out of these grungy jeans, Vincent's chambray shirt. She lowers herself onto the sofa instead, puts her feet up on the coffee table next to the pile of mail she hasn't had the energy to sort through, gathering the stack onto what's left of her lap. Tosses the Day-Glo circulars for snow tires, storm windows, and discount liquor, sets aside the seed catalogs that came weeks ago for when she has the time to even think about resuscitating the garden. She'd hoped but hasn't yet managed to plant even one of the gardens she'd designed when she was a botany major. The sultry model on the cover of *Vogue Italia* seems to sneer at Connie's split ends, un-plucked eyebrows. Neither Connie nor her sisters subscribed to fashion magazines. She still finds them both intimidating and obscene in their devotion to preening, to purchasing, to excess. Although Vince needs them for work, now that Marty promoted him from tailor to designer, if that's the word for someone who knocks-off haute couture in the garment district. She eclipses the *Vogue* with the Burpee catalog. The bump she'd presumed to be a free seed packet turns out to be a letter from Holy Name Retreat House, postmarked December 9th. From Rita.

Connie can't help it. In her mind's eye, Sister Margaret Jude will always be Rita Mooney, that too-tall little girl who'd eaten most meals at Connie's house, her big eyes ricocheting around the crowded table, trying to keep up with the boasts, the teasing, the jokes. Rose used to shoo her out of the kitchen; Rita had been so eager to help that she'd pile too many dirty dishes on the drainboard or climb onto the counter to put away a glass.

There's a separate note to Anna from "Aunt Sister," as the girls refer to her, and a brochure, the monastery grounds in fall splendor, the small white chapel even brighter amid the scarlet oaks and yellow poplars. The retreat schedule is listed in the centerfold. Rita circled the one called *Reflection and Renewal for the New Year* and the date, January 6th, and wrote "Please? I miss you!" in the margin. Two nights, three days. Connie sighs. She would have loved to. But honestly. As if she were free to do as she pleases with a husband and small children.

She munches the crackers, unmindful of the crumbs settling on the slopes of her breasts, as she reads Rita's letter about the needy: Tomás and his family, the elderly woman buying a tin of sardines, which she probably shared with her cat. Rita's such a … *force.* Always has been. Connie had loved walking down the corridors of St. Agnes, basking in Rita's fervent glow.

When they were in fifth grade, Connie's sisters tried (unsuccessfully) to tame Rita's thick and curly hair so it would grow down and not out like a clown's. All through grade school, except as a stand-in for pick-up basketball games, Connie's brothers treated Rita as another kid sister, which is to say they ignored her. Until high school when Rita Mooney's tall frame suddenly developed full breasts and lush hips. When her wild hair and broad mouth made her look more worldly-wise than the rest of the girls at St. Agnes. Then Connie's brothers, and their friends, would hang around the stoop until Connie's father chased them away. But even as teenagers, when most girls traded sanctity for the opposite sex, Rita remained inflamed with desire for sacrifice and good works. If she envied Rita anything, it was her passion, not her beauty.

At the sound of the key in the lock, Connie startles up from sleep. Vincent, his back to her, shoulders out of his cashmere coat, draping it carefully on a wooden hanger.

She hoists herself up off the couch. "You're home late, that's a good sign, right?" She ambles over to him. "Are you hungry, sweetie? I've waited dinner."

"Vince?" She reaches for him but he wheels around at her touch.

"Lay off, Connie." He scrutinizes the living room. "Christ, this house looks like shit."

She surveys the usual clutter: a pile of folded laundry perched in the crook of the club chair, coloring books, stray crayons, the purple one's tip lying at an acute angle to its shaft, a doll with no underpants, a couple of raisins half-buried in the shag. With a practiced and calm deliberation, she clears the dining room table of clutter, coupons, correspondence. Sets a place for him at the table.

"What happened?" Not really needing to ask.

"Richard was there, looking flabby. They eat out all the time now that Claire has an expense account."

Escaping to the kitchen, she tears lettuce leaves into a colander, rinses them under the tap, the water muffling his monologue. Vincent follows her. "Connie. Do you want to hear this or not?"

She doesn't answer. He snatches the lid off the pot, sniffing, and exhaling an approving sigh. She smells spearmint and scotch. He wobbles a bit when he bends to peer into the refrigerator. "I've worked with Jack Cates before. Twice. After my audition, he says 'Great seeing you, Vince.'" He rolls up a slice of bologna, bites it in half. "'Great seeing you, Vince.' You know what that means."

She hasn't been listening, just making sure the pitch of his voice was in line with 'annoyed,' not 'furious.' She hears the pause; she missed her cue. When she looks up, Vince hands her the line.

"Kiss of death." He slams the refrigerator door. "Sorry to bore you." He stalks off into the dining room.

*Jackass.* She picks up the bread knife, slices a chunk for herself, chewing as she throws the lettuce into a wooden bowl, adding slivers of carrots, cherry tomatoes. As she carries the salad and a wedge of bread to the table, Vince ignores her, as if she were some anonymous waitress. *Fine.* Retreating to the kitchen, she turns up the flame under the minestrone. She's gnawing on another mouthful of bread when she hears him bellowing like Stanley in *Streetcar.*

"I wanted this one, damn it! Not off-off-Broadway, not an out-of-town tour, not pushing overpriced crap! "

She scoops two ladles of the fragrant soup into a delicate china bowl and hurries into the dining room. "Vince. You don't know for cer—"

"Haven't you heard a word I've said?"

She can't decide whether to stay or walk away. She tries to look serene although her insides are churning. Vince totes up the reasons why he should have gotten the part. "First, the guy's supposed to be athletic," he clenches his fist, thrusts out his raised thumb. "No way Richard's right for a guy who's supposed to work out. Second," he points his index finger at her like a gun, "the guy's supposed to be Portuguese. Two-thirds of the actors in that room were either fair-haired or light-eyed. Third . . . "

*Oh, quit whining.* Wine. *Shit.* She forgot. She holds up her hand. "I'll be right back." She's in the kitchen struggling with the corkscrew when she hears his chair scrape the parquet floor.

"Connie, it's cold, goddamn it!"

She steps into the doorway, just as Vince lets fly. The bowl strikes her collarbone, the soup still warm enough to redden her skin. When it hits the floor, she hears the musical pings of china shattering. Broth darkens her shirt, bits of vegetables cling to shards of white porcelain, the rest puddles on the floor.

Something primitive in her wants to bite his flesh, tear his skin. She lunges for him but slips and lands hard on her hip. He straddles her ankles, his balled fists on his thighs, the cords in his neck like slender snakes beneath his skin. Holding her breath, she wraps her arms around herself and calls *Baby, baby, baby.* Her veins feel dilated waiting for a message back. Out there, Vince rants on and on, a litany of her shortcomings: "You always . . . you never . . . "

She stays down on the floor, in the sticky wet, curled around her womb, hating him.

# CHAPTER 4

Connie bites down on the hard details of last night, trapping the bile in her throat.

After Vince stormed out, she had stayed on the floor, imagining the baby flailing in the suddenly sour amniotic fluid. She rubbed her belly as if she could erase the bitter memory before it settled in the tender folds of her infant's brain.

"Mama, get up! Please, please get up…" Wide-eyed and trembling, Anna hovered in the doorway, a rosary clutched in her hands.

Limbs numb, Connie stumbled upright. Anna bolted, sobbing, into her mother's arms.

"Ssssh, sssh. It's okay. I'm okay."

But she's seen Anna flinch when a door slams, a car roars down the block; how she ducks upstairs when Vince rehearses dark dramas, even though Connie has reassured her it's pretend. Well, she couldn't this time.

Connie lay beside Anna and held her until she fell asleep, then dressed and curled up on the couch, staring at the snow flurry in the wedge of light from the streetlamp. But sleep never came. Just aftershocks, ricocheting off her to the children; altering the landscape of her heart, cutting off any way back to what they'd had.

This morning, instead of bright sparkly drifts, there's frozen gray lace in the gutters, helmets of soot-colored snow on the fire hydrants. The newspaper pitched sideways on the stoop, its insides spilling down over the icy steps.

'**President Nixon: U.S. Planes Bomb Da Nang By Mistake,**' she reads and wishes she hadn't. The church bells chime six knells.

She squats on her haunches, her belly resting on her thighs. Her hands tremble as she zips up Ceci's parka, snagging a stray curl at the stop. Ceci's shriek brings Anna running downstairs, her uniform jumper undone at the waist.

Connie hoists herself up. "Here, Anna, help her." Ceci, still drowsy, snuggles into Anna's embrace. Anna tucks her sister's thick curls into the quilted hood, then kneels to tug Ceci's red boots over her shoes. Connie grabs onto the banister and climbs the stairs. The baby twists inside her womb, and the stairs seem to tilt. She lurches to the toilet, vomits, then hunches over the sink to rinse out her mouth. When she closes her eyes, she has the odd sensation of watching herself on film; a wan woman, beach-ball pregnant, peering anxiously out the window; a close-up of the kitchen clock, minute hand jerking into the future; pan down to her clenched fists, then back to the clock, music rising as the tension builds. Part of her longs to sit down and watch the movie unfold. Her fingers find the swollen bruise above her breast, pressing her back into real-time. She upends the crocheted doll with the wide skirt, extracting the wrinkled bills from the cardboard tube in the center of the spare roll of toilet paper. She sweeps through the bedroom, snatches Vincent's wool scarf, tears a check from the checkbook, and lumbers downstairs.

Connie's tugging her jacket from the jumble of the hall closet when she hears a car. Mrs. Confalone's son, Nicky, dressed in Navy blues, gets out of a cab. Connie gags on the heartbeat in her throat, then jams the money into her pocket.

"Mama." Ceci jiggles and crosses her legs. "I have to go."

"Not now, sweetie, not now." She quietly closes the front door behind them. "C'mon, beat you to the corner!" They run up the street, the children bobbing in her wake. At the corner, she turns left and herds them the four slippery blocks to the church.

Outside the ornate wood doors of Our Lady of Sorrows, Connie fishes crumpled tissues from her pocket, pulls bobby pins from her hair. She shepherds the girls into the gloomy recess, blindly blesses herself with holy water from the font. She crowns each daughter with a sheet of white tissue. Anna winces when the worn tip of the bobby pin scrapes her scalp. Ceci's makeshift mantilla floats a good inch above her hairline on a cloud of thick, curly hair.

Connie genuflects without grace, her belly a beanbag pulling the rest of her body to its fulcrum of weight. She unbuttons her coat, settles herself on the hardwood pew, unyielding to her body's contours, holding her up from the cold marble floor. Her breath and heart find their mutual rhythm.

The girls, their outdoor clothing shed, practice the rituals; they bless themselves with holy water, genuflect piously, walk to the altar where they kneel, spines rigid, hands clasped. When she made her First Holy Communion, Connie walked to this same altar in her frilly white dress, snow-white shoes and socks, the short veil mimicking the bridal one. Her father had embarrassed her by snapping photo after photo, her mother by weeping with abandon.

She can't go to them now. Even Carlo, who at six two is the tallest of her brothers, seemed to shrink under their great sorrow and disappointment, folding himself up in the corner of the green brocade couch, tracing its pattern over and over with one long pale finger while Rose wept and Louis reasoned, even though Rose had opposed his marriage from the beginning, seeing the disdain in which Cathy held them. Carlo finally cut them off saying, "Don't you get it? She left me. End of story." Her parents didn't even like Carlo's wife and had no grandchildren to consider. They'll insist she stay, talk to a priest. *The sanctity of wedding vows. The blessing of family.* Well, it has been. For them.

Her father came from work the same time every night, a rolled-up, bloodstained apron under his arm, the scent of animal flesh on his shoes. Rose—proud of her handsome husband, well-muscled from lifting sides of beef and meting out chops, loins, roasts with a heavy wooden-handled cleaver—would sing out, "Papa is home! Quick, take his apron, hang up his coat, give him a kiss!"

After Mass on Sundays her mother held court in the kitchen, Connie's sisters helping, she as youngest contributing the least, but mesmerized by the joyful ritual. Her brothers ducked in and out, stealing bits of food, teasing Rose (who feigned exasperation but loved their impatience for her cooking, their impertinence). Her father sang at full voice along with the music, sometimes *La Traviata*, sometimes Perry Como, always Italian, dancing into the kitchen to whirl her mother around the red and white-tiled floor. The entire family would gather around the huge mahogany table; the long afternoon spread out like the white linen tablecloth, unhurried, lingering into dusk, with walks around the block, card games, sinksful of hot soapy water, constellations gathering and coming apart only to gather again.

Dry-eyed, Connie seeks the countenance of the Virgin Mary. For the first time, she cannot find consolation in the Blessed Mother's serene face, her outstretched arms. Resentment has eaten away every moist thread of her heart, leaving a dry veiny pit.

Anna's solemn face floats past her line of vision. Her daughter's dark beauty mirrors Vincent's. He'd stood apart from the rest of the grinning guests at her cousin Lucy's wedding. Lanky, wired, every feature outsized, eyes like shiny black olives she wanted to lick. She'd watched him all through the heraldry of the announcement of the new couple, the father's dance with the bride, the mother's with the groom, the bride and groom's first dance as a married couple. Stared at his mouth as he ate, his hands as they conducted his conversations. Watched him while she danced with Frank, her intended. Frank, with whom she'd played Monopoly and stoopball, learned to Twist, to kiss; both of them riding the wave of youthful enthusiasm they presumed would lead to this same celebration. Until they crashed against Vincent's dark solid presence. During their first dance, while Frank waltzed with the bride, Vincent whirled her into shadows just beyond the chandelier's reach where he sang every standard the band played. He'd been on Broadway. Once. Understudied on a road tour. Snagged a few commercials. It was just the beginning.

"There is nothing you could say that I wouldn't want to hear," he'd promised, making her feel as if she never wanted to speak to anyone else.

"I'm hungry." Ceci tugs on Connie's arm.

"Okay, put your coats on girls, let's go."

"Where? To school?" Anna looks at the clock. "Or back home?"

"Neither. We're going to visit Aunt Sister."

The train would be cheaper, but they take a cab to the city. She's never liked subways. At a station she'd stand as far as possible from the tracks, watching for jumpers, for signs of desperation in a stranger's face. On their way to Coney Island once, Carlo taunted her, leaning over the platform's edge. He'd backed up not a second too soon, well after the glaring light and piercing rumble of the local. She nearly fainted with relief.

Ceci finishes the last of the blueberry muffin Connie bought at the bakery. Anna eats half of her Danish, wraps the rest in a napkin. "For

Aunt Sister," she says. In a few minutes, Ceci nods off, draped across Connie's knees.

"Mama?" Anna whispers. "When I grow up? I don't want to get a husband. I'm going be a Sister, too."

"Come here, sweet," Connie says, gathering Anna close.

When she was a bit older than Anna, fourth grade maybe, Connie had announced her intention to be a nun, not realizing that Brenda, Angela, and Maria had made the same vow before her that, at some time or another, every Catholic girl wanted to enter the convent. But Rita made good on her intention. The year Connie married Vince, Rita entered the convent as a postulant. By the time Ceci was born, Rita had made her final vows and took the name of Sister Margaret Jude. Jude, the patron saint of desperate situations and hopeless cases.

She shepherds the girls past the knot of people in saffron robes chanting "*Hare Krishna! Krishna, Krishna!*" and offering flowers and pamphlets to passers-by. She'll just show up with her children, innocent as lambs. Sister Margaret Jude won't turn them away.

Vincent pulls into the alley, pops the trunk lid even before he hits the brake. He yawns so hard his jaw cracks. A vast silence envelops him when he cuts the engine. He floats for a bit on fragments of memory, last night still out-of-focus, a blurry reel he'd rather not replay. His limbs feel somewhere between asleep and dead. As he nudges open the car door, a slap of cold air revives him. He follows the banner of light that unfurls from the kitchen window.

Vince pauses at the door, steeling himself for the aftermath. More than anything else, he dreads the martyred silence, how she can, without a word, judge and sentence him with lowered lids, a pursed mouth, a half-swallowed word.

As soon as he steps into the kitchen, he knows; his synapses layer the details. The geometry is wrong: a bare Formica rectangle, no arc of spilled milk or circles and squares of cereal. The room is as cold as the fluorescent light, there's no scent of coffee. He's wide-awake now, and alert. The dining room has the usual clutter but the living room is colder, as if the front door had recently been held open. Vincent checks closets and drawers. Nothing's missing—except his family.

He runs up the stairs, leaving some part of himself behind. The hot and noisy way he feels when he enters their bedroom and finds their checkbook on the dresser, the closet door flung open, downshifts to a racy panic when he sees the jumble of clothes on the bed then stops to a cold, still point by the time he gets to his daughters' room. He picks up Ceci's teddy bear then flings it onto her bed and sinks into a hollowness that alters his face into an empty stare.

He can barely stand to remember last night, what a jerk he'd been. But he hates the way she sulks around, the ghost that she's become. Her face used to heat up and soften when they made love, like a compressed high-speed film of pink petals swelling into a radiant bloom. Now it seems more like a dream or a wish rather than history. Now he sees her face tight and drawn, like the face of a martyr tied to a stake, lit by a circle of flames.

When the doorbell rings, he starts, all the anxiety dropping away in the seconds it takes for him to answer the door. He doesn't even stop to consider why Connie would need to ring the bell. But it's only Anna's escort.

"Hey, Bobby. Anna's not here."

Stocky and squat, Bobby looks like a parody of a middle-aged businessman, dragging his book bag as if it carried a cargo of debt.

"Where is she?"

Vincent shrugs.

Bobby rubs a stubby finger along his bottom lip. "Don't you even know where your daughter is?"

Vincent restrains himself from pouncing on the boy and slamming him to the ground. Instead, he places a hand on Bobby's shoulder, leans in. "Just go on without her, kid."

"Okay. But I'll be here same time tomorrow and she better be ready."

Vincent has a feeling that not only won't his daughter be here tomorrow but also neither will he.

# CHAPTER 5

As the driver pulls out of Port Authority Connie watches the landscape telescope from stone monoliths to eight lanes of highway. The morning's a chiaroscuro of slate-colored clouds interrupted by blinding sunlight. In an hour they've shed suburbia and are tumbling in and out of the gently rising hills of northern New Jersey. Ice glazes the hillsides covered with bare trees which shine brilliantly in the morning sun.

"Where are we, Mama?" asks Anna.

"Fairyland," whispers Ceci, her forehead pressed against the window. "We're in fairyland."

The word conjures up bedtime stories, the scent of clean pajamas, the gritty sweetness of homemade cookies. Her arms ache from holding the girls close. The press of their small bodies keeps her blood pumping in steady pulses to her heart, spurring her on. But to what? As much as she tries, she can't imagine anything beyond getting to Rita.

Imagination is Vincent's gift, as was her grandfather's, actors both. Giacomo had been in the *commedia dell'arte* in the old country. He barely spoke English but taught her anyway—beautiful, magical things. She'd follow him to the tiny backyard where he would act out scenes in which new coins or wrapped candy would fall from a handkerchief or drop out of the sky. Her older siblings preferred television to his live theater but she thought her grandfather more wonderful than Disney. Merely by dint of his vocation, she'd granted Vincent access to a chamber of her heart.

She's fascinated by his other trade as well: the fine needles, the silk threads, the colors and textures of fabrics. Early in their marriage, he'd sketch after dinner while she put Anna to bed, the dining room wall a gallery for the clothes he'd designed. With cheap muslin he built ghosts of extravagant off-the-shoulder evening gowns; skirts cut on a bias, snug at the waist and hips, swirling free at the ankles; trousers and jackets like men's business suits. Singing show tunes as he shaped the fabric to her form, kissing her shoulder, caressing her through the rough cloth. Once he accidentally pierced the top of her breast with a straight pin. When she yelped, he put his lips on the gathering dark bead, sending the rest of her blood rushing to the surface. Flushing at the electric hum of the memory she looks up, wondering if anyone can read her thoughts.

After a long hot shower that does nothing to clear his head, Vincent phones the Pescatores.

"Vincent! What a nice surprise."

"So. Mom, how's everything?"

"Fine." Rose makes it sound like two syllables. "Vincent, what's wrong? Is it the baby?"

"No, no, no. I just wanted to talk about the christening party."

"I'm doing it, no?"

39

"Who else but my favorite mother-in-law? But, I was thinking, it's so much work —what if I hired a caterer? Just to help out."

"Bah! It's no trouble. You kids save your money."

"You're too good to us, Rose. But this time, we're getting the cake. I insist."

"Okay, sure. Anything you want, sweetheart."

He drops the receiver back in its cradle. Connie's not there or with any of her siblings; Rose would know.

The sky's a pewter color when Vincent drives to the office, gripping the steering wheel as if a bump could vaporize him. He takes the elevator to the eleventh floor, pushes the round chrome disk that serves as the door handle to Fields Fashions, sidles past the receptionist's desk, calling "Morning, Syl," after he's out of sight. Past the showroom, with its carpeted platform for the models and padded folding chairs for the buyers, past the office where Marty Fields sits with the phone trapped between his shoulder and ear, engrossed in what looks to be an endless stack of ledgers, the pale green paper with its darker stripes telling the company's fortunes.

Vincent figures he'll manage the day by holing up in his office, working on the sketches he started last week for the fall line, avoiding contact, skipping lunch. Then wait until everyone is gone before gearing up to drive home. Home. The word sets him back down in the bleak landscape of an unknown land.

He takes the receiver off the hook and throws it into the desk drawer then waits until the dial tone subsides into silence before picking up a pencil. Vince draws loops and tunnels, spirals and squares. He's filled a page before he realizes he hasn't even touched the patterns. The sketches hang on the wall until he takes them down to refashion a neckline, lift a hemline, add a button or a belt. When he throws them on the floor, they're done. He surveys the wall, scanning the designs. Nothing stands out: he takes one at random. He almost closes his office door then realizes that would be like putting out a welcome mat. On a fresh sheet of paper, Vincent draws a star in the center then doodles his way to the edge.

He considers calling his father but decides against it. Joseph couldn't hold on to his own wife. Not that he'd heard that from the old man. No, Vincent had to pry the story from his *compara*. She told him how Joseph Leonetti came to this country at sixteen, worked more hours in one week than Vincent does now in two. How within five years he'd saved enough money to open a tailor shop and four years after that made a trip to Italy to find a bride. He married a girl from his village. He had spoken so proudly and admiringly of the paradise of America that Filomena, barely seventeen, went willingly with her new husband to Brooklyn. She stayed only three years. Long enough to give birth to a son and then not even Vincent could keep her in the city she grew to hate with all its noise and dirt and hard streets.

Vincent's godmother told him Filomena had begged Joseph to take them back to Italy. When he could not be swayed, she sorrowed. Every morning Joseph woke up to the sound of his young wife weeping; every night he ate dinner across from her swollen-eyed face. Joseph tried to appease and cajole Filomena, to comfort and provide for her but she, too, would not be persuaded, could not resign herself to this urban exile. She stopped crying, then laughing, then smiling. Finally, he offered her passage home, but without the boy. His father once told him that they've never spoken since the day he put her on the ship. For all Vincent knows, his parents may still be married.

Unlike most immigrant fathers, Joseph didn't want Vincent to marry a girl from the old country. He wanted his son to marry an *American*, one who wouldn't flee across an ocean because she missed the olive groves.

It might as well be an ocean for all the distance between Connie and him.

The girls stagger off the bus, their legs numb from sitting; Connie's neck feels stiff and canted to one side. The now overcast sky falls sharply cold against her skin. Although it's mid-afternoon in upstate New York, it might as well be twilight on Saturn. There are no taxis, no cars, no station to speak of, only a corner store, a floodlight suspended from its peaked roof, shining down on the red clapboard storefront, a rusty aluminum sign naming it the General Store. A bell tinkles when she opens the door.

"Can you tell me how to get to Holy Name Retreat House?"

The clerk purses her skinny lips. "There's a bus goes right past it. It'll stop here in a while."

They stand in a knot near the front door, looking out the plate glass into the darkness, waiting for the bus. Connie stares unseeing at their reflection.

She's been told she leads a charmed life. As if charm and monotony were the same thing. A good family, a pleasing appearance, a range of modest talents that carried you over the little bumps and away from the black holes that could be the end of the you that everyone knew and loved. Maybe a charmed life is completely the reverse. Like Odysseus and the Sirens. Or any children's story of demonic forces, which seize you and fling you into the magical extraordinary.

The bus appears in a nimbus of yellow light, a shimmering chariot straight out of her reverie. The hiss of the pneumatic doors closing behind them sounds as if it's sealing her fate.

# CHAPTER 6

"There! Aunt Sister's house." Ceci points to the cross on the frozen lawn in front of the massive old monastery. Connie looks up the steep rise. It's a five-minute trudge from the road, and she's shivering by the time she presses the bell.

The doors of Holy Name Retreat House open to a bright light that blinds Connie's weary eyes. The tiny, ancient nun at the threshold seems similarly startled as if a band of hungry raccoons had shown up in the parlor. She looks past Connie into the driveway.

"Has your car broken down?"

"No, Sister. I'm here to see Sister Margaret Jude."

"I'm sorry, that's not possible—"

"I probably should have called first but I'm sure she'll want to see—"

"She's not here."

"I can wait—"

"Jude doesn't live here anymore."

Connie sways on her feet, suppressing her instinct to fall on her knees and wail.

The old woman relents. "You'd better bring these children in from the cold."

Ceci darts into the foyer. Anna takes her mother's hand and leads her to the deacon's bench. The little nun stands between them and the rest of the house.

"Are you one of her families?" the nun waves her hand over the children.

How many families does Rita have? Connie wonders. Is this a catechism question like how many gods are there?

"From town. One-of-the-families-from-town," the nun says.

"Oh, God, no Sister, I'm Connie Leonetti, a friend of Rita's, *Jude's*. She's Ceci's godmother. Please, I need to find her."

"Of course, you've come to Jude." The sister looks heavenward. "Everyone does. Did. I'm still not used to her being gone. None of us are."

Connie's vision blurs, her ears ring, suddenly she feels sweaty. She hears a burbling noise but not until a white handkerchief swipes at her face does she realize the sound is coming from her. Through her tears, she glimpses flutters of black serge, as the nun lifts her tiny hands in supplication.

"Why . . . when?" Connie hiccups her questions, reaches out for the small dry hand. But the nun jerks it away and sweeps her index finger in an arc, directing Connie's attention elsewhere.

Ceci's crept into the parlor. Anna's head nods, though she's upright on the deacon's bench, legs crossed at the ankles, hands folded in her lap. Connie stands up, sways, paddles the air to maintain her equilibrium. "Please. You have to help me."

"Would you like me to call your family?"

"No! Thank you, Sister."

"Would you like to speak to a priest?"

"No. Just Rita. Please."

Darting over to the nun, Ceci tugs on her habit. "I'm hungry."

Connie's too dazed to be embarrassed.

"Wait here." The old woman disappears down a dimly lit hallway.

Connie gazes at the statues planked on each wall, the Blessed Mother, the Sacred Heart of Jesus, a beautiful, gentle-faced, life-sized Jesus holding his own red heart surrounded by flames. What she needs to see instead is a life-sized Rita, welcoming arms outstretched.

From her perch at the counter at Sweetie's luncheonette, Rita watches a woman sweep the sidewalk in front of the bakery, her white hair braided and coiled into a crown, her apron pristine. She's about the same age as Immaculata, and from the looks of it, just as vigorous. Rita forces herself to look away, drains the rest of her coffee, signals the waitress.

"Hold your horses, hon," she says, holding the pot aloft and working her way down the counter.

The first thing Rita noticed when she took off her habit was that she no longer received the preferential treatment to which—no matter how irritating it sometimes was—she'd become accustomed. Never fussy about clothes, she picked up an entire civilian wardrobe at the thrift shop next to the Presbyterian Church here in Chalfont, the only town amid dozens of hamlets, seven miles past the village of Liberty and Tomás, nearly thirty miles away from Holy Name and the monastery bells. Just as well. She suspects her resolve would ebb with each sweet summons to chapel, as dear to her, she imagines, as a spouse's. Packing up that day, felt more like a divorce than the separation they'd agreed upon. One year, Mother Superior granted Rita to accomplish her mission and discern her future. More than enough time, she thought, except three weeks into her sabbatical, nearly an entire month, she's hardly made a dent.

Although nearly everyone is similarly dressed, she still feels conspicuous wearing jeans, although she knows she'd look odder in convent regalia. At

Catherine John's insistence, she wore her habit to shop for a car and was glad she did; as Sister Margaret Jude, she got a great deal on a VW Beetle. But in civilian clothes, as Rita Mooney, she had a hard time putting up with the real estate agent, who showed up late for every appointment, gossiped incessantly, and totally ignored Rita's preference for a small furnished apartment in town.

"Why pay rent," Denise scolded, "when you can buy a house with little or no down?"

Rita repeated her plans were temporary and indefinite, but that only spurred Denise to ferret out rentals with an option to buy. But in the end, Rita was happy Denise had been so stubborn.

"Here we are," Denise said, turning into a gravel driveway of a small clapboard Cape surrounded by trees, and a wooden bridge fording the stream. "The Messinger place."

Rita was enchanted by the sound of the water rippling over the rocks, the odd-shaped parcel of land, the house set in an isosceles triangle of trees. She barely registered Denise's monologue, " . . . only child so after the Judge finally died *years* after his massive stroke, Laurel stayed on, even though the mother went back to England, then *she* got sick, so Laurel, who became a nurse, by the way—"

"I'll take it," Rita said.

"But you haven't even seen the house."

Rita was sold on the grounds alone, but walked through the small house anyway, Denise trailing, not done with her gossip. "There's a few young families in the neighborhood, a new couple just moved in—different last names, so they're probably living in sin—a guy down the lane, rugged outdoorsy type, I forget his name but I could find out if you're interested…"

"No thanks."

"Oh?" Denise grinned. "Do tell."

"There's nothing to tell," Rita said truthfully.

Denise looked skeptical but shrugged and drove them back to her office where Rita signed the lease, picked up her car, and drove back to the little house in the woods. She moved in her scant possessions (a couple of suitcases and five cartons) by noon.

But despite all Denise's efforts, she couldn't find a suitable home for the food bank. Then, two weeks ago—for whatever the cause, all Rita's pent-up energy, just waiting to be loosed into the world, Divine intervention, coincidence—she stumbled onto the perfect place—a storefront here on Main Street, the first floor of an old building that was once a private house. Easily accessible from the bus stop with side entrance away from public view. Although seemingly vacant, there wasn't a For Rent sign, and no one answered her knock.

A few minutes later, from inside the bakery across the street, she noticed a guy in tight jeans putting a Now Leasing sign in the bay window. Rita left her purchase on the counter and ran to intercept him. She'd inspected the rooms, chattering away about the building's ideal location for her food bank and peppering him with questions about the cost and conditions of the lease. It wasn't until he held onto her hand after they shook on the deal and he offered to show her around that it dawned on her he was flirting. Dumb. There are other advantages to wearing the habit.

She leaves a dollar beside her cup. The waitress, no longer astonished by the more than generous tip, remains grateful. "Thanks, hon. You don't have to, but thanks just the same."

It's already nine o'clock by the time Rita resumes the work she began almost a week ago, when she corralled as much debris as she could stuff into oversized trash bags until she got down to the last layer of dirt. She makes several trips back and forth to her car, lugging in buckets filled with cleaning supplies, a broom and dustpan and a mop. No one offers to give her a hand.

Hard to believe the place is still such a wreck after days of peeling curling contact paper from the kitchen cabinets, emptying drawers of accumulated debris, pitching odd bits, a broken chair, bundles of brittle newspapers, broken picture frames. Yesterday, she removed all the cobwebs, unscrewed, cleaned, and replaced the light fixtures, and scrubbed the sinks and the toilet. Today she methodically wipes down the walls and thoroughly sweeps the floors. Just when she's up to her grimy knees in cobwebs and grit, there's a rap on the front window. A neat, compact woman points to the door. Rita opens it for her.

"What's going on in here?" she says. Her hair, nails, even her speech, are clipped—a shorthand of a woman.

Rita explains.

"Okay, I'm in," she says, handing Rita her card. Janet Brink, R.N. "I'm on my way to work, but call me," Janet says and leaves as abruptly as she came.

Rita looks at the card again. Between Janet's name and the hospital phone number: Pediatrics Oncology. Guess there's not much call for small talk there.

Rita first scrubs the floors on her hands and knees with a solution of soap and disinfectant, before mopping a second time. She surveys the pitted wood floors, pale green tin ceiling, wainscoted walls. The kitchen will double as her office. In the large former parlor, sawhorses support three wooden doors to form a counter. The place could use some pictures, a few homey touches, but it's serviceable for now. The first delivery is due in two days. She's applied for credit with Empire State Grocers, notified the churches, and begun canvassing for donations. Although she already has some pledges, she'll have to supplement the donations from her inheritance. She thinks her father would approve.

After what feels like an eternity, a younger, plumper nun emerges from the opposite end of the parlor. "Don't mind Sister Immaculata. I'm Sister Catherine John. You must be Connie." She takes Ceci's hand and leads them down a dimly lit hallway to the refectory. Connie half-expects Rita to pop out of a doorway, tries to will her into appearing.

"You make yourself at home," Catherine John says, setting out leftovers. "I'll be back as soon as I finish my chores." Anna and Connie peck at the grainy bread, the tepid casserole of leftover meat and vegetables. Ceci chews, opens cupboards, peeks into the institutional-sized refrigerator. Too weary to curb her, Connie concentrates instead on getting Anna to swallow a spoonful of mushy vegetables.

"Come," Catherine John says, guiding them back through the parlor to the opposite wing. Ceci runs ahead of them; Anna lags behind. The nun unlocks the door to one of the guest rooms, and then lifts a mattress from one of the two cots as she tucks in the frayed edges of a white cotton sheet. "Stay here tonight. We'll see what we can arrange in the morning."

At first, the plain room comforts Connie, reminds her of the retreats she'd taken with Rita, holding their faith to the flame, renewing their commitments to love, honor, and serve the church. She'd loved walking down the corridors of St. Agnes with Rita guiding, faces wrinkling into beaming smiles as they strode past. Then she remembers these rooms are called cells, and instead of comfort, she feels a lack of oxygen, the lingering scent of incense, like ether, lulling her to sleep. She shakes off the veil of rest, begs the young nun for Rita's address, implores her to call a cab, gathers up her sleepy brood, and escapes into the cold dark night.

# CHAPTER 7

Rita answers the door in faded jeans, work boots, and an oversized bright orange sweater with a prominent hole in the armpit. She shrieks and throws herself at Connie, grabbing as much as she can of the children with open arms.

"What on earth? Ooh, Anna, aren't you big? Where's my godchild? Ceci, give me a hug. What gives? Come *in.*"

They straggle into the kitchen where the girls collapse at the table, rest their heads on their coat sleeves.

"Oh, Reet, your hair . . . this place . . . " Connie looks around bleary-eyed. She feels as if she's been struggling to walk after an amputation: everything's wobbly and too difficult. Now that she's here, the import of what she's done punctures her bravado. The day rolls up and flattens her.

"Connie, what's wrong?"

"I've left Vince," she whispers. "I want to tell you everything, and I want to hear all about you, but I just can't right now." She can barely keep her eyes open.

Connie's hair is dull, limp; her pants are creased and shiny. She seems to be wearing too many clothes, but she's shivering anyway. Rita sighs. She could try to ply Connie with coffee and pleas but she's learned something about patience and charity. She leads Connie up a narrow staircase to a tiny bedroom with pitched eaves, helps her onto the bed, removes her shoes. She pulls a flannel nightgown out of a drawer that smells of English lavender.

"Rest. Don't worry about the girls, I'll tuck them in. The bathroom is at the bottom of the stairs. I'll leave the nightlight on."

By the time Rita reaches the kitchen Anna's struggling to stay awake and Ceci's drowsing in her lap.

"Come on, kidlets, let's put you to bed."

"Mama—"

"Is already in bed, Anna." Rita leads them to the couch, helps them get undressed.

"Aunt Sister?" Anna tentatively touches Rita's short locks.

"Lord, I must look strange to you, Anna. But it's me. Really, sweetie. I promise."

"Did you run away, too?"

While Rita struggles to find the words to reassure Anna, the child gives in to her weariness, lies down beside Ceci, wraps one arm around her sister's waist. Rita tucks them in, transfixed by their faces, slack with exhaustion, their bodies nestled together for comfort.

What on earth happened? Rita scans through the times she has seen Connie and Vincent in the past few years. On Ceci's birthday, Connie harried in the backyard littered with greasy paper plates, herding the kids away from the smoking barbecue grill, scooping the melting ice cream onto the birthday cake; the men drinking beer, shooting hoops; Vincent, Carlo and Louis, Jr. against their brothers-in-law; the older men egging them on.

Then Vincent, victorious, licking ice cream from Connie's knuckles, the gesture relaxing her bunched lips into a half-grin.

At Louis and Rose's fiftieth wedding anniversary party in the crepe-papered, candlelit room at the Knights of Columbus, Vincent singing "Always" as Rose and Louis danced, Connie and her sisters crying, laughing, snapping pictures. Tugging Vince away from the bar for a dance, the two of them wrapping their arms around each other, Vincent whispering into Connie's ear, her face reddening before she tucked it under his chin.

But at Anna's First Communion, after church, Rita found Connie upstairs in bed, the shades drawn.

"What's wrong?" she'd asked when she saw Connie's swollen eyes, her fist clutching a wad of damp tissues.

"I'm pregnant." Connie snuffled, patted a spot on the bed next to her.

Rita tucked in her habit, looped her beads over one arm, and stretched out beside her.

Connie turned to face her. "Maybe if I wore one of those . . . ."

Rita jumped up, started to strip. "Here you go, baby girl, I have a spare."

They cracked up then and Connie reassured her. "It's just hormones, Reet. Mother Nature has a wicked sense of humor."

So maybe it is hormonal. Why she left. Connie's the most loyal creature. She'd visited Rita's father every week until his death. And, as far as she knows, Connie still writes to the pen pal in Venezuela she's had since fifth grade. Connie only stopped getting her hair done at *Tresses* when Alexa got into a huge fight with her boyfriend and left Connie's permanent on so long that she molted like a newborn chick.

Either she's riding some biochemical tide or Vincent's done something beyond the pale. Oh, he's enormously entertaining, but also cocky, volatile, and self-involved. She'd commented once on his tremendous ego, but Connie insisted it was part of his shtick. She brushed off his moodiness as "artistic temperament." It seems to Rita that Connie held her husband up to the half-light with one eye closed, winking him into perfection.

As soon as she hears Anna's even breaths, Rita turns on the lamp. Although she opens a book, it's the girls' faces she tries to read.

By the time Connie ventures downstairs, Rita's been up for hours.

Rita hands her a thick ceramic mug. "Coffee first."

They sit at the worn oak table under the kitchen window. Birds fly in and out of the leafless thickets to the feeder dangling from a gnarled branch. Connie's skin has a bluish hue like fake milk. And she looks deflated, just the opposite of pregnant plump. She carries herself as if she swallowed something large and indigestible.

"Tell me," Rita says.

Connie lowers the bodice of her nightgown to reveal the purple lump, the angry red welt.

"Not . . . Vincent," says Rita. "Oh, Connie, this can't be . . . He adores you."

Rita notices Connie's bitten nails, the moist red rim of her eyelids. "You're staying here. We'll figure something out. We should get a doctor to look at that bruise."

"That's not what hurts. It's the way he flipped into some stratosphere of rage. The first time I thought he was just acting."

"The first time!"

"We'd been to a party in the city for his friend, Richard. He was leaving for a road tour of *Company!* You know how those parties go . . . the performers are always 'on' and they love a captive audience. Vince sang Bobby's role and everyone told him the part had his name all over it, that he'd been robbed. And it was true, Reet, he did deserve it."

"Let's not talk about what he deserves. I've a mind to tell him what he deserves. You don't deserve this."

"On the way home, he started in with the 'I coulda been a contenda' bit from *On the Waterfront*. You know him; he can go all night when he's revved. It was late, we'd had a few drinks, I was sleepy. I must have drifted off. The next thing I knew he was screaming at me to wake up, that obviously he was a lousy actor if his audience fell asleep on him. He was driving like a madman, punching the steering wheel. He dropped me home and took off. That was the first time he stayed out all night."

A sleek brown squirrel dives onto the feeder from above, sending up a burst of bird flight.

"This was when?"

"After Ceci was born."

"Oh, Con, why didn't you tell me?"

"Because then it was a one-time thing. A blip on the radar. We both couldn't believe that was *us*." She tightens the quilt around her enormous lap. "And afterward he was so contrite, tearful."

"He's an actor, Connie," Rita says softly.

"Every day for the next week he came home bearing gifts. Yellow freesias. White tulips. Champagne."

"And?"

"The gentle, vulnerable Vince erased the horrible one. I don't know how else to put it."

"Since then . . . "

"Since then, there have been two, no three more . . . incidents. Not including this one." She touches her bruise.

Rita winces. "But why didn't you go to your parents? Or to one of your sisters? Your brothers, even?"

"I don't . . . didn't want to ruin their relationship. Vincent plays bocce

54

with my father, flirts with my mother, plays ball with my brothers. Gets my sisters comps to shows. They're crazy about him."

"They wouldn't be if they knew. Why are you protecting him?"

"Because it wouldn't happen if only—" Connie lowers her voice. "Every time it's because of a role he didn't get. Or had but lost. Each time they last a little longer, get a little more intense. I swear, Reet, this is the first time I've gotten hurt."

"Physically."

"This would never have happened if he'd gotten that part."

"Please. That's like saying you wouldn't get wet if it didn't rain. He has choices here. And so do you." Rita shakes her head. "I can't believe you've allowed him to bully you."

"I have children to consider. And I took vows, too, you know. I can't just walk away from them like you."

"I haven't, I'm on sabbatical."

"Why? What's so terrible about the convent?"

Rita opens her mouth and they hear a blood-curdling scream.

Ceci's nightmare rouses Anna as well, so they each cradle a frightened girl.

"I woked up scared, Mama," Ceci sobs. "S'not my bed."

"I know, sweetie, I know. We're at Aunt Sister's, remember?"

Ceci twists around to see Anna sitting on Rita's lap. She blinks out two fat tears then narrows her eyes and looks Rita up and down. "Where's your dress?

"Upstairs in my closet."

"And your hat."

"Same place."

"You have curly hair."

"I do."

"I want to sit in your lap."

"You're such a baby." Anna rolls her eyes and switches places with her sister. She winds her arm around Connie's neck and whispers, "I want to go home."

"We're staying at Aunt Sister's for a while, Anna. It'll be so fun. You should see all the different birds at the feeder and the snow is so beautiful."

"But we don't have our stuff, I don't have any clothes."

"Tell you what," says Rita, "I'm going to make you my special lumpy oatmeal and then I'll drive you to town in my little yellow bug."

"You drive a *bug?*" Ceci says, "Euwww!"

"She means a car, stupid head." Anna's not at all appeased.

In the daylight, Connie gets her first look at their refuge. The house is a small yellow Cape that sits on the crust edge of a pie-shaped property. Hardwood trees line the perimeter.

"Look Con, this is what I fell in love with." Rita walks to the middle of a wide wooden bridge that leads to the garage. She points to the shallow brook that runs along one side of the pie slice from tip to crust, separating roughly one-third of the lot from the rest. "Listen. It really babbles."

"Is it always this quiet?" Connie shivers. "It's like another world."

The girls peer down at the mallards paddling between the icy fringes of the stream. "Look, Mama, ducks!" Ceci shouts, shattering the still air.

# CHAPTER 8

The entire town runs for two miles of Main Street: three churches, a couple of gas stations, a tavern, a luncheonette, a bakery, a clothing store, the Salvation Army, a hardware shop. And a lone movie theater featuring *The Godfather* and *Deliverance*. Rita eases into a parking space behind a pickup truck piled high with split wood. "There's Loaves," Rita says, pointing across the street. "Come on, I'll show you around, then we should be able to get most everything you'll need at the thrift shop."

"I haven't been in a thrift shop since . . . " Connie laughs, "since our Tacky Prom Nights."

That ritual Rita had designed to fly in the face of the feminine ideal. Prom night for girls only. Prizes were awarded for worst dress, worst hairdo, worst make-up, worst total effect. Connie always enjoyed the spirit of the night but secretly hated not looking her best. In fact, although she had the most beauty to conceal, it was Rita who frequently won.

They comb through the piles of clothes in the basement of the First Presbyterian Church where they find parkas, sweaters, flannel shirts. Ceci picks out red boots two sizes too big, canary yellow mittens, a fuchsia sweater. Anna falls in love with a tattered suede jacket the color of toast and a tan hooded sweatshirt just like the one she left balled up in the hamper at home.

"Ohhhhh Connie," sings Rita, "check this out." She's waving a fluffy creation of organdy and tulle, lime green with lavender accents. She holds it against her chest, drapes the skirt over one arm. "What do you think?"

"Truly gross. Butt ugly."

She grins. "I've got mine. Your turn."

Connie burrows through the limp discards from other people's lives, remembering the dress Vince made for her their first anniversary, a coppery sheath suspended by a slender noose of shimmering silk. She'd felt slinky and sophisticated, in her topaz pendant earrings, and high-heeled sandals that slid on the cobbles in Washington Square. Vince looped his arm around her waist to steady her. Then later, in the smoky scent of candles and cigarettes at the Blue Note where Vince chatted with the sax player, catching her breath when Vince took the stage at the next set. His eyes locked on hers as he sang "Since I Fell for You." She felt the other patrons staring at her in the near darkness and held herself still, both thrilled and embarrassed.

Determined to be a good sport, Connie sorts through six piles before she finds a screaming pink number with an empire waist and yards of cascading chiffon. "Ta-da!" She holds it up. When Rita shields her eyes from the onslaught of pink, Connie chokes back tears.

While Connie naps, Rita sends the girls out to play, then takes out the phone directory, index cards, a legal pad. On the cards she prints the phone numbers for Police, Fire, Hospital, Doctor, Dentist, Loaves and Fishes, Home. On the yellow legal pad, she lists the following: beds (Salvation Army?), crayons, games, etc., pillows & sheets & towels (Sears), first aid kit, other (ask Connie). Makes a note to ask Janet for referrals for an obstetrician and pediatrician.

How could Vincent do this? Why has Connie put up with his tantrums? Why has she never said a word? Rita understands disenchantment. Her own veil of illusion has been pierced. But it was a decisive moment in which she saw the divide between her desires and those of the Order. And it wasn't vile or violent. Just a difference of opinion. But this . . . minefield Connie's walked. How can she care for a man like this? How can she trust him to take care of her? Why take so many chances?

Just as Rita finishes taping an index card inside the cupboard door Connie creeps into the kitchen. "Where are the girls?"

Rita points outside. Ceci's making tracks wherever she can find a good patch of snow. Anna diligently rolls body parts for a miniature snowman.

"I sincerely hope you have a carrot for his nose. Anna doesn't take kindly to substitutes." Connie settles down at the table. "Now, tell me about you."

Rita pulls a wilted head of broccoli from the crisper. She finds a bruised carrot, hands it to Connie. "What Immaculata told you is true, as far as it goes. Children like Tomás need help, I couldn't turn my back on pain and suffering. But ever since Vatican II we've been sorting out our role as nuns, what to relegate to the past, what to keep.

"You wouldn't believe some of the tiresome arguments that go on." Rita pours some milk into a pot, turns the burner flame to low. "Interminable discussions about everything from whether or not to wear our habits to the virtues of social activism versus traditional service. We need to come to a consensus if we're to live together in anything resembling harmony. But consensus comes at a glacial pace."

Connie nods. "You couldn't even wait for the bus when it was late; I'd have to run as fast as I could to keep up with you."

Rita opens a jar of honey, spoons some into the milk. "In the meantime, with few exceptions, the laity are the ones in the streets doing battle for peace and justice, while we're still discussing our mission."

"Yes, thanks," Connie says when Rita holds up a second cup.

"And the carnage has taken a toll on me, Con." Tears roll steadily down Rita's cheeks, though her voice never wavers. "Night after night after night watching Cronkite, seeing the body count. All those lovely young men. The boys we had crushes on, the ones who had crushes on us.

"And we're still bombing the Vietnamese. Twenty thousand tons worth just last month. I'm so glad Danny left the country. The Pentagon Papers proved him right.

"Priests should be railing from the pulpits about the immorality of this administration. We should be falling on our knees in the streets in protest. I just couldn't bear doing nothing while others sacrifice their lives; walled up in the convent as if I were living on a separate planet."

"So, you're leaving for good?"

"I didn't want to leave at all. I've taken a sabbatical to open the food bank. Maybe the Order will come to terms with activism. Maybe I'll find a way to reconcile the two. For now, I'll run Loaves and Fishes and," she tugs on a lock of Connie's hair, "celebrate Tacky Prom Night with you."

# CHAPTER 9

The solitary drive to the simple clapboard church in town for Mass and the scant handful of souls scattered among the pews, serve as Rita's daily ration of sorrow. She misses most of all the convent's morning ritual, each of the sisters' prayers amplifying the others; misses that sense of buoyancy with which she began her days. These parishioners (mostly women, mostly old) keep their prayers to themselves, eyes closed, clutching their rosary beads, looking as if they're having a fierce conversation with God.

She's tried to get Connie to come along, but she doesn't seem interested in church, or much else for that matter. Rita would love to take the girls with her, but they always look so peaceful asleep. Ceci, of course, is anything but when she's awake, and Anna seems entirely too *weary* for a seven-year-old. Sometimes Rita's not sure Connie notices.

Rita left a note taped to the refrigerator.

*Will be at Loaves (1st delivery!) after Mass/back around noon*

After church, at Loaves and Fishes, Rita pulls a three-ring binder from the cupboard and goes over her checklist:

*notify churches re: Loaves days & hrs.*
*sm. sign 4 front door*
*pix(?) for wall*
*candy jar for counter*
*paper bags*
*del. Empire State Grocers, open next Tuesday!!*
*(2) volunteers.*

She crosses out the plural and changes the (2) to (1) and offers a little prayer of gratitude for that blessing. She runs across the street to Sweetie's luncheonette to pick up coffee and rolls. The least she can do is feed Janet. She's just paying for her order when the sun disappears, eclipsed by the Empire State Grocers truck. By the time Rita gets back, Janet's looking over the bill of lading, a pencil perched behind her pixie ear.

"I've checked it against the delivery. Everything's here except the case of peanut butter, back ordered for next week." She hands Rita the invoice and whistles. "Wow, this is some grocery bill."

"Don't I know it." The initial order was a combination of research and guesswork. And, since she has no established credit, Rita had to prepay the $500 before they would deliver.

It feels like Christmas to Rita, who tears open cartons of canned lima beans, solid bricks of cheese, sacks of flour. Janet works methodically, in silence, until the entire order is unpacked. Rows of canned or boxed foodstuffs fill about half of the six metal shelving units behind the counter.

They drag the empty cartons into the small room between the parlor and the kitchen, where Rita's been storing paper sacks, plastic bags, and miscellaneous donations. They sit in little mounds, like carnival targets; a dozen cans of evaporated milk, a pyramid of Spam, dropped off by women cleaning their cupboards or men who remember the Depression.

"What about the rest of this stuff?"

"Oh, just leave it, Janet, you've done more than enough. I'll break down the cartons." Rita searches the rooms for her matte knife. "Besides I'll come in again before we open, I want to put some giveaways on the counter, a candy jar for the kids, maybe some blank greeting cards folks could use, that kind of—"

"I'll see you Tuesday."

Rita turns around. Janet's already is buttoning her coat. "Wait. I wanted to ask—can you recommend an obstetrician?"

Janet's eyes drop to Rita's mid-section.

"For a friend." Rita laughs. "It's her third, and she's staying with me for the time being, but she's due soon and—"

"Dr. Flechtner. Delivers all his patients, middle of the night, holidays. I don't have his number, but he's in the book."

"Thanks." Rita walks Janet to the front door. Pale sunlight filters through ashen clouds and it feels as if the temperature's dropped ten degrees. "Look at that sky. The radio said snow but they're wrong half the time—"

"Oh, it's gonna snow." Janet claps on a pair of earmuffs. "You like to ski?"

"No. I mean I don't know, I've never—"

"Want to give it a try?"

"Why not." Rita's always wanted to. Besides, what could be better than learning from someone who could also administer first aid?

She calls home to see if there's anything Connie needs. Anna answers.

"Mama isn't up yet."

Rita checks the clock. It's after one. "Is she okay?"

"Oh, she's fine. But, Aunt Sister, I had to use your last egg for Ceci's breakfast."

"I'll get some more."

"And we need milk, too."

"Tell you what, Anna. I'll come get you later, and we'll shop together."

"Can Ceci come? I can't leave her alone."

"Of course!" Rita answers before Anna's words register. This child needs to have a mother, not be one.

By the time Rita gets home, Connie's up and dressed, nestled between her daughters on the couch, reading them a story from an invisible book. They wave to Rita while Connie turns an invisible page.

Ceci grabs her hand, giggles. "No, Mama, go back! You skipped a part."

Connie mimes flipping the page backward. "So, I did." She squints mightily. "But my poor eyes are so tired, Anna-banana, you'll have to take over." Connie pulls Anna close so she can 'see' better.

"Well, then the children talked to the birds, and then they flew with them to the South, where the ocean is warm and smooth—" Anna improvises.

"And it's always daytime," Ceci singsongs.

"Don't interrupt while I'm reading—"

"Give *me* the book, Anna."

Anna sweeps the imaginary book out of Ceci's reach.

"Mama! Make her give me the book."

Rita can't help it; she cracks up. Connie, on the other hand, maintains the fantasy, calmly taking the 'book' back from Anna. "I'll read now, girls, if you don't mind. But only if you settle down."

Rita offers Connie a silent apology for having judged her.

"Since when do you know how to cook an egg?" Rita asks Anna, as they drive around the lake.

"It's easy, Aunt Sister."

"You cook a lot?"

"Not really. Sometimes when Mama's tired. Or sick."

"Is that often, Anna?"

"Well, of course. She's pregnant," Anna says. "And Ceci's a handful."

Rita suppresses a laugh. "And what are you?"

"The oldest," Anna says, beaming.

With Anna's expert help, they gather the necessities, bread, milk, and eggs, as well as the ingredients for lunches, and a meatloaf dinner.

"How old is your little girl?" the checker asks Rita.

"Oh, she's not—"

"Seven," Anna says, slipping her hand into Rita's.

After a quick visit to the library, Rita unloads the car and puts away the groceries then settles the girls on the hooked rug in front of the fireplace with a roll of brown paper and crayons.

Connie reclines on the couch, surveying the pile of books tilting on the blanket chest Rita uses as a coffee table. "Let's see . . . Emily Dickinson, Agatha Christie, John Updike, Erica Jong? Why, Sister Margaret Jude! *Organic Gardening. Peterson's Field Guide to North American Birds. The Five Little Peppers and How They Grew*—Ooh, I loved that when I was Anna's age—Erich Fromm, Ram Dass, *The Lives of the Saints*." She picks up the Dickinson.

Retrieving her missal from the mantel, Rita thumbs through the worn, gilt-edged pages. "Exactly when is your due date?"

"February 27th."

"Great auspices. St. Gabriel's feast day. Magnificent name. Works for a boy or a girl."

Connie nods. "Vince would approve."

Rita looks up from the page.

"If I were to consult him." Connie blushes at Rita's scrutiny. "Which I'm not."

It's the blush, not the words, that worries Rita.

# CHAPTER 10

Connie wakes to a stillness unbroken by birdsong, to light diffuse, opaque. A scrim of lacy snow tumbles outside the window, the accumulation visible in the time she takes to pull on a robe, draw the curtains wide. Big flakes like cold cotton cling to twig and branch, rock and roof. *Vince would love this.* The thought closes her throat, pricks her eyes. He's forfeited his place in her enchantments.

Although Connie's grateful to be far away from Vince, she'd also missed him last night when, in the chill dark waiting for sleep, she'd heard a distant thwack. Unnerved, she inclined her body toward the window, alert as any creature to a foreign sound.

"Mama, I hear ghostses," Ceci whimpered. Connie turned on the lamp.

"She's scared of the noise." Anna was scornful but scanned her mother's face for reassurance.

Connie couldn't explain the eerie sounds, but clucked and chattered nonsense to the girls until they fell asleep. Her spine, however, stood sentry all night.

"It's snowing!" Ceci bolts out of bed, dances around Connie, then jumps back on the couch. "Anna, get up! Snow!"

"It's about time, you sleepyheads." Rita stands in the doorway, zipping up her parka. "Isn't it glorious? Come *on,* get dressed. Last one out is a rotten egg!"

From the window, Connie watches Ceci twirl, head back, mouth open to catch the falling flakes. Anna takes Ceci's hand and follows Rita to a clearing in a triangle of chestnut trees. Ceci's yellow mittens and Anna's red scarf flash in and out of the snow shower.

The picture-postcard scene draws Connie outside. She finds a pair of boots, an oversized jacket. It's not as cold as it looks. It's almost cozy—the world cut down to fit inside a dome of dancing snowflakes. Her center of gravity feels low in her belly, and the swirling snow makes her feel dizzy, disoriented. If she stands here long enough to be blanketed, she could be mistaken for any other earthly element. Rock. Tree. She closes her eyes, lifts her face. The child she used to be rushes in to claim her. She's all skin—alive only to what she can touch, to what can touch her. Her brothers and sisters used to complain about the bulky snowsuits, but she'd liked feeling snug and secure, just her eyes peeking out, impervious to the weather.

Now feathery flakes light on her eyelids, her cheekbones. The inside of her nostrils feels warm compared to the wet tip of her out-thrust tongue.

"Mama?" Anna tugs at her elbow.

"Mama's a snowman, Mama's a snowman." Ceci marches around Connie's girth. Rita gallops over, chuffing white puffs of breath.

It takes Connie a second to rejoin them.

By mid-morning, the plows make their first pass.

"You need anything? I'm making a run," Rita says.

"Just some chocolate chips. Ceci wants 'grandma pancakes' like my mother makes for her."

"Let me call them, Con. Rose must be worried sick."

"No. It's taken me years, but I've weaned them off daily phone calls, unannounced visits. We're down to Sunday dinners, so I still have a few days before I have to tell them."

"Vince won't?"

"I doubt it. He'd have to tell them why."

"Even still, why wait till the last—"

"Aunt Sister, look what I founded!" Ceci's torso is bent backward under the weight of a large squirming cat.

"E, where have you been? I've missed you," Rita rescues the cat from Ceci's clutches. It hurtles onto Rita's shoulders.

"E?" says Connie.

"I named him after St. Francis of Assisi, then 'he' had kittens so I called her 'Frances with an E,' then 'E' for short." The tawny cat clings to Rita as if she were a convenient tree. "She comes and goes. I haven't seen her with all the commotion."

Rita sets out her food. E crunches her way to the bottom of the bowl. When the cat bolts upstairs, Ceci follows.

"Don't bother her, Ceci," Rita calls. "Let her come to you."

Connie shakes her head. "It's as if the world exists to amuse Cecilia. Anna may look like her father but Ceci has his temperament. They both feel so entitled."

"Well, I remember his coronation."

"You think I've spoiled him?"

"I think you've worshipped him so long he thinks he's king."

Rita's relieved to have a list and a quest; she needs to feel constantly useful, to assuage the assault her conscience makes on her choice to abandon the convent, no matter the sanction from the Order. She gazes into the rearview mirror while the engine warms. Connie is at the sink washing the breakfast dishes, her face blank, looking out into some middle distance. She seems so remote. Rita chalks it up to the pregnancy, to Connie's obvious exhaustion. And Vincent using her as his whipping post, either literally or figuratively. Rita tries and fails to imagine that once giddy bride, that besotted groom, snarling at each other, biting down on a bitter knot of what? Jealousy? Resentment? Failed expectations? Whatever it is, it has extinguished something essential in Connie, who seems as substantial as smoke.

Rita has begun to revel in the freedom to wander downtown, just one more soul on the planet. When she wore her habit, friends and strangers alike would shrink in her presence, become stiff with self-censorship, awkward, and remote. Except for Connie, thank God, who wanted Rita to stand up for her on her wedding day, be godmother to Ceci even if she had to show up in full postulant regalia. Connie's closer to Rita than she is to her own sisters, who are a generation apart.

In the dim recesses of the Salvation Army store, Rita finds a serviceable set of bunk beds, a little scuffed, a lot ugly. But sturdy. Perfect for the girls. Rita plans on settling Connie and the children in the larger room downstairs meant to be a dining room she'd been using as a study. Even if she wanted to forfeit the upstairs bedroom (which she really doesn't, not after years of her spare convent room) it's way too small for three people, even if two of them are children.

"Hey, food bank lady," the clerk says, tossing his otter sleek hair, "you're turning into a regular."

She laughs. "Great prices. Free delivery. I'll take those bunk beds but I'm also looking for one more, a twin?"

"Uh-uh. What about a day bed with a trundle? New, just came in, still in the box."

"Even better. If I help, is there any way you can deliver them today?"

"Let me see who's around."

While he's on the phone Rita spots a dark pine cradle upended on a dusty steamer trunk. The rails feel like satin, worn smooth over the years. How many babies have sheltered under this wooden canopy, slumbered to the motion of these half-moon rockers? She imagines a pale, dreaming infant in its practiced embrace.

# CHAPTER 11

Connie finds a tattered checkerboard and enough pieces counting the three odd buttons for the missing black ones. Ceci wants the red ones, naturally. Anna patiently reminds her sister of the rules.

Connie eases herself into the rocker with a copy of *Leaves of Grass*. "*I celebrate myself and sing myself.*" She sinks into the sweeping cadence, rocking along with the poet's words. The girls' voices recede, subsumed by the vast music of the poem. Soon sunlight peeks into the living room windows spilling onto the page, the girls' hair, the checkerboard. She feels enormous with well-being, with hope. As if the next phrase, or the one after that, will unlock some mystery she cannot name.

"No fair! No fair!" Ceci hurls a fistful of black checkers, severing the fragile filament on which Connie floats.

Connie struggles to her feet. "I'll show you fair!" She smacks Ceci's bottom hard enough to pitch her forward. "Upstairs. Now!" Ceci stomps off, wailing. "And I swear to God, Ceci, I don't want to hear a peep out of you." Connie feels sweaty; her hands shake. She collects the scattered pieces on the checkerboard. Her vehemence sprang unbidden, overwhelming in its urgency, and like Vince, ambushed by rage. Mortified, she puts the checkers one-by-one back on the board. "Whose turn is it?"

"That's okay, Mama. We don't have to play."

"Oh, Anna. I'm sorry. I'm just . . . You go on out and play."

"I'll stay with you."

"No, honey, I'm fine. Just dress warm and stay where I can see you." She waits until Anna's outside and Ceci's stopped whimpering before she tries to recapture her reverie. Ritually, like a priest or a shaman, she sets the rocker back to the precise angle, turns the page to the exact point of departure, and tips the book this way and that until it's sun-striped. Self-consciously this time, she rocks as she reads. The very act of paying attention contradictory to floating free. Her thoughts drift backward instead of up and out and snag on her wedding day.

They married the first day of spring on the vernal equinox, when the earth is equally divided into light and dark, the time of Mardi Gras and Easter, Vincent's sense of ritual matching hers.

She arrived at Our Lady of Sorrows at ten in the morning in a bath of cool sunlight and left hours later, after the ceremony and celebratory brunch, through a curtain of warm rain. Just months before her graduation at which Vincent stood and brava-ed her as if she were the diva of NYU. When his flamboyance still thrilled her; before it made her cringe.

At first, her father's sense of loyalty had been offended—he thought she should have honored her pledge to her patient suitor, Frank—but Louis (as did everyone else) grew to love Vincent. There were no "warning signs" like the women's magazines listed in quizzes, shrinking love and marriage down to a series of ten or twenty questions, as if a glossy piece of paper could predict the constancy of the human heart. In fact, Vincent's sentimental nature reminded her of her father's. As a child she'd been transfixed by Louis's roughened fingers, scarred with faint white lines from the treacherous butcher knives, wrapped around the delicate tortoiseshell handle of Rose's hairbrush as he stroked her long thick hair a hundred times before lifting it up and fanning over her shoulders like a glorious shawl.

Had she ever seen her father angry? Once when a plumber came to fix the leaky bathtub and somehow switched the hot and cold taps, Louis was furious and dragged the man out of bed to repair the error. The only time her father hit any of them was when Louis Jr. blackened Carlo's eye. Looking back, it's ironic that he had chosen that time to use physical force, trying to teach his son not to, but it worked and fight as they would, the boys never punched each other again, at least not so their father knew.

Connie wanders into the kitchen, finds a clean towel, dries the dishes, puts them away. Out of some dark cavern creeps a memory of her father's fury. When she was about Anna's age, coming home from school unnoticed because her parents were huddled on the couch on either side of her Aunt Olivia. Connie glimpsed a green-striped dishtowel, lumpy with ice, Olivia's face open-jawed, as if with a bad toothache, a violet-yellow blotch on her cheek that would bloom black and blue. Her father's face grim, bunched up, so alien she must have blocked it from consciousness because now it leaps into mind with a sickening jolt; her aunt's mewling sounds, her father's short growled questions in Italian, badgering, demanding, until Olivia cries out her husband's name. Then her father said something, so soft and low that even if he'd spoken in English, she wouldn't have caught it, something that caused her mother to abandon Olivia and grasp Louis's arms, to plead with him to stay. Her father broke free, strode out, slammed the door, the women wailing, holding each other; Connie shivering in her woolen coat, book bag clenched in one hand, standing in the doorway between the living room and the kitchen, dizzy with fear.

It must have been only minutes until Brenda came home from high school, called a cab to take Rose and Olivia to the hospital, then set out apple slices and cocoa for Connie. Brenda didn't explain and Connie didn't ask any questions, not wanting to know, just grateful for her sister's company.

Late that night, well after Olivia came back wrapped in bandages, smelling of antiseptic, dreamy with drugs; after omelets and salads eaten in silent shifts, during a television show Connie was allowed to watch just before bedtime, her father came back. He headed straight upstairs trailing the cold night air behind him. Later, she heard her parents' voices in a composition of rage and anguish. From that day on Olivia stayed. And Connie only saw Uncle Robert when she happened to take the cross-town bus he drove.

Has she turned into one of those women? Olivia was an act of charity to her parents, an object of queasy fear to Connie, and a figure of scorn to Brenda. How is she different from Olivia? Is it only a matter of degree? Maybe it started like this for her aunt, one line crossed and then another without protest or consequence. She, however, has protested by abdication.

And now Vincent knows the consequences.

Snow-bright and ruddy, Rita prances into the house with her Salvation Army elves in tow to dismantle the study, as if striking a set, clomping up and down the basement steps with the benched props, then hauling in the set dressing for a new production. Although it seems they shouldn't, somehow the beds fit.

Instead of gratitude, Connie feels overpowered by Rita's beneficence, her confidence in not only her ability but her entitlement to run Connie's life.

"Well. What do you think?" Rita's face is shiny with sweat and goodwill.

"It's great, but you shouldn't have gone to all this trouble. Disrupted your life."

"What life? I'm living in limbo, remember? Welcome to my world." Rita pulls out the trundle bed with a flourish.

"I'm paying you for all this," Connie says. Rita shrugs. "No. I mean it, Reet. I have some money."

"We'll figure out the finances as we go along, sweetie. I don't want you to worry about all that right now. In your condition." Rita stretches her long fingers over Connie's belly. "And I have something for you, little one." Rita takes the cradle out of the closet and sets it rocking on the floor.

"Oh, Rita. It's lovely."

Rita kneels, runs her hand over the hood, pats the dark hollow where the baby will lie. Rita seems to shimmer in the fading light, a voluptuous fairy awaiting her charge.

That night, as soon as they make up the beds, Ceci scrambles to the top bunk.

"Anna's sleeping there," Connie says.

"That's okay, mama. She can have it." Anna offers.

"Absolutely not."

"When's Daddy coming?" Ceci sobs.

"Is he?" Anna asks.

Connie wants to reassure each of them. *Soon. Never.* She finds herself wanting to reassure Rita, too, who pounces on every mention of Vince's name as if it were a symptom of contagion.

"Shush. Go to sleep now, it's late." She tucks Ceci in. Anna climbs the short ladder and curls up against the wall.

Connie sinks into the daybed, exhausted. Her back aches, her ankles feel as if they're in leg irons. If Vince were here, he'd prop her feet up in his lap while he massaged each toe. *Vince.* The tears slide off her cheeks, pool behind her ears. *You're a fatherless child,* she tells the baby curled up under her heart.

Silence rolls over Connie like a dark beast. Back home the backdrop is constant; the whine and slam of garbage trucks, motors idling on cold mornings; footsteps; shouted greetings. *Home.*

She's dazed by Rita's alacrity and resourcefulness. How quickly she's accommodated and provided for them, whipping up quarters, designing contingency plans as if they were manning the barricades. Lending them a permanence Connie hadn't anticipated and isn't sure she wants.

# CHAPTER 12

"I heard those weird sounds again last night." Connie butters a slice of toast, hands Ceci half.

"You heard the ice expanding on the lake."

"No, Reet, this was an other-worldly sound."

"Trust me, it's the lake. If you'd budge from this house, you'd see for yourself. Come on, Con. You could use some fresh air."

"Some other time," Connie says, toddling off to the living room.

Loaves and Fishes doesn't open till ten but by nine o'clock, people have started lining up along the side entrance, their heads ducked down, their gaits low-slung. Rita doesn't have the heart to make them wait.

"You're setting a bad precedent," Janet says.

"What difference does it make?" Rita starts for the door. "It's cold out and there's so many of them."

"Because there's just one of you. If you want to make this work, you can't let their needs overwhelm you. Besides, people crave respect more than pity."

"Compassion, you mean."

"Whatever you call it, there's a limit."

Janet looks stern but Rita laughs. "Isn't today your day off?"

"Never mind. Just open the damn door."

A kohl-eyed teenager, who looks just as pregnant as Connie, tells Rita she's picking up groceries for the Sutter family. The churches have provided lists of people they've referred and Rita's made up an index card for everyone, with family size and contact information, so she can better estimate the grocery orders, and make sure people don't just fall off the radar. The index card lists this girl as the eldest of three siblings of a single working mother. Rita stuffs two bags with as much as she thinks the girl can carry.

There are walk-ins as well, and Rita asks them to fill out a contact card. "Just John," a pasty, spindly man writes, no address or phone number. He's wearing Army fatigues and torn sneakers. His long hair is matted in clumps. There is, of course, no card for him. He takes whatever she bags for him, avoiding her gaze.

Janet works swiftly, silently, bagging food and handing it out but Rita tries to engage each person, with little success. The people seem bent by shame and circumstances. She shakes her head. This is probably one of those times people would feel more comfortable if she were dressed in her habit. She hopes over time that Loaves will become more of a port than a pit stop.

During the first lull, Rita lines up the kitchen chairs along the wall opposite the counter. "I told that woman—the one with the cane—to have a seat in the kitchen until I could get to her but she seemed embarrassed." Rita snaps her fingers. "Hey! Wouldn't it be great to have a coffee urn set up? And cocoa for the kids? And I'd like to start a community garden—or wait, there are plenty of small farms around here, maybe a gleaning project this summer—or maybe spring if we—"

"Whoa! Don't you have any gears besides overdrive?"

Rita laughs. "I've been in . . . cooped up lately."

"You need to relax. I'm going skiing next weekend. You're coming."

"I'll have to check with Connie, see what's—"

A few sharp raps on the bay window reveal a tall woman, wearing a fur coat. She's carrying a carton of canned goods, which she holds up as an offering.

Donors use the front door, glad to be observed.

Even though the weather turns sleety, people continue to show up. Rita tucks her wool scarf into a bag of groceries for a woman wearing a shapeless trench coat over threadbare jeans; adds her gloves to the few items requested by a red-faced, rheumy-eyed man, wishes she had warm socks to give the little girl with holes in her sneakers.

The last person, a wild-haired woman with a pale scar slicing through one ebony eyebrow, deposits a couple of crumpled bills on the counter.

"Oh, no thanks." Rita hands her a full sack. "It's free."

The woman fixes her with a long dark stare. "Nothing is free." She takes her groceries, leaves the bills, and shoulders her way out the door.

"Who was that?"

"Card says Inez Flores: one child. And you'd better take her money." Janet points to the nearly empty shelves.

Rita's heart sinks. "I'm going to have to double the order to stay open two days a week."

"Either that or cut the hand-outs in half. Or just open on Tuesdays."

"Too late now." Rita holds up a second stack of index cards. "These are the names for Thursday." Among them: Louisa Gutierrez and sons, Arturo and Tomás.

Rita tries to sort out the paperwork on her desk, the lists of organizations to call on, strategies for fundraising, but she's exhausted. She opens letters from a social worker at the county welfare board, the pastor of the Baptist Church. More referrals. *Dear Lord, give me strength. And money.*

"Was it a success?" Connie, still in her pajamas, sits at the kitchen table, notebooks open beside her mug of cold tea.

"Define success," Rita answers. "On one hand, I'm glad so many showed up, referred or not; on the other, it's sad so many people need us. And I just thought they'd be more . . . "

"Grateful?"

"Not grateful. More, open I guess." Rita checks the thermostat, turns it down a notch. "They would have been, with Sister Margaret Jude. I'm sure of it."

"Maybe you could just wear your habit when Loaves is open."

"I wish I could wear it when I ask for donations. It's a lot tougher sledding without." Rita fills Connie in on the shortfall.

"You're not using up your inheritance, are you? For this place, for the food bank?"

"If I have to. Until I can drum up more donations. Or a grant. I'll work it out." Rita glances at the notebooks. "What's that?"

Connie taps them with her pencil. "Flora. Fauna. The trees with the shiny white bark—that look like bones?—are sycamores, the ones with the rough green-grey bark are Mountain Ash, I think. There's a blue spruce, and a couple of weeping willows, maples, of course, and oak—"

"Aunt Sister!" Ceci flings herself at Rita. "We saw some kids riding sleds. Can you take us, pretty please?"

"Oh honey, we don't have a sleigh. "

"We can use cardboard from the boxes in the basement," Anna says. "If that's okay."

"Absolutely," Rita says. She won't need those boxes any time soon.

When Rita takes the girls sledding on the hill across the road, Connie lingers at the kitchen table, watching the birds at the feeder. With the *Peterson's Guide,* she identifies the blood-red male cardinals and their less flashy mates, the tufted titmice, white-breasted nuthatches cake walking up and down the tree trunk, black-capped chickadees, purple grosbeaks, three kinds of sparrows. She watches Rita help the girls build a lumpy igloo, make angels in the snow. Outdoors till near dark, they come inside red-cheeked, wet and cold.

"My little mackerels," says Connie. "Get out of those clothes and into the tub. I'll toast your pajamas in front of the fire. Tonight, we'll put warm bricks in your beds, just like in the olden days."

She runs the tap, pours Ivory soap into the water, helps Ceci undress. Anna is reluctant to give up her sweatshirt, the twin to the one she left behind. She wants to wear it to bed, instead of pajamas.

"Don't be difficult, honey, that shirt is dirty. Let's go, the water's cooling off." She collects the damp clothes; their sour smell makes her slightly queasy. "Wash Ceci's hair, that's a good girl. Aunt Sister will be in to wash yours."

She drapes clean pajamas on a chair in front of the fire, hears them pelting Rita with knock-knock jokes. Rita's laughter triggers bouts of giggling. Connie wraps the happy sounds around her like a cloak.

The next day breaks above freezing and the snow melts enough to hear the juicy thwack of tires on wet pavement.

"I agree with Janet, Reet." Connie bags a thermos of coffee and a buttered roll for Rita's breakfast after Mass. "Give out less or just open one day."

"Come on, Connie. What if you couldn't feed your children?"

"I'd . . . I'd figure out something, Rita . . . "

"And so will I," Rita says on her way out the door.

By mid-afternoon the unseasonably mild weather has drawn all sorts of creatures out of their hidey-holes: chipmunks with their sporty racing stripes, flocks of ducks, honking Canada geese, neighborhood cats, a few humans walking their dogs. The girls beg to be taken to the lake but Connie is loath to leave the house; the baby's kicking so hard to the right she feels lopsided. Ceci carries on so vehemently Connie finally capitulates.

"Okay. *Okay!* Anna, help me into these boots and we'll go before it gets dark."

They pick their way in the squishy mud down the lane to the little lake she's not yet seen. They walk past another Cape, a tiny cottage, a large log cabin with a veranda. Two boys, slightly older than the girls, chase each other in and out of the path, around trees, over the brook. Anna eyes them furtively but Ceci runs up and down with them as if she's known them all along.

Connie settles herself on a bench at the lake, watches the light catch on the bumpy ice. Anna walks along a patch of sand meant to simulate a beach. About fifty yards out a couple of men lounge on aluminum folding chairs while they fish through a hole in the ice. She tenses with the strain of mentally holding them above the frigid depths. Connie never could wrap her mind around the concept that an element could change properties, becoming utterly unlike its previous form. That water could be yielding, then solid, then vapor—all.

Ceci, still giddy from sprinting after the boys, sails past her onto the ice and slips, her feet flying cartoon-like over her head. She slides on her back, a spinning circle of arms and legs.

Connie's pulse races at her neck as she hoists herself up, takes a step toward the lake, hesitates. "Ceci? Ceci!"

The fishermen hurry over, slipping and sliding. They bend over Ceci, blocking Connie's view. She presses her balled fists against her mouth.

The man in the blue parka helps Ceci up and leads her toward the shore. "She's okay," he shouts across the ice. "She just had the wind knocked out of her."

"You scared me to death!" Connie touches Ceci's face, her hair, her limbs as if she had just been delivered into this world. "You could have fallen right through."

"Actually, the ice is about three feet thick right now," the stranger says.

He's around forty, she guesses, a bit rough around the edges. She extends her hand. "I'm Connie."

The man holds out a hand gloved up to the knuckles. "Ed."

"And this is Ceci..."

"So I gathered."

" . . . and Anna. We're visiting Sister . . . my friend, who recently moved in—"

"The yellow house at the top of the lane?"

Connie nods.

He looks at her more closely. "That's the Messinger place. You tell your friend she's in for a treat come springtime. Laurel Messinger has one of the prettiest gardens around. It's still there under the weeds. Well, you have a nice visit. I'm going to try and catch one more before dark."

*Just like the Waltons.* Connie heads back up the lane, fixing him in her mind to share with Rita. With the children slogging around her, she conjures up flowers, leafy canopies, Laurel's garden. That's a transformation she can understand: seed and root, sprout and bloom. As they walk between the two birch trees that signal the beginning of Rita's property, the day ends suddenly in a charcoal dusk.

She herds the girls onto the cramped screened-in porch. Anna kneels to remove Ceci's boots. Connie stoops to roll up her pant legs. An arm reaches around her, a hand grabs her from behind.

"Daddy!" yells Ceci.

In slow, careful increments, Connie turns around. There are thumbprints of shadows under Vincent's red-rimmed eyes.

"I'm so very sorry, baby." He tries to embrace her. "It was an accident. I never meant—"

She rears back. Her heart races. Her thoughts freeze. The law of gravity is suspended; she's floating away.

"Where were you, Daddy?" Ceci asks.

"Working, pumpkin," Vince hoists her to his chest, searches the darkened porch for Anna. "Hey, sweetpea, where's Daddy's girl?"

She steps back into the shadows and takes her mother's hand.


Rita hauls groceries from the car to the porch. On her second trip, the front door opens.

"Let me give you a hand with that."

Rita drops the bags, pushes past Vince into the house. Connie's in a wing chair pulled up to the hearth, still in her coat, her muddy boots. Ceci is undressing a Barbie doll. Anna's gift, a Walt Disney watercolor set, rests untouched on top of a thick tablet.

Rita kneels in front of Connie, pats the hands folded in her lap. "Are you all right? Connie?"

"I'm fine. Surprised . . . not that I should be . . . I mean, of course, he figured out I'd go to you. He found the retreat notice, convinced Immaculata he was an old friend wanting to pay respects to your father. . . I wasn't really thinking . . . I just wanted—"

"Rita," Vince calls from the doorway. "Do I call you Rita, now? Where do you want me to put the chicken, in the freezer or the fridge?"

She strides into the kitchen, stands between him and the living room. "You better leave."

"It was an accident. I never meant to hurt her; I swear to God."

"She has a welt. And a bruise that's yet to fade."

He looks as if she slapped him. "Jesus."

"You're not welcome here, Vincent."

"She's my wife, Rita. Don't you think that's up to her?" But he shrugs into his coat anyway, then hugs Ceci. "Say goodnight to Daddy."

"I'll come see you tomorrow, we'll build a snow fort. If that's okay with Mommy."

Connie doesn't answer, stares down at her knotted hands.

Vince leans over, kisses her crown. "I'll take that as a yes."

# CHAPTER 13

Rita waits at the window until the taillights of Vince's car disappear. She builds up the waning fire. Connie lies on her side on the couch staring into the flames. After feeding the girls and putting them to bed, Rita clears the dinner dishes and leaves them in the sink to soak. She locks the doors, turning off all the lights except the night light in the hallway and the bulb in the metal hood over the stove. She unfurls an afghan from the cedar chest and with a snap of her wrists fans it into a fragrant cloud that settles over Connie from chin to toes.

She collapses on the floor facing the hearth, her back resting against the sofa not far from Connie's belly. "How's the weebling?"

"Quiet for a change."

"How are you?"

Connie lets out a long breath. "Have you ever seen one of those TV programs about brain function?"

"Not that I can recall."

"With some brain disorders, if an object is removed from the subject's sight, it ceases to exist. It's like that with Vince." Connie lumbers up to a sitting position and places her open palms on either side of her swollen belly. "When he's charming and thoughtful I can't picture him in a rage. And when he lashes out . . . it's like some demon's possessing him—"

"You tell me how he's hurt you, how he frightens you—" Rita lowers her voice. "Then you get the courage to leave him and you just let him waltz in here—"

"What was I supposed to do, call the cops?"

"I don't . . . I guess not. But he just seems to barrel over you. When did you get so meek?"

"What's wrong with meek? I thought we inherit the earth."

"You know what I mean."

"It's complicated, Rita. I just can't erase ten years like that."

She turns around, kneels in front of Connie, can't resist touching her big belly. "What does it feel like?"

Rita's looking at her as if she's some goddess who's swallowed the secret of life. An oracle with an ancient truth to bestow. Connie's tempted to lie to that expectant face. "The being or the getting?"

"I'm serious, Con." Rita colors. "Tell."

Connie sucks in her breath. "Your hands and feet feel like they're water balloons, and there's always a dull ache low in your back that ratchets up to sharp if you do too much or the wrong thing, and you have to pee all the time, and in the beginning, you puke your guts out, and at the end, there's stretch marks across your stomach that never go away no matter how much cocoa butter you rub on them."

Rita falls back on her heels. "But . . . what about . . . the baby, you know . . . when you feel—"

"Oh, didn't I mention the kicking? That's not a thrill if it's your ribs or bladder getting kicked." She has no idea why she's feeling so vindictive. It feels good to smash Rita's illusions.

"Connie!" Rita pales; her eyes scan Connie's face as if she's re-reading a paragraph that has ceased to make sense.

"Am I being horrible?"

"Are you telling the truth?"

"Oh, Rita, it's all true. The pain, the discomfort, the thrill, the miracle of a brand-new person. But it's not heaven on earth." She closes her eyes and lays her head back against the sofa. "Still. It's worth it to see the expression on Vince's face, how he loves being a father. I wish he could remember that."

"You can't wish this away. And demons don't leave when you close your eyes."

Vince shows up mid-morning, carrying brown paper bags still warm from the bakery and a sky-blue ceramic pot of forced paperwhites. He bundles up Ceci, coaxes Anna outside with a spectacular fort made of blocks of snow, complete with red pennants stuck into the turrets, like the one the crew built in a Canadian film Vince shot two years ago. The kids war-whoop and squeal. Each "Daddy!" plucks at Connie's resolve. When they finally stagger in, tired and hungry, the girls' faces are flushed with the kind of excitement he always manages to create for them.

Connie peeks through the yellow gingham curtains covering the kitchen window and watches Vince shovel the short macadam walkway to the bridge. His wiry frame looks good even in bulky sweats; his high cheekbones and classic Roman nose rouged by the crisp air lend him an aura of stage make-up

She glimpses herself in the curve of the aluminum teakettle. It's seven weeks past her last haircut and the dirty blonde strands curl limply at the end of each layer of what used to be stylish shag. Her olive skin looks sallow, waxy, with no hint of pink suffusing the mask her face has settled into. Her eyebrows, darker than her hair, spring spidery above eyes so dark it's hard to distinguish iris from pupil. Her sunken cheeks belie the distended belly and her lips, though plump and well defined by deep ridges, are also without color, and fade into the rest of her face.

The macadam walkway shows up now like a fat gray snake. As Vince scrapes away the thick film of ice hidden under the snowfall, the snake turns black.

"You can't spend your life behind the curtains," Rita says.

"Jesus! You scared the heart out of me."

Rita raises her eyebrows.

"My grandmother used to say that. When I'd jump off the stoop in front of her house. She'd pat me down and brush me off, then say, 'Dolly, you scared the heart out of me!'"

"So, Dolly, are you getting ready to jump?"

They watch Vince finish up the walkway, then haul firewood to the back porch from under the eaves. He's diligent, methodical, as if he were hunkering down for a siege. Which, Rita guesses, he is, in a way. Shoring up their opinion of him, stockpiling offerings on the altar of their affections.

He fills the bird feeder with scoops of seed: sunflower, millet, corn. He comes into the house, walks silently past them, finds a jar of Vaseline, and heads back to the feeder. Mystified, they peer through the window over the kitchen table. He greases the chain holding the feeder and its black plastic lid.

"To thwart the squirrels." Rita's clearly pleased to have figured it out.

"How in the world does he know to do that?" Connie shakes her head.

"Vince is nothing if not unpredictable," says Rita.

Now Connie's pleased. Pleased and slightly smug.

"For example, I would never have predicted that he'd hit you," Rita says and walks off.

Vince returns the jar of Vaseline, peeks in the living room, and says goodbye to the children. He pauses in the kitchen, hand on the doorknob, showing her he's not intending to stay.

"I've got a room at motel hell on the highway," he says. She refuses the bait. "I'll be back tomorrow, so call me if there's anything you need."

She keeps her eyes on her hands and keeps her hands busy wiping the already gleaming stovetop.

"Connie?"

She raises her eyes to meet his. With his index finger, he smoothes her eyebrow, strokes her cheekbone, brushes her lips.

"Call me if you get cravings. Of any kind."

She's shocked by the tide rising in her to follow him out the door.

As soon as Vince leaves, Rita rushes into town for day two at Loaves and Fishes. She fills as many bags as she can with groceries before they open, lines them up on the counter. There. That will save time. Until she can find another volunteer, she'll be working alone, unless . . . Maybe Louisa can help. Although she doesn't speak English. Tomás can translate. *Tomás*. She smiles. He couldn't stop staring at her when she stopped by to tell him about the food bank and give his mother enough money for groceries until Loaves opened. Rita wore a skirt and blouse and sensible shoes that day, made him promise not to tell anyone that she's a nun. *Incognito*. Louisa understood why it's sometimes necessary to keep a low profile. Not that Rita's hiding from the authorities. She just wants to be treated as a person instead of a nun. How else can she experience secular life? Know beyond the shadow of a doubt, whether the convent remains her true place?

Every time the door opens, she expects to see his mop of hair, his gangly stride. Soon she barely has time to look up. The minister from St.

James Presbyterian stops in with an elderly couple a half hour before closing. The man has a military bearing; he holds his wife's palsied hand tucked in his elbow. Rita scans the decimated shelves. She'll barely have enough for Tomás' family as it is, but what choice does she have? She starts to fill a bag with cans of soup, boxes of macaroni. "Do you like lima beans?" she asks them.

The man colors, stands even straighter. "Oh no, dear," the woman says, tapping her husband's wrist as if to silence him. "We'd like to make a donation."

Now Rita blushes and is even more mortified when the man hands her a check for three hundred dollars. "God bless you," she says coming around the counter, clasping his hands in both of hers.

"May God bless your generous souls," Rita says just as fervently, squeezing the woman's trembling hands. "I'll keep you both in my prayers." They seem a bit taken aback. The minister's expression is quizzical. After they leave, Rita realizes that she completely forgot she's wearing a thrift store purple mohair sweater over bell-bottom jeans.

At ten after four, just as she's about to lock up and drive to his apartment in Liberty, Tomás knocks on the door.

"Thank God! I was starting to worry," Rita says motioning him inside. "Is everything okay?"

"Fine, Sist—fine." He looks everywhere but at her.

"Come on, give me a hand getting your groceries together and I'll drive you." He still avoids her gaze. "Tomás, what is it?"

"My son thinks you will be angry with him."

"Mr. Gutierrez," Rita says, walking over to the man standing in the doorway. "How nice to finally meet you."

"For you, Sister Rita," he says hoisting a crate of grapefruit from the sidewalk. "I have two more in the truck. Oranges. Tomás, *por favor?*"

"Why would I be mad at him?" she asks.

"I know all you have done for my family, how you gave up your convent to start this and now I have come to take them to Florida."

"Oh. Oh, of course."

"I have a real job there. And the promise of a green card."

"That's wonderful."

"Tomás feels terrible leaving you," he says, handing her a clean bandana. She looks at the cloth in her hand, then back at him.

He uses his index finger to mime wiping away tears. "I'm sorry, Sister Rita."

"I could never be mad at him; he's such a brave boy."

"*Sí.*"

She blots her face with the cloth.

"I will try to repay you."

"No. Please. Just send me a card every Christmas, let me know how—" her voice catches. She clears her throat when Tomás staggers in carrying the two crates at once.

"Careful, *mijo*," his father says at the same time Rita tells him, "You are going to love Florida . . . ."

Rita hugs him and turns around to hide her tears. As soon as they leave, she turns off the lights, locks the door and a little piece of her heart.


Later, after she'd made their beds, vacuumed, and finished the laundry, Connie begs off a game of WAR with the girls, takes her book, and slips upstairs to Rita's room where she sits in the low chair near the window and tries to read.

The light looks blue, the sun held hostage by thick clots of clouds. She closes her book, relaxes the grip she'd had on herself since Vincent's visit.

Tries to untangle the knot of need and desire, revulsion and hate. In some ways, she uses him as a counterweight to her own confusion, something to push against, to pull with. He sets her in motion. Until he loses his equilibrium and falls into a molten rage, singeing her in the process. What she told Rita about the number of times Vince blew up and stormed out was technically true, but, she realizes now, she had seen the coming attractions years ago.

She remembers a June day so perfect that Vince had decided to take the day off from work. They'd left the breakfast dishes on the table, dressed Anna in her pinafore with the daisies embroidered on the hem, loaded the stroller into the trunk, and gone to the Bronx Zoo. The pale silky sunlight, the fuzzy green branches dappled and swaying, the breeze lifting her hair then gently setting it down again, the navy-blue stroller, its wheels whirring along the paths, her status as a mother still new enough to feel strange. Vincent practically electric with joy, rambunctious as a kid skipping school. They were laughing at the seals rocking toward the galvanized pail stuffed with silvery fish, Anna barking back at the hungry creatures.

"Got to feed my little seal pup," Vince said and went off to get ice cream.

Connie lifted Anna to the fence for a better view. By the time the show was over her arms ached to put Anna back in the stroller but when she saw Vincent stride toward them, a scowl scribbled across his face, she held onto her daughter instead.

"I lost it." He ripped the cardboard top from a Dixie Cup.

"What? Where?" she asked, alarmed, thinking he meant his wallet, or his keys.

"The goddamned part, that's what." He clenched the flat wooden spoon between his teeth, tearing off its paper wrapper with one hand.

Connie dangled the now whimpering Anna into the canvas seat, worked her rigid legs through the openings, stalling for time. "You called Arthur."

"They told him I'm too short." He jammed the spoon straight up between the chocolate and vanilla halves. "Good actor but too short for their fucking detergent commercial! They actually said my pants wouldn't be long enough for the grease stain they 'envision.'"

People were either turning toward them or edging away. Connie took the ice cream cup, squatted down, and spooned a little into Anna's mouth.

"Honey, lower your voice," she said.

The look he gave her then was so chilling that for a second, she felt disoriented, as if she had made a wrong turn onto a deserted street in a bad neighborhood. But then he abruptly grinned and crouched next to her, dug his finger into the ice cream and put it between her lips, rubbed it on her tongue, dissolving the confection, the tension, and her limbs.

"Come on, let's take Anna home, put her down for a nap. You can take one, too," he said then kissed Connie's sticky mouth.

"I need to—"

"I'll clean up the kitchen and water your flowers. Then later, we can leave Anna with your mother, walk through Washington Square, go to Umberto's and eat clams."

That's how they spent the day, with lovemaking before their nap, then again after dinner.

Even now, after all these years, the cellular memory of their best sex triggers an involuntary frisson of desire. She feels bound by the frayed strands of affection, kindness, and couplings. The truth is Vincent was lured by the promise of a clan he never had, and she by his fierce attention. Now those twin threads have twisted into a Gordian knot, the desired effect looping back upon itself, the family becoming intrusive and unwieldy by its very mass and momentum, the concentration of his gaze burning her, driving her deeper into the shadows.

It had taken nearly all her strength to walk out. She prays she has enough to stay gone.

Downstairs Connie finds the lunch dishes still sitting in the sink, Anna at the kitchen table with her watercolors. The clock reads 5:45. Rita should have been home by now.

"Where's Aunt Sister?"

"Out. She took Ceci with her." Anna carefully swirls a brush in a cup of water, then dabs the bristles with a paper towel.

"Where to?"

Anna shrugs. She's using the watercolor set Rita gave her, the one Vince brought still under the bed.

She glances at Anna's pictures: Connie, a blue hump lying on the couch under the afghan; Ceci, a dark blur of curls and arms and legs in motion; the cat in a wedge of sunlight; Rita, carrying firewood, dressed in jeans but wearing her nun's veil. For her own portrait Anna's painted herself from behind, a view of her torso, shoulders, the back of her head. In it she stands at a window, looking out. There's no picture of Vince.

"Put that stuff away now, honey, it's time to set the table for dinner," Connie fills a large pot with water. "The spaghetti won't take long."

"Is he coming?"

"Who? Oh. No."

Anna puts away her paints, washes her brushes, and places her portraits in an out-sized box that says Macy's in gold script. The last picture, the one of herself, she leaves on top of the box to dry.

Rita returns just as the water begins to boil. "Did you get any rest? How do you feel?"

Connie tears lettuce leaves into a colander and shakes her head. "He wears me out. There's just . . . so much of him—"

"I'm starved!" Ceci wraps her arms around Connie's legs.

"May I see those paws, kitten?" Ceci shakes her head and giggles. Connie tries to step out of her daughter's grasp. "Anna, help her wash up."

Rita brandishes a blue spiral notebook. "I'm making a list of the area farms to contact. Ceci's a good spotter." She tosses the notebook onto the table, hangs her coat on the back of a chair. "Anna wanted to stay and paint. Did you see her portraits? They're amazing. She must get that from you."

"Me? I never painted portraits, never even took any art classes."

"Those drawings you used to do," Rita insists.

Connie looks at her blankly.

"The botanicals?"

"Oh, those." Connie slices a tomato in half. "Ancient history."

"And your mushroom series. Connie, they were gorgeous. I still have two of them, framed back in my room at Holy Name."

Connie shrugs.

"Do I have time for a quick shower before dinner? I want to go to Sears after and see if I can find a pair of ski pants. I have a feeling I'll be spending a lot of time on my butt."

"Go ahead. I just started the sauce. You've got twenty minutes."

Rita bolts down the hallway, stops at the bottom of the stairs. "Hey, Con," she calls back to the kitchen, "whatever happened to the rest of those pictures?"

"They must be packed up somewhere," Connie says, pouring olive oil into a pot. Now that Rita has summoned them, the pictures pop into her head, as suddenly as real mushrooms after a rain. As a child that's what got her hooked: the way they appeared overnight in fairy rings under the linden trees in their earthen squares, on the damp rise along the concrete foundation at school. Undulating multicolored stripes of the Turkey-tails clinging to the oaks in Prospect Park. Puffballs bigger than a fist and bumpy as a human skull. Tiny Milk Bonnets like collapsed umbrellas on slender stems.

She loved their names: Inkcaps, Crumblecaps. Mottlegills and Brittlegills. Amanitas. Chanterelles.

She chops an onion, stirs it into the green-gold puddle of olive oil. It adds a sweetish top note to the oil's nutty aroma. She squeezes plum tomatoes into ragged chunks and extracts the yellowish core, then dumps them, seeds and all, into the pan and adds a sprinkle of chopped basil to make a quick sauce. Vince taught her how.

She taught him how to identify mushrooms. Which ones are edible, which poisonous. The death cap Amanitas, *Verna* and *Virosa,* the 'destroying angels.' So lethal they could kill. *Strega,* he'd call her, delighting in her exotic knowledge, her witchy ways.

She hadn't felt like a witch. More like a giant Alice presiding over a mushroom kingdom. Thousands of mushrooms, with tiny distinctions she'd begun to learn: the shapes of the caps, their textures, how the gills are attached, and how they're spaced, that stalks could be solid or chambered or hollow. Not unlike the human heart, but much easier to dissect, to peer inside.

When Rita appears, rubbed rosy and slightly damp, Connie takes the thick white dishes from the cupboard, sets them on the kitchen table, rummages in the drawer for clean silverware. "We need forks."

Rita fills the sink and plunges the contents of the dishpan into the iridescent suds. "You're sure you'll be okay without me."

"I'll be fine."

"That was quite a performance." Rita washes the forks, hands them to Connie to dry. "What was he playing? Norman Rockwell's winter guest?"

"He's doing penance."

"What if he comes back while I'm away?"

"I'll try to restrain him from cleaning the gutters."

"I'm serious, Con."

"It's not all show, you know." Connie takes out four glasses decorated with lemons and limes. "He's often considerate and helpful."

"And asinine and out-of-control."

"That too." Connie takes a fistful of linguine and drops the pale straws into the bubbling cauldron.

# CHAPTER 14

The children seem to take it in stride that Daddy comes to visit but doesn't stay for dinner or overnight. Over the past few weeks, they've developed a routine. Vince takes them for walks to the lake, hikes in the woods, rides to the log cabin restaurant on the old two-lane highway on the other side of town.

New clients show up at Loaves every week, it seems, and Rita scrambles to keep the shelves stocked. One day a week, she solicits donations from churches and service organizations. She sets ever more ambitious goals: a gleaning program, a co-op day care. She comes home as sleek and self-satisfied from good works as another woman would from a lover.

Once a week she meets with a dozen or so ex-clergy and social justice activists at the local Unity Church. Their causes differ in focus, but not intent: offering sanctuary to illegal immigrants, calling the administration to account for secretly funding intelligence-gathering operations against the Democrats, promoting civil and women's rights. But only the Catholics debate the fallout from Vatican II.

Sister Helen James, a middle-aged nun from the local parish, holds the most radical view. "By now we should have moved on from quibbles about how Mass is celebrated and whether or not to wear habits. How does the Church continue to justify keeping us out of the priesthood if, according to *Gaudium et Spes*, 'Every type of discrimination ... based on sex ... is to be overcome and eradicated as contrary to God's intent.'"

At first Helen James' opinions struck her as preposterous, but lately, Rita is beginning to consider *why not*? Especially since the former priests still seem to expect the women to make the coffee, supply the cookies and clean up after them. The youngest, Thaddeus, corners her after meetings, standing so close she can smell his aftershave.

The days take on a new rhythm with Rita and Vince coming and going, the children orbiting around Connie who remains like some lost planet whirling in place.

"Hi, honey, how was your day?" Connie shouts when the front door opens.

Rita walks straight to the hearth and leans into the flickering warmth. She unwinds a long scarf from her neck. "You're getting good at this."

Connie rests her ankles on a pile of cushions. "You're right, a slow burn builds a better fire. How did you know?"

"Weren't we in the same Girl Scout troop?" Rita reaches toward the ceiling, then bends to touch her toes. "Oh, right. You were always in the cabin concocting those awful campfire meals."

"I *hated* Scouts. I only joined because you did. Thank God, we only went camping twice before you got mad at Nancy Lopato for throwing rocks at box turtles."

"I was mad at Mrs. Dempsey because she didn't see anything wrong with Nancy Lopato throwing rocks at box turtles." Rita sits on the floor cross-legged with her back to the hearth. "Anyway, it was great. My day. Got a new volunteer whose son just left for college. Mitzi says she's reclaiming Rodney's bedroom for a study while she finishes up the degree she'd started before he was born. Oh, and the pastor of the Presbyterian church stopped by to tell me his congregation voted to tithe ten percent of their rummage sale proceeds to us."

"What about your commie dissident group?"

"The usual." Rita sighs. "Sometimes I think it's a cross between a lonely-hearts club and a replication of the Order we left. Most of them feel they don't fit in either world. My problem is I'm beginning to feel equally comfortable in both." She gets up, heads for the kitchen. "Hot chocolate?"

"No thanks."

Rita pours milk into a pan, turns on the flame. The aluminum burner rings gleam on the stovetop, the old linoleum reflects the overhead light, the window over the sink is no longer streaked with chimney soot. She makes up two cups anyway, takes them into the living room. "Vincent was here?"

"He took the kids for a while, brought back take-out, left some for you."

"And cleaned the kitchen."

"Uh-huh." Connie avoids Rita's gaze, sips the drink she said she didn't want.

Rita waits until Connie looks up. "What's going on?"

"I feel like I don't belong in any other world but the one I left."

"You didn't leave. You were evicted."

"What's going to happen when the baby's born? How will I manage?"

"We're doing pretty well. It'll be easier when Anna's enrolled at school and Ceci's in kindergarten."

Connie puts her mug down. "What if you go back to the convent?"

"We'll cross that bridge." Rita sits on the arm of the couch closest to Connie. "But you didn't know I wasn't there when you left him. What were you planning?"

"I wasn't. I was just too scared to stay. Not only of him. Me too. I wanted to hurt him too, Rita."

"But you didn't."

"Not that way, no. But maybe if I had been paying closer attention instead of tuning him out . . . What if I overreacted? What if it never happens again?"

"What if it does? And the next time it's even worse?"

"Loaves and Fishes. Open ten dash two, Tuesdays and Fridays." Anna reads the sign as Rita unlocks the door. "Four hours," Anna says. "That's not very long."

"Long enough to about wipe us out."

Rita steps around the stack of cartons, picks up the delivery slip sticking out from the top one, and checks it for backorders. Just the grape jelly this time. Janet comes in at seven o'clock on Mondays and waits until either the Empire State Grocers order shows up or Rita arrives around ten. Janet works the eleven-to-seven shift at the hospital, so it works out fine for them both. The delivery must've come early today; Janet's already done half the re-stocking.

Rita has to smile at the psychedelic Peter Max posters that Mitzi hung up last week. As soon as her son left for Rutgers, Mitzi started dismantling his room. "Birds do it," she told Rita. "They take apart the nest to force the fledglings out. Rodney's a great kid but since his father and I divorced, he's been overly protective of me." Mitzi shook her head. "Whether you stay married to the wrong guy, or you split up, somehow the kids pay."

Anna certainly has and Rita's heart aches for her.

Rita slits open a carton. "Anna, here, start this." She gets a crate for Anna to stand upon and sets a stack of macaroni and cheese boxes within the girl's reach. "Make them face out like in the grocery store."

No matter that it's charity, Rita likes to stock the metal shelves by category, and ask 'Now, what's your pleasure?' as if she were a clerk in an old dry goods store waiting on a favored customer. She never asks how much. Everyone gets one of everything unless she knows it's a large family. Compared to the city, there aren't that many clients in terms of numbers. But too many in terms of bent spirits. Rita crouches down to open a carton of restaurant-sized cans of tuna. When she hears Anna draw in a huge breath, Rita pops up, follows Anna's frightened gaze to the bay window. Outside there's a circus of a woman wearing layers of mismatched clothes, a rainbow of colors and patterns, mittens dangling from a half-dozen sleeves, two hats pulled tight to her eyebrows, a parasol open and held sideways as if it were a prop in a dance number. Rita stands up and sighs.

Usually, kindly, she turns people away, asks them to come during regular hours having learned the hard way that she can't stock up, place orders, keep books, and dole out food on demand. But it's Ruthie. Who may not show up for a month, then come several days in a row. So, she unlocks the door.

Ruthie keeps her eyes averted as she tiptoes to the counter. Rita knows her name from the laminated nametag she wears, as if she were a perpetual first-grader. According to Janet, Ruthie is forty-something, a schizophrenic, taking care of her elderly father who used to care for her. When her father was well and made sure she took her medication, she'd been a respected, if eccentric, piano teacher. Until she began to cower under the piano when the doorbell rang.

Rita knows not to chatter or ask questions. Human speech seems to agitate Ruthie into a state of near-paralysis. Ruthie hands her a crumpled piece of paper from one of her pockets. It reads 'A stitch in time saves nine.' After Rita puts peanut butter and the last jar of grape jelly into a paper sack, Ruthie hands her three more notes, one at a time.

'Easy come, easy go.'

'Too little, too late.'

'Pride goeth before a fall.'

Rita guesses at what Ruthie needs and bags provisions in exchange for proverbs. Ruthie clutches a bag under each arm, walks past the posters, studies their twirling banners of Popsicle colors, stops at each one as if making the Stations of the Cross.

She leaves as wordlessly as she came.

Anna has emptied the carton of macaroni and cheese and moved on to the tuna fish. The cans of tuna are shelved; stacked in threes, labels facing out. "What happened, Aunt Sister?"

"When?"

"To her. To people who come here."

"Any number of things, Anna. Someone loses his job. Someone gets sick."

"Why don't they get another job? Why don't their people take care of them?"

"Not everyone comes from a big family, honey. Or sometimes they're far away."

"Still, you belong to them, don't you? Even if you don't see them every day?"

Rita realizes bringing Anna here was a mistake. Anna seems weighed down with this new knowledge of larger losses, darker possibilities than her own. No home at all. No family to take you in.


"Did you have fun, pumpkin?" Connie says.

Anna nods, pulls off her jacket, hangs it on the coat rack, then disappears down the hall.

"I wish she'd let me get rid of that ratty coat."

"I wouldn't take anything else away from her right now." Rita selects a dark red apple from the wooden bowl on the counter. "I'm not sure it was a good idea to bring her with me. She takes everything to heart."

"She'll get over it." Connie plops a peeled potato into the bowl of cold water on the kitchen table. She shifts the soggy pile of potato skins and the knife-scarred cutting board to make room for Rita. "Tea?"

"Un-uh. I'm going to run over to the melon farm out past the crossroads and see if I can talk to the owners about gleaning their crops."

"I just put a chicken in."

"Won't take long." Rita heads back out into the cold.

It's gray and threatening but she's way behind schedule getting farms lined up and she's yet to find out their crop rotations so she can figure out how many people she'll need to glean and when. In just under fifteen minutes, she pulls into the rutted driveway beyond the simple wooden sign, lettered black on white 'Melon Farm.' The house is barely visible from the road, surrounded by the substantial trunks of old maples. The front rooms are dark but an old Volvo and a flatbed truck are parked between the house and the barn. She pounds on the front door, figuring someone's either at the back of the house or upstairs.

A bleary-eyed man in rumpled clothes flings open the door. "What?"

"I'm so sorry to disturb you . . . " She waits until his far-away gaze blinks into focus. He's wearing a Cornell sweatshirt, jeans frayed at the knees, hiking boots. "I'm so sorry. Were you already in bed?"

"What? No." He rakes his hand through his long wavy hair. "Are you a vet?"

Why would he think that, she wonders. "You mean Viet Nam?"

"Animal. My brother's seeing to one of our cows. I just conked out after spending the last twelve hours with her."

"You keep cows, too?"

"We keep cows *only*."

"This is a dairy farm? But what about the melons?"

He looks confounded for a second.

"What's so funny?" she asks when he tilts his head back and laughs.

"You're looking at one." He presses his thumb into his sternum. "Matt Melon."

"Oh, it's . . . I run a food bank . . . and I thought . . . " Now she laughs too.

"Makes sense, makes sense . . . but you have come to the right place . . . "

"Rita."

"—Rita, because I know everyone you need to talk to." He reaches back and swings the front door wide. "Come on in, it's cold out here."

He switches on a table lamp. The room's oddly formal for a farmhouse. Matching mustard-colored sofas face each other across a Tabriz rug. Framed black and white photos rest on the mantel. Above a bird's-eye maple sideboard hang a dozen small watercolors. Spare and beautiful landscapes which, upon closer inspection, reveal wispy figures, dwarfed by mountains or sky or sea.

"Yours?"

"Walter's. My brother. Come on. I need coffee." Matt leads her down a narrow hallway.

The kitchen is gloomy despite the large windows until he switches on the rooster lamp on the tiled counter. He gestures for her to sit at the table and fills a battered coffee pot with cold water, ladles in too many scoops of coffee, turns the flame high underneath it. He sets out cups, a sugar bowl, and creamer. A blue and white pattern with tiny vines and leaves and flowers tumbling every which way. The creamer is shaped like a cow; its tail the handle and mouth the spout. He fills it with cream from an old-fashioned glass bottle. "Ours," he says. "Be right back. Turn down the heat when it starts perking."

The kitchen is just as inviting as the living room. The table is a beautiful light-colored pine so shiny she can't help stroking its glossy surface. She picks up a mug and turns it over. Staffordshire. She wonders who chose the pattern, the furnishings. Mother, sister? Girlfriend?

When the coffee pot begins its raspy chirp, she turns down the flame. A ceramic crock on the counter holds a half-dozen silver teaspoons, each a different pattern. She selects a plain one for Matt, a rose-tipped one for herself, and catches sight of herself in the table's surface as she puts them beside each cup.

When he returns, he's wearing a denim shirt, his hair is brushed and his face scrubbed pink.

Rita sweeps her palm over the tabletop. "It's like a mirror."

"Pumpkin pine. I varnished it myself. Three coats." He pours the coffee and sits across from her. She tells him about the food bank and the gleaning project, making a case for the needy, the crop waste, the benefit to the farmers.

"No need to convince me." He stirs in some cream, tints his coffee a mocha color. "Damn good idea. Ashamed I didn't think of it. Most of the old boys will go for it, saves them labor. Farmers are used to waste not, want not."

Rita's reminded of Ruthie. Poor lost Ruthie. She stops nodding, drifts off.

"What's the matter?"

She's startled that he picks up on her shift in attention. She finds herself telling him about Ruthie, then Anna, and therefore Connie and Vince.

"I know the type," he says. "My father had a temper that ate him up and wore us out. He never hit us but he threw things around, pounded on walls, that kind of thing. My mother was always patching things up or buying cheap replacements."

He points to the china. "She bought stuff like this after he drove his truck off a bridge trying to pass some car merely going the speed limit."

"I'm so sorry." She shudders. Could Vince go that far? "And your mother?"

"In Australia, probably photographing the Great Barrier Reef," he says. "She's moved on to color. Those pictures on the mantel are from her Ansel Adams stage, which followed her interior decorating phase."

"So, you and your brother took over the farm."

"No. He did. With hired help. I didn't want to go into the family business. Soon as I graduated, I signed on as a social worker for the state— you know what the road to hell is paved with. I got real tired, real quick." He stifles a yawn as if remembering the fatigue. "Figured I might as well make myself useful. Now I'm glad I did. It's satisfying to work with your hands, you know?" He gets the coffeepot and is about to refill her cup.

"Oh no, I'd better be going. Connie's making dinner, I'm already late."

"Write down your number." He points to the chalkboard hanging near the phone. Rita hesitates.

"No sense traipsing from farm to farm. I'll figure something out, then call you."

On the drive home, the smoky gray sky echoes the gray of his eyes, his shirt. The air feels just like before it storms—all that pressure building, on the brink. The sky turns slate: suddenly it seems. She drives for fifteen minutes before she realizes she's missed the turn for the lake. By the time she gets back, Connie's running water for the dirty dishes, wiping the grease spots inside the oven door.

"Must have been a good meeting." Connie concentrates on a stubborn blob. "Did you get any melons?"

She doesn't see Rita's face flare into rosy patches.

# CHAPTER 15

Rita hasn't drawn breath all day. It's Janet's day off and Mitzi came in so flushed and sweaty, Rita sent her back home. For eight hours, she's been stocking shelves, bagging groceries, and taking donations. By the time the last client leaves, she's happy to lock the door and make a cup of tea before she mops the floor, muddy with melting slush, then tackles the stack of neglected paperwork. She needs to check the inventory and place an order with Empire State Grocers by five o'clock. She groans, arches her back, rolls her shoulders. She's bushed. Ceci was up half the night with an earache so Rita spelled Connie, dispensed the warm ear drops into the reddened hollow, rocking Ceci in her arms until they took effect. Rita reaches for her rosary, forgetting it's not there.

Just as the kettle begins its high-pitched whistle, there's a knock at the front door. Can't be a client, they always use the side entrance. With a sigh, she pulls the kettle from the burner. Through the window, she sees a man wearing one of those buttery-looking shearling coats, with sheepskin lining. Definitely not a client. When he looks up from checking his watch, it takes Rita a second to recognize him.

She opens the door. "Matt?"

"I called your place. Your friend told me you were here. Is now a bad time?"

"Good as any. I was just making tea. Would you like some?"

"Sure." His boots squish on the muddied floor. He follows her into the kitchen past the rows of shelving, the wooden counter with its open jar of licorice sticks, a basket full of greeting cards tucked into matching envelopes, a FREE – HELP YOURSELF sign taped to its handle.

"This is really impressive."

She laughs. "Right."

"No, really. You've found a way to make it human. Not like all those USDA hand-outs of blocks of cheese from the back of trucks."

Rita's pleased he notices, understands she's trying to lend some dignity to these people who have enough misery to bear without being humiliated by bureaucrats. She grabs two mismatched mugs from the cluttered counter. "Lemon okay?"

"Fine." Matt lifts a bag of groceries from a chair, sets it on the floor. "If I hadn't been so groggy when you showed up last week, I would have remembered there's a grange meeting Thursday night. I'm printing up the agenda and I'd like to put you on it."

"What would I have to do?" Rita sets the mugs on the table.

"Just a short presentation about your gleaning project. It's a perfect time. Before everyone gears up for spring planting."

She opens a cupboard door and checks the calendar tacked up on the inside. "What time?"

"We start at seven-thirty but new business won't be open until eight-thirty or so."

"That'll work. I just need some directions."

"I could pick you up, if you wouldn't mind getting there at seven. I do the set-up."

"I'd . . . rather see how my day goes. I can't be certain what time I'll be done here."

He writes out directions on the back of a torn envelope while she pages through a loose-leaf binder, fills out an Empire Grocers order sheet.

"So, how's your friend doing?"

"Hard to say. Sometimes she's her old self, funny and breezy. At others, she's just not there, all vacant and hollow-eyed. Her husband comes over a lot, takes the kids out; he's been very considerate, to tell the truth."

"Yeah, till someone crosses him."

Rita looks up from her paperwork, once again surprised that she finds herself confiding in this man.

"Sorry," Matt says. "That was out of line."

"No. I just realized I'm the only one, except maybe Anna, who finds it odd. Connie fell right into sync."

Matt shrugs. "The cows use the same paths over and over, even when a different one would be shorter or easier. That's why they're called ruts."

"I'm worried she'll follow him back to the barn one day."

"She might," Matt says. "What about you? Have you ever been married?"

Rita shakes her head. "You?"

"For all intent and purpose. We lived together through grad school then after for three years in New Jersey. Newark. She developed back-to-work programs for the city, I ran a methadone clinic." He looks into his cup, swirls the tea around.

"But you're not . . . she's not . . . "

"We both burned out about the same time. I decided to come back here for a while, be productive for a change, get some perspective. She wanted to take some time to travel." He swallows the last of his tea. "Two months later I get a letter from an ashram in Oregon. She wanted to stay. I was welcome to join her."

"I'm sorry."

"Don't be. It was wonderful. Then it wasn't." He hands Rita the directions. "I don't regret a minute of loving her. But when the wheel turns, you have to move on or be flattened."

Not too far off the mark from how she feels right now.

He points to the directions. "That do it?"

The map he hands her has compass points, street names, and hatch marks for bridges. "Perfect," she laughs. She glances up at the wall clock. "Almost five! I've got to finish this order and call it in . . . "

He brings his mug to the sink, rinses it out.

She walks with him to the front door, anxious to lock up before anyone else stops by.

"Whoa." Matt looks up at the posters, mock shielding his eyes. "I didn't figure you for the psychedelic type."

"Courtesy of a volunteer redecorating her empty nest." She opens the door for him. "What type then?" She can't resist asking.

"Oh, you know. More Arlo Guthrie, Bob Dylan. Or Joan Baez. That type. Only sexier." He states it plainly, without insinuation.

"See you Thursday," he says, loping off without a backward glance.

When Vince brings the girls back, he offers to give them their baths. Rita's still not home so Connie's grateful for the help. She hears Ceci command her father to "sing a song!" At first, Vince's tenor bounces lively show tunes off the bathroom tiles. But soon his tone changes and he's singing *The Way We Were* softly, slowly, a plaintive elegy to loneliness.

By the time the girls come in to kiss her goodnight, she's rigid with the effort to not soften. As soon as they're alone, Vince kneels down and whispers, "Connie, I'm begging you. Please come home."

She feels as if something sharp and jagged is stuck in her throat, that if she moves, she'll be fatally wounded.

He strokes her belly, kisses it. "I swear on our child, I'll never hurt you again." He looks up, eyes wet and shining.

In the past, that's all it took: his fervent promises, heartfelt tears. He'd reprise their courtship and lay claims to their history, their future. She'd relent and he'd live up to his words. Until the next time he lost out on a part, or Richard didn't.

"Just tell me what you want, Connie. I'll do anything you say."

On his knees, face tilted up, brows knitted above those soulful eyes, he looks like the motherless boy he once was. His need for her reaching back to before they ever met. She's torn between wanting to comfort or crush him. Somehow it feels good to know she can. "I want you to leave." Like a banished prince, he obeys.

In the rocker, feet up, a book of poetry in her lap, Connie tries to fill in the blank left by Vince. *Hope is the thing with feathers,* she reads. As if she could knit together a life with something as flimsy as hope. Not that she knows what to hope for, what she wants, or how much. She just discovers, after the fact—not this, not that. The days and nights had chased each other through the years in which she was supposed to have chosen . . . something. She wonders at the choices others make. Not their individual preferences. But at the naked fact that they've made one or two inviolable, singular choices.

She never has.

Until Vincent chose her and relieved her of the obligation. Or so it seemed. She comforts herself with the secret satisfaction of not choosing.

Of never being at fault.

It's almost nine o'clock by the time Rita gets home.

"That Melon guy called and left his number in case he missed you at work. Did he?"

"Un-uh." Rita plops down on the couch. "He dropped by to let me know about the grange meeting next week."

"He could have done that by phone."

"He had other business downtown." Rita yawns.

"Sure he did."

Rita ignores her, kicks off her shoes.

"Men usually don't go out of their way just to be neighborly, Miss Rita. You've been in the convent too long."

"Oh please. He's just a nice guy."

Connie narrows her eyes. "Does he know?"

"What?"

"That you're a renegade nun?"

Rita whacks her with a throw pillow, goes into the kitchen.

"He doesn't, does he?" Connie says, following her. "Is he cute? I bet he's tall. And brawny from wrangling cattle."

"It's a dairy farm, not the Ponderosa." Rita pours herself a glass of wine. "Actually, he's on the lean side, about my height, sort of rumpled-looking."

"Gotcha!" Connie grins, snatches an orange from the bowl. They settle back on the couch, Connie with her feet up on the blanket chest. She peels the orange in a long spiral, wrinkling her nose at the sharp citrus scent. She loops the scalloped peel around Rita's neck. "Figure you could use a lei."

"You're in a good mood," Rita laughs.

"Vincent stayed to give them their baths, put them to bed."

Rita shakes her head.

"What?" Connie crosses her arms.

"Is this what you want, to live here and have him come courting?"

"I wouldn't call it that."

"No? What would you call it?"

Connie chews an orange slice, swallows. "He needs to see the children. To make sure we're okay."

"What about your needs?"

"I need a break, Rita. He gives me that."

"Then what, he gets to terrorize you?"

"He's not, is he? You see how good he is with them." Connie escapes to the kitchen, washes the sticky juice from her hands.

Rita follows. "I'm not disputing that. But it's not a ledger, 'you can be this bad if you're also this good.' I'm amazed you've let him treat you badly then rationalize it so you can stay with him."

"What happened to your Christian charity?"

"What happened to your common sense?" Rita counters.

"Since when are you an expert on marriage?" Connie grabs a towel, wrings it. "Do you think it's all noble and sacred?"

"No, I—"

"You should talk! You can't even hack it in the convent!"

"That's different—"

"You're damn straight it's different." Connie throws the towel at Rita, stomps back to the living room.

Rita follows. "The convent—"

"The convent is to marriage what a . . . a hothouse is to a jungle. You're protected, Rita, provided for, prescribed by rules. It's calm, orderly, adult."

"You'd be surprised." Rita removes the strand of orange peel from her neck. "But you're right. I don't know anything about the complications of marriage and children. But I know aggression and denial when I see them." She takes Connie's hand, gives it a squeeze. "I just don't want to see you get hurt. Again."

"I don't know if I'm imagining it, Rita, but there's something different this time. For the first time, I feel as if I have the upper hand.s"

"That may be true," Rita breaks the orange peel into tiny pieces, tosses one on top of a burning log, "but how does that change anything?"

"What if it does?"

"You can't trust that it will."

"I know," Connie says.

But what if her one act of courage, like wresting Excalibur from the stone, restores them to Camelot?

# CHAPTER 16

Anna hangs up the phone and runs outside in her pajamas.

"You get right back here!" Connie says. "Where do you think—"

"Daddy said to look outside for my surprise."

Surprise? Will he never stop trying to win Anna's affec—*damn it*. How could she forget Anna's birthday?

"Get back in here, birthday girl, and put some clothes on. That way you'll live to be nine." Anna races past before she can give her a hug.

Ceci barrels into her mother. "What did she get? I want to see."

"Then you'd better get dressed, too."

By the time Connie's slipped into her sweats, Anna's already out the door, examining a huge cake made from snow with "Happy Birthday Anna" spelled out in a rainbow of Play-Doh. There's eight pink tapers, six of them still burning, and a green one, to grow on. A shallow aluminum disc hangs from a branch of the blue spruce, suspended like some giant Christmas ornament by yards of red ribbon.

She's almost as beguiled as her daughter. And grateful. God! If she'd missed Anna's birthday . . . Children don't easily forgive such slights—she wouldn't have when she was Anna's age.

Connie dials the food bank. "Rita? Today's Anna's birthday . . . I know, I know, I totally for—because Vincent didn't. Could you pick up an ice cream cake? It's her favorite. And something wonderful for her present. Vincent got her one of those sled thingies, like a big pie tin. Please? And a card. Not a funny one. You're a saint—sorry! A sterling human being then, whom I owe . . . Well, when you think of something, just say the word, sister."

Ceci's beside herself with envy and bolts for Anna's snow cake. Connie grabs her before she can plow through it. Ceci throws a tantrum of operatic proportions. Connie's attempting to get the sled down when Vince appears carrying a wooden crate and a pair of shears.

"I'll take care of that, Con. First let me—" He whispers something to Ceci, which silences her. Vince climbs up on the crate and cuts loose the sled. "If it's okay with you, I'll take them to Gilly's hill."

"Just what did you say to Ceci?" Connie asks.

"That for her birthday I'll make her a bigger cake, buy her a bigger sled."

"Her birthday's in *July*. She won't forget your promise."

"I know. But we've got five months to figure it out."

"Vince—"

"How about I take the kids for the day? We'll go sledding and I'll take them out for lunch, keep them busy till tonight. Then we'll all go out to dinner. Rita, too."

The thought of an entire day free of other voices, other needs and a night of being waited on instead of vice versa is irresistible. "Okay."

"Where would you like to go, Con?"

"Let Anna pick. It's her special day." Connie heads back to the house and blessed silence.

In the small window of time after work until the grange meeting at seven-thirty, Rita drives out to the Village Mall on the highway. Normally, she would have remembered Anna's birthday. But she'd barely settled in before Connie arrived and hasn't yet found her equilibrium, let alone updated her calendar with birthdays and anniversaries, the name days of her sisters.

At B. Dalton's she picks out birthday cards. Hard to believe Anna's eight years old, especially since her own childhood seems merely a glance or two behind lately. Mostly likely because she's been spending time with Connie again, Rita recognizes the careful regard with which Anna looks at Connie and remembers how it felt to tip-toe around her own mother. Rita watched her mother's eyes lose their warmth, become like green glass in the sunlight, not giving out any spark of their own. Not that Connie is that far gone but she's so withdrawn sometimes, so otherworldly. But maybe that happens when you're pregnant. Or just plain worn down. Rita will find out soon enough after the baby is born, when Anna is registered for school and Ceci's in kindergarten.

For Anna's gift, she chooses *The Little Prince* and *Where the Wild Things Are* for their parables of love and loss, and the refuge to be found in imagination. Anna will love the whimsical illustrations. At the Hobby Shop, she picks up a kid-sized artist's easel as Connie's gift and modeling clay for Ceci.

At the A&P she finds two ice cream cakes in the bottom of a freezer case, takes the one with the cellophane window still intact. It's nearly seven by the time she gets home. A note from Connie says they're at the Panda House and to come meet them for dinner. Rita scribbles a reply, reminds Connie about the meeting, peels a banana, gobbles it down, and heads out the door.

It's raining when Rita reaches the highway and sleeting by the time she pulls into the pebbled lot of the Grange Hall. Only Matt's truck and a two-tone sedan are parked outside. Inside, the floorboards creak and the room gives off a scent of damp lumber. The dark wood, the crosshatch of exposed beams, and the hanging lantern in the front of the room make the speaker's platform seem like a rustic altar.

Matt and a stocky man drag folding chairs to the center of the hall. A guy who looks like a giant version of Matt crouches in front of the pot-bellied stove set on a brick platform. A flurry of soft pings hit the windows as the sleet turns to hail. She shivers. It's too cold to wait for an invitation. She heads for the stove. The man tending it glances over to her, then away, then back again. He stands up. Still staring at Rita, he says, "Hey Matt, your friend is here."

"Walter?" asks Rita.

He nods. His face is ruddier than Matt's, his eyes are unequivocally blue compared to his brother's. He looks sturdier somehow but far less animated than Matt, who's offering to take her coat and to pour her a Styrofoam cup of coffee from his thermos.

"No and yes, thanks. I'll take off my coat after I've had some coffee. Maybe."

Matt grins and turns to his brother. "Walt, Rita. Rita, Walt."

"I think we've figured that out." She takes off her gloves and caresses the steamy cup Matt hands her. "Your paintings are lovely," she tells Walt. "So spare and beautiful. Just what's needed, nothing more."

"Thanks. I strive for that. If I try to capture everything, I just lose the feeling of it, you know?" Walt grins and crams one last chunk of wood in the stove.

"There'll be about an hour or so of old business before you," Matt tells her. "Catch you later, I'm going to finish up here." His brother stands as if to join him. "That's okay, Walt. Keep Rita company."

Rita feels sleepy despite the coffee and the hard chair. She's still acclimating to Connie's sojourn; hadn't realized tending to children cost so much because it's incremental, from the moment they're awake until they're not. The constant vigilance and stamina it requires. But having them there is also—fun isn't the right word—satisfying. Coming home to someone, even if she's still doing the caretaking. What would it be like to have someone take care of her? A complex bargain, she thinks, considering Connie with Vince, then without.

The speaker's tone claims her attention. Matt's plain-as-bread face is an animated theater of grimaces, grins, and frowns. He doesn't shout. On the contrary, his voice is low and steady. From what she can tell he's reciting a list of statistics: average to excellent yields, 200 to 250 hundredweight for beets, 200 to 240 hundredweight for watermelons, 500 to 600 for celery. Then he's talking about accommodations and transportation, wages. She can feel the tension in the room.

"I know, I know," he says. "Walt and I are dairy farmers and don't have the same kind of situation as most of you."

"Damn right," someone grumbles.

Matt holds up his palm. "But we're all decent people and we need to provide decent quarters, pay, and living conditions for our migrant workers. Most of the problem comes from the left hand not knowing what the right hand is doing. I'm willing to coordinate. Go 'round and find out who's able to provide what for the men and women who help keep us going. We can set up a picking schedule and maybe get loan of a few school buses—"

"Hold on, Matt. Just how are we going to pay for all this?" says a balding middle-aged man, salt and pepper curls springing clown-like from over his ears.

"I don't know that yet, Ted." Matt halts the slow rumble of comments by saying, "I want you to listen to Rita Mooney, who's been pulling some rabbits out of hats around here. When you hear what she's done and how, I'll bet you come up with a rabbit or two, yourselves."

He beckons to Rita who flushes at both the appraising and skeptical looks from the assembly. She'd give anything to be wearing a habit right about now. But she says a quick prayer and after a shaky start, speaks for those unable to speak for themselves.

"Thanks a lot," Rita says after.

Matt pats her shoulder. "You did fine. Just listen to all those old boys plotting and planning." The room hums and there are a few bursts of laughter.

Scribbling on the back of his agenda, Ted ambles over to Rita. "Do you think our workers could get provisions from your place?"

"I don't see why not," Rita says. "I suppose I could solicit donations for them and then, of course, we'd have to open an extra day during the summer . . . or maybe you guys could pick up provisions and we'll just load you up at the end. Or maybe some of the migrant workers could—"

"No, no. I like the idea of us picking up the stuff and bringing it to a central location. Less moving parts. What all do you stock?" Ted's curls bounce as he nods listening to Rita recite the usual inventory.

"Can you get any cornmeal?" Ted asks. "I know that's a staple."

Walt winces slightly as he walks toward her. "Hey Rita, you got any chains?"

She notices that his jeans are wet at the knees. "It's bad?"

"Black ice. The gravel's easier than the road but it still looks like we're falling down drunk out there."

"Forget it. We can't let you drive in this," says Matt. "We'll take you home."

After everyone's gone, and the folding chairs are stacked against the wall, they inch their way hand-in-hand to the truck. The cab is crowded with the three of them. Matt's driving, Rita's in the middle, and Walt's bulk is mashed against the passenger door. Matt waits until the engine warms before turning on the heater. The odor of wet wool fights with less savory aromas.

"Sorry, I forgot I turned out some manure in these boots," says Walt.

Rita snaps her fingers. "Wait. I'll need my car for work."

"What time?" Matt says.

"Eight."

"I'll pick you up at seven-thirty, and take you back here," says Matt.

"I hate to get you up that early."

"Early?" Matt hoots. "That's practically lunchtime for us."

At her house, he pulls over at the mailbox on the road rather than chance not being able to get back up the driveway, but he insists on walking Rita to the door. Actually, they glide rather than walk, Matt righting himself more easily than Rita, catching her elbow or reaching for her hand when she loses her balance.

"Company?" asks Matt, spying the Valiant at the bottom of the drive.

"Vincent. He's usually gone by now."

"He'd be foolish to drive in this." Matt delivers her to the porch. "Got any rock salt?"

Shaking her head, she opens the door.

"I'll bring some from home."

"Matt, thanks for every—" Rita turns around, but he's already scrabbling past the Valiant.

"See you tomorrow," he says, not looking back.

The kitchen is spotless and sweet-smelling. There's a candle burning in a votive holder on the counter. Rita sniffs. Vanilla. Muffled voices drift down the hall. She looks through the mail, saves the flyer for the white sale at Sears. Bills for electric and gas. A letter from Holy Name. Another forwarded from the retreat house. She hangs up her coat, makes herself a cup of tea, laces it with a little whiskey, and takes it with her into the living room. This room, too, is straightened up; books and magazines on the blanket chest; pillows fluffed; afghans folded; carpet swept. The kids' paraphernalia is nowhere in sight.

"Everyone's in bed but I can't promise they're asleep." Vince stands in the doorway. "Connie said I could stay. I tried driving but—"

"I'm not going to throw you out. The roads are really bad."

"Sorry you couldn't make it. I brought an extra order of shrimp lo mein, if you're hungry."

"I'm allergic to shellfish." She isn't.

"There are other leftovers too. Ceci hardly touched her pepper steak."

"Daddy, I'm thirsty!" Ceci calls from the bedroom.

"Third glass. Probably the MSG," he tells Rita. "I'll try telling her a story, maybe I can get her to fall off." Vincent grins, raising his nose in the air. "Her highness is miffed because Anna got all the attention today. Oh, by the way, she loved the books, Rita. Thank you."

She hears him in the kitchen running the tap. Then his footsteps down the hall. She resents him thanking her on Anna's behalf, as if nothing's happened, as if this were his house and Rita the guest.

The fire in the hearth is waning, a few flames curl around the bottom of a cedar log releasing its spicy scent. Rita pokes it till it flares then feeds another thick slab of cedar to the now lively flames. She sets her tea and correspondence on the brick-colored tiles of the hearth. Sitting cross-legged, she takes a deep breath before picking up the envelope with the cross on the return address.

*February 4, 1973*

*Dear Jude,*

*At Mass this morning, we celebrated St. Andrew who, as you're aware, was known for his great love of the poor. Naturally, my thoughts turned to*

*you and how you are faring. I think Mother regrets her veto of your project*
*but do not think you do yourself any favors by your absence, which only goes*
*to underscore your willfulness. I sense some opportunity for compromise but*
*you will have to humble yourself in no small measure. That St. Andrew died*
*six hundred years ago today also serves to remind us "this too shall pass" and*
*gives me hope that our separation is temporary.*

*I miss you dearly, as do all the sisters. We could always depend on you for*
*some practical joke or fit of pique to liven our earnest souls. Like that time*
*you positively fumed at being told to drive poor Mary Elizabeth back to the*
*shoe store for the fourth time because she couldn't decide between the*
*brogans or the oxfords and suggested to Mother Superior that perhaps the*
*three-mile walk would help Elizabeth make up her mind. And it was you, not*
*the substitute cook, who put the jalapenos in the meatless chili, wasn't it?*

*I've no doubt you will serve God wherever you are. Perhaps you are*
*needed in the larger world but I truly think we need you more. It saddens me*
*to think that if we can't keep lively, high-spirited girls like you in the convent,*
*what will be its fate?*

*You're in my prayers and in my heart,*

*Immaculata*

Rita closes her eyes and sees Immaculata's tiny silhouette like a Javanese
shadow puppet, buzzing through the halls, setting things to rights with a
fierce joy or balanced on a ladder, wiping down each ceramic fold of the
Blessed Mother's azure mantle. So certain of her duty, with a clarity of mind
that Rita envies. After dinner, in the parlor, they'd work on jigsaw puzzles,
equal in height as Immaculata stood and Rita sat, the thousand pieces
eventually forming a wildflower meadow or an Alpine lake. It took all Rita's
concentration to discern the fine permutations in the tiny cardboard
fragments, something the older nun did effortlessly, while chatting with the

others, making lists, watching the news on TV. The interlocking combinations seemed endless, arbitrary, but they seemed to reveal themselves as limited and specific to Immaculata. Rita sighs and pulls her knees into her chest, recalling the satisfaction of seeing the jumble completed, wishing all the pieces of herself could be so neatly joined.

She longs to drive there this instant, to be with Immaculata and Catherine John and the others, with whom she shares a shorthand, and a history, who are, in truth, the only constant, loving family Rita's known. What is she doing taking on a cause she may not be able to sustain? She should confess she's made a mistake; Holy Name is where she belongs. Beg Mother Superior to allow her to keep Loaves, since it's already up and running. If it weren't for Connie—and the girls.

The second letter is from her Uncle Raymond, her last living relative.

*31/01/73*

*Dear Miss,*

*I promised your father I'd look out for you (not that you need looking after in the convent) but I'm afraid I won't be able much longer. I'm getting weary, and I've more family on the other side that I'm wanting to see. I want to settle Timmy's affairs with you and turn over the power of attorney for me, as well.*

*Could you come for a visit, dear girl?*

*Your loving uncle,*

*Raymond*

"Good news?" Vincent asks from the doorway, startling her.

"Not really," Rita slips the letter back into its envelope.

"Oh?" He stands there in the long silence. "Do you mind if I join you? They're all asleep and," he nods toward the couch, "I believe that's my bed."

"I was just getting ready to go up myself." She tucks the letters into her pocket.

"No, you weren't," he says evenly. "You don't look the least bit sleepy."

"Nonetheless." She stands up.

"Rita—"

"Goodnight, Vince."

He grabs her arm as she walks past him. Rita flinches, stepping back.

"I'm not a monster for God's sake." Vincent lets her go. "I'm a jackass. That's different." He puts his hands behind his back. "I'd like us to talk."

"I have nothing to say to you." She retrieves her teacup and carries it to the sink, then turns on the tap.

Vince follows. "Then won't you at least hear me out?"

"This is between you and Connie." She sponges the cup until it squeaks.

"You know that's not true. Not completely. Because you've already heard her side of the story."

"There is no 'story' Vincent. Just bruises."

"I didn't mean for that to happen."

"So you've said." Rita runs the hot water, holds the cup by its ear-shaped handle under the scalding stream. "How in the world does that make any difference?"

"You're right. It doesn't." He reaches for a dishtowel.

"Don't. Just let it drain."

"I should have never gone off like that. It was inexcusable," he says. "But don't I get another chance?"

"It's my understanding you've had several."

"Rita, I'm not going to just disappear," he says quietly, leaning on the counter's edge. "We used to get along. Would it kill you to listen to what I have to say?"

She turns off the tap, gives the cup a few hard shakes, sets it in the slatted V of the wooden drain tray. It's true; she can't avoid him forever. He's here all the time it seems, acting as though nothing has changed except his address.

He offers her the towel draped over his forearm, tilts his upper body deferentially, like a butler or an altar boy. She tears a paper towel from its wooden spindle, wipes her hands, and braces herself against the sink, waiting for his next performance.

"Can we at least sit?" Vince asks.

"I'm fine."

"I was thinking of them." He nods toward the hallway. "The kids are finally asleep."

She feels outwitted, resenting how he always appears to take the high road. She walks stiffly, suddenly awkward under his scrutiny. In the now chilly living room, she selects the rocking chair, plants her feet on the floor, and glares at the sputtering fire.

Vince picks up the rusty poker, stabs at the charred logs. "I want my family back."

She has to bite her tongue not to say, *You should have thought of that before.* She doesn't answer; she can hardly believe his nerve.

"I know how awful this looks, but I bust my hump to make a good life for us. She must have told you that, too."

She'll be damned if she'll give him the satisfaction of acknowledging what, after all, is his avowed duty. She rocks, gripping the satiny armrests, trying to contain the heat clouding her chest.

"Once in a blue moon I lose it and she freezes me out—emotionally and physically. But the rest of the time I do my best and still, she shuts me out—"

"Don't you dare blame this on her!"

"I'm not blaming anyone. I'm trying to tell you how it is."

"And I'm telling you how it is, Vincent." She gets up. "Untenable."

"So, I'm tried and convicted."

"Is there any defense?" She walks past him.

"I give you my solemn promise it will never happen again."

She turns around, and asks, not unkindly, "Did you intend to lose your temper and fly into a rage?"

"God no, Rita, I—"

"Then you can't make that promise," she tells him. "It's out of your control."

# CHAPTER 17

Since they were already in bed by the time she got home from the grange meeting last night, Rita never had the chance to wish Anna a happy birthday. She hopes Vincent doesn't hang around until the weekend. She rushes to get out of the house before he wakes up. Puts on a ski jacket and pants, two pairs of socks under her boots, pulls a knit cap down over her ears, wraps a long woolen scarf around her neck, and slips out the front door. She trudges to the top of the driveway. The icy air feels scalpel-sharp against her eyelids, the bridge of her nose. She holds her gloved fingers over them, shivers and stomps. Finally, she hears Matt's truck. Braking and skidding to a stop, he looks surprised to find her standing in the cold.

He rolls down the window. "Am I late?"

"Nope."

He leans over to open the door for her. "I brought enough rock salt for—"

"Thanks, but let's just go. It'll probably melt anyway; it's supposed to warm up later."

He gives her a sidelong glance, makes a U-turn. The truck fishtails before the tires grip the icy road. "You warm enough?" he asks as she peels off her gloves, massages her fingers. "Why didn't you wait ins—? Vincent." He pulls over to the shoulder, turns sideways. "Are you okay? Did anything happen?"

"He's so manipulative!" she blurts out. "Campaigning for father of the year, surprising Anna with a snow cake, a tree sled!"

She describes last night, giving voice to her indignation, her fears, telling him all the things Connie doesn't want to hear and Immaculata wouldn't understand. Matt drives on without interrupting her.

She can't seem to manage any semblance of reserve or even objectivity. Vincent's cavalier attitude is galling, his tactics transparent, his resolve theatrical. By the time she draws breath, they're parked in front of Sweeties, across the street from Loaves and Fishes.

Matt turns off the ignition. "Let's get some breakfast."

"I'm not hungry."

"Coffee at least. The roads are still slippery, Rita. Your car is worthless without chains on the tires. Give me a call when you're done, and I'll drive you back to the Grange. The roads should be clear by then."

"I suppose." She rewinds the scarf around her neck.

Inside the crowded restaurant, the aroma of frying bacon reminds her she skipped dinner last night as well as breakfast this morning. They help themselves to heavy ceramic mugs from the double-decker stack on the counter, pour coffee from the glass pots warming on the hot plates of the Bunn machine, then stand patiently while the waitress clears the only free table. As soon as she plunks down fresh placemats, she motions them over.

"What'll you folks have?" The waitress blows a dark strand of hair from her face, tops off their cups from the coffeepot in her right hand. The other grips an orange-handled pot of decaffeinated.

"I'll have a small orange juice, two eggs over easy, bacon, home fries, and an English muffin," Rita says.

"Fried egg and ham on a hard roll, please." He laughs. "Man, remind me not to buy you a meal when you're hungry."

Rita flushes and grins. "Sorry for talking your ears off."

"You didn't."

Again, she's amazed at her ease with this man. "It just breaks my heart to see Connie so . . . diminished." Rita sips her coffee, grins. "She used to plant these theme gardens. One year it was crocus, iris, violets, lavender, I don't know what all—she called it 'Purple Haze.' Another year, 'Hello Dahlias.' She'd show us the garden and make us guess. Once it was ferns and roses; lilies, daisies, camellias—"

"—girls' names!"

"You got it."

Matt drains his cup. "So, Connie doesn't garden anymore?"

"She doesn't *invent* anymore. It's as if he's eclipsed her radiance. I have a sickening feeling he'll persuade her to go back to him. That maybe the next time will be worse."

"It's possible," Matt says gently. "But still, it's her choice."

"It just astounds me. Her tolerating his outrageous, self-indulgent—"

"Here we go," the waitress refills their cups, drops extra sugar packets on the table.

Matt picks one up. "You were saying . . ."

"I shouldn't be saying anything, I'm breaking the Eighth Commandment."

"But that's . . . 'Thou shalt not bear false witness against thy neighbor,' if my memory serves."

"It also includes the sin of detraction."

"Never heard of it," Matt says.

The waitress puts their plates down with a thud.

Rita pierces an opaque yolk with her fork. "Let's say Connie filed a complaint. If you were her lawyer, I would be justified in telling you what I know of their conflict. But since you're not . . . "

Matt chews slowly, calmly. Cow-like, it seems to Rita, with that same aura of tranquility.

"That's a fine distinction," he says. "Since you're splitting hairs, what about the sin of pride?"

She raises her eyebrows.

"What if someone thinks she's superhuman and can carry the weight of the world on her shoulders?"

"Ah. Perhaps," Rita says, coloring. "The road to hell . . . "

"Want some hot?" The waitress refills her cup before she can answer.


By the time she gets to Loaves and Fishes, it's 9:30, just a half-hour before opening.

She was unable to pray this morning, her anger at Vincent rising as she did, aware of his dark shape downstairs. She lays her Daily Office and Missal side by side on the table, taking comfort in their compact heft, the velvet feel of the worn leather covers. The thousands of times she's found solace in these pages, as familiar to her as her own face.

She opens her Missal to what looks like a target dividing the liturgical year into cycles, its circumference ringed with the months of the year, the inner circle prescribing the cycles of Easter and Christmas, the colors of the liturgy (purple, green, white, and red) the spokes radiating from the center. The elegant precision and reassuring sequence of rites and observances encircling her as well. Next Sunday will be the last week of the Christmas cycle; the following Sunday marks the beginning of the Lenten season. An excellent time for reflection.

She decides to make an Examination of Conscience, the spiritual practice which probes the subtler variations of the Ten Commandments and the seven cardinal sins. Of the commandments, she calls herself to account on the fifth, 'Thou shalt not kill.' Of course, she hasn't harmed anyone, but has she been furiously angry, borne malice to others, or refused reconciliation with another? Vince. She tries to get at the center of her rage. Is it solely for him? Or is it also for Connie's compliance? Should she recommend counseling instead of separation—there are five lives at stake here, after all—is there a gray area to be negotiated? But what if they reconcile and the unthinkable happens? She would never forgive herself. Or him.

As for Matt's assessment, what he referred to wasn't the sin of pride. No, that was more like an invitation to lean on him. But she is overly proud, she acknowledges, of the food bank.

As she meditates it strikes her that if she covets anything, it's the welcoming clamor of the children, their buoyant energy that lifts her as well, their endless fascination with the commonplace that grounds her daily in the sacred, the blessing of their whispers, kisses, tears.

And what about Matt, this dignified man to whom she turns for consolation? Might this be what it feels like to have a brother—a combination ally and guide? It's not simply lust, thinking back to Danny Farrell and the relentless craving insinuating itself under her skin. Perhaps some subtler amalgam fluctuating along a continuum between affinity and desire. Certainly not a sin; in no way has she compromised her vow of chastity.

Rita closes her eyes, rests her face in her palms, and for her transgressions, recites the Act of Contrition. "O my God, I am heartily sorry for having offended Thee . . . "

For the first time Connie feels at home, familiar now with the procession of sunlight as it makes its rounds through the rooms, the sound of bird flight like the shuffling of cards, the bell-shaped hum of a car approaching and receding; accustomed as well to the heart-stopping sight of deer nuzzling the ground beneath the apple trees, high-stepping through the clearing. She feels a reverence, as if she's living in some sacred wood.

Enjoyable as last night was, she felt restricted by Vincent's presence this morning, as if he were a lively houseguest who'd overstayed his welcome. It dawns on her, now that he's gone, how his attentions command so much space, how unlike Rita's unobtrusive kindness.

She hesitates when the phone rings. Connie doesn't feel like talking to her mother right now, if that's who it is, but, thankfully, it's Rita.

"So, how'd it go last night?"

"Anna had a ball, although she really missed you." Connie stretches the phone cord so she can stand by the window. "Sorry we couldn't wait up but the kids were limp with exhaustion. What time did you get home, anyway? I didn't hear your car."

"About ten-thirty. It's a long story, I'll tell you later."

"Damn straight you will. What, did that Matt guy turn you into a pumpkin? Or maybe a melon. No, wait, a lovesick cow."

"Stop mangling metaphors," Rita laughs. "What are you up to?"

"Nothing much. E's zonked out on the rug, the girls are playing outside, I don't have to cook, and it's just a beautiful day. Quiet. Peaceful."

"Vincent left?"

"I said it's quiet and peaceful," Connie laughs. "Sometimes he's as exhausting as the kids."

"I'm about ready to leave. Need anything?"

"Just your happy face."

"That was fast," Rita says, opening the front door.

"The sun is shining, the roads are clear, the chores are done," Matt says with a huge grin. "I'm a free man."

She puts on her coat, then picks up her scarf and gloves.

"Won't need those, it's twenty degrees warmer than this morning."

Once outside Rita tilts her head back and takes a deep breath. She's relieved as much by Connie's tone as by the spring-like day.

He opens the truck door for her, waving back to the teenagers packed into a yellow convertible honking their way down Main Street. "Have you eaten lunch?"

"After that breakfast?"

"It's allowed."

"This time I'm really not hungry," she says, smiling. "Besides I want to spend some time with Anna. Do something fun to celebrate her birthday." Rita snaps her fingers. "You know what would be great? A ride in a biplane. I went once, and it was incredible."

"Rhinebeck Airdrome?" Matt says. "They're closed till spring."

"You've been?"

"Yeah. My ex, Linda—oh, excuse me, she calls herself Parvati now—loved flying. Especially after she quit smoking weed. It became what she meant by 'let's get high.'"

"Have you?"

"Have I what?" he asks.

"Quit smoking weed?"

He laughs. "Isn't that like asking 'when did you stop beating your wife?'" He looks chagrined. "Bad analogy. Sorry, I—"

"Watch out!" Rita yells when a buck charges across the road.

Matt brakes hard but the deer bounces off the hood. The buck quickly gets its feet back under him and trots off, but the hood's caved in. "Goddamn brainless son of a bitch." Matt slams his fist on the steering wheel. "Great, just great. Just what I goddamn needed." Shoving open the door, he goes round to the hood and kicks the bumper.

Rita can see the vein pulsing in his neck, the sheen of sweat on his face. She's shocked by a frisson of excitement. Not fear. Since it's not directed at her? An atavistic and involuntary response. Is that part of Vince's allure for Connie?

He comes round to her side. "You okay?"

"Fine. Poor thing."

"Don't feel sorry for him. *He's* fine. My truck's the worse for wear."

"I meant you."

Matt's face relaxes into a grin. "Well, that's okay then." After he gets back behind the wheel, they ride in silence until he pulls up next to her car in the Grange parking lot.

"Thanks for everything, Matt."

"You're very welcome."

Rita reaches for the door handle.

"Wait a minute." He takes her hand, draws close. "All kidding aside, I would like to take you to dinner. Or anyplace else you'd like to go."

"Oh Matt, I can't. I'm . . . not exactly free."

He releases her, grinds out his words. "I didn't figure you for coy, Rita. You could have mentioned you're involved with someone."

"I'm not! Not the way you mean."

"Clue me in, then."

"I'm a Catholic nun."

His jaw drops. "You're not serious."

"One of the Sisters of the Holy Name."

Matt stares at her as if he's translating Urdu to English.

"From the retreat house," she adds, "at the monastery."

He finally blinks.

Rita looks down at her lap, twists the fingers of her gloves. "I've taken a leave to start Loaves but I still observe my vows, and I still belong to the Order."

"So, you lied by omission."

Rita feels herself flush. "I didn't tell you I because I knew you'd treat me differently, the farmers would have, too, even the waitress. Everybody does." She glances over at him. Matt's scrutinizing the Grange Hall, the parking lot, the sky. "Even friends and relatives," she continues. "Except Connie. No matter what I wore or called myself."

He turns to face her. "I thought you might be spoken for. I just had no idea by whom."

"When the inevitable shield goes up," she says, looking to see if it's in his gaze, "I feel as if I'm a separate species."

He regards her as he always does, with frank interest. "I'm not imagining the connection between us."

"No." She glances away. "You're not."

"Is this what you're searching for on your sabbatical? To find out what's down this road?"

"No, Matt," she says gently, "I'm searching for me."

The girls pounce on her as soon as she steps out of the car.

"Take us to the lake? Please, Aunt Sister? Mama will let us go with you."

"Girls!" Connie calls through the kitchen window. "Leave Aunt Sister alone. She just got home. Find something else to do or come inside."

They've turned the sled into a lean-to and draped their coats over it. Their leggings are wet and their hats and gloves hang from bushes like rotting fruit.

"They haven't fought once today; can you believe it? What a difference this weather makes," Connie tells Rita's approaching figure. "We don't even need a fire, unless you'd like—what's wrong?" she asks as soon as she sees Rita's face.

Rita tells Connie all about the meeting, the letters from the convent and her uncle, her encounter with Vincent, and her conversation with Matt.

She puts her arms around Rita's waist. "Of *course* he wants to take you out, sweetie. Guys were always lined up to date you."

"Yes, but half the time I think it was because they knew I was entering the convent." Rita sits down to take off her boots. "I was an affront to their masculine charm."

Connie slices an apple, then holds up a package of cookies. Rita nods.

"More than one guy told me he bet he could turn me on. As if nuns are defective females, unable to access their erogenous zones." She flings her boots onto the porch. "You don't decide to enter religious life because you can't have an orgasm. Celibacy is a renouncing of one's sexuality, not an absence of it." Pulling her sweater over her head, she sits back down. "The truth is, Connie, I didn't want to tell him. Isn't that awful?"

"No, honey. It's human." Connie sets a cup of tea in front of Rita.

Rita sighs. "Maybe it's temporary insanity. Maybe it's living with you and the kids, seeing what I've missed." Dangling the teabag, Rita watches the amber drops splash into her cup. "Or maybe it's the context, working toward a common goal at our own pace and by our own lights. Or just the timing, hearing from Immaculata and Raymond, arguing with Vince. I find myself talking to Matt about anything that comes to mind."

"Including me, I bet."

Rita feels herself flushing.

"It's okay Reet, I don't mind. I know you worry." Connie lays her palms on the table. "For my own selfish reasons, I hope you don't go back to the convent."

Rita reaches across to squeeze Connie's hand. "I was afraid Vince would talk you into going back."

"I'd be lying if I said I'm not tempted. But living here makes me feel distinct from him." Connie stares at their joined hands. "Plus, you're right. There's no reason to believe things would be any different. Nothing's changed."

"Maybe it could though."

Connie looks up.

"Maybe if he went to a counselor, figured out a way to control his temper, head it off—"

"You've had a change of heart."

"An Examination of Conscience. You were right. Christian charity requires Vincent should have a chance to redeem himself." Rita holds up one finger. "But not at your expense. Unless he can prove that he has exorcised his demons, you need to live apart."

Rita sighs and stretches, a slow ballet of limbs, then stands. "Tomorrow I'm going to see Raymond, I don't want to put it off." She dials his number. "Although, honestly, Connie? I don't think I can bear one more goodbye."

Connie spoons a bit of sugar and an ounce or so of brandy into a mug then waits for the water to boil. She finds a shriveled lemon in the refrigerator, tears off a ragged strip of rind.

Rita hangs up and bites into a ginger snap.

"What's wrong with your uncle?" Connie pours boiling water into a mug, floats the lemon peel on top.

"He didn't say. Just that he's tired and he wants to get his affairs in order."

"Oh Rita, it's too much." Connie hands her the fragrant brew.

"A toddy! I haven't had one of these in years."

"I remember your father making them," Connie says.

"It was the one remedy he knew; God rest his soul. Good for when I had the flu."

"When Danny Farrell broke your heart," Connie says.

"When I flunked chemistry," Rita says.

"The time you cracked your tooth."

"For menstrual cramps!" They say at once and crack up at the memory of Rita curled up on her bed, a pillow clamped to her stomach, Connie administering Midol and back rubs, Rita's hapless father, eyes cast down, delivering the potent drink then scurrying out the door, slamming it behind him.

Rita takes a few sips, then tears up.

"So how did you leave it with Matt?" Connie asks gently.

"The same way I left it with the Order. For the rest of the year, no pressure, no interference." Rita stares outside at the girls looping around the bushes, the trees, and each other in some giddy game.

"Then I choose." Rita watches Anna bolt, Ceci try to catch up. "One world or the other."

The children disappear.

# CHAPTER 18

"You're absolutely certain?" Rita hesitates in the doorway.

"Positive." Connie tucks cotton wool in Ceci's ear.

"Why don't I get Janet to take a look at her? Actually, I don't even have to go skiing—"

"We'll be fine. Anna's here to help, just go and have fun."

"You have the doctor's number?" Rita checks the contact list to make sure. "And the ski lodge? I'll be back tomorrow night, eight at the latest—"

"Rita!" Connie rolls her eyes. "I have managed thus far, you know."

"I know. Sorry. I'm just—" A car horn cuts her off. Rita waves to Janet, picks up her duffle bag, and heads out the door.

Just as she predicted, Rita spends a lot of time sprawled in the snow. This time she stays put, gazing upward, watching the sky turn violet with dusk. She'd spent the day dragging herself to the ski lift, colliding with the T-bar, bumping into other skiers, tripping over her own skis. Still, it was worth it for the three flawless runs with her knees bent, poles tucked under her arms, skis whispering in the spraying snow, her spirit flown open with exhilaration, her body along for the ride.

"On your feet, soldier." Janet neatly snowplows inches from Rita's head.

"No more, Janet. That's it. I'm done."

"I figured. But there aren't any St. Bernard's with brandy, dear. You still have to get your frozen self back to the lodge."

Rita struggles into a standing position, using her ski poles as crutches. "I may never walk again."

"A hot bath and you'll be good as new. In an hour you'll be raring to go."

"Yes ma'am." Rita slides along next to Janet. "Were you in the military?"

"Brothers." Janet laughs. "Four of them. Two older, two younger. Toughened me up."

Rita collapses as soon as they reach their room, but Janet prods her up, handing her two tablets and a glass of water. "These will head off the worst of it. Then take a bath, as hot as you can stand it."

Sinking down into the deep tub, Rita can almost stretch out full length. She can't wait to crawl into bed after.

"Oh no, you don't," Janet says when Rita comes out in her pajamas. "I could eat a horse and you're going to help me. I'm grabbing a quick shower. Be ready in a half-hour."

Reluctantly, Rita pulls on jeans and a turtleneck. She's tempted to tell Janet she's barking orders to a nun. Despite everything, that's how she still sees herself. Not a day goes by without observing her Daily Office, her daily prayers. If it wasn't for Loaves, for Connie and the girls, Rita realizes with a pang, she might have already made her way back to the fold. She glances at the clock. It's time for Vespers, the evening prayer. Closing her eyes, she prays for them: Catherine John,

Immaculata, Mother Superior, all of them, heartsure they are doing the same for her.

"Up and at 'em!" Janet says, switching on the lamps.

Rita hardly recognizes this apparition—a confection in a pale pink après ski outfit, white ankle-high boots and gold hoop earrings, Janet's movie-star make-up completing the transformation.

"Wow! You look—"

"I know. I get the Before and After award. Let's go."

Heads swivel as they walk into the lodge. Rita's certain she looks like an Amazon next to Janet. Or, more likely, no one's looking at Rita at all, just the newly glamorous Janet. Right about now, Rita thinks, she'd give anything for the shelter of her habit.

"You should see your face." Janet loops her arm through Rita's. "Come on, woman. Shoulders back. Chest out. Stand proud."

"Forty-five minutes. Sorry," the hostess tells them. "Wait at the bar, I'll come get you."

The last time Rita sat at a bar was with Danny Farrell, the night he left for Canada. "Liebfraumilch," she tells the bartender. Janet orders a martini.

"So, tell me more about the hospital," Rita says. "How can you bear it?"

"Because they do. The kids, I mean, not the parents. The children want to talk about dying and about the lives they've led so far, their pets, their friends. How sad they feel. What heaven's like. Sometimes it's too hard for the parents to listen. So, I do."

"Thank God they have you," Rita says.

"Yeah? Don't you think God could do better than that? Cure them. Or make sure they don't get cancer in the first place." Janet knocks back her martini, waving the tiny plastic sword at the bartender. "That's what a *real* God would do."

"Excuse me, ladies," the hostess says, "A couple of gentlemen want to know if you'd like to join them for dinner."

Rita shakes her head. "No, thanks—"

"Which ones?" Janet asks.

"The blond in the blue cable knit sweater and the guy with the beard in the black jersey."

"Here you go, miss," the bartender says.

Janet takes a swallow and then raises her drink to the men, nods.

"You might have consulted me first," Rita says.

"Oh, don't pout, you can have whichever one you want—"

"I don't want either of them, Janet. In fact, I'm not even hungry. All I want to do is sleep."

"Suit yourself." Janet fumbles in her pocket for the room key. "If I'm not back by breakfast, start without me." She struts over to the table. The men jump up to pull out her chair, to hold her drink. Janet accepts their ministrations as if she isn't the steely warrior of the highest slopes, the fierce guardian of the cancer ward.

Rita retraces her steps, feeling a race apart from the crowd of vibrant people, laughing and drinking, sating their appetites. They seem wolfish somehow, lusty animals devouring their meals with their forks and each other with their eyes. She feels the opposite, pole-axed into a stupor.

But when she steps out into the fresh air, her body snaps taut, feels sleek and sinewy, ready to spring, and so hungry she's grateful Matt isn't here on this stark beautiful mountain on this chill moonless night. Despite her vows, she's finding temptations of the flesh far more dangerous than hurtling down the icy slopes.

But as soon as she enters their room, she goes slack with exhaustion. She manages to kick off her shoes before conking out on the bed.

The sound of the key in the lock wakes her.

"Let go of the door."

"C'mon, baby, don't be such a tease." The voice is a rumble.

"I said no."

"Yeah, you came on to us, remember?" Another voice, aggrieved.

"Knock it off."

"Oh, tough girl, huh?"

Rita bolts out of bed to plant herself between Janet and the men. She's just as tall as they and totally sober.

"Whoa! Amazon," one snickers, reaching for her.

A swift elbow block and a firm shove knocks him into the other guy. She slams and locks the door, picks up the phone.

"What are you doing?"

"Calling the police."

Janet presses down the receiver.

"But they were assaulting you."

"Women come into the ER all the time with black eyes, broken ribs, beaten or raped or both. The cops, the doctors don't want to get involved."

"That's horrible."

"Agreed, but it's par for the course. Besides, I should know better: too much alcohol, one too many guys."

Janet's cavalier attitude is just as alarming as the incident. But isn't it the same in the government, even in the church? Men hold all the cards.

At the first shrill alarm, Vince jabs the snooze button, pushing himself into the chilly morning, colder still in the vacuum left by Connie and the kids.

Under the shower's hot spray, the fractured pieces of his day come into focus. He has to work all morning, pulling together another design or two, then head over to Fifth to Brentano's and Godiva for gifts, then back to midtown for the audition which he's known about for a week, which he hasn't told anyone about, which could change his life. Then he'll head out of the city before rush hour for the long drive upstate, even though it's a weeknight, for he's never missed spending Valentine's Day with Connie.

Vincent dresses carefully, aiming for the casual elegance a television doctor would have; unlike a real shrink, who could look just as rumpled as the next guy, with a bad haircut or a wrinkled jacket or an ink stain on his tie. He begins, as he always does, with the platinum medal, its smooth oval a comforting weight on his bare skin. St. Genesius, patron saint of actors, Connie's gift to him the first Christmas they were together. Charcoal gray slacks, off-white shirt under a maroon sweater, herringbone jacket. No. The herringbone won't read right on camera. Not a suit, the guy has to be a little glamorous, a little dangerous from what he can tell from the script. No jacket at all then. Black dress boots. No jewelry, except a slim gold watch. Got to keep track of those billable hours. He wonders how many times he'll have to say, "I'm sorry, our time is up." After dozens of readings in front of the mirror, pulling that one curl down on his forehead, flashing or lowering his eyes, he manages to make that line mean six different things from 'I find you revolting' to 'let's continue this someplace else.' Piece of cake. Still, he always thinks he'll get the part, never can modulate his expectations. The phone rings as Vince enters the kitchen. Speak of the devil.

"Hey, Arthur," he says into the receiver while grinding some coffee beans for espresso.

"You'd better knock them dead, Vince," his agent says. "Guess who I spent the evening with."

"The girl of your dreams? So, I better nail this so you can start shopping for rings?" He fills the small moka pot with cold water.

"Vera Stiles, Randall Brockton's agent? Seems Randall's pissed because word is his character's going into analysis and the shrink uses the information to seduce the wife. Vera figures the part's good for at least six months."

"Oh man, this cranks it up a couple of notches."

"You can do it, bucko. I'll call you after."

"I won't be here, Arthur. I'll call you."

"Okay, buddy. Break a leg."

"Thanks."

Vince searches the cupboards then stares into the fridge. Nada. Not even milk for cereal. He threw out the moldy bread last night. He pours a shot glass of anisette to accompany a demitasse of the inky brew.

The Brooklyn-Queens Expressway is smooth sailing and he sings fortissimo along with *La Traviata* on WQXR.FM. He's winding up for the finale of *Brindisi* when traffic abruptly stops halfway across the bridge. A blare of horns obliterates the music.

He switches off the car radio and leans out the window. Two cars ahead, there's a Chevy with its hood up. In the rearview mirror, he can see his lane back up, the cars behind him honking senselessly, as if their very noise will propel the Chevy out of their way. Cars whiz by in the other lanes; no way are any of these assholes going to let him in. Son of a bitch. Just his goddamn luck—if he'd left one minute sooner, he would have missed this bullshit. He stops short of punching the dashboard and takes a few deep breaths. Reaching in his coat pocket for the script, he runs lines until the flashing red light signals help has arrived.

"Ooh-la-la," Sylvia says when he walks past her desk. She reaches for the glasses she uses as a hairband. "What's the special occasion? Valentine's Day? Or are you up for a part?"

Vince leans over the counter that separates her desk from the reception area. "I'm up for anything, *schweetheart.*"

"Oh, you!" She swats him with a file folder, smoothes her skirt over her narrow lap.

"I'm having lunch with a buyer," he fibs. He doesn't want to jinx his chances. The only one he ever tells about auditions is Connie. But not this time. He's got to learn to ride this wave of anxiety on his own, to swallow the jagged sword of rejection and rage if it comes to that.

He finds a square pink envelope on his desk, made rosier by the morning sun. *Connie.* But it can't be, it's not stamped or addressed. It's a card with a bare-assed infant on the front, the words "Who loves ya, baby?" floating in a white cloud over its head. Inside, a big "I do!" and a folded hundred-dollar bill. Vince is touched; this may be the only Valentine he gets this year. Connie always has the girls make theirs from old magazines, paper doilies, red and pink construction paper. Anna's concoctions are little works of art, complicated layers of paper and paint. Maybe Anna will make one on her own, without her mother's urging. But he doubts it; Anna is the most unforgiving of them all.

From the current *Vogue*, he sketches patterns replicating a boot-length skirt and matching vest of plum-colored suede and a forest green velvet floor-length evening gown, with its faintly medieval-looking sleeves and squared neck. Then Palazzo pants and long tunic ensemble. Russet perhaps. Offset by an ochre turtleneck.

The work focuses him, tamping down the undercurrent of terror beneath the strata of craft and confidence. He jumps when Marty raps on the door. When he sees the sketches on the floor Marty does a little Zorba dance.

"Good for you, kiddo!" The mild exertion leaves him a little breathless and he plops down in a chair. "So? How are things?"

Vince notices dried egg, like pollen dust, flaking from the old man's shirtfront. And the wrapped cigar in his breast pocket. "I'm making progress."

"I meant with Connie."

"So did I." He gets some water, hands it to his boss. "Although I'm not expecting any Valentines this year." He points to the card propped up on his desk. "Thanks, man."

Marty waves him off. "I thought maybe you want to get her something extra special. Me, I do something different every year. Lynn doesn't like roses, gets mad when I give her candy. She's always watching her figure even though I tell her I'll do that," he laughs. "Today," he leans in toward Vince, "Fifty red tulips."

Vince whistles. "She'll love them, Marty. Hell, I'd love them."

"I can't wait till she gets them. First, she'll cry. Then she'll call. I know my girl."

Marty's face has a pallid sheen that worries Vince. "You feeling okay?"

Marty shrugs. "Can't live forever, boychick." He holds up his hand. "Please, no lectures. Lynn takes care of that plenty, believe me." He drains the paper cup, then tosses it into the wastebasket. "We all have our vices." Marty taps his pocket. "We compromised. I get two a day. Morning and night, if I can wait that long."

"Ah, Marty, I just want you around as long as possible, *capisce?*"

"I wish I'd never started with these." He points to his shirt pocket. "But a man makes his choices and lives with the consequences."

"Marty, you in there?" Syl asks over the intercom. "There's a rep in the lobby and Lynn's on line two."

"I'm coming, I'm coming." He hoists himself up. "She got the flowers." With a crooked knuckle, he taps Vincent's cheek.

"Choose carefully, boychick." He rests his big hand on Vincent's head a moment before lumbering out the door.

Vince tapes the new designs to the wall, then reads through the script one more time while walking the perimeter of his office. With the door closed, he vocalizes for a few minutes before heading out. The corridor is quiet, the switchboard closed, most people out for lunch. In the center of each desk sits a heart-shaped box of chocolates. Waiting for the elevator, he sees Marty shuffling toward the loading dock, swinging a Schrafft's shopping bag in his right hand, like some improbable Cupid. Vince has to laugh. Only Marty could get away with passing out candy hearts to wisecracking teamsters. Vince steps out into the bright, windy day and walks a few blocks before whistling down a cab.

Vince gets a kick from surprising his loved ones with the perfect gift. The only presents his father ever gave him were savings bonds—for Christmas, birthdays, graduations—only the amounts changed. Just once he would have liked something he could've held in his hand, shaken, ripped open. Let alone an object of his desire, beautifully wrapped.

When the cabby catches a red light at Fiftieth and Seventh, Vincent jumps out, pays him, and walks the two blocks to Fifth. The wind tunnels between the buildings, gathers momentum, making itself heard. He follows the smoky fragrance of roasting chestnuts to the corner. The red-cheeked, teary-eyed vendor hops from foot to foot while filling a small paper sack with the charred, scored kernels. Vince is hungry but he'll have to wait. As the appointed time draws near, his stomach clenches, his nerves twang.

Brentano's just another two blocks, he turns right on Fifth. The bookstore's packed; the aisles thick with men in cashmere, women in fur. Browsing in the film/theater section, he catches sight of a man who looks like Robert Redford. Maybe it is, who knows. Give the guy a break. It's easy for Vince to imagine being plagued by autograph seekers. He tries the poetry shelves. Connie already has half a dozen anthologies and the complete works of Whitman and Eliot. No dainty couplets, she loves muscular, mystical poetry. He doesn't get it, not completely, but she says that doesn't matter, what matters is the music. Well, something will strike the right note; it always does.

In the gardening section, he finds books on how to grow herbs, pumpkins, orchids. Books on organic, English, and terrace gardens. But nothing jumps out at him. Lately, he has no idea what Connie wants. His gold watch face reads ten past one. He's out of time. It's a seven-block sprint to Godiva's and he needs to be back in midtown by two.

In the crowded store, deep burgundy bows of satin and velvet adorn the signature golden boxes. A blond, bearded man with an island tan carries a stack of eight identical boxes to the counter where he flirts with an exotic-looking brunette in a tight red sweater. Looks like he's going for number nine. Vince selects tiny, outrageously expensive boxes of Godiva chocolates for each of the girls, plus one for Rita. None for Connie. It makes her queasy right about this point in her pregnancy. He takes his purchases to the shortest line where a myopic salesgirl in a pink smock carefully rings up the total.

The audition is scheduled for two fifteen; he makes it to the building by five after. They usually run late anyway, insuring he'll bump up against a few other candidates. He hates this part most of all, jousting with the competition, each of them armored in self-confidence, trying to project just the right combination of *sang-froid* and enthusiasm.

The young women glance up and then away, then back at Vince as he steps into the elevator. He grins and wishes them a good afternoon before moving to the rear of the small, hushed enclosure. The walls are brushed steel, the carpet gray. The square recessed buttons light up when pressed. Thirty-four is already lit. He can tell they think he's somebody by the way they stop talking, incline their bodies sideways to casually sneak another glance his way. *Just you wait, ladies. Just you wait.*

Behind the frosted-glass door of Day-Long Productions, past the small lobby, stands a varnished teak one leading to the casting director's suite, no doubt. The waiting area is empty, with no other actors in sight. The ubiquitous pretty young thing rolls her chair over to the appointment book when he announces his name.

"You can go on in. They're ready for you."

He glances at his wristwatch. "I'm the two-fifteen."

"I know, the two's agent called. He just signed for a film. And the one forty-five was a no-show. In fact, you're the last today. Sydney has a three-thirty shuttle to Boston."

Great. The bum's rush. He usually spends at least a couple of minutes preparing, re-reading the script. His heart feels racy and he can feel his color rising to the surface.

"Want me to hold those for you?" she asks.

"Thanks." He hands over the packages then delivers himself to Sydney.

"Vince Leone," a rumpled red-haired man says, checking Vince's face against his headshot, "meet Sydney Dayton."

Sydney turns out to be elegantly attired, long-legged, and beautifully groomed. She could cast herself in any role requiring royalty. The redheaded guy hands her the glossy.

She flips over the photo to scan the credits on the back.

To Vince, the over-bright room smells like sweat and Right Guard. Sydney walks away from the burly kid adjusting the Mylar umbrellas on the standing spots behind the camera, tilting them this way and that, trying to bounce the light off the ceiling. Up close, Vincent sees that she's around fifty. In her understated dress, with her understated heels, she towers over him. Sydney gives him a brief smile and tilts her aristocratic chin toward the folding metal chairs in front of a plain white backdrop.

"There's your mark, Vincent. Charles will read with you." She nods to the redhead and then sits in front of a monitor to watch.

Vince takes his time, slipping into the skin of a man who's heard it all, whom he imagines as some kind of evil priest, preying on his clients' vulnerabilities. He speaks so softly and kindly, that even Charles leans in, altering his monotone to feed his lines into Vincent's willing ear. At one point when Charles looks down at his script, Vincent narrows his eyes, tightens his jaw, creating the illusion of malevolence contained by force and design. When it's over the men shake hands, Charles seemingly unaware that he's beaming at Vince.

"Have you a prepared piece?" Sydney asks.

Vincent turns to face her but she's addressing the monitor. He looks into the camera. "I can do Edmund's monologue from *Long Day's Journey.*"

"Begin when you're ready."

Now it's Zen—his aim a perfect arc from his soul to the little screen, the outer world eclipsed by a private one.

"Okay Glen, we're done," Sydney says a few beats after Vincent finishes. The cameraman rewinds the tape, pops it out of the deck, and goes to stack it with the others on a table covered with coffee cups, scripts, 8x10 glossies, a Rolodex or two.

"I'll take that with me," she tells him, then walks over to Vince. "I won't cancel the rest of the scheduled auditions. However, unless in the unlikely event I see a better performance than the one you just gave, the part is yours."

He restrains himself from throwing his arms around her. "Thank you so much, Miss Dayton."

She doesn't ask him to call her Sydney.

"Have your agent call tomorrow afternoon, I'll know for certain by then."

She must be beside herself with joy; when she smiles at him now, he can see her incisors.

He floats out of the building, suspended in a state of shock. Just like that. The moment his life changed, the legendary big break, the great divide between before and after. Because this is how it begins. The exposure! Anyone could be watching on any given day: producers, directors, casting agents. He's rarely been cast for his looks, maybe a commercial or two but now he can showcase his talent, not rely solely on headshots or Arthur working the rounds. Now his agent will have something to sell. *To say nothing of the money, which is far better than Equity scale for the stage, not even in the same league.* He doesn't realize he's crying until he notices people staring at him as they edge out of his way. He doesn't care.

Everything he's ever wanted is a day away. He wishes he could know for certain tonight; he could honestly swear to Connie that things will be different from now on.

He can barely restrain himself from singing every silly tune that bounces into his brain. "I've Got a Lover-ly Bunch o Coconuts" accompanies him down to the lobby. Ethel Merman possesses him as soon as he exits the revolving door, "Ev-ry-thing's-Com-ing-up-Ro-ses." By the time he reaches Madison, he's been through the entire score of *My Fair Lady* and as he rounds 54th and Fifth "We're in the Money" elbows out a refrain of "I Could Have Danced All Night."

He's about to start back to Brentano's when a vision of Tiffany blue floats into his consciousness. Now *that* would be a great Valentine gift. But even with a hundred bucks what could he afford—a silver bookmark, two napkin rings? He walks into the wind toward the store. *No harm in looking.* Behind the plate glass, a pair of ruby earrings lie in a satin nest, small ovals like drops of wine, a single milky pearl dangling by a golden thread from each. He's tempted to charge them, to make payments with the money from his new gig. But what if by some freak chance he loses the part to someone else? What if Sydney just plain changes her mind? He turns his back on the earrings before they lure him through the door, find their way into his breast pocket, and take up residence in his pounding heart.

He walks all the way back to the garment district. For twenty-eight city blocks he wrestles with visions of instant glory or sudden death, combining the probabilities in shifting scenarios; the part but no Connie, no kids; all of them back together, a day job, nights free for talking, for listening; striking out but sucking it up and not striking out in return.

Worst case—no big break and no big happy family. Trying on the gut punch, the heartache.

Crossing over to Eighth Avenue the wind changes direction as he does, pushing at his scalp, the backs of his knees. It feels as if it's dogging him, not capricious at all. He ducks into a small vestibule and a gust blows on past him. In concert with the blackening sky, the blasts rattle the shop windows, whistle through the canvas awning, kick up spirals of gum wrappers, paper cups, bus transfers that skitter and tap-tap-tap on the sidewalks like crazed insects. In that dark cove, he stares down the fluttering phantoms, tracing instead the slick silk of his veins to his heart's desire. Then he strides again into the tempest to make his way back to her.

Vince steps inside a coffee shop to call Arthur. It's hot and stuffy, the air clogged with the aroma of fried onions. His ears sting. His nostrils let loose salty rivulets onto his icy upper lip. Massaging some feeling back into his face, he decides he'd better have a hot meal before his long drive. He orders a hot turkey sandwich from the lone cook scraping the grill behind the amber heat lamps and takes his packages to the phone booth.

"Vince! How'd it go? I called Day-Long but got the machine." Vince can hardly get the story out for all of Arthur's hoots and hollers. "You son of a bitch, why'd you wait so long to call? I've been on pins and needles here."

"Sorry, Art. I feel disoriented. Like I've been swimming and jumping trying to get upstream and all of a sudden, I'm there. Now all I have to do is flick my tail and glide."

"Yeah. Well flick that tail over here and I'll buy you a drink."

Vince doesn't answer.

"Sorry. We'll wait till it's official. I'll call you as soon as I know."

"I might be out of town." Maybe he'll hang around upstate until the weekend. Until he knows for sure. He hasn't told Art about Connie's defection. He can't bring himself to believe he won't be able to convince her to come back home. "We might take a little holiday."

"Number?"

"I said might. Nothing's definite. I'll call you."

The Valiant rumbles and chokes for five minutes before finding its rhythm, before he can turn on the heater. The steering wheel's so icy he uses his handkerchief for a buffer after he checks his coat pockets for gloves. Connie used to tuck his wool scarf in his coat pocket with a pair of leather gloves. Or pack a single lemon square in a white paper bag in his briefcase. Maybe a copy of *Vogue* with a dozen pages folded in half, Connie's comments in fine black ink, a roll of subway tokens, cardboard stubs to redeem his laundered shirts fastened to a theater review clipped from the *New York Times*. No cutesy love notes or shrill reminders. Just easing his way.

The drive up the Henry Hudson Parkway goes quickly; the traffic looks light enough that he decides to take the George Washington Bridge instead of the Tappan Zee. Bad choice. Within minutes he's wedged between a tractor-trailer and a Greyhound bus so he can't see whatever catastrophe has them at a standstill. He leans across the front seat and looks up at the bus driver who shrugs his uniformed shoulders and shakes his jowls before miming shooting himself in the temple. Vince laughs and mimes back, first winding the noose around his neck, then hoisting the rope until his tongue hangs out.

Back behind the steering wheel, the day catches up with him. He's got a three-hour drive without traffic. Maybe he should head home, get some rest, and wait until he knows for certain. But he can't bear the thought of not being with them today, at least for a few minutes. He should have taken the Tappan Zee. If he hadn't stopped to eat, he would have had a half-hour jump on rush hour. Now he'll be racing the clock to get there before the kids go to bed. He's bushed, he's late, he's stuck in a river of steel for the second time today. Maybe this is a sign to give up.

On the other hand, maybe it's a test.

He turns down the heater, opens his window a crack, and belts out 'Ain't No Mountain High Enough' to a furious medley of horns.

# CHAPTER 19

Everything seems eerily different in the pitch black. Vincent has a little trouble locating the driveway. He noses the Valiant down the long incline. Turning off the engine, he looks for the glow from a reading lamp, the fireplace, a nightlight. Nothing. If he saw even one glimmer he'd knock. But it's obvious everyone's in bed.

Back in the car, using his attaché case for a desk, he writes on the tiny gift cards: 'For Sweetpea,' 'For Princess' and 'For Rita, Peace. Vince.' In the back of his sketchbook, he finds a blank sheet.

*Valentine's Day 1973*

*Sweetheart,*

*Just so you know, I tried to get here in time to see you and the kids. I didn't want you to think I forgot what day it is. I'm looking at your window, imagining the three (four!) of you curled up in the dark and wishing I could be there too.*

*I wanted to get you something special this year and found the perfect gift.*

*I hope to be able to pick it up soon. But until then and always, you have my*
*heart.*

    *Love,*

    *Vince*

He sketches a border of trailing vines with heart-shaped leaves, dumps his
8x10 headshots from their envelope, slips the note inside, and drops it into
the sack along with the chocolates. He leaves the shopping bag on the porch
then heads back out to the highway.

Vince sleeps in as late as he can before he pulls on some jeans and a sweatshirt
to walk over to the motel's office. The surly owner keeps a pot of what almost
passes for coffee on a grimy hotplate, charging fifty cents per watery cup. Still,
it's better than nothing. Barely. She snaps open the newspaper when he walks
in and pretends to read it while tracking his every move. Her frizzy hair is
three shades darker than her skimpy eyebrows and she has the thinnest lips
he's ever seen. She's made it clear that she thinks he's up to no good. Vince
makes sure to drop the quarters into the metal box one at a time before he
pours a cup of swill.

Back in the dismal room, he decides to lie low today, afraid that if he
sees Connie, he won't be able to keep his secret. He can wait until
tomorrow. He can. There's no sense going back to the city; he's too wired
to work. Even so, he can't stay in this crummy room all day. Maybe he'll
get a late breakfast at a diner, read the paper, go exploring, drive down
some country roads. He showers but doesn't shave, then takes off for parts
unknown.

Rita's just about to leave for work when she realizes the girls are unusually quiet. "Con, the kids with you?" she calls down the basement stairs.

"Just Anna," Connie yells over the noise of the washer. "I told Ceci to bring me the hats and gloves they left on the porch."

Ceci's not on the porch. Rita finds her in the living room, her mouth glazed with chocolate, a crumpled shopping bag on the floor. Rita grabs her camera and takes Ceci's picture before sorting out the mess. Ceci's opened her own box of candy and Anna's as well. Rita salvages Anna's gift tag and fastens it to the box intended for herself. As if he could sweeten her up so easily. She's tempted to open the envelope with Connie's name on it, but her conscience won't let her. She's already gone too far over the line because of him. She sponges Ceci off then finds the soggy woolens and takes them down to Connie.

"Your father left you a Valentine present, sweetie," Rita tells Anna, "it's on the kitchen counter."

Anna looks to her mother.

"Go ahead, honey. I'll finish up here."

"I found Ceci raiding a Godiva shopping bag. Vince must have dropped it off late last night." Rita fills a basin with cold water. "Three small boxes done up in bows."

"That's odd." Connie adds a capful of Woolite. "He knows I can't tolerate chocolate when I'm pregnant."

"The third box was for me. A peace offering."

"Oh . . . Nothing for me?"

"Just an envelope."

"Fancy?"

"Business." Rita pushes the mittens and hats under the suds. "Janet has an extra ski pass for Hunter Mountain—"

"Go right ahead, Reet, have a great time." Connie pulls the warm clothes from the dryer.

"Actually, I was thinking of taking Anna."

Connie picks up a clean shirt, folds it. "I don't know . . . "

"Think about it, okay?" Rita heads back upstairs.

"Tell Anna to keep an eye on her sister," Connie says.

Anna sits at the table, tracing the velvet ribbon with her finger. "It's so pretty," she tells Rita. "I bet it's good candy."

"The best."

Anna picks up the box, puts it back down. "You should take it for the poor people. They probably didn't get any."

"Oh, honey," Rita crouches down, gives Anna a hug, "that's very generous. But what about you? Then you wouldn't have any. Besides, I have a big bag of Hershey Kisses to give out."

"Can I come?"

Rita remembers the last time. She doesn't want to expose Anna to any more heartache. "I'd rather take you someplace fun."

"Just me?" With the tips of her fingers, Anna touches Rita's hair.

"Just you."

She loops her arms around Rita's neck. "Where?"

"You'll see." Connie may not agree to a ski trip, but Rita vows to take this child someplace. Just her.

As he rounds a sharp curve, Vince sees a dilapidated barn billed as Five Oaks Antiques, Lloyd Reynolds, Prop. He brakes hard and veers into the driveway, scraping the tailpipe on a boulder. It bounces along under the chassis. *Shit.* He's not in a hurry, he has time to kill—it's just past noon. He could have just driven past then circled back. Well, now he can add a trip to a gas station to his agenda. He slams his fist into the steering wheel, gets out to assess the damage. The tailpipe dangles close to the ground, torn from its moorings. He wouldn't even be in this godforsaken place if she hadn't— he stops himself mid-kick, clenches his fists, exhales long and hard. Okay. Maybe he can salvage the damn thing or borrow some wire to tie it up. Vince wanders inside. Maybe he'll be able to find a steal, some vintage treasure Lloyd Reynolds doesn't know he has.

The barn's shelves and stacks are layered with dust. Nothing is sorted into categories; mildewed counterpanes rest atop a scarred walnut sideboard; painted metal colanders hold antique glass Christmas ornaments or silver fish forks; ceramic figurines, assorted crystal goblets and boxes of faded greeting cards and road maps share shelf space in a glass-fronted barrister's bookcase. A snip of scarlet ribbon trailing from a shoebox catches his eye. It belongs to the lacy border of a faded Valentine from the 1940s. Die-cut vines and flowers wreathe a honeycomb heart. He finds a pale-yellow porcelain tea set for the girls. Two shoeboxes and three cartons later he finds a pile of dress patterns: Butterick, McCall's, Vogue. He selects a McCall's pattern for a 1966 Halston halter dress—simple, stylish, sleek. Size eight. Connie will be able to fit into it by summer.

A clean-shaven, short-haired, slender man glides across the room. "Looking for anything in particular?"

"Are you Lloyd?"

"Stuart. Stuart Klineman," the man laughs. "There is no Lloyd Reynolds. Not that I know of, anyway. I thought it sounded very American Gothic. Better finds up here but I resell in the city."

"Guess I'm not going to get any bargains, huh?"

"Sorry." He picks up the Valentine, folds it carefully to protect the fragile pop-up heart. "Are you a collector? Or is this for someone special?"

"My wife."

"Ah." He picks up the pattern. "She sews?"

"Nope. I do."

Stuart raises one eyebrow, tilts his head.

"Garment district. I'm an actor by profession."

"What's your name?"

"Vince Leone."

"I thought you looked familiar. Didn't I see you in *The Fantasticks*? Weren't you El Gallo?"

"I wish. Probably more like a Dr. Pepper commercial. Do you have a phone I can use?"

"Behind that wall. Help yourself."

He dials Arthur who answers on the first ring.

"Childress Agency."

"It's me."

"Vince. I was hoping you were Sydney."

"No word yet?"

"I spoke to her assistant—"

"Charles."

"Right. About a half-hour ago. Nice guy. He said she'll call when she's done with auditions."

"What time?"

"I don't know."

"You didn't ask about the schedule? Jesus Christ, Arthur, what kind of fucking age—"

"Whoa! Hold on, Vince. She'll call when she calls. Charles is very aware we're waiting to hear, what good does badgering him do?"

"At least if I knew when—"

"—the last audition was scheduled. Then you'd shit a brick for every second past the appointed time."

"You know, you son of a bitch. You're just not saying."

"Where can I reach you?"

Vincent looks at the phone. Nothing's written on the little label. "I'll call you back in an hour."

"Vince—"

"An hour, Arthur. If I can wait that long."

Vince remembers the tailpipe, wants to fix it before it gets dark. "Do you have any wire?"

"For your car?"

"You heard it?"

Stuart nods. "Saw it too. Switched the monitor to the outdoor camera. You were a study in controlled rage."

Vince is not amused at having been the subject of surveillance.

"There's a Texaco about two miles up the road," Stuart says. At the register, he carefully wraps the teapot and cups, puts them in a little box, and tucks the Valentine and the dress pattern inside. Vince takes out his wallet.

"Make it twenty bucks even."

"That's hardly enough."

"Thespian rates. Besides, you made my day."

At the Texaco station, a man in a grimy jumpsuit tells him that "Todd's out on a road call and he's the only one who can fix it. Should be back soon."

"Okay, I'll wait."

He picks up a back issue of *For Men Only*. "We were Attacked by Flesh-Eating Piranhas," *yeah, right.* A really busty blonde in a skimpy top. *Always a pleasure.* It torques him that the feminists cry exploitation when half the women he sees every day dress so provocatively they're with bare inches of being on the cover of this magazine. Oh, he's all for the Equal Rights

Amendment; hopes it passes. But this men are the enemy bullshit... A cute redhead on the subway practically snarled at him when he offered her his seat. Although he's had come-ons from women—at cattle calls, on a subway platform once. Insinuating, unabashed, alluring. But he wanted a traditional marriage, so he'll keep his vows. Thank God Connie has no desire to work outside the home. And he's doing everything he can to provide for them.

At ten to three, he calls Arthur.

"You want the good news or the bad news?"

"Good first."

"Charles called. He doesn't think anybody today outclassed you."

"Great. Now I'm critiqued by a gofer."

"Assistant. He called to tell me that Sydney is unavoidably detain—"

"What bullshit! That's the kiss of death and you know it, Arth—"

"Hold your horses, Vince. She had some kind of heart palpitations or something. He called from the emergency room."

Vincent presses his forehead against the cool tile wall. "I'm listening."

"He doesn't think it's serious, she's had this before."

"And?"

Arthur sighs. "She'll call when she'll call."

"*I'm* going to have heart failure."

"Hang in there, buddy. I have a good feeling about this one."

"I'll call back in an hour."

"Better make it two. Charles says she's always ravenous after these 'attacks.' He's going to make sure she eats before he mentions us."

Vince groans and hangs up the phone.

He decides to take a run, to try to throw off the alcohol and anxiety flooding his system. He's not dressed warmly enough but the exertion compensates for the cold. The road is flat, lined with huge bare trees amputated to accommodate telephone lines. Beyond the trees lie fields patchworked with snow and low stone walls. There's a farmhouse once in a while and some scattered ranch houses squat and drab compared to the sharp peaks and wide porches of the Colonials and Victorians.

The steady whuf -whuf -whuf of his exhalations soothe him, as do the slap and kick of his sneakers, on the ground, in the air. He has always been able to depend on his body for endurance, if not for strength. He imagines he can feel the muscles in his thighs, his calves lengthening and contracting with each stride, his blood pulsing to his skin, flush and slick with sweat. At home, after a long run, he'd stand under the hard spray in the shower, soap up then rinse. Connie always wanted to make love then, after she toweled him down. He tries to remember the last time she wanted him. He has to go all the way back to a night last spring, when she came home from Rita's father's funeral. It was late; he was already in bed reading. He heard her unlock the front door and climb the stairs. He called her name but she didn't answer. She stood in the doorway of their bedroom and kicked off her shoes, then flung herself on him, knocking the book from his hands, kissing him with vehemence, pressing against him as if she wanted to lose herself inside him.

He turns around and runs back toward the gas station, still searching for the last time his wife desired him with a lust uncomplicated by fear.

By quarter to five, snowflakes start a mad dance in his high beams. He's looking for a refuge, some restaurant or bar. He's not the least bit hungry but if he has to hole up in that room all night he'll go out of his mind. Vince drives along the state road, its double yellow line the only slash of color for miles to relieve the white of slanting snow against the black night. It's time to call Arthur and find out if he's delivered or damned. But where?

A winged neon horse rises from the roofline of a roadside tavern. Two motorcycles and a pick-up truck signal at least three other patrons. Vince pulls into the lot, parking next to the truck, and cuts the engine. Why not? If he gets tanked or the roads get too bad, he can always call a cab, or wait it out with the bikers. He steps out into the swirling flakes, looks up at the sign. Pegasus rising, the perfect steed to carry him through the night.

# CHAPTER 20

Last night's snowfall has left its signature tracery on the trees and shrubs, the roof peaks, and the bridge rails. Rita stirs a pot of oatmeal as she watches the deer forage. Anna stands by the window, transfixed. Ceci opens the window and the deer bolt, crashing through the bushes.

Connie duck-walks into the kitchen.

"So, what did you decide?" Rita asks her.

"About?" She yawns.

"Anna. Hunter Mountain."

"I don't think so."

"Come on, Con. It'll be good for her."

"It's too dangerous."

"It's the bunny slope," Rita says.

"I want to go to the bunny slope," Ceci says. "I'm a bunny, too."

"I can only handle one bunny at a time," Rita smiles. "Anna first because she's—"

"The oldest, I know. No fair," Ceci pouts. "She always gets to be the oldest."

The women crack up and Ceci starts to cry. Rita gathers the sobbing child onto her lap.

"Answer that, honey," Connie tells Anna when the phone rings.

"It's for you, Aunt Sister." Anna stretches the cord, hands over the phone. Rita rests her chin on Ceci's nest of curls as she listens to the voice on the other end.

"When? Oh, dear Lord." Rita stands up. "Tell him I'm on my way."

"What is it?" Connie says.

"My uncle's in the hospital. He can't breathe. They have him on a ventilator."

"Oh no, Reet." Connie shoos the girls into the living room. "Anna, honey, mind Ceci. I have to help Aunt Sister. "

Rita starts to dial Mitzi then hangs up the phone. "I forgot. She's retaking the final she missed when she was sick." Rita runs upstairs, yelling, "Think, Con. I'm going to pack a bag, just in case."

Connie fills a travel mug with coffee, rolls Rita's toothbrush and a washcloth inside a towel.

Rita comes down with her backpack, checks her wallet for cash. "I've got to go but there's no one to open."

"I can get a cab and do it," Connie pulls some bills from the red Eight O'Clock coffee canister on the counter and hands them to Rita.

"You'd have to bag groceries and watch the kids at the same time."

"I know." Connie nods and leans over to shove the towel into Rita's pack.

"And everyone comes in all at once it seems. Plus, it's a lot of bending and lifting."

Connie straightens up. "What about Matt?"

Rita hesitates, then tosses her keys on the counter. "You call him," she says, halfway out the door.

By the time she gets to the hospital, her uncle is dozing, a white plastic tube in his mouth, an X of opaque tape on either side of what looks like a pacifier, anchoring it in place. His skin looks waxy and when she bends down to kiss his cheek, it's cool and moist.

Raymond resembles her father in looks, not temperament. Her uncle was as cheerful as her father was dour, as reckless as his brother was cautious, following his whims and fancies, he'd worked as a sax player in a wedding band, a pit boss in Las Vegas, a horse groomer at Hialeah. Raymond's wife had been a chorus girl, and they'd lived a happy, vagabond existence until they retired to New Paltz, shortly after Rita entered the convent. Rita takes out her beads and prays the rosary, closing her eyes and murmuring the prayers like an incantation.

"Amen," a voice says as Rita finishes a Hail Mary. A muscular black man in green scrubs stands in the doorway. He walks into the room, reaches for Raymond's wrist, and takes his pulse. "Your father?"

"Uncle. How is he?"

"Have you spoken to his doctor?" He counts Raymond's respirations, adjusts the tubing.

"Can't you tell me anything?"

"Just that right now he needs a ventilator to help him breathe." He jots down some notes on the clipboard attached to the foot of the bed. "He's had a rough morning." He tucks his pen neatly into his breast pocket, looks at Rita. "Why don't you go to the cafeteria, come back in an hour. He'll probably sleep for a while yet."

"Thanks, Damion," she reads from his hospital ID, Damion Truitt, RN.

"The doctor should be here by then—look for a white guy in a white coat." He grins and gives her the peace sign on his way out.

In the overheated cafeteria, she pushes an orange plastic tray down a metal rail, picks up a hamburger, some coffee. She wolfs down the hamburger then takes what's left of her coffee and finds a phone booth.

"Loaves and Fishes," Mitzi answers, a happy lilt in her voice.

"You must have aced that test."

"Rita! I did okay. How's your uncle?"

"I'm not sure, he's still sleeping and I haven't seen the doctor yet. Did everything go okay?"

"Fine. By the time I got here, Matt had everything under control. Now you're not the only tall person with biceps around here," Mitzi laughs. "Hold on. He wants to talk to you."

"Rita." He sounds like he's naming some unfamiliar object. "How are you?" A pause. "How is he?"

She hasn't realized how tense she feels until she relaxes into the low rumble of his voice. "You stayed?"

"Yeah. It's easier with two. You know. What's happening?"

She presses her back and shoulders against the booth. "Raymond's sleeping. I'm waiting to see his doctor."

"Can I do anything?"

"Could you just see if Connie needs anything before you return the keys? She's stuck in the house without me."

"I'm glad you called." He pitches his voice even lower. "That you know you can."

She manages a quavery, "Thanks."

"Take care," he says before she hears the dial tone.

As Rita gets off the elevator, she sees the doctor leaving her uncle's room, and waves for him to wait.

"It's not good news," he tells her in the hallway. "Mr. Mooney is in respiratory failure. One of his lungs is full of fluid and we'll have to tap his chest to drain it. Then maybe he'll be able to breathe on his own. Maybe not."

"Either way can I take him home?"

"Not if he needs ventilator care. He'll have to stay here."

"Will he recover?"

"Let's wait and see how he does after the procedure. Then we'll know more."

"When will you do that?"

"We're getting set up right now. You can wait in the visitors' lounge." He points to a sign with an arrow underneath. "I'll find you."

Rita turns around and ambles toward the lounge. She startles when she sees him walking an IV pole down the hallway, rushes up to greet—but it's not her uncle. Some other tall, rangy, silver-haired man, bent over, angled toward the inevitable decline. Rita peeks into the windowless lounge with its corduroy couches and artificial plants, a few back copies of *Readers' Digest* in a wooden rack. She takes the elevator to the lobby, and finds the chapel where she genuflects, then kneels in a pew close to the altar. Eyes closed, head bowed, she finds her still point. The hours collide as she stops. They settle at her feet.

She feels herself floating, unbound. Suddenly, keenly, she misses the convent, the order, her habit, and her long black rosary with the large plain cross. All the signs and symbols of that safe haven where custom prescribes action and duty provides direction. She slides onto the seat, resting her shoulder blades on the back of the pew, her hands loose and open on her lap, her breaths a metronome for the music of her heart. How has she come to be at the intersection of so many lives? Bewildered by the speed with which they shift and alter. The wait is easier here in this sanctified space and she takes full advantage before going back upstairs

The doctor glares at her when she steps off the elevator. "You were to wait in the lounge. I was just leaving. He did very well and he's breathing on his own." He punches the DOWN button and sweeps past her into the car.

"Wait. When can he go home?"

"We'll have to watch him for a day or so. Check back with me then," he says as the door closes between them.

Her uncle's sitting up in bed, pillows bolstering his back and neck. Looking older, sicker than his brother ever did.

"I thought I heard your voice," he says, "praying."

"You sure it wasn't your guardian angel?" She leans down to kiss his forehead.

"I'm sure it was." Raymond coughs. A raspy, wrenching sound.

She pours a cup of water from the pink plastic pitcher, holds it out to him.

"Funny . . . can't get used to you . . . without habit." He stops to take a few hard breaths.

"Don't talk. Take a sip." He takes two and hands her back the cup. "You just rest, I'll be right here."

The first thing Connie notices is Matt's economy of motion; his gestures as simple and direct as his demeanor. Rita has described him precisely but somehow all those bland facts add up to a presence as tranquil and substantial as a mountain lake or a riverbed. The bread she asked for is from the bakery, the milk from his farm. He holds up a glass pint bottle. "Cream. Nothing like it."

"You didn't have to go out of your way Matt. But thanks." She picks up the small bottle. "Reminds me of my grandfather. He always insisted on 'real' bread and real cream." She's putting the bottles into the refrigerator when Ceci charges into the room.

"Anna won't give me any crayons, Mama, she's supposed to share—" she stops short when she sees Matt.

"Ceci," he says. "If I'm not mistaken."

"She lives up to her reputation, I suppose." Connie laughs.

"Who are you?" Ceci asks.

"This is Mr.—"

"Matt, please." He interrupts.

"Aunt Sister's . . ."

He lets Connie struggle with that.

"Friend," She concludes.

"You smell funny," Ceci tells him.

"Ceci!" Connie shakes her head.

He laughs—a full scale. "She's right. I stepped in a cow pie when I checked the feed. Thought I scraped it all off."

"Blueberry pie is my favorite," Ceci tells him.

"Excellent choice," Matt looks beyond her to the doorway where Anna appears.

"Come here, honey," Connie says. "Say hello to Mr. Matt."

Anna gives him the once-over, her face expressionless. She says "Hi," then leaves the room.

"Sorry. My children are being rude."

"Honest. Only when you're grown is it rude to show what you really think."

"I guess that's true," she laughs. "Well, I think you're a real *mensch*. Do you know what that means?"

"Uh-huh. My friend Nathan taught me some Yiddish. We worked together in Newark and still keep in touch. He just moved to Park Slope, as a matter of fact."

"No kidding! That's where I grew up." She fills the coffeepot. "How about a cup? And some not-cow pie?"

"I'd like to but I've left Walt on his own long enough."

"Some other time then."

"Definitely."

He hands her the keys, reminds her to call if they need anything, and whistles his way out the door.

"Aunt Sister's home!" As soon as she hears the car, Anna runs to get the picture she's made for Rita. She's skiing down a snowy mountain, her nun's veil streaming behind.

"Look what I made for you!" Anna flings open the front door.

"Hello, sweetpea."

Anna turns on her heel when she sees him, goes to find her mother.

Vince unwraps the porcelain teapot and the pale-yellow cups, arranges them on the table, and props the old-fashioned Valentine between them.

Connie carries a groggy Ceci into the kitchen. She's mewling and rubbing the side of her head.

"Better late than never," he sweeps his hand over the tea set.

Connie glances at the display, then presses her lips to Ceci's forehead. "Vince, you need to call before you drop by . . ."

"I wanted to surprise you all last night but—"

"Look, Ceci's coming down with something, I'm beat. Another time, okay?"

"Let me take her." He reaches for his daughter. "Let me help."

Her ankles throb. Ceci's whimpering. After Matt left, she realized she forgot to thaw hamburger for dinner. Maybe Vince can run to the store.

"All right."

Vince walks Ceci down the hall. Connie joins Anna on the sofa.

"Pick out a book to read, sweetie," she tells Anna. "Or would you rather I help you with your arithmetic?" She needs to ask Vince to bring Anna's transcript from school but decides to wait until Rita's around. Just in case.

When Vince comes back, he sits on the floor in front of Connie, removes her shoes, and rests her feet on his lap. Anna closes the book she was reading, stands up.

"Don't stop, honey," he says. "I'd like to hear you read."

"Can I go outside?" she asks her mother.

"No, Anna. It's almost dark."

"Can I turn on the TV?"

"Okay but keep it low."

Vince takes a thick envelope from his jacket pocket, opens the flap, removes a photograph, and hands it to her. It's a candid from someone's wedding, Connie's head lying on Vincent's shoulder, both of them looking down at their clasped hands.

Then, one at a time:

The snapshot he took on their honeymoon, Connie wearing his undershirt, backlit by the midday sun on the balcony of their beachfront room.

Anna at two, rainbow-ed in finger-paint, the white wall splashed with colors Vincent later framed with black masking tape.

Ceci, radiant, her arm held aloft in a signature-covered cast as if it was the Olympic torch.

Connie can't help crying as each image taps into a larger landscape of sense memories; the rumble and thud of the surf, the oily sweet scent of the finger-paint, Ceci's silky skin under the plastered limb.

"Oh, Vincent. I know all this."

"Then come home."

"I can't. Not unless something changes."

"It has." He pulls the battered script from his pocket and hands it to her. On it, he's printed two numbers. His start date and his salary.

"But when? You always tell me. I always know—"

"Valentine's Day."

"Why didn't you say anything?"

"Because I'm not laying any more trips on you. Because I'm going to handle whatever comes my way."

She's reeling from this sudden change in direction, this reversal of fortune.

"I'm not leaving Marty; I'll just work from home. We'll be able to afford to hire someone to help with the kids and the house." His face seems suffused with the kind of light by which she used to warm herself.

"So many people have been picked up from soaps, but even if I'm not, the money's great and I can do a play on hiatus."

Vincent's ship at the dock, a more solid vessel with which to navigate the swells and troughs. Beckoning her. "I can't. I can't go through this again," she tells him.

"You won't have to, Connie." He caresses the mound of her belly. "I promise."

Maybe her baby won't have to be a fatherless child after all. If Vincent's prayer has been answered, hasn't hers been as well?

Rita pulls into the driveway and sees Vincent standing next to the Valiant's open trunk, holding two cardboard boxes, one on top of the other. What now? More bribes for the girls? Games, books, clothes? He catches her eye and turns away. She swings the car to the right, parking on the bridge. In the rearview mirror, she watches him set the boxes in the trunk then lean down to push them back.

She's out of the car in a flash, racing toward the house.

"This makes no sense." Rita grabs Connie's hands, stops them from shoving the second-hand clothes into paper bags. "What happened? What magic words did he say?"

Connie sighs and puts everything down, sits on the day bed, and motions Rita to sit next to her. "How's your uncle?"

"Out of danger. Breathing on his own."

"Thank God. And his prognosis?"

"He'll be able to go home in a few days if nothing changes."

"I'm so relieved for you Rita, you don't need any more—"

"Good-byes? Is that why you were going to take off without a word—"

"I wasn't. I didn't . . . " Connie takes Rita's hand in hers. "Vincent finally got a great part. Just what he wanted."

"What about what you want?"

"And for the first time, he didn't rely on me to prop him up or take the edge off his anxiety."

"That's a good start, Connie. But that's all it is—"

"I really like Matt, by the way, he's so—"

"Quit changing the subject. You're walking into a minefield and taking the children with you."

"They adore him."

"Not Anna."

Connie flinches. "That was cruel, Rita."

"That's the truth. And it's Vincent who's cruel, not me. Open your eyes."

"You said he should be given the chance to redeem himself!" Connie hoists herself up, continues packing.

"And one incidence of mature behavior is enough for you?" Rita stands up, faces Connie. "What about all the other times and ways he takes it out on you? What makes you think it won't happen again?"

"For one thing, this part is what he's been after all these years, like winning the actors lottery." Connie straightens up, lifts her chin. "For another, now he knows I can make him suffer, too."

Rita shakes her head. "You think you put the fear of God into him and maybe you have. I hope you did." She opens her arms and Connie walks into them. Rita gives her a fierce hug. "But leave this stuff here. If there is a next time, you'll be halfway home."

Anna clings to Rita when they say goodbye.

"Hey," Rita whispers in her ear. "I didn't forget about our special day. As soon as my uncle's back home, we'll make a date, okay?"

Anna nods, rubbing her cheek against Rita's. When Anna turns away to take her mother's hand, Rita feels the cool tracks of her tears.

Rita watches them leave, the red taillights like the eyes of a demon following Connie back home. The house feels like a tomb. The same kind of hollow echo dogs her footsteps as when she was a little girl, her father gone to work, her mother upstairs in a world of her own.

The shock feels surgical; it renders her numb. Her first thought is to pack up herself, go back to where she's needed and loved, where other hearts beat under the same roof. Her second is to call Matt.

With a flashlight, she picks her way down to the lake. The night sky like a shroud. No moon, no stars. A distant scatter of porch lights from across the water. She finds her way by sonar, bat-like. This is what she prayed for; this is what she received. A crucible of solitude in which to test her choices.

She'd vowed to take this time apart, not expecting Connie, not even dreaming how welcome other bodies would be, how insatiable her need to be needed. A character flaw, she sees now, as egregiously self-serving as is Vincent's need to be adored. She feels exposed, shorn of all delusions.

The ice creaks and groans, shifting and splitting under the surface. It sounds like sorrowing whales or lost elephants.

Grief as huge and wild as her own.

# CHAPTER 21

What sounds like thunder turns out to be the rolling boom of metal trashcans on concrete, Connie realizes, as soon as she hears the garbage truck's accompanying squeal and grind. She opens her eyes and glances across the pillow at Vincent's face, sleep swollen, a smudge of bristle along his jaw.

On the ride home last night she'd entertained the thought that they'd sleep in separate beds—presuming lying together an act too intimate, too soon—but nestling with Vincent had felt as comfortable as settling back into a familiar chair, its contours molded by her shape. Ceci took all her dolls and stuffed animals to bed with her, fell right to sleep. Only Anna was disconsolate, wanting Connie to stay with her and Ceci in their room, reluctant to relinquish her mother to her father's bed. But the night passed uneventfully, all of them seemingly exhausted by the arduous journey of reconciliation.

She prays she made the right decision, that some enormous shadow has been vanquished and laid to rest by her refusal to be bullied and Vincent's sudden good fortune. She lifts her head off the pillow and strains to listen to a series of faint peeps. A thrush? But it's Ceci piping her way down the hall. She totters into the room, crying, half-awake. Vincent has slept through all the street noise but now he stirs, opens one eye.

"We have to go back, Daddy." Ceci's damp with tears and sleep. "We forgot E."

"The cat," Connie reminds him. Vince scoops his daughter into his arms and wipes her tears with the edge of the sheet.

"The kitty lives with Aunt Sister, honey," he says. "That's her house."

"Why can't she switch houses, Daddy? We did."

Vincent looks to Connie but she snuggles back down under the covers.

"Your aunt would miss her too much, sweetie," Vince tells her, "like I missed you. From now on everyone stays where they belong."

Before visiting her uncle, Rita drives to the low-slung building with the stylized cross rising from its flying dome. St. Ignatius Roman Catholic Church. She'd noticed it yesterday, on her way to the hospital. The parking lot is nearly full for ten o'clock Mass.

As soon as she opens the heavy glass door, guitar music bounces off the polished stone floor of the vestibule. In the church proper, the priest faces the curved pews from behind the simple altar. A handful of teenagers with folk guitars and tambourines lead the congregation in song. The room crackles with high spirits and good will. The Mass, of course, will be in English. Only a few parishes, mostly ethnic, hold out for Latin. Here are lots of young families with two or three small children, teenagers and young adults, a sprinkling of middle-aged couples, a few elderly parishioners. Three women about Rita's age clap and sing with enthusiasm. From their blunt haircuts and darkish outfits, she supposes they're nuns out of habit, for the day at least.

Grown women but they look like hatchlings. She smiles at a little girl dancing away from her mother, heading toward the musicians. She looks to be Ceci's age. Rita's smile trembles and twists.

The freshest wound, the children gone. Their after-image in every room; happy ghosts wrapped in soggy towels, hair dark and dripping from the bath; faces purple and sticky with jam; or fire-lit while reading; the little room, a makeshift dormitory, their shapes lingering beneath the sheets.

Rita can't distinguish between her pangs of longing; whether they're for the convent, the children, or the Latin Mass. She's welcomed the changes in the church, but she misses some of the old ways, the ancient language, majestic and mysterious, the priest in front instead of behind the altar, the cross on the back of his chasuble directing her gaze. It's far easier to imagine the priest as the spiritual disciple of Christ when not distracted by the countenance of some ordinary man whether haggard or homely or handsome.

At the hospital, her uncle remains breathless, needs the ventilator all the time. Rita stays until he wakes, reassuring him once again she has the envelope he'd given her and the keys. After saying the rosary—Raymond's dry fingers counting off the beads—she stops at the nurses' station to say hello to Damion. On impulse, she decides to stop by Holy Name, unwilling to go home just yet.

Catherine John answers the door. "Jude! We were just talking about you, we're having chili," she laughs, welcomes Rita with a hug, then closes the heavy front door. "Come eat with us. The sisters will want to hear every little thing."

"Immaculata?" Rita asks, taking off her coat, dropping it on the deacon's bench.

"Already in the dining room, I think."

They're just taking their places at the long refectory table. Twelve chairs, ten place settings. One is quickly set for her. The other chair belongs to Mother Superior, gone to the Motherhouse for a meeting. The beaming faces look delighted to see her. Some of the sisters wear the old habit, some the new abbreviated version with the shorter skirt and veil. Two of the youngest wear street clothes. Rita's the only one wearing slacks.

"We're still deciding on outfits," says Sister Theresa. "I never thought I'd have to color co-ordinate again. That's the main reason I joined." They crack up.

Rita relaxes into the banter, the leisurely exchange of news, personal and professional. Both Mary Elizabeth and Catherine John have enrolled at SUNY for graduate degrees in philosophy and education respectively. Sister Helen Charles has resumed using her birth name, Alice Burdock. Mother Superior still refers to her as 'Charles.'

They've started a joint project with the Sisters of Charity to sponsor retreats for welfare mothers. Once a month, a small group of women and their children will come to the retreat house to be nurtured body and soul. Rita answers their questions about the food bank, tells them about the gleaning project, and her uncle's illness.

"We'll keep him in our prayers as a special intention," Theresa says. "You, of course, are already there."

They won't let Rita help clear the table, nor wash a dish. The easy camaraderie feels like a warm bath enveloping her weary limbs. The cleanup is done with alacrity and good cheer. It's true many hands make light work. After, she shares a sofa in the parlor with Immaculata.

"It's so good to see you, Jude. Your friend, did she find you?"

Rita tells her about Connie and Vincent. Her chagrin at Connie's rapid reconciliation, and how much she misses the children. About Janet and the food bank and Ruthie's sad fate. The grange meeting and Matt. Her turmoil and indecision.

"This man—is he a consideration also?"

"I'm not sure."

"Tell me what you're sure of."

"That I want to live in a community whether it's here, or with a family or in the Peace Corps. That I need to take part in providing meaningful relief to the needy, something to sustain hope. That I love being around children."

"We'll be having them here soon, starting in May. It sounds to me that, in your heart of hearts, you've dedicated yourself to good works and sacrifice. A nun's life." Immaculata rubs a worn rosary bead between her tiny fingers, sighs. "And a missionary's. And a mother's."

"Pray for me."

"Always, my dear Jude. No matter what."

The living room is in shambles. Anna's easel is propped up near the picture window, toys lay scattered on the couch and the carpet. Ceci darts in and out modeling her mother's cast-offs and costume jewelry. Connie stretches out on the couch, feet up, working a crossword. "Six letter word for 'burgeon,'" she says.

"C-o-n-n-i-e," Vince spells.

"Very funny. Third letter is 'p.'"

"Expand!" they both say at once.

"I can't wait till this one is born; this feels like the longest pregnancy yet. Ten days to go."

"If he's not early," Vince says.

"From your lips," Connie sighs and rubs her distended belly. "This one feels different, but he may turn out to be another she, after all."

"Doesn't matter, Con. There's always next time."

Next time. His words feel like stones in her pockets. She closes her eyes and turns away from him, walking into the sea.

Ceci makes an entrance wearing Anna's favorite, the tattered suede jacket, Connie's highest heels, a red lipstick O around her mouth. Vincent's aviator sunglasses cover half her face. He howls when he sees her.

Connie looks up just as Anna reaches her sister and says, "You take that off right now—"

Ceci wriggles away and jumps on Vince. Anna grabs her by the arm. "Give it back, Ceci."

She runs over to Connie, Anna chases after her. "I said give it back!"

As Ceci dives behind the sofa they hear a long thripppp—the seam splitting. Anna bursts into tears, runs up to her room, slamming the door behind her. Vincent sits up. "Come here, Ceci-bean."

She crawls out from behind the couch and scoots over to her father.

"Give me the coat." He turns it inside out, examines the seam, and rummages in the closet for needles and thread.

"I cannot get her to give up that ragged thing. It's embarrassing," Connie tells him.

"She likes it. Where's the harm?" He threads a large needle, labors at pushing it through the tough fabric.

"If my mother saw that she'd clean it within an inch of its life."

"Keep her away from it then. It means something to her, Connie. All artists have totems." He tugs the thread taut after each stitch, a line of them now, marching neatly along the seam.

"I wish you'd stop encouraging her, you know how difficult that choice can be."

"But it's paid off."

Connie looks down at her puzzle. "At a price."

When he finishes, Vincent goes to Anna's room, knocks on the door.

"Mama?" Anna says.

"It's Daddy, honey. I fixed your coat." She opens the door, looks at the garment in Vincent's hands. He turns it inside out so she can see the repair. Anna traces the scar with her finger, then takes the jacket and hugs it to her chest. She looks up at Vincent and smiles.

The Empire State Grocery truck pulls away from the curb just as Rita gets out of her car. Bill honks the horn as he passes her. Rita waves back before she turns down the narrow alley to the side door and runs into Janet.

"I'd stay and help but I have a family conference. Eleven-year-old boy, his parents, the oncologist." She shakes her head. "You don't want to know."

Rita doesn't offer Janet empty platitudes. *God works in mysterious ways* or *God only gives us crosses He knows we can bear.* Sanctimonious phrases that neither penetrate nor allay the hellish miasma of individual pain and sorrow. She hugs Janet instead, saying simply, "I'm sorry."

To Rita's surprise, Janet accepts her embrace, even leans against her for a second or two before sniffing once, tossing a 'thanks' over her shoulder, and marching off to work.

Rita's shoving a heavy carton of canned hams across the floor to the shelves when Matt shows up.

"I tried calling over the weekend, nobody answered."

"I stayed over near the hospital. My uncle is having a hard time."

"I'm sorry to hear that." He picks up the carton and moves it closer to the metal rack. "And Connie?"

Rita explains the sequence of events, while Matt takes off his coat, unpacks the hams, and carries three more cartons over to the metal shelves. He lifts a fourth, reads the label. "Rice?"

"Bottom shelf, left side." She pushes a carton of jarred peanut butter past him to the right side. They work in concert—bending, lifting, shelving. Talk about Rita's uncle, Matt's cows, the gleaning project. She cracks up when he tells her about Ceci and the cow-pie.

"I miss those kids. Especially Anna. She's so sensitive. I was going to take her skiing or someplace when Raymond went into the hospital, but now my weekends are tied up too—"

"Why don't you take Tuesdays off? You can leave the Monday order here, I'll come in early, shelve it and work with Mitzi—"

"No, I couldn't let—"

"For my benefit as much as yours. I miss this, Rita. It's what I had in mind when I went into social work."

"But what about your farm?"

"It's there morning, noon, and night, each and every day of the year." He sighs. "I like the work. But it's relentless. Walt and I have been talking about hiring someone, maybe in exchange for room and board and a small salary so we can take some days off. Vacations even."

"Some vacation."

He laughs. "I'm not counting this as one. Call this an avocation."

"You say vacation, I say vocation." Rita sings, suddenly lighthearted at the prospect. "If you're sure—"

"I'll start tomorrow."

The bottom shelves are full and they begin working in the middle.

"Here." He puts the case of Spam she just opened on the countertop. "It'll be easier this way."

They're done in less than half the time it would have taken Rita. Despite her loneliness, however, or maybe because of it, she refuses his invitation to lunch. "I think I'll go visit my uncle, maybe stay over tonight since you'll be here tomorrow," she says, soaping her hands under the faucet in the kitchen.

"There's no rule that says we can't spend time together is there?" He shrugs into his coat. "Because frankly, I'd like to be part of the equation when you're figuring out what you want."

Rita stops washing her hands, turns to face him.

"Do you ever mince words?"

"Guess not."

"There is no 'rule.' I'm finding my balance, Matt. I have to do that first. On my own. Let me call you."

"Anytime," he says as he walks out the door.

And she does call him. The following evening, after another discouraging day at the hospital. After changing her clothes, she scrambles an egg for supper. "He must be exhausted; it's such a struggle for him to breathe. They had to put him back on the ventilator last night before I left. He was off it for only an hour today."

"How's his state of mind?"

"Lucid, calm. He made it clear he's ready to leave. He gave me the key to his apartment, a sealed envelope with his final wishes, and the number for the funeral home."

"What about you? Are you ready?"

"I don't want him to suffer. But it's hard to know I'm the last one left from my entire clan." Her voice catches. "It helps that I believe in an afterlife."

"Heaven."

"If by that you mean pearly gates, harps and thrones—no. I imagine it to be more like a metaphysical state of awareness and awe. On the same order of magnitude as being born into a physical state from a spiritual one."

"Sounds heretical."

Rita smiles. "It has gotten me into a wee bit of trouble with my spiritual advisor." She stirs her hot chocolate and sits down at the kitchen table. "But there are Christian mystics, Catholic ones even, although they're in disfavor."

"You're just a trouble-maker, Rita Mooney."

"That's me," she agrees. "How did it go today at Loaves?"

"Fine. Ruthie showed up toward the end. Mitzi took care of her. Everyone asked for you. Hold on," he says.

She hears an animated exchange but can't make out the words. When she turns on the overhead light, she catches sight of her reflection in the kitchen window—her hair grown long but not down, its unusual thickness giving her a clownish mop; her misshapen sweater ripped at the armpit, her jeans sagging low on her thinning frame; her eyelids plump from crying.

"Sorry," he says. "Walt just came in. He spoke to Mom earlier. Said she met a sheep rancher from Maine. They plan on visiting each other when they get back from Down Under. She made a joke about 'animal magnetism.' Walt said he's never heard her so . . . 'giddy' is the word he used."

"That's wonderful, Matt."

"Yeah, she deserves some happiness after all she's been through. Speaking of which, how's Connie?"

"Okay, I guess. I'd have heard if she wasn't."

"When's she due? She looked about to burst."

"A week from today."

"Hey, a Tuesday! Now that you're off Tuesdays, you could go be with her."

Rita laughs. "Right. Things don't happen that way in real life."

"You know, sometimes they do."

"But statistically, Matt, what are the chances the baby will be born on the predicted day?"

"Slim to none, probably. But so are the odds of my mother meeting a sheep rancher from Maine in Australia. Or me falling for a nun."

# CHAPTER 22

Connie lies on her side in the hospital bed watching the silhouette of Vincent cradling Gabrielle. Vince is singing softly, "The First Time Ever I Saw Your Face." Connie thinks he's burning this memory into his brain and into Gabrielle's as well, a perpetual loop of adoration. Narcissus stares at his reflection as she escapes into the arms of Morpheus.

She dreams of fields of poppies: tall as lilies, red as blood. She is Lilliputian running through the stalks, trying to escape their spell but is overcome with lethargy. Wrapping her arms around a flower, she pulls its belled petals over her head and drops into oblivion.

The first time she nurses Gabrielle, Connie imagines that the baby struggles to make sense of the eviction from her mother's womb. She's the only child with the subtler palette of Connie's coloring: fair-haired, skin more sallow than ruddy. She nestles the baby close to the swollen sac of her breast, already leaking in anticipation, then nudges the nipple toward Gabrielle's mouth. It opens and closes on the tip of Connie's finger. Another nudge and Gabrielle has the nipple but doesn't suck. She massages the baby's cheek. Still nothing. She milks her breast into her daughter's mouth and Gabrielle suckles calmly, as if she knows that whatever she needs will come to her.

Connie sighs, knowing she's in for months of people talking to her while they stare goofily at the baby in her arms. Connie could be bald or blue and people wouldn't notice. It's different with Vince, though, and it's not her imagination. She first noticed it with Anna, then with Ceci, how women focus on the baby and then shift their gaze to Vince.

Women fuss over Vincent even when he isn't holding a baby. Though he's not tall and by no means classically handsome, not even good-looking, really, when he enters a room, she's seen women moisten their lips, lower their voices, and rearrange their hips. He has a banked heat, the same intensity that gives him stage presence, a phrase with which she's become all too familiar, a quality she knows she lacks.

"Reet? I've been trying to call you all day. We had a girl: six pounds, seven ounces. At one thirty-eight this morning."

"Gabrielle?" Rita's throat closes. It's all she can say.

"Just like you wanted." There's an awkward silence. "Please don't be mad at me. Can't I have you both in my life?"

"I'm not. You do," Rita says. "It's just that I miss you guys."

"We miss you too. Anna's painted dozens of pictures of you, your house, your car. How's your uncle?"

"He has good days and bad. He needs the vent often enough that they won't send him home. I've been spending weekends at the hospital. Tell Anna I haven't forgotten my promise. He's just so frail. How's it going with . . . you two?"

"Great. This job has made all the difference, Rita. Actually, I've been the temperamental one lately. Baby blues. How's Matt?"

"He's been volunteering on Tuesdays to give me a break."

"And?"

"We talk on the phone sometimes. I stopped off at Holy Name last week."

"Any thoughts?"

"Too many. Things are beginning to seem muddier."

"You'll come for the christening?"

"I promise."

"Write it down. The eighteenth. At my mother's. Bring your appetite. And Matt, if you want to."

When Rita arrives at the hospital early on Saturday morning, Damion follows her into the room where her uncle used to be. She wheels around; the nurse is right behind her.

"When?"

"About an hour ago," he says. "I tried to call you."

"Where is he?"

"In the—downstairs. Would you like to see him?"

She nods, and he tucks her hand in the crook of his arm, leading her down the corridor filled with people for whom time has not fractured, then to the elevator and down to the morgue.

"I'm sorry, Rita."

"I'm grateful you were the one taking care of him, Damion. So was he." She hugs him. "God bless you."

Damion speaks to the attendant, a slight, turbaned man, who escorts her into another, colder room.

Her uncle's face is serene, not so different in pallor, in fact, than it has been these past weeks. She lays her hands over his, prays the Our Father, and then kisses Raymond goodbye. She's glad he's given her precise instructions because her brain feels useless. Weeping steadily as she leaves the room, she hears the delicate-looking Indian man ask who is to pick up the body and then roots around in her knapsack for her wallet, handing him the business card from Duffy and Doyle Funeral Home.

She's still crying when she gets to her uncle's apartment and unlocks the front door. His apartment smells stale, as if he'd stopped living here long before he went into the hospital. It's exceedingly neat and orderly, like Raymond himself. She sits on the couch and waits until she stops sobbing before she opens the envelope. A sheet of lined yellow paper lists his last requests.

He'd cataloged with precision a rota of tasks: notify the landlady, the utilities, Social Security. Cancel his insurances. Whatever Rita finds useful or dear, she is to keep. The rest gets sold or goes to the Salvation Army. His passbook is in his sock drawer, along with her aunt's wedding ring. For his funeral: cremation. Then scatter his ashes over the sea. They're not to hang around indoors like some gloomy keepsake of death. Please pray St. Patrick's Breastplate for him. No music. And "not to be sad, dear girl, it's a party we'll be having, your dad and I, with our brides again, all shining and whole."

Rita opens the drawer, finds the worn gold circle, slips it on her ring finger, and then drives back to the hospital to pick up her uncle's personal effects. In the bottom of the plastic bag, weighing down one corner is his wedding band. She puts it on her finger next to its companion. At Duffy and Doyle's, she gives the funeral director, a plump cheerful man, her uncle's instructions: no casket, as soon as possible.

"Will you want a viewing first? For the family."

"I'm it," she says.

"Please accept my condolences." He opens a large appointment book on his desk. "We can schedule the facility Monday. At noon?"

She nods.

The days go by in a gray blur. She calls Connie, the convent, Janet, Mitzi, and Matt; accepts their condolences and declines their offers of companionship. She needs to get used to standing alone.

Monday couldn't be more beautiful. Outside the simple stone crematorium, the breeze flings the tree tips in a merry dance. Fat white clouds chase one another across the endless bright blue. As Raymond's body passes through the flames, Rita lifts her voice in prayer.

> *"Today I put on a terrible strength*
> *invoking the Trinity*
> *confessing the Three with faith in the One*
> *as I face my Maker."*

As she stands in the radiant light, the wind catches her words along with the smoke from his funeral pyre, tossing them skyward. By the time she gets to the fourth verse, she can't see through her tears but she can hear a distant plane, can feel the cool gold rings on her hand.

> *"I arise today*
> *Through the strength of heaven:*
> *Light of sun,*
> *Radiance of moon,*
> *Splendor of fire—"*

After, she wanders the grounds until she finds a caretaker. For some reason, she thought she'd be handed an urn with her uncle's ashes. She didn't realize they'd be too hot to touch, that what she would pick up in a few days would be surprisingly heavy, his remains wrapped in plastic, inside a small cardboard box.

Matt is waiting for Rita when she gets home from the food bank on Thursday. Connie has called every day, the nuns have sent Mass cards, and Janet and Mitzi have made donations to Loaves in her uncle's name but this is the first time she's spoken to Matt.

"You look like you could use a good meal," he says.

"I'm not hungry."

"When have I heard that before?" He follows her into the house carrying an A&P bag under each arm. "I'll cook; you eat what you can." He sets the bags down on the counter. "Go sit down. I'll call when it's ready."

By the time she's hung up her coat and washed her face, he's unpacked the groceries and is kneeling at the hearth, lighting some kindling under a charred log. She steps outside, gets a couple of split logs, and hands them to him then sits in the rocker. As soon as they catch, he goes into the kitchen, uncorks a bottle of wine, and brings her a glass.

Rita takes a deep swallow. "Did I tell you Connie had the baby? A girl."

"Uh-uh. When?"

She just looks at him.

"No kidding? On the appointed day?" He laughs all the way to the kitchen.

Rita leans back and closes her eyes. How is Matt always right? She finishes her wine and battles between hunger and exhaustion. Exhaustion wins and she drifts off to sleep until lured awake by the mouth-watering aromas of frying potatoes and broiling steak. Her stomach growls.

She brings her wine glass to the kitchen. "Is dinner ready?"

"As soon as you set the table." He smiles.

After she's set out cutlery, napkins, and salad bowls, he takes the plates from her, sets them in the center of the stovetop to warm, spears the fat porterhouse steak from the broiler, slices it in half, and loads their plates with golden fries.

"I hope this isn't one of yours." She waves a chunk of juicy beef on her fork.

"Nope. Just milk-cows."

"You always seem to make a liar out of me, Matt. This is delicious."

"You've had a rough go of it."

"Raymond wants his ashes scattered over the sea. I guess that rules out the lake."

He refills their wine glasses. "You know, I've been meaning to visit Nathan. He's still in the trenches at a clinic in Canarsie. I can drive you, stand by you or not—whatever you want."

"I don't know."

"You could visit Connie while I spend time with Nathan. We can kill two bir—" Matt grimaces.

Rita waves her hand. "I know what you mean. Actually, Gabrielle's christening is a week from Sunday. You've been invited. That makes three birds. I don't suppose Raymond minds waiting a few more days. May God rest his soul."

She lifts her glass to his memory swallowing the last of her wine with her tears.

# CHAPTER 23

The roar and thump of the surf, Rita imagines, sounds like the voice of God: powerful, glorious, never-ending. She's been sitting on this bench on the deserted Coney Island boardwalk ever since Matt dropped her off hours ago. He wanted to stand by her and then take her with him to visit his friend Nate, but she can't allow herself to accept the respite of his comfort, his care. There's nothing she can give him in return.

She clutches the box of ashes, wishing she could place her uncle in the same Brooklyn cemetery where her parents are buried, to have her family gathered together, even in death; however, she couldn't bring herself to betray his final wish, even though the Church forbids the scattering of ashes. Will the sin be his or hers? It doesn't matter. There's no turning back now.

The Cyclone's undulating humps and the Parachute's skeleton serve as her sentinels as she walks across the beach. Along with her heart, the dense weight of Raymond's remains seems heavier with each graceless step in the shifting sand. At the water's edge, the wind buffets her awkward attempts to commit his ashes to the sea, tossing them skyward, and sideways, and back at her, as if Raymond were just as reluctant to say goodbye as she.

When it's over, she leaves the container in the surf, then huddles under the boardwalk where, in summers past, she and Connie shielded each other with towels as they changed out of their wet bathing suits, or she lingered with Danny Farrell in the cooling dusk, her body vibrant and tingling, never dreaming of this day, unmindful of her own mortal fate.

Footsteps trounce and stop overhead. Matt is running toward the little box bobbing in the surf.

"Matt!" She walks out from under the boardwalk.

"There you are. You okay?"

She nods, then shrugs.

They walk in silence to the truck, where he opens the door for her. "Would you like some coffee? Or breakfast?"

"Connie's mother would have our heads," Rita says, smiling. "Wait till you see the spread." She combs her hair in the rearview mirror. "Besides, there's nothing in this world that I'd rather do right now than hold Gabrielle."

Rose sails into the room, the warming tray of lasagna held bare inches in front of her formidable bosom. She resembles the figurehead on the prow of a ship, chest jutting, chin held high, thick black silver-shot hair piled on top of her head, her broad bottom balancing the impression she could topple over.

The mahogany table has been pushed against the dining room wall under the enormous mural of the Last Supper Connie's brother Carlo painted when he was in high school. The table is covered with platters of pinkish cold cuts, a cutting board stacked with cubed cheeses surrounding a green pepper porcupine with frilled toothpick quills, piles of rolls, batons of bread.

"*Concetta! Veni ca.*"

The gravelly voice coils itself around Connie and jerks her over to where a tiny figure in a pink lace dress, a corsage pinned to its sagging bodice, perches on the armchair. Nonna Rosemarie, at 94 the eldest living Rinaldi, has beautiful white hair still thick enough for decorative combs to catch into a small bun at the nape of her neck. Connie bends down to kiss her grandmother, getting a whiskery kiss in return.

With a bent knuckle, Nonna taps Connie on the wrist. "Everything okey-dokey, dolly?"

"Fine, Nonna." Connie holds her grandmother's crooked fingers.

"You no look happy. Today you should look happy."

"I'm just tired, Nonna."

"No lie to me, *figlia mia.* Something no right."

Connie sees Rose open the door and take Rita by the shoulders. "My dear girl, what happened?" Rose says in tragic tones. "Connie tells me you've lost your vocation."

Rita scans the room and finds Connie who shrugs and rolls her eyes.

"It's okay Rose. I'm fine and my vocation is just on sabbatical."

"Is that something in the Jewish faith?"

"What? No. Sabbatical means a hia—a break. I'm just taking a break until I can work things out."

Rose's eyebrows wrestle with her hairline. "You can take a break from the convent? It's allowed? I never heard of such a thing. It must be new."

"Speaking of new, Gabrielle makes how many?"

"Fourteen." Rose's chest expands appreciably. "My fourteenth grandchild. What a beautiful baby, just like a little doll. She's got my Connie's features but her Papa's build. And his lungs! You could hear her at the back of the Met. Come, Vincent's holding her all day. She won't let him put her down."

"Wait, Rose, I want you to meet a friend of mine."

Rose looks up at the man who's been idling at Rita's elbow holding a misshapen lump of tissue paper trailing pink ribbons. Her eyebrows disappear.

Rita takes the present from Matt and leaves him to fend for himself.

Connie gives Rita a fierce hug. "I'm so glad you're here."

"Rose is freaking out about the convent."

"To say nothing of Matt." Connie waves to him. "I'm glad he went with you this morning; I would have if it were any other day—"

"I know. Here." Rita hands Connie the present.

Connie opens it and holds up a green canvas pouch. "Marsupial mom."

"Roo baby." Rita grins. "I can't wait to meet Gabrielle."

"There she is." Connie points to the other end of the living room.

Vincent's making the rounds with baby, the elaborate ivory christening gown draped over his forearm as if Gabrielle were the centerpiece in some fancy window display. The gown, made of satin and lace and silk ribbons, has been worn at every family christening since great-grandmother Rinaldi made it almost a hundred years ago.

"So." Rita doesn't take her eyes off the baby. "Has he been behaving himself?"

"Why wouldn't he? He loves his work, the money. He's been attentive, generous, helpful. He even does the grocery shopping since one of the clerks asked him for his autograph." Connie laughs.

Rita studies Connie's face. "And you?"

"Me?" Connie looks around the room. "I'm the envy of all I survey."

As Vincent approaches, he holds Gabrielle out like an offering to Rita, who takes the infant into her arms, brushes her lips against the baby's downy hair, as silky as the ribbons on her christening gown.

"She's exquisite." Gabrielle blindly takes hold of the thin silver chain around Rita's neck, its filigreed cross in her grasp.

"It's good to see you, Rita," Vince says, "in happy circumstances."

"Very happy. Aren't you a happy little girl?" Rita nuzzles Gabrielle. The baby stretches, squints, and then rubs her face with one fist like a kitten washing itself.

"Time for someone's nap." Connie holds out her arms for Gabrielle.

"Not yet! I just got here," Rita clasps the infant to her chest.

"You can have her back as soon as she wakes up. I promise."

Rita reluctantly hands the baby back to Connie.

"I'll be back as soon as she drifts off, and we'll catch up, Reet. Go rescue Matt."

Vincent follows Connie upstairs to the spare room Rose and Louis have furnished for their grandchildren's visits and sleepovers. There's a spindle crib, a set of bunk beds, and a rocking chair. After Connie nurses the baby and settles her in the crib, Vince pulls Connie onto the bottom bunk, brushing his cheek against a golden sheaf of her hair. "I like this new color, the way it complements your dark eyes."

He turns her face toward him, then watches it soften as he lightly caresses the contours of her breast, her hip.

"Not now, Vince."

"Shhhh," he says, pulling her against him, lifting up her skirt.

"Cut it out. We have guests—"

A shriek like an ice pick punctures the air.

Vince races toward the sound. In sickening slow motion, Connie makes her way downstairs where her relatives stand bunched up near the back door. They scatter to make way for Vincent who stumbles into the kitchen carrying Ceci, her hair slick with blood, her face smeared red. Connie hears Vincent yell for towels, for ice, before she crumples to the floor.


Something wet and cold lands on Connie's forehead. When she opens her eyes, Rita's face recedes.

"She's okay, Connie. She'll need a few stitches but she's okay."

Connie sits up slowly, removes the washcloth, and takes a sip of the water Rita hands her. "I fainted?"

"You always hated the sight of blood."

She holds the cool glass against her neck. "What happened?"

"The kids were roughhousing, Ceci fell and gashed her temple. It looks a lot worse than it is. Vince took her to the emergency room. Your father drove them."

Connie tries standing up but the room tilts. Rita steadies her, then sits her down on a chair. "Maybe you should lie down. We're going to hit the road. Call me tomorrow."

Connie nods weakly. "I will. Safe home." She watches Anna follow Rita into the backyard. Connie wobbles over to the couch, lies down, and waits for the dizziness to subside.

Suddenly Rose looms over her with a glass of wine, Brenda hovers close behind—the first wave in the undulating sea of family surging to her side.

They're on the Palisades Parkway, the Hudson River beside them, Rita notes when she blinks into the present. Her thoughts scroll through the day—the long ride, the dreary rain, the gruesome task on the desolate beach. Gabrielle's skin, Ceci's blood, Anna's tears. Rita stretches and yawns.

"She wakes!" Matt says, in mock horror.

"Hmmmm. Sorry. I dozed off."

"She speaks!" he crows.

Rita opens her window to inhale some fresh air.

"Feeling better?" He reaches over to caress the back of her neck.

His hand feels warm and solid, a magnet for the shards of sadness collecting in her chest. She shifts away from his touch. "I'm worried about Connie."

"Why? I never got to talk to Vince, but I saw him in action. He's great with those kids. Maybe things will work out for them."

"Maybe. Everyone has some redeeming qualities."

"Then it stands to reason, we all have a dark side, too."

Rita looks over at him, waits. A mile rolls by. Then two. "What is it you want to tell me, Matt?"

"Hold on." He pulls off the thruway at the next exit, turns down a side road, parks. "Let's walk a bit," he says getting out of the truck.

She joins him on the dusky street, allowing him to tuck her hand in the crook of his arm. They stroll past a neighborhood of neat little bungalows with bikes in the driveways and they end at an empty ball field.

"Cold?" Matt asks.

"A little."

He wraps her in his arms, leaning in to kiss her.

"Matt. Don't."

He throws his hands in the air. "Just how can you decide anything without knowing what's being offered? How can I talk to you about that without infringing on your integrity?" He lowers his voice. "Look, Rita. I'm not a saint, just a mere mortal who has come this close to insisting your body listen to mine, just knowing it will answer touch for touch the way I feel about you."

"Please try to understand," she says, taking both his hands in hers. "I think I know 'what's being offered.' I'm not choosing whether we could have a future, Matt, whether we would please each other. There are many ways to love, each with its own blessings and sacrifices. I just need to know which path is mine."

He releases her hands, tucks his in his pockets, and starts back to the truck. "You know, I've heard this bullshit before. From another headstrong woman on her way to spiritual enlightenment."

She hurries to keep up with him. "That's not what I'm looking for. I don't want to remove myself from worldly concerns. Just the opposite. I want to find out where in the world I belong."

"Fine." He opens the passenger side door for her. "You do that. But I can't do this anymore."

"Understood," she manages to say around a lump in her throat. She gets into the front seat, unassisted.

He climbs behind the wheel, pulls back onto the highway, the silence between them unbroken, mile after mile after mile.

# CHAPTER 24

Walking across the bridge to retrieve the mail, Rita notices the fading clumps of daffodils along the brook, the stands of shell pink tulips at the foot of the bridge. The trees are furred with pale green buds, the grass a sharper green than the day before. The forsythia branches have a chartreuse cast, weeping willows drip lime green wands. She steps carefully around the fronds and shoots poking up through the damp earth. As she bends over a mound of huge green and white striped leaves unfurling, she notices a slender. green stalk, like an antenna protruding from the center of the plant.

A man stands a respectful distance away. Coils of rubber hose hang from his shoulder.

"Good morning," Rita says, walking toward him.

"Ed." He extends his hand. "I live down the lane, met your friend with the kids—on the ice?"

"I'm Rita." She shakes his hand. His fingers are yellow with tobacco stains, scaly with calluses.

"Promised Laurel come spring, I'd replace the cracked hose, if you don't mind."

"Sure." She points to the plant. "You wouldn't happen to know what this is."

"Hosta. It'll get a lot bigger and that center stem will flower. The deer love it. But then they seem to love every damn thing that grows. Laurel used to stick pinwheels in the ground. Seemed to work for the most part."

"That sounds very . . . festive."

"Actually, it looks like hell." He almost smiles. "But set them out. Should be a box of them over the workbench in the basement." Ed hooks the hose up to a spigot Rita hadn't noticed, and walks back down the lane, leaving her stranded in paradise.

Lately, she's been battling the self-pity that creeps into bed with her, greets her in the morning, jumps out in unguarded moments. She finds herself cataloging her losses, beginning with her mother's illness and ending with Matt's retreat into the periphery of her life.

She took some comfort this morning looking at her missal. This Sunday falls into the white wedge of the liturgical calendar marking the beginning of eight weeks of Easter Time, leaving behind the melancholy purple of the Lenten season. Some days she's certain she'll rededicate her life to the Church. Others she feels a desire to bring forth from her own flesh the family she'd never had.

The only bright spot on the horizon is Anna's visit. Vincent has promised his daughter that if she catches up on her schoolwork, she'll be allowed to spend her first week of summer vacation at Rita's. Anna sends pictures she's painted, reports of her grades, while Rita writes Anna stories about E, or the ducks, or the deer.

She crosses the bridge and opens the metal flap on the mailbox. On top of the pile sits a manila envelope with Anna's signature drawing on the back.

This time it's a clay pot crowded with daffodils. Inside there's a family portrait depicting her parents sitting side by side, Gabrielle on Connie's lap, Ceci sitting next to her father, and Anna next to her mother. Rita trusts Anna's perception. It looks as if Connie and Vince have found their equilibrium. Now if only she can do the same.

The driver leans against the Empire State Grocery truck. "I'm really sorry, Rita."

"Come on, Bill, just give me another week, and I promise—"

"Not up to me. Credit department has you as a C.O.D. customer now. Nothing I can do."

"But I only missed one payment."

Bill consults his paperwork. "Two. Says here the last check bounced."

"And I told them to redeposit it last week. It should have cleared by now."

"Sorry, hon. Certified only. Rules are rules."

"Can you wait, then? While I get to the bank?"

"I'm not supposed to." Bill looks at his watch. "Tell you what. Make it worth my while, I'll make the rest of my deliveries, then double back on the way home."

Rita flushes. "Look. I don't know what you have in mind but I'll have a certified check for you. Period."

"Whoa. Lighten up." Bill climbs into the truck. "I'll be back around five." He starts the engine. "And Rita? All I had in mind was dinner."

Her face flares red and Bill pulls away before she recovers enough to apologize. What's wrong with her? He's not the most elegant guy but she should know better than to think . . . oh, God, there's Ruthie. She's dressed in a plaid flannel nightgown, a pink feather boa, and flip-flops. And Rita still needs to go home and get her passbook before she goes to the bank and . . . it will have to wait. First, she needs to take care of Ruthie.

The house is sleep-quiet; everyone's in bed. Vincent throws his gym bag on the floor, takes off his shoes. He washes up at the kitchen sink, decides he'll eat in here as well. But the dish she's left warming in the oven makes it easy to skip dinner. Meatloaf, string beans, and a shriveled baked potato. He pedals open the pop-up trash can and slides the meal into the garbage, although if Connie notices, she'll have a fit. She's developed a fierce social conscience since Rita's. Vince grins recalling yesterday's dinner at his in-laws—as if Easter Sunday hadn't been enough, they were summoned the following week for Nonna Rosemarie's ninety-fifth birthday—Connie holding forth about the needy and how sinful it is to waste food and resources because the face of hunger is *real*, how everyone should volunteer at a food bank if they want to know how fortunate they are, one disaster and pow! (Rose actually jumped) that could be you. He likes this new fire of hers, pain in the ass that it may be to him. He ties up the trash and takes it out to the alley, drops it into the aluminum can, softly replacing the lid.

He pours two fingers of brandy into a tumbler, tucks the paper under his arm and makes his way into the darkened living room, taking care to sweep his foot in small arcs to feel for discarded toys or the laundry basket or the baby walker. Backing into the wing chair, he turns on the pharmacy lamp and picks up The Washington Post.

## WHITE HOUSE STAFFERS RESIGN.
## NIXON COUNSEL FIRED.

President Nixon, after accepting the resignations of four of his closest aides, told the American people last night that he accepted full responsibility for the actions of his subordinates in the Watergate scandal.

"There can be no whitewash at the White House," Mr. Nixon declared in a special television address to the nation. He pledged to take steps to purge the American political system of the kind of abuses that emerged in the Watergate affair.

The President took his case to the country some ten hours after announcing that he had accepted the resignations of his chief White House advisers, H.R. Haldeman and John D. Ehrlichman, along with Attorney General Richard G. Kleindienst.

He also announced that he had fired his counsel, John W. Dean III, who was by the ironies of the political process a casualty of the very scandal the President had charged him to investigate.

The dramatic news of the dismantling of the White House command staff that served Mr. Nixon through his first four years in the presidency was the most devastating impact that the Watergate scandal has yet made on the administration.

*Something is rotten in Denmark,* Vince thinks. Fascinating how the walls keep tumbling down. Just ten years ago, the assassinations started with JFK, then MLK, and lastly RFK. Then LBJ (when did everything turn into initials?) and this endless 'conflict' that whacked people into postures and stances that started a civil war, in a way, on campuses, at work, and at dinner tables all over the country. He and Joseph had argued over the war, Joseph wanting his son to enlist after he was no longer eligible for the draft. Although the old man has never said so, Vincent thinks his father feels differently now, looking back at the carnage, the revelations of misinformation, and doomed battle plans.

He sips the brandy, dropping the newspaper on the floor. Vincent never wanted a life like his father's or a wife like his mother but certainly, a woman who would make a home for him, provide the shelter and succor he never experienced as a boy or man.

But women now, oh man, ballbusters, some of them, but fierce and sure and alluring in their new claimed power. That buyer from Macy's made it plain she wanted him, married or not. And when he took his taxes down to the accountant's, a new one, Jackie, he thinks, in that power suit with that gorgeous mouth and those soft brown eyes, checked off details and came up with a strategy that gets him a big fat refund this year. He fantasizes about these capable, competent, sophisticated women. Women who could share the load. Half the work, twice the fun. But with kids . . . well, some women choose to work anyway, taking advantage of daycare and grandmas. But no, Vincent knows that's not for him, for them. His wife should be home with their children. Later, there'll be time for Connie to take on whatever she wants.

A slip of paper falls out of the newspaper.

Your father called (twice)
Marty - "shrink the yardage on the green suit"
Don't forget to pick up circus tks for Sat.

He sighs. Isn't it enough a man has two jobs, three kids, one wife? Does he have to account to them all for his time and money? And report to his old man, too? He finishes his drink, turns off the light, closes his eyes, and unreels a movie in which Connie checks her watch, puts down her briefcase, strips off her suit, holds him down, and makes slow, sexy love to him before heading downtown for a day in the office.

"Don't let them eat a lot of junk, Vince." Connie buttons Ceci's sweater. "Make sure you watch you-know-who with the c-l-o-w-n-s. Last year she f-r-e-a-k-e-d."

"What's the point of going to a circus if they can't have treats and she doesn't like cl—them?" He checks his pockets for the tickets. Connie hands them to him, along with a clean handkerchief.

"She may have outgrown it and they can have some junk, just not enough to make them sick. Right, Anna-banana? She knows. Help daddy with Ceci, sweetie. And have fun."

Connie's been looking forward to using this time to go through some of the cartons in the basement. She puts Gabrielle in the sling pouch, then walks down the wooden steps. She likes the dank of the basement, always has. She often used the cellar as a hideout when she was a kid; it felt like a secret cave, cool and musty, full of artifacts. When she learned about root cellars, she understood why she felt so free; she could unfurl in private. That's the drawback with large families, no privacy. Even now, there's the constant pull of the children, to say nothing of Vincent's needs. Sometimes she feels like a hapless moon, only reflecting the fiery suns around her.

Her post-partum funk seems unusually lengthy—more than two months now—and treacherous this time, a bleakness that yaws into great black holes. Perhaps due, in part, to Vince's desire for a son. She can neither imagine herself as a mother of four, nor as the sort of woman who pops birth control pills behind her husband's back, committing a mortal sin in the process.

There are not many boxes labeled CONNIE'S STUFF—a dozen or so. Less than a carton a year considering they date back to when she graduated from eighth grade. Rose has all of Connie's baby and girlhood memorabilia, drawings, certificates, Girl Scout uniforms, photo albums, dolls, Teddy bears. Her mother's attic looks like a back room in the Smithsonian, hand-lettered signs for all six children; Concetta Pescatore, Louis Pescatore, Jr., and so on for each of them, which Connie has come to regard as a shrine to Rose's maternal devotion and sacrifice.

A faint snore alerts her Gabrielle's asleep, so she slips off the pouch and places the baby on top of the folded towels in the laundry basket. Connie hasn't looked in these boxes for years. What will she find under the silt? She gets a matte knife from the top drawer of the gray metal utility cabinet. It feels cool and dangerous; the razor's edge a thumb-flick away. She sneaks up on a carton and tears open its cardboard throat.

An hour later, the floor is littered with worn-out skates, roller- and ice-, color-coordinated outfits for each (short, twirly skirts, headbands to match); St. Agnes school uniforms; botched garments from sewing class, a half-started sweater, knitting needles stuck in the balled yarn; six albums for coin-collecting, five of them empty; old test papers, many of them telling her she wasn't working to her capacity; a brand-new calligraphy set.

She rips open the remaining carton and scrabbles through the contents, frantic for the cherished objects she's certain must be in here somewhere. But no. She saved all the wrong things.

Where are her college textbooks with the margins filled in with who she used to be before marriage and mothering, her favorite cowl-neck sweater, a book of poems she'd loved? All gone to church basements, younger cousins, the trash. Even the dainty opal ring Frank gave her, she passed on to Brenda's oldest daughter Camille, an October baby. No locks of her children's hair or their baby teeth. She was sure she'd put them in a safe place, but where? But maybe she hadn't, maybe it was Rose who wrapped the wispy filaments in waxed paper, the enamel kernels in cotton batting.

In a passionate—and unrequested—gesture to Vincent, she'd erased all evidence of the boys that came before. Prom pictures, the powdery remains of corsages, ticket stubs, love letters pressed into scrapbooks she never got around to making.

Photographs lay in a mound redolent of dust and developer. Some are stuck together as if the respective subjects had been kissing in the dark carton. She pries two photos apart. Rita and Connie sit on top of an open convertible, their saddle-shoed feet resting on the back seat, part of Rita's skirt is stuck to a much older snapshot of a group of children dressed up for Halloween. Whose car? What year? Which ghost was she? Or was she the witch that year? She turns the photos over. No clue. Her mother's photos had legends on the back: *Aunt Gemma & Uncle Dominic with Grandpa & Grandma Rinaldi at cousin Donna's wedding 1958.*

Connie kneels and pushes her palms down under the pile of photos, closing her eyes, trying to conjure up the past. She feels as if she's lost pieces of herself: a fingertip, a spongy wedge of liver, a cluster of brain cells. Whatever she has left of who she was lives in the warm, salty stream of her tears.

# CHAPTER 25

Connie wanted to spend the Memorial Day weekend at Rita's, but Vince couldn't wait for this party at Richard and Claire's new place, a townhouse on the Upper East Side. He circles the neighborhood five times then cuts off a cab to nab a parking spot.

"Vince!"

"What? Did you want to drive around all night?"

It's so hot and humid she feels limp by the time they walk the three blocks to the front door.

Vincent whistles at their new digs. "Far cry." After punching the doorbell, he steps into the foyer.

Richard, looking flushed and damp, comes down the stairs, pauses on the landing.

"I'd like to thank my beloved wife, Claire, for shielding me from the corridors of power and influence so I could work on my craft. Darling?" he calls upstairs.

"Just a minute!" Claire yells back.

Since her promotion to VP of marketing for a national packaging company, she'd started pulling down the kind of money they all used to sneer at. Connie sometimes thinks that Vincent would prefer her to be more like Claire. Not go to work but have a sphere of influence somewhere, outside the house and kids.

"You guys are unfashionably early," Richard says.

"It's the first time we've been out on the town since the baby," Connie apologizes. "As soon as the sitter came, we left. Didn't think you'd—"

"Of course not!" Claire runs down the stairs, gives her husband a playful boink on the head. "When he's off-book Richard just blurts out whatever's in there. C'mere handsome." She sidles over to Vince and gives him a big smack on the lips. Claire's done up in black: a sheer silk blouse, mini-skirt, and platform heels.

Vince does an impression of Groucho Marx ogling a pretty girl. "What kind of business didja say she's in, Rich? Looks like monkey business to me."

"Hey, this makes up for the rack of gray flannel suits in her closet," Richard says patting his wife's barely covered bottom.

Claire looks anything but executive now. Connie feels suddenly dowdy.

"Connie! You look fabulous," Claire says, as if reading her thoughts. "C'mon let me get you something to drink."

She tucks Connie's arm under hers and leads her into a high-ceilinged room shadowy with candlelight. The narrow end of a dining table butts up against one wall, leaving enough room behind its length for the bartender who's just setting up.

"You remember Colin. He understudied Vincent in *Godspell*," Claire says, stopping to flirt with the pale angular man with long wavy hair and unfocused gaze. Claire kisses him tenderly, then runs her fingers through his locks. "You remember Connie, Vince's wife?" He nods, uncertain. "Colin's bartending tonight."

"I can do a killer martini, if you want," he offers.

"No thanks," Connie says, "maybe just a little wine."

He points to the antique sideboard across the room where bottles of wine stand on silver servers, next to rows of overturned glasses on crisp white linens. When a buzzer goes off, Claire excuses herself, waving her hand over the sideboard, saying, "Help yourself. The hot stuff will be ready in a little bit."

Along with the wine and the hors d'oeuvres, Thai sticks rest in a shallow silver dish next to a teepee of twisted joints in a crystal goblet. Not for her, not tonight. No escape for nursing moms. She pours a couple of inches of Valpolicella into a glass and makes up a small plate of cheese and crackers. She scans the living room for an out-of-the-way perch and settles for a club chair near a window. The rings are short and perfunctory now, announcing new arrivals like a ship's bell. Chick Sabatino is greeted with cheers and he goes straight to the piano while Richard fetches a tray with a bottle of bourbon, a carafe of water, and a squat heavy glass. Once the singing starts Connie knows she can relax; they'll be camping and vamping for each other all night. The enormous windows frame the reflections of the guests who look exotic or beautiful or both. People wander to the bar to pick up their drinks, then crowd around Vincent to congratulate him and hear gossip from the set. Claire latches onto Vincent as if he's a particularly chic accessory. They all manage to touch him, as if his good luck may rub off on them.

Claire quotes his lines verbatim, to Vincent's great delight. Pleading a lack of time, Connie rarely watches the show, even though she knows it hurts Vince's feelings. Unlike his other roles, she finds the one of the venomous psychiatrist too disturbing, as if within her husband's familiar form dwells an incubus. A man she doesn't recognize taps Vincent on the shoulder, then hands him a joint. It's comical to watch, the short deep tokes, the pursed lips, the held breath exploding in a long stream. If it hadn't been for Vincent, she would never have smoked grass. She never would have experienced that wavy feeling of space, not bending but pulling close then moving out, an undulation full of epiphanies and hilarity, freeing but scary too. What if she never came back? What if she just kept on drifting and floated off the planet into some netherworld and couldn't return?

After the fact, she wishes she had gone to Woodstock as Vincent had wanted, but she worried about the parking, the weather, and the bathrooms. And she wishes she had tried LSD, just once, in college, to see what all the fuss was about. But what if she'd had a bad trip or brain damage? She'd waited to have sex until she met Vincent, when it seemed that everyone else at NYU was sleeping with everyone else, sex as sport or a game of musical chairs. Although, who knows, it may not have been that great with anyone else. Most likely sex with Frank would have been as predictable as their Sunday drives; Frank who used to keep an umbrella in the backseat, rolled coins in the glove compartment, and road maps tucked into the visor.

With Vincent, she'd wound up on dance floors with no band playing or backstage at the Village Vanguard amid the cables and crew, or in the kitchen drinking coffee with the chef in some restaurant in Little Italy.

These theater people are no different from Ceci, entertaining and exhausting, following instinct and whim. Part of her longs to let loose, get crazy, forget for a night she's a mother of three with a sturdy brick house in a working-class neighborhood. Some other part of her, however, keeps pulling her side of the fulcrum down, so she and Vince won't fly up and out of that neighborhood into parts unknown.

Richard claps his hands. "Come on you grunts, help me clear the decks." He grabs one end of the sofa and Vince picks up the other. The rest push furniture out of the way to make way for dancing. Connie's forced to walk the perimeter to find a new perch.

She sits on the living room steps just below the landing, watching the party build. Chick quits playing piano and the singers disperse. Someone puts on Sarah Vaughn and the guests become languid, so used are they to interpreting whatever score is playing. A couple of the chorus boys head for the shadows of the staircase. A leotard-clad woman renders a sensuous interpretative dance on the parquet of the foyer. Colin adds his flutelike tenor to Sarah's ballad as he pours drinks at the bar. Claire wraps her arms about Vincent's shoulders, her bra-less breasts squashed against his chest, his left wrist resting low in the hollow of her back, her long legs spilling down from the brief twitch of black fabric riding her hips. They're both stoned, swaying with their eyes closed.

Connie hates when it gets like this, a party she can't be a party to. Richard sits down next to her, gently strokes her sternum with his knuckles.

"Tit for tat?"

"Very funny."

He withdraws his hand from between her breasts, clasping her knees instead.

"Getting jealous?"

"A little." But it's more like envy of Vincent's ability to cut loose, to throw off conventions while she's moored to propriety.

"Don't be . . . it's their shtick." He strokes her hair.

She swallows the rest of her wine, hands Richard her empty glass, then pulls his face to hers and kisses him. His lips are thin and slippery; not the twin fullness of Vince's against hers, blotting out all but their silent language of need and desire. When Richard's pointy cool tongue plumbs the seam along her teeth, she stands abruptly, climbing over the men necking on the landing, and heads for the bathroom.

She looks good—sleek and tawny—reflected in the candlelight, but the overhead light cancels the special effects, revealing her plump cheeks under the contours created by make-up, the pallor beneath the lipstick, and rouge. She squeezes the bubble of soft flesh bunched under the long black satin vest Vincent had made for her, after she'd tried on and rejected every dressy outfit in her closet in anticipation of tonight's party. "Goes with anything," he said. "I'll take it in when you drop the weight." When he had said, not if.

"What if I can't, this time?" she asks the older woman in the mirror. "What then?"

The party's shifted tempo as if she'd been gone for intermission and they'd changed not the act but the show. Now, straight-backed chairs line the living room and Vincent marches toward the steps welcoming her to "Cabaret." Claire's ensconced in the Sally Bowles part, probably because of her sexy legs and spiky black hair. Claire is high enough to make it work. Vincent has slicked down his hair, his face contorted into a melodramatic leer. When Connie reaches the bottom step, he leans backward from his knees and extends his arm to her, waggling his fingers suggestively.

She never knows what to do when he tries to include her in their spectacles. The few times she has joined in, she was drunk, but sober, it makes her cringe. She latches onto Vincent's arm and steers him to a loveseat where she deposits herself. She feels weary, wants to go home to snuggle in front of the TV, eat ice cream, and watch Carson. But she knows he's just getting started so she circles back upstairs, finds a bed without a pile of coats, lies down—grateful for the luxury of being alone—and falls fast asleep.

"You're such a little bitch. Do you think I'll put up with anything? That your goddamn money means that much?"

The shouting wakes Connie. She opens her eyes but doesn't move. Her heart pounds hard, as if she's the one found out.

"And you. Get the fuck out of my house."

Connie holds her breath waiting to hear the next voice.

"Richard, this is dumb. We didn't do anything. It was the grass, man, you know we'd never—"

"I don't give a shit, Vince." Richard's voice breaks. "She's my wife, goddamn it. Get out of my sight before I—"

"Okay, okay, okay . . . but I'll call you tomorrow or today . . . later. Because I swear on my children, man, we didn't get very far—"

"Vince. I'm warning you. Don't . . . say . . . another . . . word."

Connie's stomach lurches and her face feels hot. She hears Vincent go into the bathroom and pee a long time, then the faucet. She swipes her tears with Claire's Porthault pillowcase, leaving a slurry of mascara and snot. Footsteps cross the hall, a door slams, then another. Claire's crying, Richard's shouting. Muffled sounds come from Richard and Claire's bedroom, the bedsprings sigh and creak. Vincent peeks through the few inches her door has been left open.

She stares through him.

"Were you sleeping, beauty?"

*For way too long.*

She walks to the car in silence, doesn't even look at Vincent. Even though it's nearly three in the morning, the night air sticks to her skin, clings to her hair. "I'll drive." She holds out her hand for the keys. He gives her a bleary-eyed look, takes a minute or two to find the keys, then hands them to her, making a wobbly bow.

The ride home is cathedral quiet. Just once, he says, "Con . . . " but she shushes him.

Downtown a few couples stroll languorously in the heat, arms draped around each other faces inches apart. In midtown, groups of teenagers roam, shaking off the school year, goofing around, getting high. She drives past Washington Square, crowded with free spirits, revelers reluctant to give up the night. On the bridge crossing the East River, the temperature drops, then rises again on the off-ramp, on the avenues and streets that lead to their neighborhood. Occasional knots of people gather on stoops drinking beer, too restless for summer to sleep.

She leaves Vince to wake the babysitter, pay her fee, and walk her home. Upstairs she strips and showers. Despite the heat, there's something cold and hard growing inside her, colonizing her belly, working its way through her system. By the time he gets back, she's on the living room sofa in the dark, beneath a cool cotton sheet.

"Connie—"

"Not now," she tells him, in a tone of voice she didn't know she had.

Up before the children, she starts the coffee, and takes a can of frozen concentrated orange juice from the freezer, plopping the glistening orange mush into a green plastic pitcher, which she fills with cold water. Connie stirs the glop of concentrate with a wooden spoon until it becomes a tiny, icy clot. She balls up the wrinkled sheet from the sofa and throws in the washer. The dark house feels narrow, as if she is being squeezed into a sharp-edged block. She opens all the curtains to let in the light despite the continued heat which according to the forecast will build through the weekend, kicking off an early heatwave that will melt the tar in the streets, burn the top layer of skin, and cause Con Edison to overload and blackout.

Carrying a cup of coffee into the tiny backyard, she sips it while gazing at the bare patches in the grass, the weeds grown long and thick in the borders, the jumble of toys. Her plant stands and trellises empty this year, the baby claiming the last of her energy. She sits on the bottom step, her feet bare on the cool ground, hoping for a squirrel or a songbird. When something rustles the dense leaves in the mulberry tree, she looks up. Staring down at her is the shiny black shape of a grackle, a bird as ugly as its name.

The girls wake as they always do: Anna half-dreaming, wading into the day; Ceci chirping, bounding down the stairs. Mercifully, Gabrielle is still asleep. Connie doesn't expect to see Vincent for hours yet, judging from his condition last night, the bass notes seeping from their bedroom this morning. The girls drink juice while she fixes them breakfast. On Sundays, Vince usually goes to the bakery, picks up the papers. Customarily, Connie takes the girls to a late Mass.

She half-listens to the children's voices and half-listens to the sounds of the night before, waking up in a panic in the strange spare bedroom, hearing Richard shout, Claire whimper, Vincent plead. Each one held hostage by their vehemence, desperation, lust. She can't decide what revolts her, their naked need, or their betrayal.

"I said if I can wear my Easter outfit to church." Ceci pulls on Connie's arm.

"Hmmm? Yes. Sure, honey," Connie answers, not sure what Ceci's asked for, not caring either.

Connie feeds Gabrielle and puts her in the bassinet near Vincent's sleeping form, then puts on a long, flowered skirt and a peasant blouse. She's getting the stroller from the hallway when Ceci comes downstairs wearing her Easter dress, a pale pink coat, with matching hat and gloves.

"Oh, honey, it's much too warm for all that."

"You said I could. I asked you and you said yes."

"But Ceci . . . Fine. Wear whatever you want."

Anna has draped her mother's black lace mantilla over her head and hung her rosary beads from the sash on her dress. "Guess who I am."

Connie stares at her blankly, her thoughts a million miles away.

"Aunt Sister!" shrieks Ceci and collapses laughing.

They sit in the back of the church, which feels like a cool cavern, the priest's words elongated as they career off the stone pillars and vaulted nave. Connie tries to see the face of the Blessed Mother enshrined on the side altar, but too many people intersect her line of vision. She waits until the Mass is ended, after she's been told to 'go in peace' before she kneels in front of the tier of blue votives at the statue's feet. As Our Lady of Sorrows, Mary is dressed in black, a sword run through her heart, holding the three nails used to crucify Jesus, her face ravaged by grief. How different, Connie thinks, from the sweet countenance of Our Lady of Grace, or Our Lady of Guadeloupe in her vibrant cape, or Our Lady of Good Counsel's sympathetic gaze, so serene, radiant, comforting, wise. Our Lady of Sorrows depicts the pain of motherhood, the only Mary with tears on her face.

If not for the children she could be free of Vince forever. Instead, no matter where she goes or what she does, she'll always be the mother of his children, bound to him by their beating hearts.

They stop for newspapers on the way home, for bakery rolls. She lets the girls each pick out a treat.

"What about Daddy?" Ceci says. "He likes those things." She points to a cinnamon bun, a thickly iced spiral of sweet dough studded with raisins. Connie buys one then carries it out into the noonday heat.

At home, the girls change their clothes and eat their doughnuts before going outside to play. After making a fresh pot of coffee, she retrieves Gabrielle from the bedroom where Vincent still lies sprawled out on the bed, changes the baby, and brings her downstairs. In the kitchen, Connie gnaws at the cinnamon bun as if its sticky sweetness could dissolve the bile rising in her throat.

They're all in the yard when Vincent finally straggles out with a cup of coffee, squinting, red-eyed, unshaven. He wears faded Levis and the undershirt he'd slept in.

He pulls up a folding chair next to Connie's.

"Thanks for going to the bakery, honey."

She goes inside and empties the coffeepot, then washes the breakfast dishes. She's sponging off crumbs from the table when he comes in and puts his arms around her, kissing her neck. She doesn't move or say a word. When he releases her, she picks up where she left off, sweeping the grit into her palm and brushing it into the trashcan.

"You're not still mad."

She rubs her palms together over the sink to get rid of the last clingy bits then washes them thoroughly under the tap.

"Connie, hand to God, nothing happened. I got a little stoned, had a few too many, but we didn't do anything more than make out, I swear on our— Hey!" He taps her on the shoulder. "I'm talking to you—"

She whirls around. "I'm supposed to be grateful?"

"Am I? For the scraps of affection, that once in a while you tolerate my making love to you. For—"

"So now it's my fault?"

"What am I supposed to do? Grovel and beg? You came home but you haven't forgiven me. You act like all I do is play and you're stuck here with the kids all day. Well, what do you want Connie? Tell me, so I know what we're all keeping you from."

After drying her hands, she flings the towel on the floor and stomps out of the room. He follows her up the stairs and grabs the door before she can slam it in his face.

"Really. I want to know," he says, gripping her arms, forcing her to face him.

She closes her eyes and turns her head away. She can't tell him; she doesn't know want she wants beyond an end to being subject to his passions, to his needs, and the chance to kindle the spark of desire to find her own.

He throws her down on the bed and crouches over her. Squeezing her jaw with one hand, he pushes her cheeks together to open her lips. "Say something, goddamn it!"

She presses her lips together, staring through him.

"Like blood from a stone!" He releases her. Jumping up, he kicks at the mattress, sweeps the bedside lamp onto the floor, and jerks the phone before flinging it across the room. He punches a hole in the flimsy closet door, snatches his wallet and keys from the bureau, and crashes down the stairs.

She waits until she hears the car door slam, the engine rev, and the tires squeal before she takes a breath.

Connie knows Vincent would never miss his morning call on the set. By 7:00 a.m. she's packed the baby's carryall, stuffed a couple of changes for each of them into a duffel bag, and called a cab. He'd cashed his check Thursday; she takes all the bills from his dresser drawer. Connie arranges Gabrielle in the sling pouch so she can see her daughter's face.

"Here, Anna, take this." She hands her the carryall. "Ceci, get the door."

The moment they reach the sidewalk, the cab pulls up. Safe in the shabby back seat, surrounded by her children, Connie tells the driver, "Port Authority. No rush."

This time it's different. She's not running away but to something: Rita's capable arms, the yellow house with the wooden bridge, the soothing lilt of the stream, and Laurel's garden.

# CHAPTER 26

Rita isn't at all surprised at the turn of events, just at how little time it took for Vincent's resolve to collapse. Though Connie and the girls are a welcome relief to Rita's solitude, her funds are diminishing faster than she dreamed possible, between her expanding household and supplementing donations to Loaves, which somehow seem to fall short every month. Still, there's no way she can turn her back on the children.

Anna and Ceci are fascinated by the transformation of their winter playground. Rita becomes the carefree girl she never was, exploring the grounds with them, lying in dense thickets of cool green caves, the leaf canopies carving the sky into blue squiggles, the grass like lush carpets speckled with tiny violets, wildflower wisps.

Outdoors—reading a book under the apple tree, lunching at the picnic table, or walking the stream with Gabrielle like a papoose in the pouch slung across her back—is the only place Connie seems at peace.

Since the children are with their grandparents for a few days (Rose had handed Connie a breast pump and demanded to spend time with Gabrielle), Rita attempts to coax Connie out of the doldrums with a reprise of tacky prom night. One evening she springs it on Connie.

"No way."

"Come on, Con. We always had fun." Rita circles the couch, dangles the hideous dresses.

"The last time was ten years and three kids ago. Besides, it was never just the two of us. We'll look ridiculous."

"You worry too much about what other people think."

"It's easy for you to—"

Connie's words are absorbed in a blast of sound when Rita cranks up the tape deck. Rita mimes a mad duet to "I Get by With a Little Help from My Friends" swinging the lurid gowns by their hangers, bobbing them up and down, asking and answering the 'what would you dos?'

Connie laughs. "Okay. But I'm not wearing juice can rollers in my hair."

"Up to you. I'm going all out."

Connie gives her a baleful look.

"Who knows us here, anyway? I rather like being thought of as eccentric." Rita drapes the hot pink chiffon gown over the back of the rocker. "Remember the rules?"

Connie recites them in the cadence of a recruit answering a sergeant. "Absolutely no make-up. Juice cans and/or rubber bands must be worn in your hair. Athletic shoes are the only acceptable footwear. Least attractive wins."

"Now all we need is a judge."

"Rita!"

"Kidding. We'll do it on the honor system."

"What's the prize?"

"Loser cleans the bathroom for a month."

It is a job they each hate; everything else gets divvied up easily, but neither wants to swab the bowl, scour the tub, scrape the mold, or mop the tiles in the tiny bathroom.

"Get going, missy." Rita throws the putrid lime green and lavender number over her shoulder and heads up the stairs. "You have a half-hour to make yourself ridiculous."

Connie's tempted to try and win the bet but once she's alone, she pinches her cheeks and applies cherry Chapstick. The dress is beyond redemption, though. She'd worn the most exquisite gowns to her proms. She remembers that unsteady feeling of gliding into dimly lit rooms in shoes so new the soles offered no resistance; the dreamy slide into the tuxedoed arms of some boy made magical by the blue pulse of the saxophone, the scent of carnations and roses, flowers that still linger in her memory as a prelude to warm wet tongues and hot breaths, feeling aroused but blind to the particulars.

She decides on pigtails as a hairstyle that will satisfy Rita but leave her looking halfway decent.

"No cheating," Rita calls from down the hall.

It's a weeknight so the restaurant is only half-full. Connie shuffles in behind Rita, then sits with her back to the other diners. A fair-haired woman with a slight limp brings them water and menus.

"I'm Trudy—the oldest dish in the place," says the waitress as if she were reciting the daily special for the hundredth time today, then does.

"I'll have the Cornish hen," says Rita, which Connie seconds. "And a bottle of Beaujolais."

"We'll never finish a whole bottle."

"I know but—thanks, Trudy." Rita waits for the waitress to leave. "But the house wine is always awful."

It's difficult for Connie to reconcile Rita the sensualist with Rita the nun. Rita's clothes may be threadbare but they're all-natural fibers, cottons and flannels, and linens. She relishes warm peaches, just-baked bread, snapped off the vine tomatoes. Rita can work for hours lifting rocks, raking leaves, then stride around the lake for fun. Connie's seen her pitched flat on a blanket, wriggling down into the warm wool, arcing her face toward the sun. It's Rita who soaks in the scented tub water until it cools, who anoints herself with fruited lotions and perfumed talc. There's a lot more sacrifice in married life. Even in the convent, Rita was doing what she loved, had some time to herself, even without the bubble baths.

Rita waves her hand in front of Connie's face. "Where are you?"

Connie looks up to see their wine has been served. She lifts her glass. "To the girls we were."

"To the women we are," says Rita.

The Cornish hens sit on a fan of asparagus spears adorned with glistening medallions of pickled beets, an emerald pea in the center of each ruby disk.

"Peacocks! My compliments to the chef," says Rita.

"He said to tell you 'to match your outfits,'" says Trudy.

Connie blushes; Rita hoots.

"I'd like to meet this paragon of bad taste."

"That's him." Trudy nods toward the kitchen before refilling their wine glasses.

A large man peers through the glass porthole in the swinging door. Connie swivels around and catches a flash of white teeth in a forest of beard. Rita raises her glass and bobs her head in his direction.

"Rita!"

"What? The man has a sense of humor and a wicked way with vegetables. He sounds like a perfect prospect for the food bank."

The stares from the other patrons are curious but not hostile, although Connie can hear one fiercely whispered conversation among three men a few tables away. When the men get up to leave, Connie spies a familiar reflection in the plate glass, inclines her head toward Rita, and speaks in a low urgent tone.

"That's the man I told you about. Don't look! The one at the lake who helped Ceci . . ."

"Which one?" Rita asks.

"Long hair, plaid shirt, mid-forties."

"Oh, I've met Ed. He lives down the lane and stops by once in a while. Not to chat, though; more like to supervise. Rugged good looks. Not that you noticed."

Connie flushes and reaches for her purse. "I've got to go."

"Lighten up, Con—"

"To the ladies room, you jerk."

This strikes them both as hilarious and they tumble back to being teenagers, their shared history fueling their rounds of laughter until they're limp.

After dinner, Trudy serves them large snifters of brandy, which glow amber in the light of the hurricane lamp.

"Compliments of the chef," a voice rumbles behind Connie. The burly man bows slightly from the waist. "May I?" He pulls out a chair. When they nod, he sits. "Augustus."

"I'm Rita. She's Connie."

"Lovely Rita, meter-maid." He turns to Connie. Frowns. "Sorry. I can't think of one for you."

"We loved the peacocks!" says Rita. "No offense but I was surprised to see that sort of presentation in such a . . . casual place."

"Oh, I don't do that for everyone. I thought I recognized some kindred spirits," he extends his upturned palms to their respective midriffs.

"We don't always dress like this," says Connie.

"No offense, but I should hope not." He smiles.

Augustus signals Trudy to bring the bottle of brandy and a third snifter and they sit and sip and talk, slipping into the easy intimacy of expatriates stumbling upon one another in a foreign land.

Rita explains their appearance and the wager. Suddenly, she snaps her fingers. "Connie, how about letting Augustus judge?"

He turns to Connie. "I'd be honored."

Connie examines her reflection in the window. At least her hair looks somewhat normal and her dress is only one color. Rita's rubber-banded her thick curly hair into dozens of upright tufts. Her two-tone dress is even flouncier than Connie's.

"Okay."

Augustus holds out a beefy hand. "Please stand so I can appreciate the full effect."

Connie looks around the dining room. Except for a middle-aged couple exchanging sour looks and scant words, all the other patrons have left. She takes a swallow of brandy and stands up. Augustus motions her to twirl around. As she does, she catches a glimpse of Trudy who's stopped clearing a table to watch.

"Lovely." He claps. "I particularly like the white tennis shoes with the pink laces."

Connie curtseys and sits down.

He nods to Rita. "Now the meter maid."

Her face flushed with wine, Rita's eyes glitter with barely contained high spirits. She takes the ferns from the vase on the table, leaves the single rose, and fastens one on each side of her head like exotic feathers. Drawing herself up to her full height, she clomps away from the table. Her dress stops above her ankles and rests on the tops of her brown hiking boots. When she spins around the ruffles flutter and float, their colors blending into a rare shade of green, like seafoam at twilight.

Connie looks over at Augustus to see his huge head cocked to one side, his expression that of a man struck dumb by this bizarre apparition, a secret dream made flesh. *Great. A month of scummy tiles and stubborn porcelain stains.*

He raises his glass. "A toast to the winner, the lovely Rita, meter maid."

"Why, I shore thank you, Mister Gus," Rita says in a terrible Southern accent.

"I should tell you . . . it's Augustus. Not Gus. Never Augie. "

"Fair enough. And I should tell you that it's Rita, also known as Sister Margaret Jude."

Augustus looks pole-axed. "As in—?"

"Yup."

They turn to Connie but she's clutching her glass, staring, not seeing, tears spilling down her cheeks.

Rita reaches across the table to clasp Connie's free hand lying limp on the tablecloth. "Con?"

"You both know who you are and I don't. I'm . . . Con. *Con*fused. *Con*spicuous. *Con*cave."

Augustus gets a clean linen napkin from the sideboard and hands it to her. "But my dear, this is how it begins. With sorrow."

Something inside her curls up and skitters away from his words. She tries to pull herself together but her hands remain clenched around the thick wad of napkin.

Augustus lifts the hem of the tablecloth and gently blots her tears. "A toast," he says softly. He looks to Rita.

"In *vino veritas*," Rita lifts her glass.

Connie does the same as her muzzy brain translates: in wine, truth.

What a disaster, Rita thinks as she pulls out of the driveway on her way to church. Instead of lifting Connie's spirits, last night sent her into a downward spiral. She heard Connie crying herself to sleep. She was still in bed this morning after Rita had made coffee, showered, dressed, and dawdled as long as she could before being late for Mass.

There are still two days till the next food bank delivery and only enough money in her checking account for thirty bags of rice and half as many dried lentils. The store manager lets Rita write an I.O.U. for a case of canned hams. By the time she gets to Loaves and Fishes with the emergency supplies, Mitzi has set out new lettuce, cucumbers, and sweet onions; the fresh produce almost festive on the long wooden counter. Rita gives her a quizzical look.

"From Matt." Mitzi stacks the last of the onions on top of the mound. "He won't take any cash for it. I think he pays for this stuff out of his own pocket although he makes it sound like he just happened to have extra."

"It looks wonderful. And, Lord knows, we need all the food we can get." Rita realizes she's pleased that, even though he's washed his hands of her, Matt's generosity is not contrived to impress her, that he's a far cry from Vincent.

With Mitzi's help, she unloads the grocery bags from the car, adding to the dwindling stock on the shelves. "I hope we have enough volunteers to get every last bushel from Ted's farm."

"Let me see how my summer courses go, Rita. I may be able to pitch in once in a while." Mitzi swings the side door open and stops it with a brick, washes her hands, and joins Rita behind the counter. "Have you ever considered enlisting our people?"

Rita bolts up from the floor. "You're brilliant!" She gives Mitzi a hug. "Why didn't I think of that? Of course! A perfect solution."

By the end of the day, more than a dozen people have signed up to volunteer for the gleaning project. In addition to the hand-lettered notice they'd hastily made, both women mentioned it to the regulars as they bagged groceries and caught up on their family news. When a woman with two young sons wanted to know if she could bring them along, since she couldn't afford a babysitter, the elderly man behind her volunteered to watch them 'as long as we can stay in the shade.' So, they incorporated daycare into the mix and several more mothers signed up. Soon the atmosphere became charged with an animation Rita had never witnessed at the food bank, as if those gathering were neighbors bumping into each other at the supermarket, instead of standing in line for 'welfare' which no one fares well from. One man, a former teamster, who couldn't speak, his lips quivered so, wrote his name in large letters, upright and bold.

After everyone left and she'd thanked Mitzi for the fifth time ("Enough!" she'd laughed. "It wasn't rocket science.") Rita sweeps the floors then gets down on her knees to scrub them by hand. She feels a need to humble herself, do penance. When has she consulted Janet and Mitzi, even Connie for that matter? What makes her think she knows how to make the world a better place, what's best for everyone? She can't even decide her own fate. What arrogance. Maybe Matt was right. She scrubs harder, working her way across the room in small sudsy arcs.

Since the christening, she's steered clear of the food bank on Tuesdays when Matt volunteers, but it's a small town, so they've run into each other at Grange meetings or the bakery, or while standing in line at the bank. A couple of times she noticed his truck in her rearview mirror and waved hello; he waved back, a perfunctory raised palm.

They never seem to strike the right balance, she thinks, remembering a drizzly day in early April when, before starting the county grant proposal, she'd dashed across the street to pick up a sandwich. The rain turned torrential by the time she reached Sweeties. He was at the register, paying for his meal when she walked in. She felt her face lift into a smile.

"Matt!" she said. "How have you been?"

He took one long look at her then fled, after fumbling with his change, muttering something about being late. She felt disconcerted by his demeanor until she toweled her hair in the bathroom and saw her shirt plastered to her skin, revealing her full breasts and the darker-hued nipples through the thin cotton bra.

At the May Grange meeting, he was brimming with news: Walt hired an Ag major for the summer; Matt's mother, now engaged to the sheep rancher, was up in Maine; Walt and he will take turns going up to meet him, to check out the ranch; he's organizing the gleaning schedule, so she should get ready to start her teams in June. He said all this in a rush after the meeting while folding the chairs, wearing his gray Cornell University sweatshirt, shuttling back and forth with two flattened chairs under each arm, looking so much like a penguin she had to laugh. He walked her to her car. Both of them caught in the sudden silence; neither willing to make small talk.

She empties the dirty water from the bucket outside, refills it, then works her way across the floor again with a damp mop.

The last time she spoke to Matt for any length was at the library, the week after Connie came back. Rita had been lugging two sacks of books when he pulled into the space next to her VW. She filled him in, omitting the details, only saying there had been another, more grievous incident. They lingered, leaning on the warm metal doors of their respective vehicles, under the shimmering new leaves of a silver maple. He'd been to Maine, met Graham, his mother's intended, and surveyed the ranch, the flock. Easier than a dairy herd, he said, worth exploring. She had added fieldwork to her schedule and the extra hours at Loaves to serve the influx of migrant workers.

"Plus, Connie and the kids, you must be exhausted."

"Getting there," she said, sitting down behind the wheel, her body absorbing that very fact. She found herself mesmerized by his forearms, the tendons strung taut under barely tanned skin, the slightly articulated musculature, his capable hands—veined on top, callused on the bottom. She wonders now whether she was entranced because she wanted the comfort of his embrace or his help carrying the heavy load. Or was it merely aesthetics? Beautiful day, beautiful tree, beautiful arms. All she knows is that she's always happy to see him. But the same is true for everyone she's fond of—Connie and the children, Janet, Immaculata, Augustus.

She doesn't, however, contemplate their forearms.

She realizes her arrogance in thinking that she can reason this through and find her way on her own. She closes her eyes and asks God to open her heart, to guide her to her righteous path. "Thy will be done," her prayer with every stroke of the mop.

On her way home, Rita stops at the Four Corners farm stand. A small shed and a greenhouse sit at the crossroads of four huge fields striped with various shades of green. Inside she finds bushels of potatoes, onions, and other vegetables, as well as apples, rhubarb, pears. Rita fills a paper bag with fruit, and a basket with lettuce, tomatoes, and cucumbers. When she reaches down into a bin of onions, she spies a box full of wriggling kittens.

"Better not look." A youngish woman, hair piled high in a curly topknot, carries in a flat of white begonias from the greenhouse. "You'll be a goner."

"I'll take my chances," Rita smiles. "I work with Ted through the Grange. Are you his daughter?"

"You, honey, just made my day." She puts down the flat, dusts her palms on her jeans before offering her hand. "I'm his wife. Ginger. You must be

Rita. Ted's mentioned your name. You all are coming here next week, right? To clean the south field?"

Rita nods, her eyes back on the kittens.

"It's back-breaking work. Worse than the picking, and there's so little to show for the effort."

"Enough though, you think, for our little food bank?"

Ginger considers then sweeps her arm around the room. "I'd say about half this much give or take a bushel or two, without the variety of course. You'll be culling one or two crops at a time, three at the most."

Rita almost weeps picturing the counter piled high with tomatoes or cabbages or pears, of summer-long bounty, the boon of nutrition, the blessing of taste. She ducks down to the cardboard box. "May I pick them up?"

"It's your funeral." Ginger grins as she heads back out to the greenhouse.

Four little faces peer back at Rita. Two orange kittens clamber on top of each other, the black one rolls onto its back, the calico nips at her outstretched finger. Rita cups the squirming calico in her hands, imagining the look on Anna's face when she gives her the kitten. She'll take it home, and if Connie vetoes it, she can return it before Anna gets back from her grandparents.

Ginger carries in another flat, scarlet geraniums this time. "The black one is spoken for."

Rita holds up the calico. "Well so is this one, aren't you sweetie?"

"Here." Ginger puts the kitten in the bottom of a bushel, rings up Rita's purchases.

"Oh, wait." Rita adds a dozen each of geraniums and begonias for Connie, a consolation prize.

# CHAPTER 27

Red-eyed but calm, Connie stands at the sink de-veining shrimp. A platter of sliced tomatoes and cucumbers, halved hard-boiled eggs, and black olives sits on the counter. "I made a light supper, after last night . . . ."

"It was supposed to be fun."

"I know, Reet. It's me. Post-partum, I guess. As long as my mother has Gabrielle anyway, I think I'll wean her." She opens a jar of cocktail sauce and pours it into a small bowl. "Does that make me a terrible mother?"

"I get jealous every time I watch you nurse. Does that make me a terrible friend?"

Connie looks up from her work. "Seriously?"

"Seriously."

Rita tells Connie about her realizations today, apologizing for talking her into going out last night.

Connie smiles. "You are hard to say 'no' to."

"That said, I know I'm pressing my luck, but I promise if you say 'no' I'll turn right back around." She retrieves the bushel from the porch and hands it to Connie. "For Anna, if that's okay with you."

Connie picks up the kitten, strokes its fur. It purrs so loudly the women laugh. "She'll love it."

"I got you something too." She shows Connie the flowers.

Connie riffles their petals with her fingertips. "Healthy plants. Lovely. I'll pot them after we eat."

"Mmmm, good," Rita says, her mouth full of shrimp. "I'm famished. It's great having a cook."

"You could have a professional chef if you wanted one. Augustus looked like he wanted to wrap you up and take you home." Connie helps herself to an egg white, leaves the yolk. "Why do you always wait until you're starving?"

Rita shrugs, bites down on a roll, and stabs another shrimp. "Rough day?"

"Every time I think I'm done crying, there's more. If what Augustus said is true, then I'm off to a great start. I wonder how he ended up here, of all places. You'd think after three years on ocean liners, he could have found someplace more exotic."

Rita ladles cocktail sauce onto her plate, blood-red against the white dish. "Maybe he got tired of exotic. Maybe he wanted some plain and simple."

"Speaking of which. That Ed," Connie puts two shrimp, a tomato slice, and a cucumber spear on her plate. "What's he like?"

"Sometimes I feel like he's spying on me but mostly he keeps to himself. If it wasn't for my gossipy realtor, I wouldn't know he lives alone; that he never married; that he's a Vietnam vet. He must have volunteered; he's too old for the draft. I tried to talk to him about it once. He wouldn't say anything more than it cured him of patriotism." Rita snaps her fingers. "I almost forgot. He gave me some diagrams of Laurel's gardens." She feels around on top of the refrigerator for the drawings that she hands to Connie.

Connie studies a diagram, chewing on a cucumber spear. "Oh, here." She points to a circle close to the stream. "Oriental poppies, those enormous orange flowers that look like butterflies in the breeze? And here, at the foot of the bridge, the yellow bush? Japonica."

"You going to eat those yolks?"

"Help yourself." Connie doesn't look up from the chart. "Bellflowers. The blue ones by the picnic table. I think they're called Canterbury Bells."

"He said he probably missed some but that's a good start."

"I can fill in the rest after everything blooms. I've wanted to experiment with perennials. Wouldn't it be fun to learn the Latin names? " She looks up when Rita laughs. "What?"

"You look like a young botany major I used to know. It's good to see her again." Connie flushes and grins.

Rita clears the table. "Finished? You hardly ate anything."

"I'm determined to lose those last five pounds," Connie murmurs, not lifting her eyes from the paper.

Whether it's because she's stopped nursing, or started working in the garden, Connie seems more like her old self again, regaling Rita with the children's exploits, the garden's progress, and preparing wonderfully simple fare from the produce Rita carts home. Connie looks bright-eyed, sun-kissed—happy. Other than the hissy fit both Ceci and the cat threw over the new kitten—which Anna named Tabitha—their household is harmonious.

Whenever she can, Rita watches the congressional hearings on the Watergate break-in. The machinations of the corrupt White House is, by far, the best drama on TV. So many lies and misappropriations exposed by the special prosecutor.

If the little ones are napping, Connie joins her.

"What do you think happened, Con? Do you think Nixon knew about the break-in, that he sanctioned it?"

"I haven't been following it all that closely. But it seems possible, doesn't it, that he could have been unaware, that this could be the work of his misguided supporters."

"What about John Dean's testimony? And the Ehrlichman memo? The plans to steal the Pentagon Papers?"

"Still. It doesn't prove the president knew about the cover-up."

Rita sighs, shakes her head. "You should have been the nun. You're so . . . "

"Gullible?"

"In a way, I suppose." Rita gets up and turns down the volume. "Have you been avoiding Vince because you're afraid he'll be able to change your mind? Because you'll have to deal with him someday."

"No. I know he won't," Connie wipes her tears with the back of her hand. "He finally destroyed any illusion I had that his 'lapses' weren't his fault. Now I know he's not the one who needed an excuse. I did."

"Whoa, Rita, let them be. Those are the peonies."

"Sorry." Rita stops mid-shear, a handful of stalks already lying at the bottom of a rusty pail. Sitting back on her heels, she watches Connie stroke the severed nubs as if saying goodbye. "I thought they were weeds."

"*Paeonia*. Herbaceous peony. These will smell like roses and look like ball gowns stuffed with a dozen crinolines, all cream or pink or burgundy." Connie surveys the damage. "Well, you've left most of them at least. I'd better add them to the diagram."

It's been a hotter than average June and they want to weed before the heat adds its measure to their work. The playpen sits under the dappled shade of an apple tree; the baby's hands look as if they're conducting a symphony of leaves. The girls ferry each other around in the wheelbarrow, its bulk heavy enough to keep them at a snail's pace.

A rhythmic creaking sound turns out to be the plodding steps of a man in dripping rubber waders. Ed's got more gear hanging from his fishing vest than most anglers have in their kits.

"Hey, Ed. Any luck?" asks Rita.

"Just getting started. Oh, you're back . . . Connie, right? How's your little girl?"

"Intrepid as ever," says Connie. "Last time I saw you, you were fishing too."

"Ice fishing in the winter, trout fishing in spring, blue fishing in August when they're running down the Jersey shore."

"Gee, how do you make it through fall?"

"Hunting. Duck, pheasant, deer. Don't make those faces at me, ladies. Just as important as the weeding you're doing if you don't want each species running the other one off. Cycle of life. Besides, I eat what I hunt. And share it out if it's too much for one man. Mind if I try my luck from your bridge for a bit?"

"Not at all." Rita hoists herself up. "Get a folding chair from the garage, Ed, make yourself comfortable." She leans close to Connie and murmurs, "As if I have a choice."

"He's quite the mountain man," Connie says.

Rita tilts her face toward the sun. "He acts like he owns this place. He spent one whole day last month cleaning the gutters, replacing the broken stair to the porch, fixing the running toilet." She picks up Connie's sketches. "I'm so glad you stopped me from destroying those . . . "

"Peonies." Connie spots a dandelion, pulls it out by the root. "He's so protective of this place. You think he had a thing for Laurel?"

"Could be."

"What do you know about her?"

"That she's a lot younger than he, mid-twenties or so, from what the realtor said. That after her father died, her mother couldn't bear the memories and moved back to London but Laurel stayed here taking care of the house and gardens."

"So, what happened to her?"

"She'd just been licensed as a nurse when her mother was diagnosed with Lou Gehrig's disease."

"Oh, no! So . . . she's in England, right?"

"Uh-huh. It's a slow degenerative disease, so poor Laurel has the unhappy fate of nursing both of her parents until their deaths. Which is why she had to rent this house. Denise told me Laurel felt terrible leaving her garden."

Connie shivers despite the rising heat. "Now I feel even more guilty about the poor peonies. Hand me those diagrams, Reet. I want this place looking great if Laurel happens to come back to see how her garden grew."

Connie studies books and catalogs, calls the county agricultural extension office, and learns the botanical names for the flowers and plants on the property. She keeps journals, dividing a loose-leaf binder into categories for charting weather, bloom time, color, and height, pressing petals between sheets of waxed paper, tucks them into phone books until they dry. As soon as the kids are asleep, she commandeers the kitchen table, which barely accommodates the amount of materials she's accumulated.

"Rita, do you think she'd mind if I planted a garden?" Connie sits near the open window, a slight breeze fluttering the glossy pages of the Spring Hill catalog.

"I don't know. Talk to Ed."

"I'll only do annuals so it wouldn't be permanent. Do you know if you soak the seeds in water before planting, they do better?"

"No, I—"

"I wonder if Ed would build me a cold frame so I can get an early start next year. This is so much fun, Rita. You and me, this place, all the—"

"Con."

Connie looks up from the stack of books, an array of seed packets, the graph paper studded with different–colored dots for globe amaranth, delphinium, phlox. With a black smudge on her cheek, she grins at Rita.

"I haven't decided yet, remember?"

"Oh, Reet, how could you give this up?"

Despite the heat, Rita waits for Immaculata in the dusty courtyard, where she feels protected by the buildings, soothed by the carillon of the monastery bells. Six months ago, she was filled with energy and certitude, now she's empty of both. She hadn't counted on the constant attention fundraising demands, nor had she anticipated sheltering Connie and the children. The money Vince reluctantly provides is sporadic at best. "Come back home, and you can have anything you want," he wrote Connie.

Rita sinks onto the curved stone bench. Although a divorce would mean court-ordered alimony and child support, Rita can't encourage Connie to commit what would be, according to the Church, a mortal sin. On the other hand, Rita can't bear the thought of reconciliation and losing the children, especially Anna, whose sensitive nature unravels Rita's memories of caring for her own mother. But Connie's definitely on the upswing and Rita has three grant proposals in the hopper and just enough money left to float them through year's end. Maybe by then, she'll know just where she belongs.

She looks up when Immaculata calls her name and is filled with a nameless joy when the tiny woman enfolds her in a fierce embrace.

"You're too pale," Immaculata says when she holds Rita at arm's length.

"And too thin. We would never allow you to wear yourself down like this. What good are you to the poor if you—"

"It's not Loaves. It's Connie. She's left her husband."

"Again?" Immaculata sniffs.

"For good as far as I can tell."

"How far can you tell your future?"

"Not very."

"Is it so dependent on Connie's?"

Rita sighs. "No. Maybe. It's so many things . . . "

"It can't be. I thought you understood that."

"I do. What I mean is I'm trying to line things up so the food bank can be self-sufficient and Connie can make it on her own . . . "

"You're not her savior." Immaculata stands up. "There is only one true Savior and as long as you keep making others' problems your own, you will never discern whether or not you belong here. And believe me, my dear," Immaculata says placing her hands on Rita's shoulders, looking into her eyes, "you will not have a second chance."

"She's not here." Connie opens the door and relieves Augustus of the white boxes tied with string. "She's at Holy Name."

Augustus looks crestfallen. "That's the second time this week."

"Because this week two of the sisters have their name days."

He gives her a blank stare.

"Instead of birthdays, nuns celebrate saints' days. For the saint whose name they've taken."

"When's Rita's? Would that be Margaret or Jude? Oh no, that's a bad idea, isn't it? Although—"

"Relax, it isn't until October." Connie cuts the string and lifts the top of the smaller box. "Blueberry pie, Ceci's favorite. You don't have to bring something every time you come over, Augustus."

"But I do. It's my propitiation to the gods."

Connie opens the box of cookies. "Which ones?"

"Ganesha and Cupid. Fortuna . . . "

"Ganesha?"

"God of doorways—beginnings . . . "

"You sound more like a scholar than a chef." She takes a bottle of formula from the refrigerator, sets it in a pot of water on the stove.

"Can't one be both?"

"Yes, of course . . . I didn't mean—"

"'gustus!" Ceci carries in a handful of colorful weeds, which she quickly discards to sit next to him at the kitchen table.

"Where's Anna?"

"Hiding seek." Ceci reaches for a cookie.

"Wash your hands, first," Connie tells her. "Augustus, about the scholar thing. I didn't mean to imply that —"

"My dear, I am not so easily offended."

As soon as Gabrielle wakes up, they go outside. Settling into a lawn chair, Connie gives the baby her bottle. Augustus swings a gleeful Ceci onto his immense shoulders and walks toward the lake.

Connie scans the property for Anna. She's used to her daughter taking refuge in her hideouts. She's seen Anna emerge from a dense thicket, leaves sprinkled in her hair, or climbing up from the brook with muddy sneakers and dirt on the seat of her pants. God knows, she understands Anna's penchant for solitude. Besides, she's a good kid, smart, dependable. Let her have her little secrets. Connie peers into Gabrielle's infinitely calm face. Unlike the others, she relinquished the breast without a fuss. Well, why not? As soon as she cries, she's changed, fed, picked up.

Rita dotes on her. As do her big sisters. She has more than enough mothering for one little girl.

During the happy confusion of the returning wanderers, Anna turns up. "Can I hold her, Mama?"

"I asked first," Ceci says.

"Go get the quilt. I'll put Gabrielle down and you both can watch her, okay?" The girls race into the house. "And bring me her hat."

"May I?" Augustus holds out his hands for the baby. A passer-by would think she's an incredibly life-like doll cradled in his massive arms. The girls spread the quilt on the grass, and he sets the baby down in the middle, as carefully as he would a soufflé straight from the oven.

"So, what do you study?" Connie asks when he settles into an Adirondack chair.

"Folklore, mythology, philosophy. Whatever strikes my fancy."

"Rita and I were wondering why you settled here. Of all places."

Augustus looks up at a turkey vulture riding the thermals high above the treetops.

"Not that it's any of our—"

"A matter of the heart." He doesn't try to conceal the sadness that moistens his eyes, contorts his face. He leans back in the chair, rests his hands on its wide wooden arms. "I was in Vienna, soaking up the music and the pastries when I met this incredible woman; she was striking, eccentric, gifted. A classical musician. Her tour was over, and I still had three weeks before my next voyage from Genoa to New York, so we went everywhere—Paris and Milan, Mykonos, Dubrovnik. She spoke three languages; I get along in four; we argued, cracked-wise, and ordered room service in all of them. A mad fling, I thought. A summer romance, she thought. At the end, I simply went home with her. She lived here."

He tents his fingers, peers into the empty triangle. "You save a lot of money working on ships; my room and board were covered. I'd been well paid. I could afford to tour with her, at least for the foreseeable future. An oxymoron. One can only see the present."

Augustus closes his eyes as if he doesn't even want to see that. "We were in Minneapolis; she'd had a performance, and I'd gone to the Guthrie to see a play. We were to meet after at a jazz club. After waiting an hour, I went back to our hotel thinking she'd forgotten or perhaps I had it wrong. There were frantic messages from the concert hall, the front desk, the police. She never showed up to perform; instead, she went to the hotel's restaurant and cadged food from the patrons' plates, then wandered downtown where the police picked her up. They found her in a pet shop where she'd opened all the cages then crawled into one—naked."

As soon as he opens his eyes, Connie averts hers.

"Adult-onset schizophrenia." He accepts the ball Ceci hands him, then tosses it back. "As an artist, she was always allowed her idiosyncrasies. As an intellect, her judgment was presumed to be superior, by me as well as her colleagues, her friends, her father. We stumbled along for a while— psychiatrists, mental hospitals, medications. I'd wake up in the middle of the night to find her gone. Outside, barefoot in winter. Or locked in the bathroom, terrified."

"Oh, Augustus." Connie hurts just hearing this.

"It can't be cured. It can be tamed by medication but as soon as she felt at all herself, she'd stop taking it. Her father insisted I leave her in his care. 'She'll always be my little girl, son, it's easier on me,' he told me. So, I did. Before I lost my mind, too."

"Where is she now?"

"With her dad. For a while, she taught piano when she was stabilized with medication, but then even that stopped."

"Oh my God. Ruthie." Connie blurts out. He clenches his jaw, nods. "I'm so sorry, Augustus." She holds his hand. "What a tragedy."

"Worthy of the gods," he sighs.

Connie watches Gabrielle doze on the quilt and Ceci fill a toy dump truck with pebbles, leaves, grass and then crank the lever so it all slides out again, the kitten leaping at a yo-yo Anna dangles. Her children are happy. With Rita's help, she's kept them safe. She wonders what the gods will bestow on them.

Augustus stands, some trick of sunlight blotting out his features, outlining his frame. "One can't really survive without friends, I've learned. Especially when life cracks apart like the fragile illusion it is."

"How did you manage?" Connie asks. "Besides friends, I mean."

"After a black void—about which I remember very little except Billie Holiday and bourbon—I started performing rituals."

"Like what?"

"Little ones at first. Lakota Indian smudging ceremonies, yogic sun salutations, simple mandalas made of river rocks."

"And that helped how?"

"It made me feel connected to something universal, timeless. The collective unconscious? I don't know. All indigenous peoples use ceremonies to mark significant passages."

"What were the big ones? The rituals?"

"Are. Once a year I go off by myself for a week or two. Commemorate in some fashion the summer and winter solstices. Have at least one bacchanal a year.

"Oh. And every once in a blue moon, I try something that scares the shit out of me."

# CHAPTER 28

"Isn't that terrible?" Connie follows Rita upstairs.

"It's one of the saddest stories I've ever heard. I can't imagine what it must be like to see someone you love become . . . Ruthie." Rita takes off the clothes she wore to the convent, steps into her oldest jeans, pulls on an orange tee-shirt that advertises 'Empire State Grocers—serving the five boroughs since 1958.'

"One day I'm going to get you some decent clothes." Connie lies down on the bed. "You don't even try and these great guys are crazy about you. And you're not even sure if you want a man."

"And you are?" Rita sits on the bed with her back against the headboard.

Connie rolls onto her side, props herself up on her elbow. "Fat chance. With three kids. That's even presuming Vincent would agree to a divorce. For which I'd be excommunicated."

"This is the sort of thing that makes me crazy," Rita says. "Why do Catholics have to sacrifice their faith to have a life? Or their life to keep their faith? There must be some sort of dispensation."

"Well, I'll cross that bridge . . . it seems so far off. I haven't even seen him since . . . that day, let alone talked about a divorce."

"I can't keep fending him off, you're going to have to face him, you know."

"I will. I promise." She gets up. "Come on. Let's sit outside, it's a beautiful night."

Above the leaf canopies, Connie finds Venus, the North Star, the Big Dipper. "I was thinking . . . "

"Hmmm?" Rita lights the candles, blotting out the stars.

"About Augustus and his ceremonies and this glorious place." She inhales. "Oh, God, Rita, can you smell that? Night-blooming jasmine."

Rita laughs. "Con, you say that every night."

"How about we have a big party? It's Ceci's sixth birthday next month. I could see Vince in a crowd instead of on my own, we could invite my family, have a barbecue—"

"I have been wanting to invite the sisters over here."

"Ed and Augustus, of course," Connie says.

"Janet, Mitzi," adds Rita.

"Then you have to invite Matt."

Rita considers this.

"Come on, Reet, he's one of the volunteers, and you won't be alone with him—"

"Then Walter, too. And Ginger and Ted."

"Hold it." Connie chews on her thumb while she does the math. "That's thirty-three adults if everyone shows. Plus, the kids." She looks up at Rita. "Pray it doesn't rain."

Rita, Connie, and the girls spend all morning getting ready; they scrub down the bathroom, loop crepe paper over low hanging branches, sculpt disks of chopped meat into hamburgers. The refrigerator's filled with salads: potato, macaroni, coleslaw. Rita lugs the old washtub from the basement, dumps in blocks of ice, cans of soda, bottles of beer.

Connie cuts daisies and yellow lilies, adding a bright red geranium to each bunch, for the picnic table, the card table, and the folding table they set up outside. Anna fills a basket with paper plates and napkins, plastic cups, and utensils. By eleven o'clock they're grimy and sweaty. The guests are due around one.

"Do you think we should get more hot dogs? Another case of beer?"

Rita collapses on the grass. "Con. Your mother alone will have a trunk full of food. To say nothing of your sisters."

"True. And Janet and Mitzi will probably bring something. To say nothing of *your* sisters."

"I don't know who will show. Immaculata, I hope. And some of the others. I'm so glad Augustus volunteered to man the grill. I don't want your father working all day in this heat."

"Anna, honey, go check on the baby? See if she's awake." Connie sits next to Rita. "Think Ed will show up?"

"Might."

"What about Walter and Matt?"

Rita shrugs. "Haven't heard. But Ted and Ginger said yes."

Ceci's on the bridge coloring a Happy Birthday! sign to put on the mailbox along with the pink and white balloons.

"Vince better remember he promised her a bigger 'cake' and a better 'sled' or there'll be hell to pay." Connie stands and brushes off the seat of her pants. "Mind if I shower first?"

"Are you nervous?"

"Sort of." Connie squints as the sun clears the tree line.

"Go. Shower. I'll clean up the mess in the kitchen then set up the sprinkler for the kids."

Rita's up to her elbows in the sink washing the mixing bowls when the doorbell rings. It's Vincent. She doesn't say a word. Neither does he. He gives a wrapped package to Anna and scoops Ceci up in his arms, covers her with noisy kisses.

"Come on birthday girl, help me set up your present."

He coaxes Anna outside and moves the playpen into the shade. Rita watches him blow up an inflatable raft, then set up a wading pool, the two objects replicating Anna's winter gifts. Ceci prances around her father, clutching the green and yellow raft shaped like a frog. In all these weeks he hasn't attempted to win back Connie's favor but Rita's certain he'll try, and today he'll have a chance.

"Your turn," Connie comes up behind her.

"Look outside," Rita says, without turning around.

"He kept his promise," Connie whispers. "I never would have thought of that, Rita. Would you?"

Before Rita can answer, Connie steps out into the midday sun. She's wearing the halter sundress Vince made. Her skin looks burnished against the beige linen, her hair glints as if woven with gold thread. Her topaz earrings catch the light and toss it back. Vince says something Rita can't hear, takes Connie's hand and kisses it, holds it while he continues to talk to her. Instead of shrinking from him, Connie moves closer and says something that silences Vincent. Then she withdraws her hand, retrieves the clippers from the grass, and turns toward the bank of daylilies. Vince looks as if he's swallowing stones.

Rita feels like applauding.

Just as Augustus lights the coals, Rita sees the Pescatores arrive in a caravan. Brenda and her husband with Louis and Rose and Nonna Rosemarie, Carlo with Louis Jr. and his family. Marie and Angela, their husbands and children. The men unload the trunks carting coolers of food, softballs, and bats, toys for the kids. Louis and Augustus debate the barbecue rotation for the hot dogs and burgers along with ribs and flank steak from the butcher shop. Immaculata arrives with Catherine John. Janet's wearing the shortest shorts Rita's ever seen. Then Ted and Ginger with a bushel of corn. Mitzi carrying a covered dish. Ed at the last. No Walter, no Matt. If she's honest, Rita has to admit she feels more disappointed than relieved.

By two o'clock, the air is filled with the aroma of grilled beef and cut grass. The kids screech and shout their barefoot joy, the tape deck pumps out rock 'n' roll, the grown-ups settle down in bunches at the tables or on the grass.

Rita surveys the party as she makes up a plate for herself. Augustus and Janet are deep in conversation, the contrast comical. Janet, shrinking by comparison to an even tinier version of herself, Augustus taking on Bunyanesque proportions. Immaculata, in the abbreviated habit sans veil, is at eye-level with Ginger's bare midriff, Connie's tanned shoulders are in stark relief next to Catherine John's fish-white limbs poking out of her pink short-sleeved blouse and a white pleated skirt. Rose, animated and garrulous, corners the taciturn Ed. Rita's not sure but she thinks Mitzi's explaining the concept of a food bank to Nonna Rosemarie, who nods and smiles as she fans herself with a paper plate. Carlo and Vincent sit on the hood of a car, halfway up the driveway with hangdog expressions and bottles of beer. The children make merry on and around the blankets Connie's sisters have spread in the shade, the husbands ferry hot dogs and hamburgers back and forth from the grill where, in his butcher's apron, Louis spells Augustus. Ceci twirls from group to group. Brenda, who believes in such things, declares her niece a true Leo—enthusiastic and temperamental.

Just as Rita takes a huge bite of her burger—the first food she's had all day—Matt walks into her field of vision.

"Hello, stranger," he says.

So, she has to just stand there chewing and swallowing while they have a separate conversation with their eyes. She holds up the hamburger, points to it, and then her throat.

"You're choking?"

She rolls her eyes, watching a slow smile light up his.

"It's indescribably good?"

She shakes her head.

"It's—"

"Breakfast," she says at last.

"Ah. You do wait till you're ravenous before you chow down like a truck driver." His laughter feels like cool blue water where she can sink deep and swim free.

Matt holds out what looks like a paint-splattered watermelon. "For you."

She puts down her plate to take it. It's small but heavy, dark green except for the yellow dots.

"It's a Moon and Stars." He turns it until she sees the large yellow spot. "That's the moon and the rest are stars."

"Wherever did you get it?"

"Grew it. Them. There's plenty more." He smiles. "You did think it was a melon farm, remember?"

She nods, cradling the warm fruit.

"Plus, it's hard to resist a man who brings you the moon and the stars."

"Matt—"

"I'm going to get something to eat while you catch up on your caloric deficit," he says as he walks away.

Rita smiles and slowly runs her hand across the melon's sky.

She takes another bite of her burger and tracks Matt's movement to the grill, to the folding table covered with all manner of side dishes, to the metal tub to pull out a can of beer before making his way back to her. He lowers himself onto the grass where she sits cross-legged, polishing off her potato salad.

"Who's that big guy talking to Janet?" Matt asks.

When Rita looks over Augustus is staring at her. He cuts his eyes back to Janet. "The chef at the Snow Goose. On the other side of the lake?"

"And those two?" Matt points.

"Sisters Immaculata and Catherine John."

"I had a feeling."

Rita scans the yard. "Where's Walt?"

"On his way back up to Maine. Our soon-to-be stepfather wants to gift 'Kate's boys'—as he refers to us—with a mare and her foal. Can you imagine, trying to buy grown men's affection with a pony."

"You don't like him?"

"Hell, yes. It's working." He laughs and sips his beer. "No really, he seems like a decent guy who works hard and plays hard. He loves my mother. She's happy, so I'm happy." Matt digs into his food.

Ceci, still damp from the pool, climbs onto Rita's lap. "Today's my birthday," she tells Matt.

"So I hear. Happy Birthday."

"Everybody brings me presents."

Rita hugs her. "Not everybody, Ceci."

"Uh huh. Everybody. Even the sisters brought me presents. I got three Holy cards and one Holy rosary. Ed got me a fishing hat and 'gustus made me a blueberry pie."

"If you don't mind waiting a bit, you can have a pony ride for a present."

Ceci jumps up and looks around. "You have a pony?"

"Not yet. It's on its way to my farm. You can come over and ride it."

"When?"

Matt looks at Rita. "Anytime you want."

"Hey Mooney, how's your jump shot?" Carlo yells from the top of the drive. He twirls a basketball on his finger. "One game of h-o-r-s-e. For the all-time world championship."

"You're on." She re-ties the laces on her sneakers and gets up. "Excuse me. I'm going to have to beat that boy—for the thousandth time."

Matt dumps their plates into the trash and goes to get another beer.

"You must be the sainted boyfriend," Vince hands Matt an icy bottle of beer from the galvanized tub, takes a long pull of the cold one dangling from his other fist.

"You've been badly misinformed, my friend," Matt says.

Vince wipes his palm on his jeans and shakes the other man's hand, squints up at him. "Matt, right?"

"Right. But I'm not 'the boyfriend' least of all a sainted one."

"Rita's still on the fence?" Vince throws his head back, flings open his arms. "Torture, thy name is woman."

Connie glances over, a quizzical look on her face. Matt waves.

Vince puts a hand on Matt's shoulder. "Save yourself."

"I'm trying my damnedest," Matt laughs.

Taking another long swallow, Vince finishes his beer. He digs around in the half-melted ice for another bottle of Heineken. All he finds are cans of Budweiser and soda. He rubs his reddened hands together. "That was the last one. I'm gonna get another case." He looks at Matt. "Want to come?"

"I'll drive."

"Suit yourself."

Vincent climbs up into the cab of a truck so old and battered it reminds him of a movie prop. He gazes out the window as Matt drives around the lake, past the open fields of local farms, inhales the burnt earth smell of fading crops composting in the heat. Sunlight dusts the pale crook of Vincent's arm poking out into the air stream carved out by the truck's hot metal hood. He stares at his hand until he can see the minute triangles and trapezoids, tiny maps and legends that seem as mysterious to him as his wife's newfound ferocity. No, more like her tenacity. 'We're too far gone' her first words to him in two months.

"I was the sainted boyfriend once. Now I'm the rotten husband. Maybe it'll be different with Rita; she's used to sacrifice and compassion and all that shit. It's like Connie's changed frequencies and nothing I say gets through to her. There's nothing she wants from me."

"Rita doesn't have kids."

"Like that's a trial, man?"

"Not a trial. But ceaseless. Like farming. You've got to be dogging every detail, each new twist and bend of the crop and the weather. Every cliché you can think of from 'nip it in the bud' on down. Those words are worn out cause they signify."

"Ever been married?"

"Nope."

"Doesn't matter. Can't tell you anything, anyway. Every man for himself."

Matt pulls into the dirt lot of a long low building, 'Mavericks' written in a braided rope font the only indication it's a bar and not an abandoned storefront. Inside, the spicy, moldy smell of spilled beer, a darkness that isn't cool exactly, just not hot. The bartender's jeans gap around his pelvis, his tee-shirt clings to the bony ridges of his ribs. When he smiles, Vincent sees a patch of shiny gum where three teeth should be.

"Do for you?" he asks them.

"A case of Heineken. Cold if you got it." Vince looks at Matt, nods toward the barstool. "You mind?"

Matt shakes his head, sits down.

"Give us what you have on tap." Vincent lays a twenty on the bar in the time-honored tradition of men indicating that they want to talk, get wasted, or both. 'Can't live, if living is without you,' plays the melancholy dirge from the jukebox.

"You know what her hobby used to be?" Vince stares at the mirror behind the bar. "Me."

The bartender deals out cardboard coasters, napkin squares, two foamy mugs. He takes the twenty, rings up the sale, and lays the change on the bar.

"Her sisters used to call to invite her over. 'Come for coffee, come for lunch, bring the kids.' But Connie turned them down till they stopped asking. She took naps with the kids, so she could stay up late with me. Christ, what was I supposed to do, push her out the door? She seemed content. Happy even."

He picks up a couple of quarters, walks over to the jukebox, and stares at its carnival colors, its song list of love and longing. L-3, their second date, G-5 the first time they made love, D-6 at the beach, accompanied by rolling whoosh of the surf. He closes his eyes, remembering when her day began and ended with him.

Vince finishes his beer, then sets the empty mug down with a hollow thump. "She has the upper hand. For now."

He leaves a tip for the bartender, pockets his change. Matt picks up the case of beer and they walk out into the rank heat.


The party winds up for a few more hours then begins a slow slide into twilight, cranky children, and long rides home. After many maneuvers and one dented bumper, the Pescatores get back on the road. The nuns are long gone. Ed's slipped off down the lane. The rest help clean up, return objects to their rightful places then hang out for a last beer or a cup of coffee. Connie puts Gabrielle to bed; Anna and Ceci chase fireflies in the dusk. Augustus is holding forth when Matt takes his leave.

"Early day tomorrow and Walt's not here," he tells Rita. "You going to be all right? Want me to wait till he leaves?" He points to where Vince sits just outside the rest of the group drinking coffee and staring at Connie, who's smiling up at Augustus.

"We'll be fine. Thanks." She walks him to the foot of the bridge.

"I'll call when we get the pony."

"Good." She feels his eyes on her. "Thanks for the Moon and Stars." She hazards a brief glance, turns away. "Safe home." Not at all certain if she's talking to him or herself.

After Vince kisses his children goodnight, he walks over to Connie. "I'll stop by tomorrow to see the kids."

"What time?" Connie asks, not leaving the circle.

"You're setting the agenda, so why don't you tell me."

Augustus, stopping mid-sentence, glances over.

"We'll probably go to a late Mass, then for pancakes, so about two, two-thirty?"

"I barely got to see them today. And tomorrow I have to leave by five. Can't they skip church?"

"I'd rather they didn't."

He leans over and says softly, "Connie, you're not going to deny me my children, too." Straightening up, he calls, "Goodnight, everybody," as he walks into the sudden dark.

Soon everyone leaves but Augustus. The three of them sit outside and talk long after the girls fall asleep. Slow easy talk of other summer nights when they themselves were children.

Augustus recalls the hours he'd spent on the roof of their mobile home, his face pressed against his father's arm sighting along its length to the extended finger pointing to the stars. In the Arizona desert. On the beach in Mexico. In the Canadian wilderness. Each latitude and longitude revealing a different piece of the constellations.

Connie remembers the small backyard, crowded with her parents and grandparents, her sisters with their girlfriends or dates, her brothers too, sometimes. She'd sit under the fig tree with her grandfather. The pleated paper cup of Italian ice collapsing as the sharp pain in the middle of her forehead expanded. The sweetish smell of the anisette in the espresso. The delicate china cups ringed in gold objects of intense longing.

For Rita, it was playing stickball under the streetlights in front of her house, the pwock of the pink Spalding, the nonsense chitter-chatter of the boys. Sitting on the stoop until the sweat turned into cool patches on her face. Coming into the dim house where the standing fan fluttered the sheer curtains, the light from the television like a black and white strobe on her father's face.

The memory leads Rita to the edge of melancholy. She backs away. "I don't know about you two, but I'm ready to call it a night."

Augustus stands up, holds his palms together with his thumbs close to his chest, and bows his head. "*Namaste.*"

They look at him expectantly.

"It's a Nepalese salutation, translated many ways. My favorite is . . . " He resumes the pose. "I honor that place in you where the whole Universe resides."

"Oh Augustus, that's beautiful," Rita says. "How do you say it again?"

"Na-ma-stay."

In a lovely duet, the women press their palms together, bow to Augustus, the single word magnifying as it escapes their lips.

# CHAPTER 29

"Does that hurt?" Rita asks as she brushes Anna's hair into a ponytail.

"Not one teensy bit," says Anna. "You brush softer than Mama. Grandma even."

"I'm a slow-poke is why." Rita ties a ribbon around Anna's locks. "There you go, pony-girl." Anna whinnies and prances. Although Ceci is theatrical, Anna has a true talent for mimicry.

"Me, too," Ceci begs. "Make me a ponytail, too."

"Okay, but then we have to vamoose before it gets too hot." Rita does her best to corral Ceci's thick curls into a lopsided ponytail while Connie packs a diaper bag for Gabrielle.

It wasn't Ceci's relentless reminders about the pony ride Matt offered that finally impelled Rita to chance another awkward encounter with him, but rather Anna's growing fascination with 'wildlife.' To a city kid like Anna, everything from ducks and deer to horses and cows are exotic. When most children her age were drawing upright, pink-eared bunnies, Anna sketched rabbits in muted grays and browns so cleverly blended in with the rest of the landscape that Rita had a hard time finding them all. A trick of Anna's also, to blend in, to disappear, reminding Rita of her own childhood, invisible to parents, lost to illness and despair.

They all pile into the Beetle for the trip to Matt's farm. Although it's not yet noon, the temperature already feels close to the ninety-degree forecast.

Fifteen minutes later, Rita parks in the shade of a maple and they walk over to where the horses stand tethered and saddled in the bright sun. Rita feels sorry for them.

"I thought it would be cooler here." Connie dabs at her face.

"It's August everywhere," Rita says.

Ignoring the black pony, Ceci runs right up to the chestnut mare and stands on tiptoes trying to touch the coarse mane.

"Whoa, little girl!" Walt scoops her up; Ceci reaches out for the saddle horn. As he walks her back toward the women, she lets out a scream that stops him in his tracks. He stands there helpless as Ceci blares in his ear.

"Guess you want to ride this one." Matt seats Ceci on the mare, steadies her with one hand, and grabs the reins with the other. He offers Rita a tight smile and says hello to Connie.

"How about you?" Walt says to Anna who's inching her way toward the pony.

"Go ahead, Anna," Rita says.

When Walt puts Anna on the pony, she grips the saddle horn with both hands, smiling weakly at Rita.

"Go slow, Walt," Rita says.

"Will do." He walks the pony toward the meadow chatting to Anna the whole time.

Connie and Rita settle Gabrielle under the canopy of a crooked elm tree. It's nearly an hour before the girls can be persuaded to dismount and by then even Ceci's wilting. Matt carries her over to the women. Walt and Anna trail behind. They all straggle into the cool farmhouse kitchen where Walt sets out pitchers of cold milk and iced tea and Matt stands at the counter making sandwiches. After lunch, Matt offers to take the girls to the barn to show them how to milk a cow by hand, the way it was done before the milking machines.

Ceci, revived, runs ahead of Matt when he holds open the door.

"I'll stay here with her." Gabrielle's eyes flutter slowly as Connie brushes the baby's brow. "Keep an eye on Ceci, Reet, you know how she is."

Anna, sketchpad in one hand, hooks her arm into Rita's as they head out to the barn where Ceci gags on the smell. Matt gives her a handful of hay to hold up to her nose. Rita takes some, too. It has a tangy sour scent.

"Cows have to drink two gallons of water for every gallon of milk they make. And they make about nine gallons of milk per day," he tells them. "It takes twelve and a half gallons of milk to make just one gallon of ice cream . . ."

During Matt's recitation of 'Where Milk Comes From' Anna sits down on a hay bale to draw while Ceci interrupts with a dozen questions.

"Uh, Matt," Rita interrupts, "I think they're on overload. You'd better get right to the milking."

He grabs a pail, sits on the milking stool, and presses his shoulder against the cow's massive mahogany flank. The girls giggle when he shows them the udder, then squirts milk into the metal pail. He gets flustered when he tries to instruct the girls how to pull the teats. "See? Like this. No, no—yes, that's right. Tug a little harder. Easy!" When Ceci sprays them both, he laughs his long open-throated way, turning around then to include Rita in their antics, still laughing; his shirt now sprinkled a darker blue, one arm around Ceci, his other hand swiping flecks of milk from his face.

It's all Rita can do to stop herself from helping him.

The girls chatter all the way home. The warm milk is 'yucky' according to Ceci, the long teats 'gross,' declares Anna. Rita steers the car around the bends, shifting up and down. Stops at red lights. Signals to turn. Pulls down the driveway, parks on the bridge. It's not until she turns off the ignition that she realizes she has no idea how in the world they got there.

After Rita showers, she puts on clean shorts and a t-shirt, then lies down on her bed. The window is level with the top branches of the pear tree. The few pears that fall to the ground are stunted, hard as nutshells, mottled with spots. Still, the tree emits a faint clean fragrance that soothes her, and its leaves scatter the sunrays into gold discs that shimmer on her legs, the sheets, the cat curled up by her feet. With her bare toes, she ruffles E's fur. The cat stretches and purrs. Concentric bands of tension relax their grip on Rita's temples as she savors this constellation of small pleasures.

The days have been pushing her along through the weeks and now the months of summer. Between the kids, the food bank, the gleaning project, and her devotions, she's barely had a minute to herself, keeps getting ambushed by waves of longing; washing Gabrielle's silky skin, singing hymns at Mass, watching Matt work. Maybe he's right and she can't make this decision in a vacuum, without traveling down that road some. But that feels like a lack of faith, like hedging her bet. There must be a part of her that knows which road is hers, that doesn't need an escort to find it.

The next weekend Vincent brings the girls back from a day at a local carnival, laden with trinkets and too stuffed to eat. It is 6:30 p.m. when Connie meets them at the front door. He holds it open. "Let me stay till they go to sleep."

"Vince—"

"I haven't spent any time with the baby. I can't stay till tomorrow. Marty needs me at the shop."

"All right. Since you won't have them tomorrow."

By nine, he's put the children to bed. Connie pretends to read a magazine under the bright overhead light at the kitchen table. When she hears him in the hallway, she studies an appliance ad.

"Ceci said it was okay with you if I bought her a pony," he says. "You're sure now? Because I wouldn't want to have the Shetland shipped all the way from—"

"Are you out of your—" She looks up and sees the big grin on his face.

He sits down at the table. "Now why would I do that, Con? You can't have horsies in Brooklyn."

"Vince, quit it . . ."

"Isn't there anything you want from me anymore?"

She goes to the sink to get a glass of water. He follows. "We need a car," she tells his reflection in the window. "I can't always rely on Rita."

Bill unloads the last cartons while Rita adds up the Empire State Grocers invoice for the third time. There must be some mistake. The demand at Loaves has slackened now that the migrant workers are beginning to move on and she's cut down on her order. She pulls last month's invoices for comparison. With the price increases, she's barely realized any savings. Just when she thought she was getting ahead. She signs the invoice and hands it to Bill. "Do you need a check today?"

He shakes his head. "Nah, we're even. I'll need one next time, though." He climbs into the cab, no longer hanging around since that time she practically accused him of lechery, even though she's tried to apologize. In the convent, acts of contrition are offered and accepted with alacrity. The secular world, it seems, is less forgiving.

She starts in on the stack of cartons then, suddenly weary, decides to wait for Janet to tackle shelving the order. In the convent, someone else is always around to lend a hand. At the kitchen table, Rita props her feet up and faces the paperwork instead, a chore she's been dreading. Needlessly, it turns out. Even with the price increase, between donations and grants, the food bank is finally holding its own. She jumps up and runs across the street for some celebratory jelly doughnuts, Janet's favorite.

It's still fairly warm but the sun is at a lower angle this time of day and the light is softer. Back-to-School Sale banners adorn the clothing, shoe, and stationers' stores. Tomorrow, she'll take Anna (who looks forward to school) shopping and let Connie deal with Ceci who regards kindergarten as incarceration. Rita grins, ducks into the bakery, and buys doughnuts enough for them all. When she gets home tonight, Ceci will clamber all over her, doughnuts or not, and Anna will wait patiently for Rita's embrace. She traces her steps back to Loaves, wishing the day was already over.

Janet's not due for a half-hour, so Rita works on reconciling her personal checkbook, biting into the sugary treat for sustenance. A glob of jelly blots out some of the entries, so she has to reconstruct them from the bank statement. With sticky fingers, she does the arithmetic. She wants to stretch what's left of her inheritance to tide them over till she decides her future and Connie gets on her feet. Another six months would be realistic. Let's say till spring. Rita recalculates. The powdered sugar–smudged sums add up to a monthly shortfall of nearly $200. Something else she never had to worry about at Holy Name. How much more can she stretch the budget? And herself?

"Dear God, give me strength," she prays, certain that He will.

Connie's as reluctant as the girls to let go of summer. After she put Gabrielle down for her nap, Connie hears the weather report call for heavy rains and high winds. Just when the gladioli are in their glory and the late summer tomatoes at their peak. She's mulched and planted, fertilized and watered all summer long, loving Laurel's garden, adding a few flowers of her own, some tomatoes, peppers, a few eggplants. There is no way she will let these last go without a fight.

"Come on, chicklets, let's get cracking." Connie doles out gardening stakes to Anna and Ceci, tucking a ball of string in her basket. "Let's get this done before it pours."

"These already have stakes." Anna points to a three-foot-high pepper plant.

"Only two. Let's do four." After Connie unwinds the string, she hands the end to Anna, sets two more stakes, looping the strand around each one, and tying it off when she gets to Anna. With all the plants tied up, the garden looks as if covered with cobwebs.

"Spidergirl!" Connie swoops Ceci up, twirls her around, and sets her down before chasing Anna who shrieks off, running around the house. Connie catches her before they collapse, giggling, onto the grass.

Rita stops at the Snow Goose on her way home.

"Augustus around?" she asks Trudy.

"Nothin' rounder." Trudy nods toward the kitchen. "Go on in."

"Don't distract me," he says over a stack of sliced onions, "when I'm cooking."

"Do you need help?"

"Too late. I'm almost done."

"I mean in the dining room."

"Ask Trudy if she wants a hand—"

"Augustus!" He stops mid-slice. "I need a job."

"Then you shall have one," he says, and Rita's grateful that he takes her at her word, not offering anything more than what she needs.

"How about waiting tables on the weekend? You'll still be feeding people Rita," he says, "and, on a good night, you'll take home a tidy sum."

At home, Rita takes off her coat and delivers her news along with the bag of doughnuts.

"It's too much!" Connie protests.

Rita shrugs. "It buys us time. And it's only Friday and Saturday nights."

"I'd talk to Vince if I thought it would do any good." Connie's tried, she has, but he's so damned clever. He agreed to supply groceries, as well as clothes and toys for the girls. He gave her the Valiant, and a gas allowance, but he won't give her money for rent or utilities. "Come home, where you belong," he tells her over and over. "I'll hire a housekeeper. You can go back to school if you want. Or get a job or stay home. I don't care. Just come home." She could attempt a divorce, do battle with him, her family, the court, and the church but she hasn't the strength.

So, Rita works weekends at The Snow Goose, weekdays at the food bank, with any free time devoted to helping with the children, determined to put aside her own decision for their sake.

Connie, just as determined to find some way to generate an income, installs a second-hand desk full of cubbyholes and drawers which she stuffs with seed catalogs and garden logs, articles on cold frames and greenhouses, and charts and graphs of her own design. She shares the desk with Anna, buying her a sunny yellow ceramic vase to hold her brushes, gives her a file drawer—with a lock and key—to store her artwork. They spend hours at the desk. Connie planning her gardens, Anna drawing. Whole afternoons with the radio playing old dance music or rock and roll. Cookie crumbs dust their respective papers.

Sometimes Connie's up half the night, shifting imaginary landscapes: monochromatic, crazy-quilt, aromatic, seasonal. She designs gardens for the stream bank, for Matt's farmhouse, for the deck outside the Snow Goose, a container garden for the sidewalk in front of Loaves and Fishes, and the back yard of her parents' house, working out from her grandfather's fig tree. She'll have the fall and winter to drum up business and come next spring, she plans to be ready.

# CHAPTER 30

It's a glorious day, brisk and bright with fiery autumn foliage, orange and red and gold. Connie enjoys driving, likes feeling the car respond to a twist of her wrist or her foot on the pedal. Vince always drove so she seldom had the chance. They started out late enough to miss most of Thanksgiving Day traffic, and the girls are behaving under threat of missing Grandma's turkey dinner.

Connie planted the last spring bulbs yesterday, an extravagant one hundred daffodils scattered throughout the perimeter of the property, which she's been burying surreptitiously for the past week, when the girls are at school and Rita's at work. She can't wait to see their faces when the flowers appear like golden coins in the new grass come spring. Rita has promised to stay that long, no matter what. *God. What would she do without Rita?*

Rita gets the car serviced, cuts the girls' hair, helps Anna with her homework, orders oil for the furnace, has the chimney cleaned, and checks the cats for fleas. Connie shops, cooks, cleans. Every once in a while, they slip a cog, run out of bread or diapers, have to run to the little store across the lake, but mostly they hold their own.

"Doesn't anyone cook anymore?" Rita blots her face with her apron before shouldering another tray of turkey dinners.

"Not if they can help it, apparently." Augustus, red-faced and sweltering, plates the next order and slides it under the heat lamp. "We're backing up. *Vamanos.*"

If the Snow Goose hadn't been booked solid for Thanksgiving, Rita would be at Rose's in Brooklyn with Connie and the girls. But after he's been so accommodating, Rita could hardly leave Augustus in the lurch. She serves a party of six, three adults and three children, scanning their faces, trying to sort out relationships. Single parents, stepfamilies? Makeshift groups of relatives and friends? Whatever, they are freely chosen. If she could choose hers, who would sit at her table? Connie and the kids, of course, and Immaculata. Catherine John. Ed. Janet. Who else? Someone's missing—

"Excuse me," says the man at a table of four, a couple with two small sons. "We'd like some more cranberry sauce."

"So would we," calls the elderly woman seated with five other women her age, and a lone, middle-aged man. Rita tries to figure that one out. Trudy bumps into her at the side station, knocking over Rita's tray filled with water glasses and dishes of cranberry sauce.

"Sorry, sorry. Damn it, sorry."

"That's okay," Rita says. Trudy looks beat, her limp more pronounced. Rita guesses she's not all that much younger than Immaculata. "Look, why don't you stay here, keep up with the water and condiments, and I'll run the dinners."

"Bless you," Trudy says.

"Back 'atcha," Rita answers with a wink, Trudy-style.

Tired of sitting so long, the girls jump out of the car as soon as Connie parks.

"Wait! Anna, here take the pies. Ceci, don't run!"

Connie lifts the baby from her carrier, grabs the diaper bag, and shoves the door closed with her hip. Despite the chill, she walks slowly toward the already crowded house.

Everyone's gathered around the dining room, waiting for their arrival. Seated at the far end is Father Mulvaney. To his left, Vincent. Connie whirls on her heel, finds Rose in the kitchen.

"What's he doing here?"

"It's Thanksgiving."

"And the priest?"

"What? He's our pastor." Rose puts down the turkey baster, clasps her hands together. "Please, *Cara*, let Father talk to you. Vincent agrees. What's the harm?"

"The harm? You want to know the harm, Mom? Okay, I'll tell—"

"What? The soup? It was an accident, sweetheart. The girl? He's a passionate man, your husband, hard-headed but he loves you—"

"Whose side are you on, Mom?" She can't believe she said that as if she were eight and squabbling with Carlo.

"The children, that's who," Rose says, as if that settles it, then pulls the bird from the oven.

Connie manages to get through dinner for the children's sake, although it's obvious that everyone except Carlo—who hugs her and whispers 'hang in there'—hopes for some holiday, Hollywood, happy ending. Vincent cozied up to the priest all through the meal, his eyebrows tented in supplication. He insists on washing up afterward and wrests the greasy turkey pan from Rose, then shoos her out of the kitchen. Connie dumps a stack of dirty plates on the counter so hard the bottom one cracks then flings the silverware into the sudsy sink.

"Tem-*per*," Vincent cautions, his face rosy, his smile sly.

She takes a deep breath, forces herself to saunter back into the living room where her sisters nest on the sofa, their husbands watch football on TV, the children play board games on the floor. While Rose cradles Gabrielle, Louis pours Amaretto for the priest who abides in the wing chair.

Connie gets her coat, slipping out the back door. She's halfway down the block before Carlo catches up with her. She shakes her head.

"Don't I know it," he laughs. "They're impossible."

"What do I have to do to make them understand?"

"They don't have to understand; they just have to accept your decision. Hold your ground."

"They've covered the field with reinforcements."

Carlo shrugs. "Make an end run. We'll stay out till the wee hours and you can split while they're asleep."

"The voice of experience."

"Yup."

They've reached the avenue. Across the street, a jaunty neon martini glass spills out Hide-a-While over and over. Carlo takes her hand.

"Sounds good to me," she says. "But let me call Anna. I don't want her to worry."

To her credit, Rose looks a little sheepish this morning and accepts without protest Connie's sudden departure a day earlier than planned. Connie figures it's all for the best. At least she'll have the weekend to get the kids back on some sort of schedule before they go back to school on Monday. Her tension unravels along the radius of the drive home, dissolving when she rounds the arc of the lake. She pulls up next to Rita's car, happy to be moored. They tromp into the house. The nightlight is still on in the kitchen.

"Reet?" Connie calls out.

"Up here." For once, Rita is still in bed, muscles aching, footsore.

Anna tiptoes into Rita's room. "Aunt Sister? Are you sick?"

"Hey, sweetie, come here." Rita pats the covers and Anna snuggles against her. "I'm not sick. Pooped." She gives Anna a squeeze. "You're home early."

"Daddy came to Grandma's. With the priest. To make Mama stay."

Rita's stomach clenches. She keeps her voice neutral. "Well, you're home now, Anna, safe and sound." She can feel the child's body relax before she hears Anna sigh. Rita holds her until the child drifts off to sleep, then pulls the quilt over her, wishing she could as easily shield Anna from her parents' sorrows. At least she can comfort and reassure her. It would have made a tremendous difference to Rita, had someone taken an interest when her mother was dying her long death, when much of her father faded along with his wife.

Although now she's wide awake, Rita stays in bed, reluctant to forfeit the uncomplicated joy she always feels caring for Anna. She hears Connie downstairs, putting Gabrielle down for her nap, setting things to rights. The house feels warmer somehow, looks brighter. The scent of coffee lures her to the kitchen where she and Connie drink to all the things they're thankful for.

Since the Friday and Saturday nights after Thanksgiving are unusually slow, Augustus encouraged Rita to work the busy Sunday brunch (the easiest shift, he'd told her, the best tips) but she still holds the day sacrosanct, as much for ritual pancake breakfasts with the girls as for her Christian duty. She and Connie take turns improvising pancake shapes and ingredients: mouse-ear pancakes, ghost pancakes, blueberry-banana-chocolate chip pancakes. Today she's making pumpkin pancakes with whipped cream on top.

Rita leaves for Mass at first light, but Connie languishes in bed until the baby starts whimpering then grabs a quick shower in the minutes before Gabrielle begins howling for her bottle. Connie scrounges in the refrigerator for the carton of milk. When she opens it, the foul smell makes her gag.

"Anna, honey, would you run to the store? We're out of milk."

Anna pulls her jacket over her sweatshirt, grabs Connie's change purse, and runs out the door. The cold pinches her ears and crawls down her neck. She pulls up the hood of her sweatshirt, tugs on the ties to seal her head inside the bubble of fabric. With each step the noise and urgency fade. Cutting through the woods, she comes upon some deer and stops. Pretending she is the doe and the fawn belongs to her, Anna creeps along behind them, The world shifts with the light in the wooded glen now filtered so finely that only a few shafts of sun hit a spotted flank or a dried spike of fern. Stepping as carefully as the deer, Anna avoids crunching deadfall, looking instead for pine needles patches to tiptoe on.

The doe, her hide rippling, tail switching, makes a slow circle around the roots of a tree, checks her fawn then ducks her nose into a fragrant mound of rotten apples, nibbling, lifting her head while she chews. Anna slowly, slowly, enchanted, suspended in time and place, circles a sapling not far from the deer, arches her neck, and chews on the tip of a low-hanging branch. She closes her eyes and wriggles her nose—milk, baby, noise, all lost.

A loud snappy crack in the woods opens her eyes and she sees the doe with her ears up and still. Anna copies the pose but just then the deer bolt, their white tails bouncing high as they rocket away. Dismayed, Anna plummets back to the milk, the store. She starts trudging through the thicket when a hot punch of metal slams her into the dirt.

Connie is just stepping into her jeans when an earsplitting noise snaps her straight and swivels her around to face the direction from which it came. She races out the door like a runner at the starting pistol, only it wasn't a pistol.

Too full of reverb, too big. *Shotgun.* Arms pumping, pajama top flapping, hair still wet from the shower she races toward the woods, her heart like a wild thing struggling to get loose, only her legs sure, churning the rest of her back to that shattered silence. Only now, there's not a sound. Just the pumping whoosh in her ears, the thud of her feet on the earth more felt than heard. In an endless loop of dread, she barrels to that intersection of time and space, seconds ago.

But Ed races up the lane past Connie, crossing the road before she does. When she gets there, he steps in front of her, tries to block her, slow her down, tell her . . . something. She crouches next to Anna, whose dark eyes drift unfocused, whose lips are almost as pale as her ashen cheeks, whose jacket is soaked and sticky with maroon. She holds onto her daughter's feet. Ed peels back Anna's jacket to apply pressure to the wound. Connie glimpses a flash of white in a field of red, pinkish matter exposed, then throws up into a pile of leaves. She wipes her mouth on her sleeve, refuses to budge, forces herself to watch her daughter's face as it loses so much color it passes pale to blue.

It seems an eternity before an EMT gently removes Connie's hands from Anna's ankles and places them on the rail of the gurney, guiding Connie into the ambulance as if she were a second victim. Later, she'll remember seeing Ed combat crawl into the woods and disappear. Now from the back of the ambulance, she watches Ed march a man dressed in hunter's camouflage down to the road. The hunter, a kid with a scraggly blond beard, is shaking and sobbing as two paramedics wrap him in a blanket and sit him down on the ground.

Hearing the siren so close to home, Rita fears the worst. She barrels past the cruiser's flashing lights and down into the driveway, races into the house. *If Vince, if he* . . . she chokes on the knowledge that in this moment she's entirely capable of killing him. Rita hurtles toward Ceci's screams. Ed is trying to calm the hysterical child. Snatching her up, Rita holds her tight while Ed explains what happened.

"No, no, nooooo!" Ceci cries and clings to Rita. Rita wants to go to Anna but she can't leave Ceci like this. "You go, Ed. Tell her I'll come as soon as I can."

Ed finds Connie shivering by the windows in the emergency room. She's in her pajama top and her hair is still damp from the shower. He takes off his flannel shirt, puts it on her, and snaps the snaps. "How is she?"

"I don't know, they won't tell me. They won't let me see her." These are the first words she's spoken out loud since the ambulance when the only word she said over and over was 'please.' The EMTs blurred past her, through the glass doors and straight down the hallway where men in green scrubs took Anna and then veered out of sight.

When Ed puts an arm around her, she presses her face into his chest, whispering "Please, you must know how bad? No, no don't tell me! Please, God . . . Ed, please."

He holds her as she lets loose, gagging on her tears and mucous until she goes limp against him. He sets her in a chair.

She sits down only to spring up the next second. "The children! No one's there. I can't leave Anna. My baby, my best girl, my—" Her throat closes hard and tight.

"Rita's there," Ed says. "She'll come as soon as she can. I'll stay with you till she gets here. Do you want me to call anyone?"

"Vincent," Connie whispers. "Call Vincent."

The only way Connie knows the difference between hours and seconds and days is by the industrial-sized clock-face, black and white, impartial.

Nine-thirty. Two forty-five. Four-fifteen. Seven hours. Eight. The day inks up to black. It's not only dark, but windy, and the emergency room echoes with groans from the trees outside the windows. Every so often, a woman with crow black hair tells her that the doctors are still working on Anna.

Connie paces and prays. A walking meditation: the Stations of the Cross, Hail Marys, the Lord's prayer, the Act of Contrition. Every prayer she's ever learned. She begs God for mercy, offering herself in Anna's stead, vowing eternal devotion to the Blessed Mother, if only she would intercede on Anna's behalf. As if on some surreal merry-go-round she circles the room: sliding glass doors, steel gray admitting desk, corridor to emergency room, long green wall, clock, rows of chairs, restrooms, wall of windows, wind, and dark, sliding glass doors—

Rita's frantic to get to Anna but it takes hours to calm Ceci and now she won't let Rita out of her sight. Rita can't take her to the hospital; it would only make things worse. She called Vincent when Ed told her to and left a couple of messages at Fields since there was no answer at the house. She hopes she's gone by the time he calls back. Who can she get to stay here? Janet's away for the holiday weekend, Ed's helpless with the kids, Augustus can't leave the restaurant . . . She has no choice. She dials Matt's number.

The doctor's words ricochet in Connie's brain.

"Slight concussion . . . punctured lung . . . bone fracture . . . torn tendons . . . ligaments . . . metal pins . . . morphine . . . lucky . . . ICU . . . second floor . . ."

She hesitates on the threshold. A pool of light spills from the hallway onto Anna's sleeping form even smaller on the raised hospital bed. She looks so pale and still. Loops of plastic tubing drape from her chest, her nose, her small helpless wrist. The thick swathe of bandages resembles a Girl Scout sash, only white. Connie strokes Anna's hair and holds the hand without the IV, then bends to listen to her daughter's shallow breaths. Deep breaths must be too painful, pulling at the shattered flesh, the knotted stitches.

She presses her lips to her daughter's forehead. It feels cool but clammy. Connie breathes her daughter in, a sharp, chemical scent, which seems somehow worse than all the bandages and tubes, an invisible, indelible alteration of Anna's essence. Connie trembles with the sudden and terrible truth that from this day forward, a part of her child is forever damaged; that Anna will mark this day in her memory: *before and after.* Her chest feels crowded with all the Annas before this one lying torn and broken. Connie weeps as silently as she's able, for as long as it takes. Until she can see clearly, speak steadily. Then she arches her body above Anna's, one hand on each rail, leans in, and promises, "You're going to get well, sweetheart. I'm going to watch over you, Anna, like a fleet of angels, like a thousand suns."

Connie drops to her knees, closes her eyes. "Holy Mary, Mother of God, heal my child and I pledge to you a daily devotion from now until the hour of my death, amen."

When Rita finally gets to the hospital, Connie's asleep in the chair. Rita draws a ragged breath seeing Anna, still as stone, swaddled in sheets. Her own body imagines every insult to Anna's. Rita's chest hurts, and her shoulder, her skin throbs just looking at the IV needle stuck in Anna's vein. Shaking, Rita tracks down a nurse, learns what Connie found out an hour ago. Anna's lucky. Lucky she's alive. Rita can't stop her tears, can't stop shaking, a long exhale of tremors she'd been holding onto since Ed told her Anna was shot.

Connie is standing over Anna when Rita gets back to the room. "She was moaning," Connie tells her, "but she hasn't opened her eyes."

"She will."

"I know."

Rita puts her arms around Connie. "You look like a zombie."

"I know."

"But a cute zombie."

"I know."

"Con?"

"Who's with the kids?"

"Matt."

"Did Vince call back?"

"Not before I left."

Connie looks up teary-eyed. "Oh Reet, I've been so selfish. When Anna gets well, I'll find a way to support them, you can have your life back, I won't be a burden—"

"You're not."

"An obstacle then."

"Not that either."

"Of course I am."

Rita's never heard Connie sound so fierce.

"Now you go home, and you thank Matt and you kiss my babies for me."

"What if Vincent shows up?"

Connie gives her a clear-eyed look, tilting up her chin. "Of course he'll show up, he's her father." Connie crosses her arms over her chest. "Don't worry, Rita. I can handle him now."

Hauling her weary self into the dark house, Rita turns on the kitchen light, then the nightlight in the girls' room. Ceci's curled up in a nest of blankets.

Gabrielle is snoring lightly, a clear bubble of saliva inflating with every breath, which smells faintly sour. Rita checks the baby's diaper. It's dry but unpinned. Rita smiles at Matt's handiwork.

She finds him asleep on the sofa, and sinks into the rocker, trembling with exhaustion.

He wakes at the sound. "How's Anna?"

"Oh Matt, we could have lost her," she says. The very words sabotage the last of her composure.

"Rita," he says and stands up but then hesitates. "Come here." Matt opens his arms.

She staggers over and tilts into them, her limbs loosening as his tightens around her. She clings to him, hungry for his weight on her, as if to hold down her suddenly frail self from capricious fate. Gratefully, she succumbs to the succor of his mouth and hands and receives him and rocks with him until thought and memory cease and there is only this.

Vincent arrives at the hospital at two in the morning. Connie struggles up bleary-eyed from the black hole she'd sunk into an hour ago. Instinctively she holds out her arms but Vincent walks past her to Anna. He lifts a damp clump of hair from her forehead, strokes her forearm, puts his ear to Anna's chest as if to reassure himself her heart still works.

"Vincent . . . "

When he turns to face her, his cheeks are wet, his mouth clamped down.

"What happened?"

"A hunter mistook her for a deer. He sh—she was wounded, right below her shoulder. The doctor said—"

"I know what the doctor said. I just spoke to him. Tell me how it happened."

Connie looks at Anna, "Not here."

They walk into the glare of the hallway and Connie starts toward the visitors' lounge.

Vincent stops her a few feet from Anna's room. "I want to be near if she wakes up."

They stand opposite the nurses' station. Connie watches them consult their charts, pad in and out of rooms, whisper to each other in calm, earnest tones. She adopts the same tone as she tells Vincent about the milk, the store, the shotgun, the horrible echo. He listens but does not look at Connie, staring instead at the doorway to Anna's room. He's still staring when Connie finishes.

"Vince?"

"You sent her to the store alone."

"She used to go all the time."

"In Brooklyn. Down a block where everyone knew her. Not on a freezing cold day in the woods during hunting season."

"I didn't know it was hunting season. And Anna knew she wasn't allowed to cut through the woods."

"So, it's her fault?"

"No! I don't know . . . the boy who hurt her."

"He couldn't have if you were watching her." Vince talks in low measured tones.

"You blame me," she whispers.

"I hold you responsible."

His words spring open the trap door she's been trying to avoid and she plummets into the dark cell where, in her heart of hearts, she'd already condemned herself.

# CHAPTER 31

As if from a great distance, as soundless as pantomime, Rita registers Matt's arm draped across her bare hip, his body spooning hers in a warm and solid embrace. She turns around, slowly to not wake him, although she can't resist touching him, describing the line from his brow to his jaw with her fingers, his skin smooth from his hairline to the bristly eyebrow, smooth again before whispery scritch of new beard. She rests her open palm on his sternum, splays her fingers to feel his heart thrum. Then breathless, bold, she caresses his hip, the length of his thigh, holds the velvet weight of his sex in her cupped palm, is just about to nuzzle the hollow above his clavicle when Gabrielle whimpers, breaking the spell, slipping the film from its sprockets, slapping Rita awake and into a state of longing so intense that turning her back on him seems sacrifice enough to expiate her sin.

She peels herself from Matt's embrace, pulls her eyes away from his naked beauty, and, without even a sheet to cover her, picks up Gabrielle. The baby clutches at Rita's breast, her lips working in unison with her grasp, as primal, perhaps, as her own overwhelming need for contact and comfort last night.

That exquisite pleasure and powerful connection she felt with Matt must have started Connie down this same road with Vince, a road that veered into disappointment, heartache, finally dead-ending in despair. No guarantee that won't happen to her.

Quickly and quietly, she heats up a bottle for Gabrielle, cradling the baby while she feeds her. An intense pleasure of a different order of magnitude: this tiny, perfect creature. But this, too, is fraught with peril Rita thinks, picturing Connie holding vigil at Anna's side.

Immaculata once asked Rita what's she sure of. Funny how the answer remains the same, but the circumstances continue to elude her. Rita knows this much. In her heart of hearts, she hasn't chosen, not yet, despite her weakness last night. God will certainly forgive her this singular, all too human transgression. She's not so sure about Matt.

As soon as the baby falls asleep, Rita puts her back in her crib, checks on Ceci, then showers and dresses. By the time Matt gets up she's ready.

He ducks into the bathroom, then comes out ten minutes later, in his rumpled jeans, his hair slicked down with water, his face scrubbed but unshaven. He kisses her forehead, her cheek, her lips, holds both her hands in his, and stands there smiling. He doesn't seem to realize that she isn't.

"Matt."

"What is it, sweetheart?"

"That wasn't . . . ought not to be, a commitment. It was a lapse—glorious and thrilling—but not a solemn promise—"

"It was for me."

"Oh, Matt, I'm so sorry. If that's what's meant for me, for us, I want to get there unencumbered, after I decide about Holy Name." His smile fades, his shoulders hunch as if to ward off the words, his fingers strangle his keys. Now she stings with shame, as she watches Matt leave in a fog of regret.

Connie allows no one except Rita to spell her, defying the hospital rules, staying overnights. Rita takes up the chores that Connie forfeits: laundry, housework, cooking.

When Rita visits, Anna lets her stroke her hair, spoon some simple nourishment between her lips—ice cream, oatmeal. After a week, the chest tube is removed and Anna's appetite increases. She's more clear-headed and less weepy. By the end of a second week, she's well enough to go home with a schedule for rehabilitation therapy and a prescription for painkillers.

Rita makes up her own room for Anna, filling it with books and sweets, and stuffed animals. She'll take the bunk bed until Anna's well. Connie finds Tabitha sprawled out on the hearth and carries the mewling cat upstairs. It squirms out of Anna's arms, settles at the foot of the bed. Connie fits herself into whatever space is left.

"It'll be better when she can paint again, Con, you'll see." Rita plugs in the heating pad and puts it behind Connie's back, kneads her shoulders. Rita hasn't told Connie about Matt. That's between her and Matt. And God. Besides Connie has enough on her plate.

"She's still having nightmares." Connie sighs. "Last night she wet the bed."

"I wish I didn't have to be gone so much." Rita is developing a begrudging respect for Vince, who often worked two jobs and always provided for his family. Between the food bank and the restaurant, the house and the children, Rita has little or no time for meditation, or visiting Holy Name or rest. Still, it's worth it. Anna's getting stronger. So is Connie.

Connie answers the door one bitterly cold December day to find Augustus delivering cinnamon buns. Anna joins them at the kitchen table, cozy now with the three of them drinking tea, the mouth-watering scent of the buns warming in the oven. Leafing through one of the seed catalogs, she finds a picture of a radish she wants to copy, so with tea in hand, she returns to the desk.

"She's doing wonderfully well," Augustus says.

"Divine intervention. I made a vow of devotion to the Blessed Mother," Connie says. "I've thought about a statue but I hate seeing them like knick-knacks around the house, or worse, as lawn ornaments. But I want to do something . . . ceremonial."

Augustus taps the Burpee catalog. "What about a Mary Garden?"

"You're making that up." Connie laughs.

"Not at all." He reaches in his jacket pocket for his pipe. "According to folklore, after Adam and Eve were banished, only Mary, who was without original sin, was allowed into the Garden of Eden."

Augustus holds a match to the pipe's bowl and Connie inhales its smoky herbal smell. "Look at Medieval religious art. In Mary's Garden the Virgin and Child are surrounded by symbolical flowers. Columbine is said to have sprung up wherever Mary's foot touched the earth, thus it's called Our Lady's Shoe. Marigold: Mary's Gold. Morning glory: Our Lady's Mantle."

"How do you know all this stuff?"

"Because I am the Wizard," he intones.

She laughs. "You are, you know. At least to me." She reaches for his hand.

He gives hers a little shake. "But if you remember the story, my dear, he's a fraud."

Connie checks out library books on folklore and legends, propagating seeds. She and Anna make a list of Mary flowers. They find hundreds of them:

Anna chooses the ones they'll plant: Bachelor's button (Mary's Crown), aster (Mary's Star), forget-me-not (Mary's Eyes). Anna paints a picture for each. "Write down all their names, Mama," Anna says and waits, plucking at the fabric near her wound.

"Does it hurt, honey?"

"Not a lot."

Connie adds the Latin names as well to the bottom of each page. "By the time these flowers bloom, Anna, I promise you'll be good as new."

They all decorate the balsam fir Rita hauls in one day and sets up near the fireplace. With ornaments Anna makes, strings of popcorn, a papier-mâché angel Rita bought at Sears along with twinkling lights and tinsel.

A few days before Christmas, while Rita's out with Ceci, Vince shows up with shopping bags of presents from his in-laws and himself. He sets a good-sized box at Anna's feet.

"Don't lift it, honey. Just open it," he says.

Anna kneels down and unwraps a dark wooden chest. She lifts the lid and gasps. Inside, there's a tray divided into big rectangles and tiny squares filled with erasers, a set of color pencils, another of pastels, a pencil sharpener, a half-dozen brushes. Vince kneels next to his daughter and picks up the tray. Underneath, a compact watercolor field kit, water container, rubber cement, sponges, dozens of watercolors, each palette distinct, boxed in grids under clear plastic lids.

Anna opens the little field kit, unfolds the clever arrangement of the assorted paints, the pocket brush, sponge, the fold-out mixing basins, and the little reservoir, her face a portrait of rapture. After she puts everything back, she hugs Vincent's neck. Then kisses him. For the first time in almost a year. She leaves her present on the floor and scampers out of the room.

"To get you a present," she tells her father.

"How's the scar?" Vince asks Connie, wiping his eyes. "She won't let me see it."

"Not terrible. But she avoids looking at it, and she hates when I do." Connie runs a hand over the wooden chest. "What a lovely gift, Vincent. She's thrilled."

He rummages in one shopping bag after another and pulls out a present.

"For you." He tosses it onto Connie's lap.

"You shouldn't have. The children, okay. But not me. I didn't get you anything." She hands the present back to him.

"It's just a little something, Con. If you don't like it, you can just chuck it."

She laughs when she sees the goofy earmuffs, hairy with fake fur. "I'll probably need these," she grins, "even though I'll look like Sasquatch."

When she takes them out, she sees the tiny blue box. Her eyes travel to Vincent's then back to the box. She can't resist opening it. Inside lie the ruby and dropped-pearl earrings. Connie holds them up to the light and they give off a fire of their own.

"I wanted to get them for Valentine's Day but Christmas will do." He tells her then what he had planned to say ten months ago, how they remind him of the rosy flush of her skin when they make love.

"Oh, Vince they're exquisite." She slowly puts the earrings back in their satin nest, closes the blue box, and puts it on the couch next to Vincent. "But I'm sorry. I can't. We're not—"

"Here, Daddy," Anna hands him a tube of paper tied with a green ribbon. "Merry Christmas."

It's a picture of Connie in the rocker holding Gabrielle. Anna and Ceci sitting on the floor in front of their mother, the kitten on Anna's lap. Rita dressed in jeans and her veil, standing sentinel, E curled up at her feet. They're all watching Vince on TV.

# CHAPTER 32

"Doesn't your friend have family? Parents, siblings?" Mother Superior finally says, looking up from the papers on her desk.

"Yes, but they all live in Brooklyn, too, and her husband's insidious," says Rita. "Besides, Connie is starting a plant business and the city is no place for that."

Mother sits back in her chair with a faint click of her rosary beads. "You think she's capable?"

"She majored in botany."

"That's not what I meant," Mother says, studying Rita's face. "I mean will she be able to sustain a job and a family on her own."

"Women do."

Mother sighs. "Again, that's not what I asked."

"I think so. I hope so."

"Six more months."

Rita nods. "The funding for a coordinator for the food bank starts the first of July. I can hire someone to take over, maybe even Connie if that's what she wants."

"And you, Sister, do you know what you want?"

At this moment, in this austere room with its bare white walls, and worn planked floors, it seems to Rita as if she does. "It's not the poverty that's daunting, Mother. People's lives are so complicated, compromised in a thousand ways by the claims they make on one another."

"The difference between love and charity."

Rita nods. "Here, we're outside all that, somehow."

"It can seem that way, I suppose." Mother Superior says, reaching for a pen. "You may take the time. Just be careful your concern for your friend isn't an excuse to avoid making a decision."

Rita walks over to the window. "I don't see how I can abandon them."

"I'm not questioning her need. You're too fond of helping, Jude," Mother says, not unkindly. "God also loves a grateful receiver."

Rita watches a couple of women dressed in colorful ski parkas and knee-high boots make their way across the courtyard. "I didn't know we were having a retreat this weekend."

"We're not," Mother Superior says, fighting a smile. "Look closer."

Rita catches up with them outside.

"Jude!" Sister Catherine John says, hugging her. "You're back! And none too soon, you look like a rail."

"Are you unwell?" Sister Theresa asks, looping her arm through Rita's.

"Tired. And I'm not back." Rita fills them in as they make their way to the refectory where Sister Immaculata, in full habit, stands on a stepstool rinsing salad greens.

"Let me help."

Immaculata turns around. "You look exhausted."

"I'm taking six more months."

Immaculata turns back to her work.

"I know you think I'm on an ego trip and maybe I was, but Anna is healing and Connie's getting back on her feet and I'm making plans, I am, to hand over the food bank and I can't think just of myself, not yet . . . Immaculata? Please. I need your blessing."

The monastery bells peal as the last of the light leaves the sky. "You have my prayers. Come," Immaculata says. "We'll pray together for you and your friend and her children."

In the little chapel, the sweet sound of the sisters' voices renders Rita mute and she can only mouth the familiar prayers. Everything seems to gleam in the candlelight or maybe that's just because she's holding back her tears.

The phone rings as soon as Connie walks into the kitchen. "Happy New Year," Vince says. "And how did my girls celebrate?"

Connie pinches the phone to her ear with her shoulder while she folds a raw egg into the ground beef. "They stayed up till midnight and toasted each other with Shirley Temples. And you?"

"What do you think, Con? I was out on the town?"

She sighs. "I don't know, Vince."

"How's Anna?"

In a greased pan, Connie shapes the meat into a loaf. "Better physically, but still withdrawn. The scar upsets her. I'm not sure if it's just how it looks or that it's a constant reminder."

"You sound beat."

"I'm fine."

"Come home, Connie. It would be so much easier. I could take Anna to the best plastic surgeons in New York—"

"Is that a pre-requisite for helping your daughter?"

"Of course not. But, please, Con . . . It's a brand-new year, let's wipe the slate clean, start over—"

"I already have." Connie takes a deep breath. "I'm not going backward, Vince, and nothing you can say will make me change my mind."

He hangs up so quietly that only the dial tone tells her he's no longer there.

"We got slammed tonight," Rita says, shrugging out of her coat. "Are the girls still up?"

"Anna must be. She just finished her bath."

"Augustus sent this home."

Connie opens the paper sack Rita hands her, pulls out a flaky, golden lemon bar, takes a bite. "Yum. He made these? Marry him, Rita, the hell with Matt."

Rita hasn't disabused Connie of the notion that Matt's still waiting for Rita to make a choice. She'd have to tell Connie what happened that night and she won't expose either Matt's distress or her own shame.

Rita sets a pastry on a tray. "Okay if I take one up to Anna?"

"Be my guest."

Rita adds a glass of milk and carries the tray upstairs. She's amazed that Connie still advocates marriage after what she's been through. Whatever the reason—the weather, his schedule—Vince hasn't been around much lately and Rita is profoundly grateful. His visits leave Anna anxious, Ceci revved up, Connie exhausted and Rita just plain furious at how he upsets their hard-won equilibrium.

Anna's kneeling on the floor, paintbrush in hand, poised over what looks like a map. Her pajama top gaps at the neck, exposing her scar. It tattoos her flesh like a grotesque flower, the dark red center and its paler petals, fixed precisely where a corsage may someday be fastened to her prom gown, just above the rise of her someday breast.

"Hey, sweetie," Rita says, setting the tray on the desk then kneeling next to Anna. "What are you working on?"

"Look, Aunt Sister," Anna says sitting back on her heels.

It's an aerial view of the house, including the bridge and the stream, even the little lane all the way down to the lake. "This is incredible Anna, just the way everything looks from a bi-plane. I still owe you a ride. That's the first thing we're going to do when it gets warm. Deal?"

"Deal," Anna says, wrapping her arms around Rita's waist.

"Oh look, there's my car, at the top of the drive, you clever girl. But what's that?" Rita points to a splash of color she missed at first glance.

"That's my Mary garden. The one Mama's making for me," Anna says. "See. Blue for Forget-Me-Nots, orange for Marigolds, a pink Morning Glory . . . "

Rita's willing to bet anything that Anna's got it just right.

"You must know someone." Rita sorts through the mail at Loaves while Janet writes up the backorder.

"Not really, there aren't any pediatric plastic surgeons on staff," Janet says. "You'd have to go to a bigger hospital. Children's in Boston, maybe, or NYU Medical Center."

"Sounds expensive." Rita stacks the bills in one pile, correspondence in another.

"Isn't Anna's father a big shot actor?"

"Small shot. He probably could swing it. But the less Connie has to rely on him, the better off she is."

"The scar's probably not the worst of it, anyway," Janet says, leaning against the counter. "I see parents who fixate on the physical symptoms—the baldness, vomiting, weight loss—but can't deal with the child's grief. Adults delude themselves into thinking they can protect their children even when the kids know that's just not true."

"I think with Anna it may be the other way around. She's always been very protective of Connie."

"The little adults. It's worse for them. They have a hard time relying on anyone but themselves." Janet thumbtacks the order to the bulletin board.

"That's not the worst fate," Rita says.

"If you don't mind going it alone."

"You go it alone."

"But I mind, Rita."

Rita looks up.

Janet waves her off. "No sermons."

"I wasn't—"

"You and I tend to the sick and the poor and there's nothing wrong with that. But we don't draw any lines between our work and our personal life because we don't have one." Janet slings her purse over her shoulder.

"But you go skiing, have boyfriends—"

"I blow off steam, Rita, I don't have boyfriends." Janet opens the side door. "But I'd be interested in Matt if he was available."

"He isn't?" Rita blurts out.

"Not according to Inez. She works at the hospital now. That anonymous hundred-dollar donation? I bet it was from her."

Rita waits until Janet leaves to go through the client cards. *Inez Inez.* She only came to Loaves for a couple of months. There was something about her . . . here's the card. Inez Flores. Rita scans her notes. Oh. The beautiful, wild-haired woman. The one with the ebony eyebrows. The one who told Rita that nothing's for free.

It's not yet dark by the time Rita finishes calling in the backorder and balancing the books but it's still February for a few more days at least, and so wintry that all she wants to do is relax in front of the cozy fire she prays

Connie has started, and sip cocoa and play Parcheesi with the girls. Shivering, she turns the car heater on full blast.

Not only is there no fire or wood smoke, Rita nearly trips over the suitcases in the hallway. "Connie? Con?"

"I'm down here," Connie calls from the basement.

Rita races down the stairs. "What's going on? Where are—"

"I *told* you Vince would come through," Connie laughs. "He got Anna an appointment at Beth Israel in the city next week. He can't leave the set, so I'm going to take her."

"Next week. Why are you packing now?"

"Because you and I are driving the girls to my parents' tomorrow morning."

"I can't. I'm working—"

"I already called Augustus. You can have the day off, Rita. We both could use a break."

"Rose looks like the mother ship," Rita says, laughing.

She and Connie have said their goodbyes but linger for one last look at Gabrielle napping on Rose's shoulder while Ceci traces the Kiss The Cook letters on Rose's industrial-strength apron. Even Anna is nestled against Rose's bosom, whispering God-knows-what tender secrets, as her grandmother nods with her eyes lasered onto that serious little face.

"Yeah, they're docked," Connie says. "Let's go while the going's good."

It's one of those winter days so crisp and brilliant, the sun looks like shards of light cutting the landscape into stark relief.

"You realize we're going to hear '*Grandma* let me' for weeks to come," Connie says, pulling away from the curb. "But five whole days, it's more than worth it."

"Want me to drive so you can start relaxing?"

"What's the opposite of relax? That's what I want," Connie says. "The seeds are all ordered, except for the heirloom tomatoes. I'm still waiting to hear if Four Corners will lease me the greenhouse space. I can handle all the herbs between the basement under grow lights and the cold frame Ed's helping me build, but if Ginger comes through at the farm, I may be able to double or triple the savory yield in addition to growing heirloom varieties but at the very least I can get a jump on the growing season especially—"

"Slow down!"

"Believe me, five days is not that long—"

"*Now.* Slow down now. You're doing seventy-five."

"Let's stop at the Snow Goose," Connie says as they approach the lake. "Augustus should be free now, right?"

Rita glances at the dashboard clock. "For a couple of hours."

The restaurant is empty except for Trudy, who's topping off the salt and pepper shakers at a table by the window. "Thought you took the day off, hon," Trudy says.

"I did, but this one," Rita says, pointing to Connie, "has cabin fever. Where's Augustus?"

Trudy nods toward the frozen lake where dozens of skaters circle a safe distance from a gaggle of boys playing ice hockey.

Rita can't spot Augustus, big as he is, until he gets up on his knees. He manages to stand, wobble off and skate for a minute before he lurches and falls again. "You're kidding."

Trudy shakes her head. "He's a lot better now that he's been at it for a couple of days. See, already he's up again, and there he goes—whoa, whoa—c'mon stay up there—ooouff, that's got to hurt."

"He's going to crack his thick skull," Connie says. "Make him stop, Rita."

"I'm busy," Rita says pulling up a chair next to Trudy. "You try."

Connie makes her way down to the lakeside. "Augustus!" she calls. "Over here."

She watches his bulky torso hurtle toward her across the lake, his face crimson from the cold or the effort; it's hard to tell. He shoots past her and collapses on the shore. Connie hurries to his side. His skin is flushed and glistening, his breathing's labored.

"Don't look at me that way," Augustus gasps. "I haven't lost my mind."

"Then why on earth are you risking your fool neck?" Connie tugs at his scarf.

He grabs her hand, tucks it inside his jacket, and places it over his heart. Its rapid lub-dub bounces against her palm. "I told you. Because this gets stronger every time you take a leap of faith."

"Faith in what?"

"That you'll survive," he laughs.

"God, it smells wonderful in here," Connie says when they get back inside. "What's on the menu tonight? Some kind of meat. Beef. With . . ." she sniffs, "cinnamon?"

"Good nose. Beef shanks braised in cinnamon and star anise," he says.

"Star Anise. Do chefs use a lot of it? Maybe I could try growing that, too."

"You'd need about fifteen years, even in China. It's not grown here."

"Don't put it past her," Rita says. "I've seen what she's done with a backyard in Brooklyn."

Connie cooks and freezes spaghetti sauce, bakes two batches of cookies, chocolate chip for Anna, peanut butter for Ceci, then finishes the laundry. She's pulling linens from the dryer when she hears a knock at the door. She runs her fingers through her hair, dumps the towels on the kitchen table, and opens the door. A squat little man, his jacket straining across his paunch, stares up at her.

"Constance Leonetti?" he pipes.

When she nods, he hands her a thick envelope, turns on his heel, and scurries away.

Connie rips it open and scans the document.

*Vincent Leonetti (AKA Vincent Leone), petitioner*

*Vs.*

*Constance Leonetti, respondent*

*RE: Custody of Anna, Cecelia, and Gabrielle Leonetti*

*Petition for sole custody.*

*Reckless endangerment. Neglect. Anna's gunshot wound. Cecelia's fall on the ice last winter and repeated ear infections. Dates and times petitioner found the children crying, distraught, ill, unkempt. The six weeks Anna missed school. The respondent incompetent, unstable. Entertaining male persons.*

She's shaking so hard it takes three tries to dial her parents but the line is busy. Then she tries Vincent but he doesn't pick up. When she calls Rita, she races home from the food bank in ten minutes flat.

It's Rita who redials the phone until she gets through to the Pescatores and pieces the story together. Connie tumbles in and out of rage, despair, grief. She waits for a lull in Connie's sobbing and screaming to tell her what she's found out. That Vincent had treated his in-laws with last-minute tickets to *Pippin*. How he offered to stay with the kids. That when they came home from the theater last night, they found the note saying he took the children home with him. How they weren't worried, assuming he would drop the children off on his way to work. When he didn't show up this morning Louis drove to the house. Vincent answered the door, said he's taking custody of the children, that he was sorry but he had no choice.

"That's the first time I've ever heard your father curse. Your mother's beside herself. Vincent just informed her he hired a housekeeper."

Connie finally gets him on the phone. "How can you do this?"

"What? Protect my children?"

"Take them away from their mother, you bastard."

"I brought them home, their mother is welcome to join them," he says.

She can hear Ceci in the background. "What did you tell them? Put Anna on the phone."

"Sorry, Con, Mrs. MacLeod just got here, I've got to go."

"Just let me say hello to—" Connie says before the line goes dead.

"He sat right there," Connie punches the air toward the couch, "handing me rubies and pearls, biding his time, knowing if I didn't give in, he'd go to plan B."

"We'll get a lawyer, fight him in court."

"Who's going to pay him? Vince?" Connie spits out the word.

"I'll find a way to get the money, he can't get away with—"

"Rita. It's Vincent, remember? He always wins. No matter what."

They talk to a lawyer anyway. Connie and Rita. Louis and Rose. Carlo. As if their sheer numbers could tip the scales in Connie's favor.

Had Connie reported Vincent's violent outbursts to the police? No. Were there any witnesses? No. Did she seek medical attention? No. Were the facts stated in the subpoena true? Not the characterization of Connie as incompetent but the dates and incidents? Yes.

Absent the shotgun wound Connie would have had a chance to regain custody. Given the detailed documentation and the severity of Anna's trauma, the best they can hope for now is to contest his petition for sole custody and to argue for unsupervised shared custody, or for Vincent to change his mind.

"You'll be fine, Con," Rita says in the corridor outside the courtroom. "Just tell the truth."

Connie, looking as pale and delicate as lilacs, clings to Rita before allowing the lawyer to escort her to the defendant's table. Rita takes a seat behind them, closes her eyes, and silently prays the Breastplate.

> *May God's strength pilot her*
> *God's might uphold her,*
> *God's wisdom guide her,*
> *God's ear hear her,*
> *God's word to speak for her,*

As soon as she hears the little gasps of recognition, Rita's heart sinks. She turns around to see two women whisper to each other as Vince walks into the courtroom. The court stenographer gawks at his familiar face.

He testifies first. "I took the children to protect them, your honor. Their mother had removed them from the home twice before, without my knowledge or consent."

"When was this, Mr. Leone?" Vincent's lawyer deliberately uses his stage name.

"The first time was a little over a year ago, Your Honor. Then again last May."

"How would you characterize your wife's emotional state at the time?"

Vincent recites, seemingly with reluctance—the liar!—a catalog of

Connie's faults and shortcomings. Affidavits. Times and dates. Medical records. His demeanor humble, his voice soft but firm, his eyes blinking back tears. Convincing.

By the time Connie takes the stand, she's shaking. Her voice trembles, belying her attempts at composure, giving credence to Vince's portrayal of her as unstable, overwhelmed.

Rita hears the judge's voice echo down what feels like eternity. "Temporary custody granted to the petitioner. The respondent is allowed supervised visitation until further notice."

# CHAPTER 33

Rita has known the prayerful silence of Vespers, the deliberate silence of anger, and the helpless silence of illness. This silence is unlike any she has ever known, the children's music subtracted from the universe.

Around the house, she and Connie speak to each other in choked whispers as if there's only so much oxygen and they have to make it last.

Connie drives to Brooklyn to steal hours with her children. If Rita can get away, they go together. The ride down is like a roller coaster, the ride home like a wake.

Connie's not permitted to see them alone. Either Vince or a court-appointed guardian accompanies them to her mother's, the playground, or an overheated restaurant.

"Now you know how it feels," he tells her.

In the middle of the night, a plaintive cry forces Connie out of bed. She's cried herself to sleep so often her eyes feel like sandy marbles. It's E meowing to go out or maybe just because she's lonely for Tabitha. The one time Connie defied the court order. When she'd brought the kitten over to Anna after her surgery. Even Vince hadn't objected. Anna needed her mother's touch, the kitten's velvet presence.

Connie lets the cat outside. Moonlight lattices the bridge, casting shadows of overhanging branches onto the cold blue light. A waterfall of clouds cascades down to the black horizon. The sky so bright that after she looks away, everything else seems darker than before.

She crawls back to bed and flattens herself against the mattress. The more desperate she feels, the more still she becomes, unable to move, barely able to breathe. There have been fleeting moments when an unexpected surge of strength infuses her limbs and she springs up only to be knocked over by an errant thought as powerfully as if she's standing in a turbulent surf. The times she resented the children. The freedom she felt when she foisted them on Rita or Vince. A moment she'd wished them gone or never born.

There's not enough work in the world to fill the cavern in Rita's heart, but it's the only thing that keeps her sane. She takes on as many shifts as Augustus will give her, shows up at Loaves and Fishes every day, whether she's scheduled or not, to work on grants or meet with donors or just sweep the floors, careful to leave before Matt gets in on Tuesdays. One day she runs late when Matt arrives early and she barrels into him at the side entrance.

As soon as she sees him, she flinches, expecting the contempt she deserves for not understanding, as dear God, she does now, how much it hurts to be denied. She is sorry for taking for granted the implacable fact of his decency, so sorry and ashamed, she backs away, hurrying past him.

"Rita," he says.

She cannot make her body take another step, nor is she able to turn around and face him.

"I'm sorry," he says.

"No, no, it's all my fault, I never meant to—"

"About the children."

For some reason, she can scarcely breathe. "Poor Connie," she manages to say.

"Poor Rita." He clasps her shoulder as if to grant her courage or benediction.

As soon as he lets go, her pulse thunders in her ears and her face goes rigid with the effort not to crumple. She crosses her arms over her chest as if to restrain her wayward heart and waits until she's able to speak before she turns around. By the time she does, he's gone.

In the blustery wind, Connie walks the old neighborhood. The yellow heads of daffodils struggling in the blasts, the purple crocus blinking up at her, remind her of the Easter she had been showing her grandfather her drawings of the *Ficus carica* when he started lurching around in classic *commedia dell'arte* style. She'd been laughing at his theatrics when his face blazed red and he fell flat, his palms still clasping his shirt pocket into a nosegay of plaid. Before she could say his name. Before she understood.

The day turns wavy and opaque. Blinking it back into focus, she stomps across the street, cutting away from that chasm of pain.

She resists walking past her house, fearful that Vince will get a restraining order, further hampering her appeal. But she always visits the Church of Our Lady of Sorrows, where she lights a votive candle and prays to the Blessed Mother to save her children once again.

Each time Connie leaves, Ceci sobs, clinging to her mother's knees, Gabrielle flails in her arms. Anna's eyes fill with tears, uncomprehending, reproachful. As if this were Connie's choice, not Vincent's mandate.

Week after week she forces herself to drive into Brooklyn, to watch Gabrielle develop in staggered leaps instead of day by day, to hold her children then let them go, anticipating the entire cycle of reunion, deprivation, and despair like a hapless subject in some scientific experiment to test the limits of the human heart. '*Now you know how it feels.*'

The coming together and pulling apart damages her children as well. Vincent refuses to give an inch, his victory more important than their welfare.

Finally, she stops going to see them. To spare them she locks herself into a chamber of hell.

Connie phones her parents every week, instead, for detailed reports on each child, to reassure them their child's okay, surprised they agree with her decision, and seem to understand the toll it takes on her.

She leaves the legal battle to her father, the novenas to her mother. Augustus doesn't intrude but she's found offerings on the porch: a book on Shamans, a white feather, a bundle of dried sage.

"How can you bear it?" Rita asks. To her, Connie's sacrifice is as noble as any saint's and as incomprehensible.

"You think I should go back to him?" Connie says, hammering in the last stake marking off the area for the Mary garden.

"Of course not."

"This helps." Connie loosens the soil with a spade, breaking up the clods. "It's how Augustus managed," Connie reminds Rita. "Sacred rituals, remember?"

The cat pads around in the overturned earth, sniffing at a clump of weeds. Rita picks up the rake.

"Don't," Connie tells her. "This is mine to do."

"But it will take you hours," Rita says.

"Good," Connie says, standing on the spade to push it deeper into the ground.

"But—"

"Just go, Rita. You do your job, I'll do mine." Connie says.

By the time the clouds roll in Connie's done turning over the soil and warm enough to be grateful for the lack of sun. She edges the borders then un-pots the thriving seedlings. All the flowers Anna chose: Bachelor's Button, Morning Glory. Petunias and Marigolds. Forget-Me-Nots. *Forget-Me-Nots.*

Fighting back tears, she arranges them in two arcs, tallest in the back, shortest in the front. She plants the Morning Glory in the center, wrapping the new tendrils around a teepee of stakes. She stands, exhausted, then gathers up the gardening gloves she'd abandoned after the first row, preferring the spongy feel of the soil, the feathery threads of the roots. The little greens look so fragile and . . . expectant. She thinks Anna would see them the same way. Then wonders if Anna will get to see them at all.

After she showers, Connie sits at her desk with a glass of wine, unlocks Anna's drawer, and as she does almost every night, plucks out a picture at random. This one she's never seen. A man pointing a shotgun, smoke rising from the barrel. Anna stretched out on the ground, a bright red circle on her shoulder, Connie on her knees.

A searing image she does her best to blur with the rest of the bottle of wine.

Long after Rita leaves the next morning, Connie wakes to the sound of rain on the roof, not a gentle lilting rain, but torrents pounding the shingles, spilling over the gutters. *Oh, God. The greenlings.* She pulls on sneakers and rushes outside as rivulets flood the neat rows; the little plants are plastered to the ground, some snapped at the base. She turns the wheelbarrow upside down over one corner of the bed, then runs into the house and tears the shower curtain from its plastic rings. Now more are covered, but most remain exposed. She remembers the rickety sawhorse stored in the garage loft and the tarpaulin in the basement. She gets the tarp first and then climbs the narrow ladder to the loft.

It takes a few seconds for her pupils to adjust to the gloom but she feels triumphant when she spies the faded, splintered wood. It'll probably break into bits if she tosses it. Resting a pair of the sawhorse legs on her shoulders, she backs down the stairs in its stiff embrace.

Even after rigging up the tarp, a three-foot gap remains. Connie mounds the earth around the roots of the exposed plants, tunneling out ruts to channel the water away from them, her nightgown plastered to her body like a winding sheet. Her sneakers squish with every flex of her foot. Oddly exhilarated, she kicks off her shoes and sinks her toes into the muck.

The sudden storm abates to a misty shower. Connie sits up on her muddy heels and shakes her head like a dog to throw off some of the wet. She rakes her eyes across the rows, but except for a couple of zinnias, a few Bachelor Buttons, and a short row of marigolds, all are present and accounted for. Her spirits rise so quickly, dizzyingly, she's forced to acknowledge the resilient hope hidden in her heart; the Blessed Mother will protect her children and bring them safely home.

Connie's gaze wanders into the middle distance and her heart stops. She blinks hard but it's still there on the bridge—a woman draped in a long blue mantle. Connie holds her breath as the vision glides toward her. When the lady raises her hand in greeting Connie nearly faints.

"I didn't mean to startle you. This is my house. Well, yours of course, while you're renting. I'm Laurel. Laurel Messinger."

They sort out everything in the kitchen. "Have you any tea? I've grown accustomed . . ."

"Of course. Here," she hands Laurel a mug and a box of teabags. "If you wouldn't mind. I really have to wash up."

"Take your time."

E shows up to keep Laurel company while Connie quickly showers.

Damp but clean, Connie sets out plates, unwraps a pound cake, and joins Laurel at the kitchen table.

"It's a Mackintosh cape that's very popular in England," Laurel laughs. "I wondered why you looked as if you'd seen a ghost. I mean the flight home was ghastly but I didn't think I looked that bad."

Connie starts to explain about Rita and the new garden but Laurel stops her.

"I know about almost everything from Ed. We correspond."

Connie stops cutting the cake and stares at her.

"We have for years. Even when I lived here. My parents thought him too old for me, too rough. We'd manage to sneak away every once in a while. Down the shore. Up to Lake Champlain."

"That's where he is now."

"That's what I get for trying to surprise him. Best laid plans, eh?" She takes a sip of her tea and then grips the mug with both hands. "My Mum died last month, and I stayed to settle her affairs. Didn't think I'd get quit so soon. I fancied this romantic reunion, you know?"

"Talk about still waters."

"Ed doesn't say much, I grant you, but he writes the most beautiful letters."

As soon as Laurel leaves for Ed's house, 'I know where he keeps the spare key,' she'd said, Connie rescues Anna's paintings from the locked desk drawer and tapes them up in every room. She digs through the mail until she finds the envelope from Rose, fat with photographs, which she tucks into the mirror's frame, behind refrigerator magnets, under clear domed paperweights.

She dials her old number, hears the phone ring through the loud thumping of her heart.

"Leonetti residence." A woman answers in a Scottish burr.

"Anna, please. Or Ceci—"

"No one is home right now. May I take a message?"

"Tell them . . . tell them their mother called."

# CHAPTER 34

The Mary garden blooms wherever the deer have spared it. "I forgot to set the pinwheels out," Connie says. "All that work! And less than half the flowers to show for it."

Rita points to the army of potted plants marching along the grass. "These all for the farm stand?"

"Yes. From here," Connie sticks a plastic tag into a pot then lays a trowel at a plant several feet away, "to here are the Brandywine Reds." Connie hands Rita a marking pencil and a handful of tags. "I'll label the Cherokee Purples. I've set aside some to grow just for the Snow Goose. Augustus placed a standing order."

The plants give off a spicy scent as the morning heats up. Trays of three-inch pots cover the picnic table, its benches; dozens more are scattered on the grass. Chives, thyme, savory, marjoram, the trays are marked. Cilantro. Dill. Parsley.

"This keeps up, you're going to need a greenhouse."

"Got one." Connie flushes. "Ginger's allotting me one at Four Corners, in exchange for all the tomato plants and whatever herbs she can sell."

"But that leaves Augustus as your only paying customer. How are you supposed to make any money?"

Connie brushes the soil from her hands, reaches into her back pocket, and hands Rita a card.

### Constance Gardens
### Supplier of Herbes Fines

"Augustus says the better restaurants will pay for hard-to-find herbs delivered straight to their kitchens. I got a list of Empire State Grocers' customers in Manhattan. If I get the orders, Empire will pick up my weekly supply when they drop off at Loaves, deliver the goods, process the paperwork, and pay me."

Rita stops tagging plants. "When did you do all this? Where have I been?"

"Working your butt off, as usual. Look, Reet, I haven't called on the restaurants yet but I plan on charging them New York prices so if this works it'll be enough to keep me afloat. So, you're finally off the hook."

"But Con, the rent alone is—"

"Laurel and I made a deal to trade landscaping and gardening services for a reduced rent. I'll need the space for the children even if you go back to Holy Name, if that's what you decide you want." Connie squats opposite Rita. "Is it?"

"It really hasn't been an option until now. It still may not be. I think I should wait and see. I mean, if you get the children back, how will you support them? You can't count on him, you know. Have you even heard from him?"

Connie shakes her head. "Not a peep. I bet the housekeeper spends more time with the kids than he does." She pinches a leaf from a plant. "I think Vince would have been so different if he'd had a mother to care for him when he was growing up, although you didn't have yours, either . . . never mind, sorry."

"It's okay, Con. I'm a big girl now."

"But when you weren't—"

"I didn't understand." Rita plucks at a blade of grass. "As I got older, I did but then I was angry anyway. At being cheated. Until I realized how much more she suffered than I did."

"I hope Anna will understand someday." Connie swipes tears from her face, smudging it with dirt.

Rita wraps her arms around Connie. "She will. I'll tell her just how brave and strong her mother is."

At 60 mph with the radio cranked and the windows rolled down, Connie's so pumped up, she almost misses the exit for the Tappan Zee bridge. Turning down the volume, she decides she won't let the Rolling Stones dictate what she can't get and cuts over to the right lane. The car's packed with coolers of florist boxes containing nosegays of exotic herbs—wild bergamot, fenugreek, dark green Italian parsley. French sorrel, Greek oregano, Russian tarragon. They're sheathed in pale pink tissue paper and tied with satin ribbon the color of celery. She plans to call on a half-dozen chefs before lunch, and then as many as she can in the lull before dinner. Then do it again tomorrow. Thursdays and Fridays are best according to Augustus. She's rented a room midtown. She can't bear to stay at her parents' or even step foot in Brooklyn. Her old house a magnet, a fortress, a promise she can't keep.

Chef Claude breaks off a leaf of wild bergamot, rubbing it between his long, bony fingers. He holds it under his formidable nose and inhales. After washing his hands, he repeats the sequence with each of the other offerings. "*C'est bon, Connie. Trés bon.*"

He sets out two bowls of café au lait and warm, crusty rolls accompanied by white crocks of sweet butter and orange marmalade. "If I make the list of others, you can grow them, *non?*"

"As long as I can find the seed. Yes."

"Not to worry. If you cannot, I call my *Maman* and she will find them for us." Claude writes rapidly, which herbs, by what date, how much. He looks up and winks. "Maybe I come visit your *jardin* someday."

Praised and fed and flirted with, she ends the day with a fistful of orders. By the time she checks into her room, the woman in the dresser mirror looks vibrant.

Each month more pregnant teenagers seem to show up at the food bank.

"Why is that, do you think?" Rita asks Mitzi.

"Sex?"

"Seriously." Rita bags groceries for the regulars who will stop in today.

"The Lutherans opened a group home for pregnant girls. We must be listed as a resource."

Rita freezes mid-bag then puts down the sack of rice and scoots under the counter. She riffles through the file cabinet in the kitchen. Mitzi follows her. "What?"

"Hold on a sec," Rita says, tossing folders onto the table.

"*What?*"

"Here it is. The specs for a daycare grant. Those girls will need a place to bring their children and Connie, please God, is going to need a place to bring Gabrielle when the girls are in school. Technically, we're only open Tuesdays and Thursdays so . . . " Rita scans the document as she strolls into the front room. "Mitzi, can you grab the tape measure?"

After they close at four, Rita stays at Loaves to work on the grant until it's time to change into her restaurant uniform. She arrives just in time to help Trudy set up a table for a party of twelve.

When the dinner rush finally ends, Rita notices the dull headache with which she began her shift has crescendo-ed into timpani. She serves her last customer before swallowing a couple of aspirin.

"Can you pick up the deuce, hon? I'm beat," Trudy says. "I already gave them menus."

"No problem," Rita says, arranging a tray with ice water and warm rolls. She carries it to the table where the exotic Inez, her dark curls brushing her bare shoulders, is studying the menu as intently as her companion studies her.

"Good evening." Rita just stands there until they look up.

"Rita!" Walter says. "How are you getting along? And Connie? Those cute kids, what a shame. Matt told me."

"Hello, Walter. Inez."

Inez looks up, smiles. "I'll have the prime rib, please," she tells Rita, then reaches across the table and strokes Walter's hand. "I'll be right back."

"Will Matt be joining you?" Rita says as soon as Inez is out of sight.

"Hey, I love my brother, but three's a crowd."

She offers him a weak smile. Janet must have got it wrong. Inez is with Walter, not Matt.

"Besides, he'd never come in here. It messes him up when he sees you." He stares at her until she looks away. Rita fumbles in her apron pocket for the order pad sitting on her tray.

The next day goes so well, Connie's out of samples by one o'clock. On impulse, she drives to Fields Fashions. God, she hasn't been to Vincent's workplace since she took Anna there, six months old and cranky from the subway ride. Vince had paraded Anna throughout the office onto the loading dock where the booming voices set the baby into such a hysterical state that Vince took them into his office so Connie could breastfeed in private. Connie doubts the receptionist would recognize her but, just in case, she makes it fast.

"I have an appointment with Mr. Leone," she tells Sylvia. "Please tell him Laurel Messinger is here. I'll wait in the showroom."

It looks much the same, except the little platform is worn down on one edge and the carpeting smells faintly musty. Connie hears footsteps then Vincent's voice, hearty and hale.

"I'm afraid I don't remember our appointment—"

"I wasn't sure you'd see me," Connie says. "I need to talk to you."

"Talk to my lawyer." His voice is tight.

She sees through him now despite the theatrical line, tossed off with aplomb. "I will if that's what you want. But I'd rather speak with you."

He hesitates, off-guard. "So, speak."

"I'm sorry that I sometimes kept you from the children. You're right. Now I know how it feels. And I'm sorry for resenting your considerable talent, for always feeling second best to you. That part's not your fault."

She talks in gentle tones. "Do you remember what it felt like to be left with sitters, to not have your mother? Is that what you want for your daughters?"

He looks away.

"The children deserve to have at least one parent with them all the time. You can't give them that. I can. You can see them every minute you're free, I swear."

For once, he has nothing to say.

"Think about it, Vincent. Please?" she whispers before slipping away.

The red flash flaring in the dusk, accompanied by the perfumed musk of Augustus' pipe tobacco, reminds Rita of the night of Ceci's birthday party, nearly a year ago. A magical time when Connie was buoyant, flush from her escape from Vincent, the children enthralled with the lush summer green landscape, when Gabrielle was a daily miracle and Matt a dear friend.

The screen door slams, interrupting her reverie. Connie carries a bowl of peaches and a bottle of wine. She pours them each a Dixie cup of Riesling. "You're here early," she says to Augustus.

"Light crowd for a Thursday." He shakes his head. "This heatwave better break before my provisions go bad."

"So, what did I miss?" Connie rests her feet on the picnic table's bench.

Rita picks up a peach, rolls it around in her palm. "Holy Name's losing two sisters to graduate school in the fall. With my being gone, that's twenty-five percent of the convent out of commission. They want to know if they can count on me." Dropping the peach into her lap, she takes a sip of wine. "I'm just so weary of being in limbo. The truth is I feel so close to knowing, like it's a membrane away."

"After all this time, I guess you're due." Connie pats Rita's arm. "Believe me, I know the feeling. Too bad you can't induce labor."

"Ah, but you can." Augustus pushes his thumbs into the seam of a peach. "Western civilization has flattened the arduous rites of passage into merely symbolic gestures—a slap on the cheek, a public performance, a party."

He breaks open the fruit exposing the glistening pulp, the crenelated stone, licks the juice from his fingers then presses the pit's pointed tip into his palm until it yields a drop of blood. "Beyond initiation rites, vision quests

319

are designed to pierce the veil of innocence—to induce a mystical experience which reveals one's purpose."

"A visible sign," Rita murmurs.

He shrugs. "Anything's possible. Actually, it's not dissimilar to the sensory deprivation practiced by shamans and mystics, even biblical prophets."

"At this point, that sounds appealing," Rita refills their cups. "Too bad there's not a desert handy."

Augustus holds his palm over his cup. "Would a mountaintop do?"

"You're kidding," Connie says.

He shakes his head. "Come, ladies," he pulls them up from their chairs. "Let's go inside and prepare the way."

From his perch on the ladder-back chair, Augustus draws up a map of his private preserve—forty acres of forest, fields, and streams. "Here's the well and over there's the outhouse. You'll see the fire ring and grate. I don't think there's much in the way of firewood but you'll find plenty of deadfall. It's easier to use a Sven saw to cut up the thicker branches, then haul them to the campsite."

Rita studies the map. "No cabin?"

"I have a dome tent, a propane stove, kerosene lantern, Coleman cooler, the whole kit and caboodle."

"Augustus, I've never set up a tent, or used a kerosene lantern."

"I'll teach you. It shouldn't take any more than an hour or so before you get the hang of it. Which will leave you plenty of time to make a grocery run, drive up, and pitch camp well before nightfall."

"But what about Loaves?"

"What do you need, Rita? Let me help," Connie says.

"Everyone will. Now tell us what needs doing." Augustus presides over the sprawl of legal pads, pencils, and calendars at the kitchen table. They extinguish the harsh overhead fluorescent and circle, like some ancient tribal council, around the softer lamplight.

After Rita outlines her schedule, Augustus decides he'll take over the ordering for the food bank. "Works perfectly. I have Mondays off. I'll meet the truck, check off the inventory, place the backorder, make out the work schedules for whatever fields the farmers deem ready. Then Janet can switch to cover the Friday hours. Mitzi and Matt have Tuesdays. The field teams will have to do without you for a couple of weeks, and maybe Connie can handle the solicitation and donation arrangements by phone."

"No problem, just tell me who to call."

"Well, this is a lesson in humility. I see I'm quite easily replaced."

"By about ten people!" Connie says.

Rita tries and fails to quell the intoxicating rush of pride she feels in bringing Loaves to fruition.

"Wait. What about the bills and the banking?"

Augustus adds that to the list. "You can write the checks in advance for whatever vendors have to be paid. I'm sure Mitzi will mail them when due and make the necessary bank deposits."

By the time they open a second bottle of wine, their various lists are complete.

"Tomorrow first light, I'll bring my stuff over."

"I don't know if Janet can arrange that on such short notice," Rita says.

Augustus looks at the clock. "Midnight. Her shift's over at eleven, isn't it? She should be home by now. Call her."

Rita hesitates.

"Go ahead, Reet," Connie says softly. "Carpe diem."

# CHAPTER 35

It's a splendid morning but Rita feels like hurling the bright yellow rods at Augustus. He's sitting at the picnic table, sampling the French toast Connie made.

"You've almost got it," he says. "The trick is to thread all three poles through the loops while the tent is collapsed on the ground, then fasten one arc at a time. The last one's the hardest. Don't be afraid to throw your shoulder into it."

"Now you tell me."

He shrugs. "You need to know you can figure stuff out on your own. Improvise."

After three hours she knows how to lay the ground tarp, pitch the tent, attach a dining fly, inflate the air mattress, fill the kerosene lamp, light the mantles and blow them out, hook up the propane stove, assemble the Sven saw. He makes her stow all the gear in the Beetle's trunk and hands her one more box.

"Miscellaneous cookware, utensils, first aid kit, flashlight, waterproof matches, etc." He closes the lid. "Trust your intuition, my dear. And have a wonderful journey."

Setting out she feels much the same way she did the day her father drove her to the convent on her first day as a postulant. Only then she joined up with other young women as scared and excited as she. Now she has to depend entirely on herself. And Him. Which is the point, she tells the open road, her words tossed out on the wind. She pulls into Custard's Last Stand and eats her fill of chili dogs, onion rings, and ice cream before heading for the hills. To camp out with the critters. She grimaces and hopes she won't have to spend the entire time trapped in a rerun of *The Beverly Hillbillies*. After a few hours and a couple of wrong turns, she finds the rutted road into the property and barely has time to look around before the clouds darken and the wind shifts. For what seems like the tenth time today she sets up camp then stops rushing for the first time since dawn, the sky overhead now clear.

At the end of this long day, she lowers herself into the sleeping bag hours before dark.

Next morning the first thing Rita notices is—not silence, exactly, because she can hear various chirps and whistles and peeps—but the absence of mechanical sounds signaling human activity. The second is the intense heat. As soon she unzips the tent flap it's ten degrees cooler. She's about to pull on her jeans to go down to the stream when it dawns on her—nobody's around. She puts on sneakers and walks barelegged to the shallow spot where she dragged the cooler and takes the rocks off the lid to get to the only perishables she'll see for a while. Other than a sack of apples, a bag of potatoes, and bunches of carrots, this is it. In a couple of days, it will be powdered and canned everything.

After she fires up the stove, perks coffee, and fries bacon and eggs, Rita sits on the grass with her breakfast and watches the birds. Some land incredibly near her outstretched legs. A vibrant blue jay marches right up to her lap and she rewards his fearlessness with a chunk of bread. She fills a basin with well water—thrillingly cold! —washes the dishes, then pumps another basin for cleansing herself, puts on shorts, gets her Daily Office, and heads off to the woods. About 100 yards past a stand of paper birch she finds a pair of massive fir trees splitting the sky into ribbons of light, boughs like fringed buttresses holding up an evergreen dome, the shadowed naves as vast and majestic as any cathedral.

She nestles against the rough bark and begins her morning prayers.

The room is so crowded that Vincent has to stand near the back, behind a vaguely familiar group of men he suddenly realizes are some of the teamsters that work the loading dock. Replicating her role from the office, Sylvia stands in the lobby greeting people and directing them to the large chapel, though she needn't; the constant stream of mourners points the way. He notices several perfect-size-eight models wearing the Fields version of the suitable-for–any-occasion black dress, along with accountants, secretaries, and sales reps. Marty's children and grandchildren surround Lynn whose eyes appear as if they're straining to read the fine print in fading light, as well as scores of people Vincent doesn't recognize.

He's never been to a Jewish wake. *Do they call it that? Funeral service, maybe. A plain pine box. Closed. No kneeling and saying the rosary.* A rabbi says a short prayer in Hebrew and then turns the dais over to a man so resembling Marty that Vincent gets gooseflesh. Marty's brother

Benny's eulogy is tender, funny, tearful. The tributes continue: Marty's other brother, a brother-in-law, his sons, a neighbor, members of his minyan, business associates, friends, and employees. Although no two anecdotes are the same, they all praise his joy, his generosity, his goodness. *Mensch.* A good decent man. Vincent stands up to tell the story about the Valentines but the cold, hard fact of Marty's death lodges in his throat and leaves him mute.

As soon as Vincent steps inside his front door, he smells charcoal and ash. He rushes through the living room to the kitchen where Anna, sobbing, stands in a puddle of water, a charred, soggy potholder at her feet.

"I'm sorry, Daddy, Ceci wanted hot choc—"

"Where the hell's Mrs. Macleod?"

"Upstairs with Gabrielle."

"I'm sorry, honey." He wipes Anna's wet cheeks with his thumb, checks her hands for burns. "You okay?"

She nods. Vincent charges up the stairs. In the bathroom, water is rushing full force into the tub. The baby's face is reddened from the steam, she gazes listlessly over the housekeeper's hitched-up shoulder. His daughter's torso jerks through a spasm of wracking coughs.

"How long?" Vincent asks.

"Since she woke up from her nap." Mrs. Macleod sits on the edge of the tub draping Gabrielle face down across her lap and, open-palmed, softly thumps her back. "I called the doctor." She looks at her watch. "You can take her over in half an hour. I can stay till you get back."

"Thanks." Vincent rolls up his shirtsleeves, picks up his daughter. She coughs again, and the sound hurts Vincent's heart. It's not even four o'clock but he feels as weary as midnight.

In six days and five nights, Rita has moved past novelty to boredom to exhilaration, and finally back to boredom again.

Isolation and idleness erase the shape of her days, the edges of the form she's used to filling. She doesn't feel unfettered as much as evaporated. The relentless heat steamrolls her physical energy.

This heat. Dear Lord. Only in the early mornings does she have energy enough to hike through the shadowy woods. Then the temperature and humidity deflate her bit by bit. She spends most days in her 'church' in the woods or wading the stream.

Her only connection her daily prayer and daily bread. For supper, she eats a couple of apples dabbed with peanut butter and stares through the clouds at the waxing moon. The clotted sky and still air forecast another night with neither stars nor rain.

The next day—is it the seventh? the ninth?—she wakes in a misery of sweat. Her hair feels like wet wool clinging to her skull. She walks barefoot to the stream and splashes wildly, too impatient for relief to pump the well. By the time she gets back to the tent, she's hot again. She rummages through the box Augustus gave her and finds a pair of shears. She cuts off clump after clump of her thick mop until a pile of curls lies at her feet like an abandoned nest. *There. Better.* Her temples and neck now free to catch a bit of breeze. Too out of sorts to eat, let alone brew coffee, trek back and forth to the cooler, the car for supplies, she steps into her sneakers and heads for shade of the green glen. After reading her Daily Office, she nestles in a cradle of ancient fir roots to meditate.

Rita sees them as soon as she walks out of the woods. Huge leaden thunderheads like avenging angels swallowing the sun, lowering the horizon to a greenish-yellow stripe. Then heat lightning, like electrified stickmen. She counts the miles. One. Two. Thr—the thunder washes over her with the rain. She opens her arms and twirls in the welcome benediction of the fat cold drops bouncing off her grateful skin, the thirsty leaves, the dusty earth.

Not until thoroughly soaked does she get into the car to wait out the rest of the storm, reveling in the racketing explosions of sound and light. As she pulls her feet up on the seat and hugs her slippery legs against her chest, a pulsing joy beats along with her heart.

The storm keeps her company through the afternoon and long into the night. When it tapers off to a steady thrum she makes her way to the tent, cozy now—some heat still trapped inside the dome despite the rain, which slides off the nylon canopy inches above its roof. By flashlight, she strips and towels off the wet, finds a wrinkled tee shirt, a pair of flowered pajama bottoms, and snuggles down inside the sleeping bag into a warm, dry, velvety sleep.

She dreams she's a child, asleep in her old bed in Brooklyn where a hooded woman, draped in long black robes, stands sentry. Rita's mother is there, too, the age she would be now if she'd lived, white-haired and stouter but so lively she dances an Irish jig, her green eyes sparkling. In her dream, Rita longs for her mother to hug the little girl but she embraces the black-robed woman instead, swings her around in a do-si-do, laughing, around and around until the woman laughs too and tosses her head back, throwing off the hood and Rita sees herself, her own wild hair, her own green eyes and now the bed is made of dirt and filled with what looks like plump cabbages, rosy tomatoes, big leaf runner vines sheltering whatever lies beneath the rich soil.

Rita wakes to a morning so glorious, so cool and crisp, she longs to sing its praises. Each earthly element has been scrubbed into a piercing clarity. The small clearing beyond the stream laced with bird flight among the trees: oak and maple, hickory, beech, spruce. The trees giving way to the foothills then the mountains crowned by a cloudless sky. Tiny bright blue butterflies wink on and off like fairies around her ankles as she walks through the tall grass. The westerlies race through the woods where the leaves sound like a thousand kites and lift her heart as high.

With the waterproof matches and pieces of wood she has gathered and stored under a tarp, she builds a dancing fire to warm herself and roast a few potatoes to break the fast—she now realizes—she began the night before last. For matins today she counts her blessings, enough to last the length of time it takes for the potatoes to char and burst into the most delicious meal she's ever had.

When she's finished eating, she lingers near the fire—as fragrant as incense to her heightened awareness—and feels the sun and breeze and damp and watches the blue bowl expand into an infinity so vast she feels as if she's falling up, as it dawns on her:

She knows.

And her body, trembling with the knowledge, leaps up to take her home.

She leaves the fire burning till the last. After she takes down the tent, the tarp, and the fly, folds and stacks them in the trunk. She dismantles the propane stove, secures the kerosene lamp in a carton, empties the cooler and hauls it back to the car, scatters the few leftover apples and potatoes, the sole bunch of carrots for the wood creatures. After washing and drying the kitchen gear, she makes one last visit to the pine grove. Only then does she extinguish the flames and wait until the last plume of smoke releases her to her destiny.

Unwashed, unkempt, and reeking of campfire smoke she drives straight to the convent at Holy Name.

Rita practically skips into the house to tell Connie her news but can't find her. She takes a quick jog down to the lake to see if maybe Connie's at the little beach, and on the way back runs into Ed, his waders dripping wet from the stream.

"Where have you been? In combat?"

She laughs and runs her fingers through what's left of her hair. She's grimy and her clothes are a wrinkled, pungent mess. "Camping. Have you seen Connie?"

"With Laurel," he says. "Now they've got plans for my property. Grape arbors. Couple of years, those two will have us making wine."

"Right." Rita laughs, heading back up the lane to the house where she showers, then wraps herself in a towel and flip-flops, and throws her dirty clothes in the washer. Upstairs she finds her bed freshly made but covered with clothes. A long skirt of a pale blue gauzy material and a matching tunic top, a pair of brand-new sandals, the kind with straps that tie all the way to the knee, two pastel tee shirts with the tags still on, a pair of aqua slacks, and a beautiful hand-tooled leather belt. Centered on the pillow lays an envelope with her name on it. She wraps the towel tighter around her, sits in the chair, and reads the note.

*Sister dear (because you are to me, whatever name you choose),*

*Consider this a small token of my gratitude. I wanted you to have, even just for once, some outfits that aren't totally utilitarian. (Don't worry, except for the tee shirts and sandals, I found everything at the thrift shop!)*

*I hope you found the answer you've been searching for and that you take some solace from knowing we are family, Rita, in every way that matters.*

*Love,*

*Connie*

The words go wavy as she re-reads the words. She can't recall ever feeling so beautifully and extravagantly provided for. She steps into the feathery light skirt, the delicate blue tunic, laces up the leather sandals, and floats down the stairs and out of the house. She can't put it off any longer. She has to tell Matt.

She finds him in the barn, hanging a pail of feed for the horse. The colt nuzzles him as he holds out a fistful of sweet hay. Dark patches dampen the back of his shirt. Bits of straw cling to his jeans, dust his hair. When she crosses a shaft of sunlight in the threshold he turns around.

"Rita? What are you doing here?" It takes a few seconds for his eyes to travel from her cropped hair to her long skirt, then the sandals. He smiles. "You look like a medieval saint." He stops smiling. "You've decided."

She nods. Before he can say anything, she wraps him in a fierce hug, and then backs away, her hands still cupping his sides. She feels the smile he presses on her lips before it disappears and they slowly begin to inventory their storehouse of kisses.

"Now what?" Connie sits among the scattered outfits.

"Thirty days until I get formal papers from Mother Superior, then the grant kicks in, and I can start to draw a salary as director of Loaves and Fishes. With that, plus waitressing, plus your business, we'll find a lawyer who can get the children back."

She had left Matt when he could no longer postpone the evening milking. He hadn't been able to foist the job on Walt, who was out scaring up parts for the backup generator that fizzled out during last night's storm. 'I'll be done no later than nine,' he said, with his arms around her, his lips pressed to her ear, 'eight-thirty if I don't shower and change.' 'I can wait,' she'd laughed then kissed him again as if she couldn't.

"When I saw your hair, I thought you decided on the convent for sure."

Rita hangs up the slacks. "So did poor Matt."

"Poor Matt? Poor Augustus, you mean."

"He'll be fine. Besides, he spends more time with you than with me." Rita unbuckles the leather belt, steps out of the denim skirt and into the gauzy one. "It's perfect, Connie." She sweeps her hand over the lot. "They're all perfect. I don't know what to say. Thank you."

"If you thank me one more time, I swear I'm going to sock you. You've done everything for us, Reet. It's the very least . . . Wait, there's one more thing." Connie holds up a gorgeous cotton eyelet top with a square bodice and satin straps.

"What's this?" Rita asks.

"Besides beautiful, too big for me. It'll go great with that skirt."

"But this is purple."

"Lavender, Rita. Pale lavender and powder blue. You'll look like twilight."

A few minutes later, Rita stands in the kitchen in her new clothes looking out toward the driveway.

"How about some leftover turkey? I could make us sandwiches, and I think there's some minestrone in here somewhere . . . " Connie peers in the refrigerator door. "Reet?"

"What? Oh, no thanks."

"Too nervous to eat?"

Rita laughs. "No. Immaculata practically hauled out the fatted calf today. We ate and talked and cried." She sighs. "A wake of sorts, I suppose."

Connie puts the container of soup down. "You know, I could do some simple make-up. Just a little blush—"

"I'm fine, Con." Headlights bounce against the kitchen window as the truck makes its way down the drive. "Truly."

And she is, Connie realizes. Rita looks radiant.

She hugs Connie and then walks out in the moonlight to meet Matt halfway.

Connie can't restrain from snooping. Rita, as serene and unaffected as the nun she was, embraces this man with a natural ease. As delighted as she is that Rita will be staying, Connie feels a twinge of envy that Rita seems to effortlessly navigate the waters from one world to another when her own crossing has cost so much.

The price she's paid for the wisps of wisdom that trail her through the hours, as she weeds and prunes her gardens. In the lengthening evenings she walks around the lake or through the woods, gathering the remnants and debris of all her years, the blossoms, too, and jewels, both genuine and paste. Fashioning a different tapestry of her own design. More complicated. Of deeper hues. Blood red, grass green, sky blue.

At Loaves and Fishes, Rita sets out the last of the produce of the season, some of it from Connie's garden, some of it from Matt's. He's so vital to her now; she can't imagine a universe without him. Who would bring her warm grapes, whose silhouette would be the same at dusk, or rumbling voice sound the same on the phone? She loves the way he holds her wrist between his thumb and forefinger as if her hand was some exotic fruit suspended on a bulky vine.

Rita never understood Connie's obsession for Vincent until Matt, until she sinks into the sea of him and floats along in warm fluid feeling of being connected with another, the outlines of their separate selves blurring in the light the beloved wears like an aura. She's felt this way sometimes in prayer, the room dissolving, sound and touch falling away as she lifts off into the atmosphere of the heart. That shift of focus. What else is the religious life but moving into another, unseen world of the spirit? Why couldn't love transform in a similar way? Love, like faith, is a matter of direct experience, she supposes; when it happens to you, you know.

Connie stops swishing the dishcloth in the sink and closes her eyes to revel in the warm breeze slinking through the kitchen window. She feels a deeper heat and knows the sun has just this moment cleared the sycamore at the end of the walkway, savors her intimate knowledge of the rhythms here.

She opens her eyes when she hears the little boys from down the lane. They've taken to tormenting the cat. Connie dries her hands as she rushes outside into the flood of sunlight. Squinting, she holds up one hand as a visor and sees Anna standing in the driveway, Ceci racing to the porch.

Connie squats to catch her in her arms, hugs and kisses her until she's breathless, then looks around for Anna, to pull her in, bring her home. She's standing where she was, stock-still. Connie gets on her knees and opens her arms. Anna takes one step, another, stops. Connie rushes to her then, grabs her, holds her tight.

"First, she didn't want to come." Vincent appears, carrying Gabrielle.

Connie looks at Anna's face and knows it's true. "Oh, Anna. I never stopped loving you. I . . . " Her daughter's gaze is closed, although her lip quivers. "Look, there's our Mary garden. With everything you chose." She forces herself to release Anna, to allow her to walk through the garden on her own, although Connie has long pictured herself holding Anna's hand as she delights in each drawing sprung to life, their shared triumph. Anna leans into the last of the fragrant columbine. Connie waits for Anna to call her over but it's Ceci that Anna beckons. So be it. Anna's home now, that's all that matters. Connie takes Gabrielle from Vince's arms and nuzzles her neck, inhaling the baby scent.

"What's all this?" He indicates the rows of stacked flats, sacks of potting soil and limestone, little hillocks of sand and gravel.

"Herbs. I sell them to restaurants through a distributor."

"No shit." Vince stares at her. "Since when?"

"Since spring."

He narrows his eyes. "That roly-poly cook do all this for you?"

"He's a chef. And no. No one did this for me." She sits on the grass, sets the baby in her lap, and shows him her palms ridged with calluses.

He turns away from her. "Marty died."

"Oh, no! Vincent, I'm so sorry. When?"

"Last month. You wouldn't believe how many people stood up at his funeral service to say how much he meant to them. What a kind and generous man he was." Vincent's voice is strangled now.

"Yes, he was."

"I knew there'd be no one to say that about me. Not even my children, if I kept them from their mother."

She looks at him. "You mean . . . "

"It's not fair to them with me gone so much."

"For real?" Her brain races to keep up with her happy heart. "For good?"

"You heard me." His voice is hoarse. "But I get to see them whenever I can."

"Bless you, Vincent. God bless you." Connie swings Gabrielle up toward the sky and drinks in the baby's sudden joy.

"What is it? Oh, Con, what now?" Rita says, when she finally gets home from a late dinner rush at the Snow Goose and finds Connie, her eyelids pink and swollen, her face splotchy and damp with perspiration. The kitchen smells like burnt sugar, dirty dishes crowd the counter, and Connie's shirt is streaked with blood.

"Good God," Rita says, reaching for a towel. "Let me see—"

Connie drops the spatula and grabs Rita's hands. "I'm fine, it's spaghetti sauce—"

"Why is the oven on? It must be ninety degrees in here."

"I've been cooking for the girls, oh Reet, they're here, they're home, Vince brought them back just—"

Rita yells before Connie can shush her, squeezes Connie until she yelps, and then, a finger to her lips, tiptoes down the hall to hold the children in her gaze, even if they're sleeping, even for a second.

"So that's why you look like a deranged lunatic," Rita says after Connie fills her in and they laugh and cry and hug each other. "Don't worry, Con, Anna will come around."

"Yeah?" Connie asks, bleary-eyed.

"Go to bed. I'll clean up. It'll help pass the time till they wake up."

"Yeah?"

"Go ahead, you're delirious."

"I know. Thanks. Happy face in the morning," Connie says, and they smile at Rose's good night wish when they were little.

It's after midnight by the time Rita has put away all the dishes, scrubbed the counters, and swept the floor. Even with the oven off, and the windows open, it's humid. She slips outside—no way she'll be able to sleep anyway—to sit in the cool dark and give in to the torrent of joy.

A flash of light captures her attention, followed by another, and in the space of a breath, two more. *The Perseids.* She races into the house. Connie's passed out flat on her back, one arm dangling off the bed, and the other curled around Ceci. Gabrielle is gurgling and playing with her raised foot. Anna, owl-eyed and upright in the top bunk, flings herself into Rita's open arms.

"Aunt Sister!" Anna sobs.

"Shhh, Anna, it's okay. Everything's okay now. I promise." Rita carries her outdoors, grabbing the quilt on the way. She sets Anna on the grass, spreads out the quilt, then lies down, patting the space beside her. "Look," she says, tilting Anna's chin, directing her gaze.

Anna, star-struck, gasps in little bursts of pleasure, held captive by the incandescent fire light-years away.

Rita brushes Anna's hair away from her face, kisses her forehead. "Would you like to hear the prayer my mother taught me when I was your age?"

Anna nods and snuggles closer.

Rita wraps her arms around the child and, to the accompaniment of the meteor showers, begins,

"I arise today,

Through the strength of heaven:

Light of sun

Radiance of moon,

Splendor of fire . . . "

# Acknowledgements

My agent, Tracy Crow, is a force of nature. She has opened doors, forged paths, and, just possibly, found wormholes in the space-time continuum. Her enthusiasm for and dedication to this book have made all the following acknowledgments possible.

Deep gratitude to Dianne Nauer, who held the lantern as I navigated this journey, and to my North Star, Anita Virgil, who knew I was a writer before I did.

To Susan Paredes, who has talked me off ledges and up mountains, for her wisdom and strength.

To John Marcus, as well as John and Carolyn Paredes, for their years of generous support and encouragement, to Tom Paredes for his counsel, to Teresa Lanowich and Lynda Leo for their faith, and to Joanne Brunnquell, Mary Hom, and Guy Paredes for cheering from the sidelines.

To Judi Hendricks for her unwavering belief in this book. To Val Nieman for providing sustenance, literally and figuratively.

I'm indebted to authors Judith Guest and Rebecca Hill, for lessons learned during their wonderfully welcoming Inkwell Intensives; also, the Bucks County Writers Workshop, especially Don Swaim, Chris Bauer, Les Berkley, Carmen Ferreiro, Peg Gallos, Candace Barrett, and Carolyn Merlini. Many thanks to my thoughtful and thorough editors, Margaret McInnis, and Kimberly Coghlan.

Everlasting gratitude to my innamorato, Al Sirois, for everything that matters.

# READING GUIDE

1. How does Sr. Jude's experience in the convent compare with your expectations of what religious life is like? Were you surprised by any of the stances she took toward the church, other nuns and priests, and changes in culture?

2. In the novel's first scene, Sr. Jude prays for a sign. What other signs has she received and what did they signify?

3. How did Rita and Connie's childhoods influence their adult choices?

4. Early in the novel, Rita is described as "a force . . . inflamed with desire for sacrifice and good works. If [Connie] envied Rita anything, it was her passion, not her beauty."

   How does this manifest the many obstacles in her life? How do other characters prove to be resilient in their own ways, and which characters are most successful?

5. What seems to be the biggest cultural shifts between the time Connie and Rita took their vows and the time of the novel?

6.  Discuss Rita's sense of responsibility and obligation to her loved ones. How does this role, which she adopts from a young age, influence her decisions throughout her life?

7.  Discuss the portrayal of romantic love in the novel: between Rita's parents, Connie's parents, Connie and Vince, Rita and Matt. What are the ways that affection and passion manifest themselves between couples?

8.  How do Connie and Rita respond differently to the task of parenting that falls on them, biologically or otherwise? In what ways are they both mothers to Anna and Ceci and the other people in their lives?

9.  Does the novel expand the traditional definition of motherhood?

10. Did the shifting points of view affect your understanding of and sympathy toward the characters? Did your feelings about any one of them change by the end of the story?

11. Is the question of faith in God, in oneself, in the people you love a matter of choice or experience?

12. Describe the shift in gender dynamics from the time of the novel until today. What's changed about men's and women's roles and what hasn't?

Photo credit: Al Sirois

Her checkered past includes stints as an actress, waitress, social worker, newspaper editor, and radio and cable TV show producer. Her work has been published in *Philadelphia Stories*, *The Bucks County Writer Magazine*, *Adanna Literary Journal*, *TheWritersEye*, *Women on Writing*, *Me First Magazine* and *Embark Literary Journal*.

A Brooklyn native, she has lived on both coasts, and presently calls North Carolina home where she is working on a new novel and a collection of short stories.